PRAISE FOR MELISSA PAYNE

In the Beautiful Dark

"Melissa Payne's *In the Beautiful Dark* is a heartfelt delight of a story, often adorable, sometimes tastefully creepy and even bone chilling, certainly never predictable. She's created a cast of lovely characters, led by the vibrant and determined Birdie, who remind us that it's never too late to seize life. Richard Osman, look out, there's a new geriatric sleuth in town."

—Boo Walker, bestselling author of *An Echo in Time*

"*In the Beautiful Dark* has everything you could possibly want in a novel: page-turning suspense, laugh-out-loud banter, an endearing ensemble cast of characters, and a long-unsolved mystery, tucked into an unforgettable setting. Melissa Payne has expertly crafted a moving, unpredictable novel that will keep you guessing and leave you smiling. The relatable (if nosy) residents of Sunny Pines found their way into my heart and will live there for a long time."

—Jessica Strawser, *USA Today* bestselling author of *The Last Caretaker*

"What an unexpected treat this novel is! Everything from the characters to the setting to the twisting plot kept me off balance and loving it the entire way. In turns heartwarming and thrilling, *In the Beautiful Dark* has something for everyone."

—Suzy Krause, bestselling author of *I Think We've Been Here Before* and *Sorry I Missed You*

The Wild Road Home

"Fans of Andrew J. Graff's *Raft of Stars*, Catherine Ryan Hyde's *Just a Regular Boy*, and Lee Smith's *Silver Alert* will find lots to like in Payne's tender and heartwarming novel about unexpected connections in surprising places."

—*Booklist*

A Light in the Forest

"The authentic characters and their realistic struggles make this introspective tale entirely believable. Vega's resilience is sure to endear her to readers."

—*Publishers Weekly*

"*A Light in the Forest* is a thrilling portrait of women finding their footing when all odds seem stacked against them."

—BookTrib

In the
Beautiful
Dark

OTHER TITLES BY MELISSA PAYNE

The Wild Road Home

A Light in the Forest

The Night of Many Endings

Memories in the Drift

The Secrets of Lost Stones

In the Beautiful Dark

A NOVEL

Melissa Payne

LAKE UNION
PUBLISHING

Text copyright © 2025 by Melissa Payne
All rights reserved.

Published by Lake Union Publishing, Seattle

www.apub.com

Amazon, the Amazon logo, and Lake Union Publishing are trademarks of Amazon.com, Inc., or its affiliates.

EU product safety contact:
Amazon Media EU S. à r.l.
38, avenue John F. Kennedy, L-1855 Luxembourg
amazonpublishing-gpsr@amazon.com

ISBN-13: 9781662515750 (paperback)
ISBN-13: 9781662515767 (digital)

Cover design by Shasti O'Leary Soudant
Cover image: © Adina Iftimie / ArcAngel, © ElenaChelysheva / Shutterstock

Printed in the United States of America

To Ella, Keira, and Sawyer: The gift of your adult friendship makes the heartache of missing bedtime stories and scraped knees sting a little less. I love you.

One

February 29, 1972

Allison walked arm in arm with Birdie, dodging a cold sleet that tapped against the plastic headscarf she had tied around her shaggy hair. A fat drop slid inside the collar of her raincoat, freezing slime that spread goose bumps from her back all the way down her newly shaved legs.

"I swear, this cold makes my leg hair grow twice as fast." She gripped Birdie's arm tighter with a shiver. "I'll have prickly shins before I even take the stage."

Birdie laughed. "Maybe it'll keep Sleazy Ted's hands from roving."

Allison snorted. "Fat chance. Sleazy Ted gets handsy even if the Giant is working." The Giant, the kindest and strictest bouncer at the club, had an actual name, but Allison preferred the nickname because it made her think of Felix and his favorite bedtime story, "Jack and the Beanstalk." And thinking about her four-year-old son reminded her why she was walking toward a building on Colfax with a marquee that boasted BOTTOMLESS TOPLESS TALENT. Above the marquee stood another kind of giant—an Amazon clad in head-to-toe red: pantyhose, high heels, and a leotard, with a pillbox hat atop her brown hair.

The money she earned dancing for Sleazy Ted and the like paid for a sitter, kept the heat and the lights on, and added to a growing savings. And soon she'd use it to go to school to become a teacher. High school, she'd decided, so she could be like Miss Anderson, her English teacher. Young Miss Anderson had guessed Allison's pregnancy before she'd even told her parents; had taken her aside, held her hand between her own. *If you need anything, I'm here for you.* Allison often wondered what might have happened if she'd gone to Miss Anderson for help instead of running away.

Allison grabbed Birdie's hand and squeezed. They'd reached the marquee and paused, protected from the rain by its thick overhang. The moody gray and wet afternoon reflected the crowd of rumpled and shifty-eyed men already gathered inside the dark bar; Allison would rather shiver in the cold for a minute longer with Birdie. She was still new to dancing, having left her low-paid receptionist job where she'd danced around a hands-on boss like his personal showgirl. At least Sid King's had bouncers.

"Freedom," Birdie said.

"Freedom," Allison agreed, and turned to face her friend. Birdie was a bombshell: shiny auburn waves and eyes a golden green. In her yellow raincoat and umbrella, she resembled a grown-up version of the Morton Salt girl. But she was stable, honest, and hardworking, and why Allison hadn't fallen flat on her face when she ran off to Denver pregnant and alone. Birdie hated that Allison worked at the club now too. But they'd needed the income, and Allison had grown tired of doing what was expected. This was her choice, and it felt damn good to finally be making decent money. Must be how men felt all the time.

There was another reason she needed a moment outside the smoky club: she had something she wanted to give to Birdie. Allison's hand trembled as she pulled a small box from her pocket.

Birdie's dark eyebrows arched. "What's this?"

"Happy birthday, Bird."

"You remembered."

"Of course I remembered. How many leap year babies do I know?" She held up a finger. "Exactly one. Open it."

"Now?" Birdie sounded nervous.

Allison playfully stomped her foot. "Yes, now!"

Birdie slid off the paper—careful not to tear it in case they could use it again, Allison knew, and smiled at Birdie's thriftiness. She opened the box and Allison's heart thumped.

Inside was a necklace with a tiny gold bird in flight. Birdie held it up, blinking, her eyes wet. "It's beautiful, but how—"

"I didn't spend my savings, I promise. I got it at a garage sale, and it was so cheap. Well, I mean, for me it was. The lady selling it must have paid a bundle when she bought it." Allison shrugged. "Their trash, our treasure."

"Thank you," Birdie said, holding the necklace like it might break.

"Let me put it on you." She stepped behind her, opened the clasp, and when she clipped it around Birdie's neck, she paused, hands lingering across her back. She breathed in pine needles and roses, a scent specific to Birdie, like she flew among the trees and gardens every night. Allison brought her lips close to Birdie's ear and spoke what had lingered on her heart, played at the tip of her tongue for almost a year now. "I love you, Bird." A sentiment she believed Birdie felt but was too afraid to say out loud.

Birdie stiffened and tapped Allison's hand. "Love you too, Al."

"No, not like that, not like a friend." Allison's pulse raced. "Like the way men and women love each other. With my whole heart."

Birdie didn't move; Allison wasn't even sure she was breathing. Then she felt Birdie's shoulders soften beneath her hands, and Allison's entire body tingled with relief. Until Birdie ruined it. "You don't want this, Al," she said.

Anger slid hot down her throat. "You don't know what I want."

Birdie stepped away from Allison, and cold air slithered between them. Of the two of them, Birdie was the levelheaded one. The one who had taken Allison in when she was pregnant; who'd provided a home for her son, loved him as though he were her own. Who wouldn't give in to the feelings that had grown between them. Allison gathered her nerve and, under the overhang where the nearly naked mannequin stood alone in the rain, she said, "If you're afraid of what people will think, know that I'm not." She lifted her chin. "Look at me, Birdie. I'm an unwed mother with a fatherless son, and I wouldn't change a thing about where we are now and I don't care a lick about what people think of us. Do you know why?"

Birdie was staring at her, rouged lips parted, a flicker in her eyes.

"Because it's my life to live. And I choose you. You make my heart want to fly out of my chest. And you love Felix so much it makes me want to cry." She took a step closer to Birdie, and when she didn't turn away, Allison moved until they were inches apart. She put her hands on either side of Birdie's face. Their eyes locked. "To hell with everyone else," Allison said.

A look of pain stole the glow from Birdie's eyes. "You have no idea how much it can hurt," she whispered.

Allison let her hands fall to her sides; she could feel Birdie closing down. "And you do?"

Birdie's mouth opened. "Al, I—"

"What the hell you two doing standing here like a coupla morons?" Their manager filled the doorway, his greasy stink dampening the crispness of the winter air. Ruining the moment between them.

Allison spoke through her teeth. "Just give us a minute, Jerry, can you?"

He exhaled a grunt. "No."

Birdie shook her head and brushed a hand through her hair, giving the man a rueful smile. "We're coming in now," she said, shaking her umbrella violently as she walked past him and sending a deluge of water at his shoes. "Oops, sorry!"

Allison followed, frustrated by the interruption. She tried to stay angry but found she couldn't because the conversation had sparked hope. Birdie had been about to share something with her, and her gut told her it was the thing that kept Birdie so locked up when it came to love. Allison tightened her jaw. Tonight they would talk about everything because she was done pretending, and if Birdie wasn't ready, well—her chin trembled—then Allison wasn't sure what she was going to do.

∼

Birdie thought the daytime crowd at Sid King's was the worst. Horny drunks downing cheap liquor with glazed eyes and greedy hands. Then again, she thought the nighttime crowd was the worst too. Men in suits with a little bit of money and privilege that whetted their egos and expectations. But the shift she hated the most was working alongside Allison. Then she had to endure the sleazeballs who licked their lips and touched their pants, leering at her every crease and curve. Today she couldn't stop thinking about Allison's declaration, and it kept her mind off the sticky floor, the air tinged with sweat and onions, and the eyes on Allison. There was a tightening in her stomach whenever she thought of the tenderness in Allison's touch, the simplicity of her words. *I love you.*

Birdie wasn't a fool. Allison had alluded to her feelings before, growing braver each time, and now today coming right out and saying it like that. That was Allison, brave and bold, and it left Birdie breathless and a little afraid.

Birdie tiptoed her fingers down her stockinged leg to the tip of her shiny black heel, the exaggerated bend emphasizing the curve of her hip and keeping the customers' eyes locked on her body. She preferred it that way, hating the ones who tried to make eye contact. The dancing was automatic, letting her mind wander back to her friend. The idea that they could be together the way Allison dreamed of was pie-in-the-sky. She was naive in her boldness. Birdie knew the cost of being her true self, and it was devastating. She couldn't bear the same thing happening with Allison.

She looked down the stage at Allison twirling her hips, just out of reach of Sleazy Ted, and noticed a gray pallor to her cheeks, a sheen across her forehead. She didn't look well. The song ended and Birdie made her way down the stage.

"Are you okay?" she whispered.

Allison shook her head. "No, I think I might have a fever. It came on so suddenly."

Birdie touched the back of her hand to Allison's forehead the way she had learned to do with Felix. It was clammy, hot. "You must have whatever Felix had last week."

Allison nodded.

Birdie took her elbow and led her off the stage, Sleazy Ted grunting in displeasure. "Hey! Bring her back!"

Birdie gave a quick glance to Jerry, who was looking the other way, and then shot her middle finger up at Ted. He hunched his shoulders over his beer, frowning. Behind him, the Giant grinned.

Backstage, Allison collapsed into a chair.

"Oh, Al, you look terrible. Go home!"

She shook her head. "I can't! I left early last week to pick up Felix from the sitter when he got sick. Jerry will fire me."

Birdie shook her head. "You can't work like this. Go home. I'll call Cora. She owes me one."

Allison's shoulders slumped. "Yeah, okay."

Birdie helped her into her coat, tied the rain bonnet around her hair. "I'll bring home some chicken noodle soup."

Fever tears sprang into Allison's eyes. Birdie touched her cheek, her vulnerability in the moment reminding her of how she'd first met her friend—inside a Kmart, her dark hair parted in the middle and falling down her back like the hippies Birdie had seen in *Time* protesting the war.

Birdie had been shopping and couldn't help but notice the girl's shoulders squared above a swollen belly. She'd looked young, too young to be in that predicament, and the absence of a wedding ring hinted at the direness of her situation. A manager followed her: boring brown suit pants, white shirt, tie, shined shoes, eyes big behind thick glasses. Birdie felt a flare of recognition. She knew him from the club. A regular. He spoke to the pregnant girl loud enough for others to hear. On a moral

6

high ground. *We can't have that here.* He shook his head, disgusted, glancing around him to see who was watching. *This is a place of family values.*

Birdie should have left; it wasn't her fight. But the sallow disdain on his face, the desperate yet straight-backed defiance of the pregnant woman made Birdie's hackles rise. She strode up to the man, his cologne thick, eye-watering. Yeah, she remembered him, and from the surprised lift of his eyebrows, the mottled pink of his cheeks, he remembered her from the club too. His mouth hung open, and oh, how Birdie had wanted to hook it with her finger, yank him out of the store, and toss him to the pavement. She wasn't so brave as all that.

In the end, all it took was the one look from Birdie for the man to stop his showboating. In a much quieter voice, he said, *We don't have an opening for you. Please go.*

Birdie had followed the girl out of the store and found her leaning against the building, cradling her belly with one arm and smoking a cigarette, hand trembling when she inhaled.

I'm Birdie.

The girl's forehead wrinkled when she looked at Birdie. *Allison.*

Birdie smiled, gestured toward the smoke curling into the air. *Is that okay for the baby?*

Allison blinked and stared at the cigarette in her hand. *I have no fucking clue.* It fell from her fingers to the sidewalk; she stubbed it out with her shoe, and her tears fell with it. Birdie ached for the girl's predicament. She wasn't much older than Allison, and understood without needing a single detail that life hadn't worked out at all the way the girl had planned. Birdie took Allison by the arm and walked her back to her apartment, where they drank coffee, talked, and laughed. Even then, Allison had been frank and unapologetic about her situation. *Turns out my parents care more about their reputations than their own flesh and blood.* She'd rubbed her belly. *This baby will never know what that feels like.* Then she'd smiled. *So what's your sob story?*

And Birdie had almost told her. About her first love and a stolen kiss. Instead, she'd shrugged. *Oh, it's nothing so dramatic as all that.* Allison had laughed, and by the end of that first afternoon together, Birdie had offered her a place to stay.

Backstage, the heat had been cranked up, the dressing room stinking of old stockings and takeout. She handed Allison her umbrella. "You don't need to catch a chill on top of this."

Their hands touched when Allison took the umbrella. Birdie paused, words on the tip of her tongue: *I love you too.* Shook her head and crossed her arms instead.

A beat of silence. Allison sighed. "Oh no," she said.

"What's wrong?"

"We're supposed to celebrate your birthday with Felix tonight."

When Allison had learned that Birdie was a leap year baby, she'd been beside herself, excited at the chance to celebrate something so rare. On her last leap birthday at home, Birdie's mother made steaks for dinner and ordered a special cake. They ate on the fine china that night. Her father had slid a small box across the table. Pearl earrings. Birdie shook away the memories. "Please, I'm not a child."

"But you are! You're five today."

She laughed softly. Allison was always doing little things. Celebrating birthdays with abandon, giving little gifts—she touched the bird resting against her chest, blinked at the woman's kindness. Birdie had had to sell the pearl earrings one month when money was tight and she'd had no other nice jewelry. Allison remembered things like that. "We'll celebrate when you're feeling better."

"I ordered a cake. Your favorite too: lemon poppyseed."

"From where?" Between the two of them, they had little money to spend on frivolous things.

"The landlord's son."

"Who?"

"I met him on the stairs the other day; he was painting for his father. Apparently, he was a baker of some renown in Chicago."

"Is that so?"

"And he's making you a cake for free. Said it would be good to do what he loves."

"Who am I to turn down free cake?"

Allison laughed, then grimaced. "Oh, my head hurts."

"Hey, girls!" the manager's cigarette-thick voice boomed backstage. "What the hell's going on back there?"

"Hang on a minute, Jerry! Allison's sick," Birdie yelled, and helped Allison to the back door. "Go, rest. I'll see you at home. And don't worry about Felix. He's all mine tonight." Birdie loved Felix as if he were her own. Having been there since his very first breath, all the sleepless nights, first foods, first steps, first words—her love for him was just a fact.

Allison's grateful smile dimpled her cheeks.

From behind her: "One of yous better get her skinny ass onstage or you're both fired."

"Go," Birdie said. "Get some sleep so we can eat the painter's cake tonight." She watched Allison walk down the alley; sleet had turned to snow that pattered softly on the pavement. Her leg muscles twitched, and Birdie fought against a desire to run out, put her arms around Allison, and hold her. Instead, she closed the door to the alley and returned to the dressing room.

Today she turned twenty-four years old. Seven years since she'd left home. Five since she'd last spoken to her parents and realized their love had conditions she'd never meet. And a lifetime since her very first love had tried to kill herself because of her feelings for Birdie.

When Allison had walked into her life, Birdie had given up on love. She was content to be Allison's friend, Felix's doting "aunt." She was not prepared for the growing affection that took up all the space inside her chest until she couldn't breathe from longing. She'd never dreamed Allison would return her feelings. But in the last few months Allison had tried to tell her in one way or another, and Birdie had done her best to put her off. She sat down, arms folded across her stomach. Allison's words curled around her heart: *I love you.*

Could things be different for her and Allison?

For a moment, she let herself dream. There were those communes out in California where all the free love lived. Times were changing. There'd been riots, protests, marches, and demonstrations demanding rights. Could the future hold a place for people like them?

I love you.

Birdie had been that bold once. And it had led to so much heartache she'd sworn to herself she'd never live that kind of life. She touched her cheek where Allison's hands had cupped her face, the sweet smell of cherry lip gloss lingering in her nose.

To hell with everyone else.

She made her way back to the stage, a tentative hopefulness creeping into her heart. Allison loved Birdie and she didn't care what anyone else thought. She touched the gold bird, and the dankness of the bar turned magical with possibility. Today was her birthday. Maybe it was the best time to start something new.

~

Later, she rushed home from work, stopping first for chicken noodle soup at the corner grocery, then hurrying past their apartment to Mrs. Dempsey's down the hall. Felix rushed to greet her the minute it was opened. "Mama!" He threw his arms around her legs, smelling of Play-Doh and cookies. He called them both *mama*, no matter how many times Birdie had tried to correct him.

"It's Birdie, silly boy, and watch the soup. It's hot." His arms around her legs only tightened. She waved at Mrs. Dempsey. "Hope he was good for you."

The older woman waved back from the kitchen, where she was feeding mashed peas to a baby in a high chair. "A dear as always. See you tomorrow?"

"Same time." She closed the door and turned to see a man in paint-splotched overalls walking away from them and toward the stairwell, carrying a bucket and other supplies. Allison's words from that morning—*baker turned painter*—flashed in her mind. Was that him? She smiled, warmed by Allison's thoughtfulness. She'd get Felix settled, check on Allison, and then go get her cake.

Holding the soup in one hand, Birdie slid her key into the door. It spun uselessly, and her shoulders fell. The broken lock. She cursed herself for dragging her feet, and made a mental note to phone the landlord right away.

Felix's hand tugged on her shirt. "I have to pee."

"Okay, honey, just a minute." She pushed open the door and was stopped short by a smell she didn't recognize. Something chemical, like a cleaning product. Maybe Allison had been nauseous too.

"Al?" she called, and headed straight into the bedroom. Unmade, rumpled sheets: empty. Allison was up.

Felix danced at the closed bathroom door. "Mamamamamamamama! I have to pee! Now!"

Birdie set the soup onto the kitchen counter and hurried to his side. "Hold on, buddy. Al? You feeling any better? Felix-boy needs the bathroom, if that's okay."

No answer.

Felix's hopping stopped abruptly. "Oh no, Mama." His pants darkened and his cheeks reddened. "I'm sorry."

"It's okay, sweetheart. Come on, let's get you cleaned up." She made a pile of his dirty clothes and helped him change his underwear. "You want to pick your pajamas tonight?" He ran to a small chest of drawers in the room he shared with Allison and pulled out pajamas with trains on them. "Choo-choo tonight?" she said.

He giggled.

She helped him into his pajamas and sat back on her heels. "Why don't you play in your room while I get dinner going? Mama's not feeling good, so we're going to leave her be for now, okay?"

He ran to his room, and soon she heard train noises and a conductor speaking. She smiled, and on her way to the kitchen, she stopped at the bathroom door and knocked again. "Allison?"

Still no answer.

"Can I get you anything?" Her fingertips tingled, *I love you too* on the tip of her tongue. Her heart squeezed through her ribs. This life, this woman, Felix—all she ever wanted was right here. But now was not the time, not when Allison was so sick she couldn't leave the bathroom.

Birdie sucked in her cheeks. Her passion had been what had gotten her in trouble. In fifth grade, overcome by her first real crush, Lynette Patterson, and having no guidance on how to navigate those feelings, she'd given the girl a valentine with a simple sentiment: *To the most beautiful girl in school.* At home that night, with a cold steak pressed to her eye, she'd told her mother there'd been a fight over a boy. Her mother had tucked a loose strand of hair behind Birdie's ear, smiled. *You're supposed to let the boys fight over you, silly.*

And then in high school with Sarah Wyler—her girlfriend, even if it had been in secret. Birdie had kissed her first but Sarah had responded, her hands roaming down Birdie's back, their combined moans, the shock of white light when Sarah's father flung open her bedroom door. Sarah sent away, returning months later changed, quiet, pale. Birdie slipping her a note in school. *I love you. Run away with me.* Sarah's father finding his daughter in the garage with the car running, his accusations flung at Birdie—*your fault.* Not a word of defense from Birdie's parents.

Birdie pressed a cheek to the door, suddenly anxious to say the words before she lost her nerve. "I have something I want to sa—" She tugged on her lower lip; it could wait. She gave the door a gentle rap. "Allison?" Still no response. It was the quiet that set Birdie's pulse ticking a beat faster. Goose bumps across her back. Allison wasn't one to play games. She knocked again. Hand on the knob, light pressure. It turned. Pushed the door in an inch. "Allison?" Her voice absorbed. The feeling of someone in the small room. No answer. A drip. Light, weightless, like that of water on the tile.

She breathed in. Tasted something metallic, bitter. Her throat was closing. Pushed the door all the way open, and at first she didn't understand what she saw, her mind immediately creating order in the chaos. Allison was taking a bath. There was nothing wrong with that. She moved closer, her feet dragging, a ringing in her ears that muffled everything. A tub empty of water, white porcelain smeared red, and Birdie fell to her knees, hand across her mouth to stifle a scream that wouldn't alert Felix.

She didn't remember the hours that came later. Somehow, she'd kept it together enough to take Felix back to Mrs. Dempsey. He was confused and crying, but he hadn't seen anything. The woman said later that Birdie had hardly been able to speak. When the police arrived, they set her down on a kitchen chair. Someone gave her water, another a damp rag to wipe the blood that had caked in the creases of her palms. She stared at her hands, and through the thickening fog, a conversation diminished her stupor. ". . . neighbor said she's an unwed mother."

Another voice. "Works at Sid King's."

Someone snorted.

A stillness followed, then the first voice. ". . . apparent suicide."

And Birdie pushed to her feet, put her hands on the arm of the officer who stood in the doorway to the bathroom. "No!" Her voice raw, pitiful. His expression when he looked at her a reflection of it.

"Ma'am." Hands on her shoulders, gentle but forceful. "We need you to stay in the kitchen."

"No, you don't understand. She would never hurt herself; she loves Felix too much, and me—" Her stomach revolted and Birdie's mouth watered. She felt like she was going to be sick. "Someone did this to her." Her whispered protest hung limply in the small apartment, and the policeman's eyes softened.

"Ma'am, back to the kitchen. Please."

The strength slipped from her legs, and Birdie allowed herself to be led to the chair, where she sat, numb.

Later—after the police, after they took Allison away, after Birdie asked Mrs. Dempsey to keep Felix overnight so she could scrub clean the tub and tiles—Birdie lay on her side on the floor outside the bathroom in the dark, eyes bleary but dry, arms holding her stomach, fingers smelling of bleach. Murder. It was murder. A sourness lingered in her mouth. They were wrong about her. A sound from the hallway, and she scooted her cheek along the wood to look. Someone outside her apartment, a scuffle of shoes, an object placed on the floor that blackened the slit of hallway light underneath. She crawled over, opened the door.

In a cardboard box, her cake. Blue and yellow birds in icing across the white frosting. In delicate script, *Happy Leap Birthday, Bird!*

With a scream that blistered into something guttural, Birdie hurled the box against the hallway wall opposite her door. It splattered white icing across the wallpaper, chunks of lemon-yellow cake plopping onto the floor. In the morning, when the sun buffeted her swollen eyes and she had to get Felix from the sitter because the world didn't stop for anything, every single crumb and slick of icing was gone, cleaned up by some thoughtful neighbor who didn't understand how cruel it was to wipe away something like it had never existed.

Two

Sunny Pines Retirement Community

February 29, 2024

Birdie sat in the recliner, computer open on her lap, reading through the local news sites. She missed the days of ink-stained fingertips and printed articles. Now the actual newspaper was too thin, and all the real news lived on the internet. But she'd adapted, as people of her age must, and got all her news online or through one of the many apps on her phone.

She mindlessly scrolled, looking for nothing and anything that might keep her mind off another birthday. She coughed, and in her tidy apartment with the nice kitchen and two bathrooms, it was loud and lonely to her ears. Birdie breathed in. After only six months at Sunny Pines, she was lonelier than she'd ever felt in her two-story home with stairs she couldn't climb and a yard overgrown by weeds. At least the house had memories of the good years with Felix. But here, in this independent-living community for the *Sixty-Two and Better!*, where not a soul under the age of seventy-five lived, was where Felix hoped Birdie might have opportunities for friendships, now that she was retired and had all the time in the world (or what was left of it) to enjoy the fruits of her labor. At the very least, he hoped this place, with its activities and structure, might keep her from dipping back into the depression that had tried to swallow her. It seemed poor Felix had drawn the short stick when it came to mothers, because it wasn't any better here than it had been in her house. Without her company to run, Birdie had lost her way, quickly becoming another gray hair among the many, drifting without a purpose. And moving here hadn't made the difference Felix had hoped for.

Birdie sighed and kept scrolling, hoping to find something lighthearted. Like a lost dog found hundreds of miles from its home and reunited with its family. Anything would do. Instead, her eyes went to the last kind of article she needed to read, on today of all days.

Body of Exotic Dancer and Mother of Three
Discovered in Dumpster

A catch in her throat. She scanned the text. *No, no, no.*

The body of twenty-five-year-old Geneva Smith was discovered early Thursday morning behind the Paragon apartment complex on Colfax. The Paragon is no stranger to murder. In 1974, Cora Jones, a dancer at Sid King's, was discarded in a dumpster, drained of her blood. In 1975, Freida Yarrow was found in her bathtub, also drained of blood.

Before she could stop herself, Birdie tapped the printer icon on her computer and pushed to her feet, hands on her walker. She opened the door to the second bedroom; the printer whirred and hummed, spitting out the article. She stared at the paper in her hands, Geneva smiled back from her small black-and-white picture, no clue that this happy photo would be used in an article about her gruesome death.

She tugged at her lip, looked over her shoulder as though Felix could see her. Nettles of anxiety in her stomach didn't stop her from carefully dropping to her knees to look under the bed, where it was overcrowded with old boxes that had no other place to go when she'd moved. She pushed aside a taped-up shoebox; dust tickled her nose, her eyes squinting into the dim space. It was here, she knew, because Felix had lugged over boxes when he helped her move. She'd been shocked when he'd carried in the plastic one with the yellow top. One he obviously didn't remember helping her fill thirty-five years earlier. He'd been too angry at the time, she supposed.

A glimpse of yellow sent a rush of adrenaline down her arms. She gripped it with her fingertips, scooting it across the carpet until she could pick it up and place it on the bed.

She stood above it, holding her breath. She shouldn't open it. Felix had begged her. *Throw it out, please, all of it.* They'd stood outside the police station where he'd had to bail her out for breaking and entering. He'd only been twenty, but so sure of himself, and he'd given her an ultimatum: Allison or him. *Some mysteries don't have answers,* he'd said. *Despite everything, you built a good life for us.* His voice had broken, his blue eyes glowing. *Isn't that enough? Can't that be enough, Mom? Please?*

She'd touched his stubbled cheek, jawline straight and strong. Handsome and so like his mother. *Okay,* she'd said, because there was no way she was going to lose him too.

Felix had grown into a worrier. Birdie had often wondered if the trauma of losing his mother at such a young age had been the cause. Felix insisted he didn't remember his mom. What he remembered was Birdie in the years that followed. Overprotective. Manic about locked doors and windows. Dogged about the truth. That was the other problem with retirement—the clarity of her mistakes that came with it, her fractured legacy in this man she loved so much it hurt.

It hadn't been easy to stop looking for who had murdered Allison. Birdie had always believed that once Felix knew the truth, he'd be at peace about his mother's death. But Felix had insisted it was Birdie who needed that peace, not him.

She touched the box—sealed shut, a place she hadn't gone since her promise to him, yet it had played in the background of her thoughts, perhaps waiting for a moment like today.

Birdie's hands shook when she opened it. Pictures in newsprint, faded but not aged by time; young women—Allison among them—dead, murdered, drained of their blood by a depraved psychopath who was never caught. She held the printout of the Geneva Smith article; was her death a coincidence or something more? Old urges rose like flames, and her stomach soured. This wasn't healthy, had never led to answers and only created problems, a rift between her and Felix. She tried to close the box but voices stirred, imagined pleas, Allison's drifting to the top: *Help us.*

Her hand slipped inside, touching first a picture of Felicity, who had forty-one first cousins and a twin sister who shared the exact same birthmark on her upper-right thigh. Using a tack from a box she found in the bottom of the bin, she pinned Felicity's picture to the wall, along with interviews Birdie had done herself with the woman's sister and any other family who'd talk to her. In 1989, Felicity had been the last known victim of what police had coined "the Vampire Killer." The serial killer Birdie believed had murdered Allison first.

She pulled his victims out one by one, getting lost in the past. The first one, Cora, had danced with her at Sid King's; the second, Freida, had lived at the Paragon too. Birdie coughed, her throat feeling dry. The wall had quickly filled, and with Judy's picture in her hand, she sat on the edge of the bed. Outside, small groups of Sunny Pines residents walked toward the community center. Sunlight glinted across metal walkers and canes, a couple of women chattering loud enough that she caught pieces of it through the window, along with the occasional peal of laughter. Birdie's ground-floor apartment had a perfect view of the parking lot and the comings and goings of all the residents.

She stared down at the picture of Judy. Murdered in 1981, she'd owned five dogs and four cats that her neighbor had had to take to the shelter because Judy had no family that anyone knew of. She'd been alone in life and alone in death, with no one to remember her but Birdie. She swallowed and stood, pinning Judy's picture next to Barb's. Before long the walls were papered in a familiar pattern. Allison and the ten women who'd followed her. Birdie added Geneva next to Felicity and stood back to take in her work.

At one point, it had felt as though these women had needed her. She'd said as much to Felix when he'd questioned her fixation on the murders. She'd forgotten what it had felt like, this sense of purpose that gave way to prickles of energy down her legs.

Her eyes roamed over their faces, most of them she'd only gotten to know after their deaths. Except for Freida, a German immigrant who'd moved in two doors down a year after Allison died and whose homemade strudel had spiced the hallway with cinnamon and baked apples. And Cora, a fellow dancer at Sid King's who wore geometric-patterned scarves around her Afro and favored denim bell-bottoms and huge platform shoes. The loss of her friends had hit her hard. It was only later, when the police announced that a serial killer was at large, that Birdie zeroed in on how closely their deaths mirrored Allison's.

Still, nobody had ever believed her. They pointed to the inconsistencies. Allison's blood had been all over the bathroom, her wrists ragged from her efforts. It was clear to them what Allison had done. The other women's blood had been methodically drained. They were obvious victims.

Birdie's gaze landed on the photo of Allison when she was still pregnant with Felix. Hair long and straight down her back, hands resting on her belly, and a smile playing around the corners of her mouth. One hand on the walker to keep her balance, Birdie felt both sickened and relieved to see her walls alive with the past. Like a recovering alcoholic with a stolen sip.

Her doorbell rang, and Birdie jerked away from the wall, clumsy with her walker, and exited the room, closing the door behind her. An electric shot of pain up her spine from the quick movements. She rubbed her lower back, irritated. Arthritis slithered inside her joints, back, hips, demanding all her attention. It was embarrassing to have deteriorated to the point where the walker had become her constant companion. Maybe that was another reason she kept to herself.

A soft knock followed the doorbell, and Birdie smiled. She did have one friend here at Sunny Pines, and when she opened the door, that friend gave her a disapproving frown.

"Birdie," Faith said, "I smell bleach."

Birdie shrugged, secretly pleased. "So?"

The woman shook her head and pulled a couple of rags and a spray bottle from her cleaning cart. "You're not supposed to clean for me! That's my job." Faith smiled, her youth giving off a magnetic glow.

"I've cleaned enough toilets in my day to know that folks should clean their own damn toilets," Birdie said.

Faith laughed and waited for Birdie to walker herself back a few steps before she came inside. The woman had pulled her glossy black hair into a sleek ponytail, her dark brown eyes delicately lined in black. She went straight to the kitchen.

"Coffee?" Birdie offered. *"Con leche?"* The words were uncomfortable on her tongue.

Faith laughed again. "I'll make you a proper *café con leche* one day. The kind with real Puerto Rican coffee too." Faith sprayed the kitchen counter. "But no thank you, not today. A new tenant moves in tomorrow, and I had to spend extra time cleaning. They replaced the carpet, but I swear . . ." She made a face. "Mrs. Radna's cat must have peed everywhere but the litter box."

Birdie sat in her armchair and inhaled lemon and lavender. "Is that one of your sprays?"

Faith held up the bottle, a glass one with a simple black-and-white label, CLEAN FAITH, typed across. "Don't tell management, but I refuse to use the cleaners they buy." She shook her head. "Full of nasty chemicals."

Birdie nodded approvingly. "How's business?" Birdie had started out cleaning houses, eventually building her own cleaning company into a regional success story—Allison's Maids. Her eyes slid to the spare bedroom; a rising wave of guilt. She'd take it all down tomorrow.

Faith wiped the inside of the microwave. It cooked all of Birdie's meals, spaghetti sauce splattering its insides like a crime scene. "It's slow but good," Faith said. "I have an Etsy store now too. Who knows? Maybe one day Clean Faith will be in Walmart."

"I have no doubt," Birdie said. She respected self-starters like Faith. In her opinion, the world needed more women like her. "Have you convinced your mother to move to Colorado yet?"

Faith shook her head. "She says it's too cold here and Puerto Rico is where she wants to die."

"I understand." Birdie hadn't wanted to leave the house she'd worked her fingers to the bone to buy for her little family. "You must miss her."

"Every day. But I have my work and my business, and every time I send money to Mamá, I feel peace." She shrugged. "It can be lonely, but that's life, eh?"

Birdie nodded. "Yep, she's a bitch."

Faith laughed. "Oh, Birdie." And returned her focus to cleaning.

Birdie pulled at her fingers, not wanting to appear needy for company but sensing the quiet of her apartment linger on the outskirts of their conversation. She hadn't been a loner her entire life—or she hadn't thought she was, with her days filled by work and Felix. In fact, she hadn't realized how few relationships she'd cultivated until she'd retired and the phone had gone silent, except for calls from Felix and the boys.

Faith collected a vacuum cleaner from her cart and crossed the apartment quickly. The space was modest, nothing fancy, except for the perk of bimonthly cleaning. The first time in her life that someone else cleaned Birdie's space. Felix had been the first to suggest Sunny Pines. *The house is too big. Too many stairs. I worry about you.* When she'd protested that she didn't need round-the-clock babysitters, he'd sighed. *It's independent living. No step-up facility or other kind of care, just apartment buildings for people your age.*

People my age, she'd grumbled. She'd been seventy-four at the time, not a hundred and six. She knew of *people her age* and older running marathons, and wasn't there that video of the ninety-year-old woman doing gymnastics? She'd resisted for as long as she could, until the quick progression of arthritis and a hip surgery narrowed her options. But it was the bleak state Felix had found her in that sealed the deal. Birdie had lost motivation to do anything—clean, leave the house, keep in touch with a friend or two—and it had been evident to Felix whenever he called, even though she'd tried to pretend otherwise. His surprise visit hadn't let her hide it from him and he'd seen her at her worst. Stuck in a downward spiral he thought a move would fix.

It *was* nice here, she'd reluctantly told him during one of their evening phone calls. There was yoga, book clubs, trips to the theater, and all manner of social activities designed to keep the white-haired folks from focusing on the elephant in the community—their front-row seat to the end of the road. Not that Birdie bothered with all the activities. She wasn't about to be paraded around like a schoolchild on the community van.

I'm never riding in that van. She'd been emphatic about that, and Felix had laughed, indulgent.

I wouldn't think any less of you if you did, he'd said, and she'd clucked her tongue, smiling on her side of the phone. A charmer like his mom, that Felix.

Faith stopped at the closed door to the spare room, hand twisting the knob, and Birdie made a sound. Faith turned, an eyebrow raised.

"No need to clean that room today."

Faith shrugged. "Okay."

Guilt made her back itch. This was worse than depression, even she knew that. This was excavating something old and destructive. Back then she'd pursued the truth for Felix. He should have had his mother with him all these years. Not Birdie, who forgot to get the lock fixed, who wasn't as brave as Allison, who sometimes still felt like she'd been gifted a son she'd never deserved. Proving Allison's murder was a promise she'd made to herself—to Allison—so Felix would never believe that his mother had left him by choice.

Birdie's chin wobbled, shaking the flesh just below her jawline. When her grandson Cody was five, he'd liked to rub the pad of his finger along the loosening folds of her skin, stopping at age spots and moles, fascinated by the texture and color of *old*.

"Birdie?" Faith crossed the room and knelt in front of her.

Birdie rubbed gooseflesh from her arms, chilled despite the heat from the gas fireplace. This day, rife with memories and regrets, unbound dark thoughts and made her glad for the woman's company.

Faith touched Birdie's arm. "Are you okay?" Such compassion, such kindness from someone so young.

Birdie patted Faith's hand, warmed by the affection. "It's been a day of ghosts. That happens with age, you know. Lots and lots of ghosts."

Faith was nodding. "Mamá says they come at night." She looked serious. "I try to ignore them."

Birdie cleared her throat, trying to regain her composure. "Not literal ghosts for me, dear. Just the ones that come with memories."

A moment of silence followed, with Faith still kneeling; then, from the spare room, a sound. A knock? A creak? A rattle? Birdie couldn't tell because her hearing aids were in the charging station by her bed. Faith's head shot up, her eyes to the door.

"Got a cat lately, Birdie?"

"Cats are spawns of Satan," Birdie said. Feral hunters—the house kind most likely to eat their owners, if given half a chance. "That's the toilet pipes from that woman upstairs. She's got the bladder of a baby, and makes so much noise at night I'm certain she's rearranging the furniture."

Faith stood and her knees responded like well-oiled hinges. "Ms. Trudy ascended Mount Everest twice. She's a badass regardless of her bladder size," Faith said.

Birdie sniffed and studied the age spots scattered across the tops of her folded hands.

"You know," Faith said, "this place isn't so bad."

"It's a dead end." She pulled a pillow onto her lap. The one she bought at the home-goods store for 75 percent off because *Liv, Lagh, Lov* had been printed across the front.

Faith shrugged. "My brother died when he was three. My papá when he was forty-eight. We're all facing the end, Birdie. Some of us get there sooner than others."

Birdie wanted to be angry at the young woman. To accuse her of youthful condescension. But Faith wasn't wrong. Birdie blinked. And blinked again. "At the very least, they could insulate the place better," she said.

"That's the truth," Faith said, and moved toward the bathroom. "It's cold in here!"

Birdie relaxed into her chair, kneading her hands together. She glanced at the spare bedroom and then back down to her lap. She shouldn't have spoken about Trudy like that. The woman was friendly and waved hello every time she saw Birdie. She blamed it on her leap birthday. An endless day. She checked the clock and wished for the moment when she could climb into bed and see another leap day to its end.

Three

ALLISON

We are bound to the truth.

But Birdie is caged by it.

Time has changed her. She is delicate. Her body betrays her. I feel the grinding of her bones against ligaments. In the middle of the night, she wakes in pain that radiates from her tailbone. I am there the day she injures it. A blue plastic sled at the top of a snow-crusted hill. Felix between Birdie's legs, her arms clasped tight around his puffy winter coat. His nose a Rudolph red, Birdie's curls frozen across her shoulders. I try to warn them. My fingers graze the back of her coat.

I would do anything to spare them pain.

Except it can't be avoided.

We know that.

They hit the bump and fly off the sled. Birdie cocoons Felix from the fall, absorbs the brunt of it on her tailbone. She takes Epsom salt baths, sits on cushioned doughnuts, and sleeps with a heating pad for weeks. It heals. But the fissure in her heart only widens. Because Birdie knows the delicateness of each breath. It ticks. It diminishes. It is not a promise.

Birdie sits in her chair, staring at her hands. She is embarrassed about the way she spoke about her neighbor to Faith. It's not who she is. I know this, but others do not. Except Faith, who is empathetic and intuitive and scrubs Birdie's clean toilet anyway because she wants the older woman to have the peace that comes with clean.

Birdie picks up a silver frame from the end table by her elbow, touches my face in the photo. The sting of our lost moment never subsides for her. Regret is powerful in that way. A rabid dog with its teeth sinking deep, impossible to shake off without losing flesh. Sadness is in the rise and fall of her bone-thin chest. She stares at her hands. I rest mine over the top. Today Birdie lives in the past, her thoughts set firmly inward. She can't see what we see. A collection of souls. A gathering of truths. A future where something comes for her.

I can't leave her until it's done.

We won't leave until it's done.

Four

Birdie flipped through the newsletter while Faith vacuumed, the young woman smiling at her anytime their eyes met.

PICK UP AFTER YOUR PET!

ALL GUESTS MUST PARK ON THE ROAD!!

IF YOU SIGN UP FOR AN ACTIVITY, YOU WILL STILL BE CHARGED EVEN IF YOU DON'T ATTEND!

She blew air through her nose. Birdie hadn't signed payroll checks, offered health care to her employees, built her own 401(k) to be talked to in all caps and exclamation points. She turned the page, the edge tearing with the force of her annoyance. Noticed the arthritic curve of her pointer finger. Turned another page, and right before she threw the damn thing across the room, she saw the announcement, and only because it was in regular-size letters. Book club. Bring a sports book to share. Thursday 4:30 in the community room. Birdie snorted. This person had no clue how a book club worked.

"Found something?" Faith's voice startled her, the vacuum cleaner silenced and the cord wrapped up.

Birdie closed the newsletter, tossed it onto the side table. "Not a thing. Other than I'm too young to be here. Didn't you know that, Faith?"

Faith pressed a hand to her chest and gave her a look of pretend shock. "You live here?"

Birdie's laugh morphed into a grunt when she pushed to her feet and steadied herself by gripping the handles of her walker. "I noticed a new camper moved in down the street." Denver had become an expensive place to live—prohibitively so for many folks—and of late, an RV or two could be seen parked along the length of empty street behind the community. A home was a home, even on wheels. And while Birdie had never experienced being homeless, she'd been damn close at times.

But not everyone held her same view. She'd heard the grumbling from folks who refused to walk that way anymore. Worry that people who choose to live like that could be dangerous. That was one thing about getting old: they were slower, more vulnerable to everything, more afraid of the unknown. After Allison's death, Birdie had lived so much of her life in fear of something happening to Felix. Of letting her guard down and losing him too. As he grew older without incident, she was able to let it go. She worried far less about herself.

Faith nodded. "A girl lives in the new camper."

A tingle down her spine. A girl. "Does she live alone?"

Faith shook her head. "I don't know. I saw her coming out of the camper with two little dogs," she said. "But she's very young and she seems shy."

Birdie hated to think of a young girl living alone like that. Flimsy locks, to be sure, with only a building full of mostly deaf folks within screaming distance. She shivered. "She's not safe out there if she's alone."

"I'm going to bring her some of my empanadillas. Maybe find out a little bit more about her."

Birdie's mouth watered. Faith had shared her empanadillas with Birdie several times, and she could taste the buttery, smoky goodness just thinking about them. "Let me know what you find out."

Faith tilted her head to one side. "You worry about her like you do me, huh?"

Birdie's fingers ached from her grip on the walker. "I just don't like the thought of you young women alone. It's not safe for you." She could tell that Faith thought her concern kind, if a little misplaced, but Birdie knew more than most about the bad things that lurked in broad daylight. She tried to shake off the feeling that settled heavy across her shoulders and pulled a small envelope from her pocket, held it out. "Thank you."

Faith shook her head. "You know I can't take that."

Birdie sniffed. So much for independent living. Management had rules for everyone. Like no tipping the cleaners.

She walkered across the carpet and pushed the envelope into Faith's hands. "This is mine to give to you. The rules be damned. You do your work with exceptional care, and you deserve a tip. My choice." Birdie winked. "But if you're a rule follower, then think of it as a micro-investment in your product line."

Faith's shoulders dropped with her smile, and she took the envelope, pocketing it. "Okay, but you can't do this every time I clean here or you'll run out of money."

Birdie shrugged. "When I run out of money I'll take that as my cue."

A wrinkle formed in between the woman's eyes. "Cue for what?"

Birdie linked her thumbs and fluttered her fingers to make the shape of a butterfly. "To dearly depart."

Faith made a sound in her throat. "That's not funny."

Birdie picked up a peacock-blue pashmina from where she'd laid it across the end of the sofa and wrapped it around her shoulders. "If you can't laugh about death at my age, what's left to laugh at?"

"Oh, Ms. Birdie. You're too much." Faith loaded her cart with the sprays and dirty rags, and hefted her vacuum cleaner onto a hook on the side. "See you in two weeks."

They cleaned twice a month, more than Birdie needed since it was just her. So different from the days of raising Felix and running her own company, when dishes crowded her sink and dirty clothes piled up among the toys. She was too busy cleaning other people's homes to bother with her own. But those were good days, despite the clutter. Her heart beat at the remembered weight of Felix's small body in her arms, how he rubbed circles on her cheek when she read him books. The smell of his hair after a bath. His warm breath against her neck.

The apartment had turned cool, and Birdie started to walk over to turn up the heat, stopped. The light outside was the thin kind that came from a winter afternoon and a sun that disappeared behind the opposite apartment building well before sundown. Suddenly, she didn't want to be alone. She stared at the closed bedroom door, thought of the pictures tacked onto the wall, anxiety tugging on her stomach. They called to her, Allison and the women, their voices swarming inside her head, as though the unboxing had freed them. She spied the newsletter face down on her coffee table. Any distraction would help, and she loved reading. Not sports books, but it was better than staying here and scouring the internet for more information on Geneva Smith, which was exactly what she'd do. Felix wanted her to get involved. And on today of all days, she'd do anything to keep her memories at bay. From her bookshelf, she pulled a book, slid it into her shoulder bag, and walked out the front door.

~

Birdie's walker glided over the carpet, a quiet swooshing sound accompanying her wherever she went. The community room was just down the hallway from her apartment. She checked her brand-new watch—a birthday present from Felix, and one that had taken her only a few moments to set up and pair with her phone just that morning. She'd been quite proud of herself for the feat. According to the fancy watch, she was only ten minutes late.

Voices drifted toward her. Outside the community room, she hesitated, brushing a hand through her hair. When she was younger, the only thought she gave to being old was the color of her hair. What shade of gray would she be? Bright white and silky? Dirty gray and coarse? Birdie's dark locks had changed gradually, auburn shifting to dark gray, threads of snow white weaving throughout. Changing but not too much. Like Birdie herself. Inside, she was the girl who left home at seventeen, who favored jeans before they were fashionable for women, and wore brightly colored headscarves to keep her rust-colored waves out of her face when she cleaned. But here she was, the old woman with the walker, nothing much to distinguish her from the others.

She should turn around and go home. People here would say she was friendly and interesting, but that was because she wasn't a joiner. They didn't really know her, and she was fine with that. Felix called her a loner, judgmental at times, and he wasn't wrong. There were things she kept to herself, things that nobody understood—not even Felix anymore—but had become such a part of her it was impossible to hide from anyone who knew her well.

Birdie's arm muscles fought with the walker, wanting to give up on this foolish idea and go home, watch reruns of *Suits*. That was a good show. But when she thought of her apartment today, she felt a hollowness expand inside her chest. Today was the day when thoughts of Allison scratched at the callus built by years apart, the loss made fresh if only for a moment.

"Who's there?" A man's voice—impatient, curt, and Birdie felt like she'd been caught skipping by a truancy officer. "Are you here for the book club?" This time his voice was a skosh kinder, like he'd remembered himself.

She pushed her walker forward and entered the room. Two men sat opposite each other on the overly floral couches. One smiled at her above a white beard, white hair to the middle of his neck, round belly flanked by skinny legs and arms. Like a pregnant Santa Claus. The other man was fit, shirt tucked neatly into brown trousers, full head of hair trimmed close to the sides. He'd be handsome, too, if it wasn't for his nose. Crooked, bulbous, like he'd broken it more than once.

"Come in." Broken Nose Guy said it like a command.

Birdie stayed put. She didn't acquiesce to commands. "Is this the book club?"

He blinked. "Yes."

"You wanted me to bring my own book?"

"A sports book, yes."

"Are you aware that most book clubs read the same book?"

The man shrugged. "No one's come before."

Santa Claus laughed. "I just joined, myself." He stood. "I'm Glen and I'm brand new here. Although, to be honest, I don't officially move in until tomorrow. But I was here for a walk-through and was just leaving when I saw Joseph sitting alone, and I invited myself into his book club." He kept standing, waiting for Birdie to take a seat. Polite. She still liked that tradition, even if it did reference a time when men believed themselves to be the superior sex. Some still did, but at least they were challenged more on it these days.

The other guy didn't laugh or smile, but his face didn't hold the arrogance that his tone and body language suggested. Birdie decided to give him another chance to make a first impression. She sat down in one of the blue wingback chairs and took a book out of her bag, laying it across her lap. Glen sat down.

"I'm Birdie." She turned to Glen, thinking about what Faith had said earlier. "Are you moving into 115?"

His smile was easy. "I am!"

"I live just down the hall."

"How wonderful! We're neighbors. And Joseph here lives just across the hall. Like a regular neighborhood gang."

His optimism was slightly off-putting. Birdie turned her attention to Joseph. She'd never met him before—or seen him around the building, for that matter. He must use his patio door exclusively. "What book did you read?"

Joseph cleared his throat. "I read *The Soul of a Butterfly.*" The book sat untouched on the couch by his thigh. "You two are the first to show up to the book club, so I mostly read what I want."

Birdie found herself fighting a smile. "Defeats the purpose of a book club, though, right?"

"Or maybe the category is a bit too narrow," Glen offered.

Birdie nodded, but Joseph looked unfazed. "I like sports," he said.

Her second first impression of Joseph led her to believe that he was an introverted oddball, and she immediately liked him. "I didn't know I was joining your book club until about five minutes ago, but thankfully I've read *Harry Potter and the Goblet of Fire.*" She held it up.

Glen's laugh shook his belly. Joseph shifted on the couch, squinting, a bit irritated like she'd gone off-script. "That's not a sports book."

"Of course it is. It's got the big quidditch tournament. The World Cup of quidditch tournaments, to be clear."

"Creative take on sports fiction, Birdie! I like it." Glen held out his hands, palms up. "I was woefully unprepared for my first sports book club meeting. But if I may, I could discuss the book I just finished, as it has some elements of sport sprinkled throughout."

"What's that?" Joseph sounded hopeful, and Birdie guessed her quidditch reference had missed the mark.

"A Sherlock Holmes novel." Glen's deadpan expression made Birdie snort a laugh. She found herself liking this Glen guy too.

Joseph sighed.

"He does *hunt* down a criminal in every book," Birdie said.

Glen nodded at Joseph. "Hunting is a sport, is it not?"

"So, you like birds?" Joseph seemed to have given up on the books. He pointed to the birds printed across her bag. Cardinals, blue jays, and finches. And then to the owl stitched across the breast of her button-down shirt.

"Comes with the territory, I guess." Birdie had been asked about her name often enough to have her standard reply. The truth was that her given name was Dorcas, a name her father had chosen for her because it had been his mother's name. A fine woman, he'd told her. She'd once been close to her father—a daddy's girl, her mother would say. When her father rejected her, it was so painful Birdie needed a change. So she started with her name and picked something that made her believe she could fly on her own.

"Not a typical name, is it?" Glen said.

"There's Birdie Tebbetts," Joseph said.

"Who?" Birdie asked.

"He was a catcher for the Cleveland Indians." Joseph's voice had softened, and Birdie suspected it was because he was on stable ground when he spoke about sports.

Glen laughed. "And we're back to the topic at hand! Well done, Joseph!" He took the lead. "Shall we discuss our books, then?"

An hour later, Birdie rose to her feet. The time had passed surprisingly fast, with topics ranging from boxing glory and quidditch tragedy to criminal investigations à la Sherlock Holmes. "Quite the interest you have there, Glen," she said.

He smiled, sheepish, like he was sharing a secret that might make them think differently of him. "A hazard of the job, I suppose."

"Were you in law enforcement?" Joseph said.

Glen held up his hands. "Guilty. I just hope neither of you are retired criminals." Glen smiled. "Because I quite like our little book tête-à-tête-à-tête." A self-satisfied smile; he was pleased with his quickness.

"Me too," Birdie said. It had been a blissful hour in which she hadn't once thought about Allison or the faces that she'd spread across her wall, but now that it was ending, the images were creeping back in. "Glen, did you by chance see the article about Geneva Smith?" She figured a retired cop might keep up on local crime.

Glen's eyebrows rose. "Why, yes, I did."

An uptick in her pulse. "I read that there was some speculation that it's the Vampire Killer returned."

"I suppose that makes sense, given where she was found," Glen said, tugging at the end of his sleeve. "But the serial killer returned? I very much doubt that."

Birdie straightened. "She was found in a dumpster, like his very first victim, Cora Jones, and she had quite a bit of blood loss too." Although the article had been unclear about how she'd suffered it.

"More likely a husband or boyfriend did it," he said.

Birdie deflated, hating herself for even a moment of disappointment. The last thing she wanted was for a serial killer to be on the hunt again. Yet, for a moment, talking about it made her feel relevant; this was a topic she knew something about. She pinched the fabric arm of the chair. There was no good in digging up the past. None at all. And Glen was probably right anyway. The husband or boyfriend had done it. A small voice protested—the police had said the same about Cora and Freida until Carol's murder made it painfully clear that something far more sinister was at play. She shook her head and turned to Joseph, who had listened to the exchange in silence. "So, when do we meet again, Joseph?"

"Oh." He looked surprised by her question. "Um, next month?"

"And you're still married to this sports-book theme?" she said.

Joseph nodded.

"Okay, then. What do you think about reading *The Hunger Games* next?"

A low groan from Joseph, and Glen laughed. She smiled at Glen. "Good luck on the move tomorrow."

"Righto!" He glanced out the glass doors and frowned. "My brother's here to pick me up." His face soured. "A few years younger than me and he treats me like a child. I can still drive, you know." It seemed Glen argued with an invisible dissenter.

She felt a twinge of empathy for the man. Sometimes the sum of their years, the whiteness of their hair, the frailty of their bodies, reduced them in the eyes of others.

A smile returned to Glen's face. "Well, then, I'll see you soon, neighbors."

Early-winter night pushed against the windows; Birdie was suddenly drained. She turned to Joseph, who stood silently beside her. "It was nice to meet you."

Joseph cleared his throat. "I'm going that way too."

"Okay, then." They walked side by side, Joseph keeping pace with her slow progress. He could walk faster, she knew—that was obvious from the steadiness of his legs. But it was nice.

Outside her door, she said, "Good night, Joseph."

His cheeks crinkled with his smile, slight but warm. "Night, Birdie." He stood with his hands in his pockets, like he was making sure she got home okay. A polite gesture, maybe. But to Birdie, it seemed like he didn't want to go into his apartment any more than she did. It softened her, and very nearly pushed her so far out of her comfort zone that she almost invited him inside for a cup of decaf. Almost. As lonely as Birdie was, especially in the bleakness of a winter evening on a leap day, with Felix and his family on the other side of the country, book club was a big enough step for her today.

"Good night, Joseph," she said again, and tried to insert her key, missed with a slightly shaky hand, missed again, then finally seated the key inside the lock and turned. "Blasted hands," she mumbled to herself, cheeks heating at her unsteadiness. Her walker knocked against the doorframe, and she was happy to let the door close on the hallway and Joseph.

The small lamp in her entryway burned golden, keeping the dark at bay. She preferred a light on, especially at night. Memories swirled, waiting to slip inside her waking thoughts, her dreams, her nightmares. In her bedroom, Birdie changed into a nightgown printed with owls. They protected her at night—or so she liked to believe—and tonight she needed the protection, on her birthday, when the past was a person with her wrists smeared red.

Five

ALLISON

We listen to Birdie and the others, and we are stirred by the blood washing through their veins. The echo of heartbeats, inhales of breath. They are the lucky ones. Years pave their paths, joy in moments of community, grandchildren, birthdays.

But not all birthdays.

No, not all birthdays.

Loneliness swims around them, sticking to some hearts more than others. Pockmarks of love and loss.

A bittersweet mixture.

We are not jealous. We don't begrudge them their breaths.

Yet we yearn for the years stolen from us.

They yearn too.

Joseph sits in his big chair and watches sports. Any sport will do, but he prefers boxing. The room is empty of pictures and knickknacks; the only other piece of furniture is a heavy bag that collects dust. He makes fists with his hands. Joseph doesn't realize he does this, incessantly, like a tic.

He steeps in regret. We can smell it. Stale, sweat-soaked. He wakes up in the early-morning hours thinking about his wife. When this happens, he can't go back to sleep, so he drinks strong coffee and reads a book until the sun reminds him that it's another day. Most mornings he goes to the gym in the community center, which is empty much of the time.

He regrets the book club. He didn't mind that no one showed up before tonight. Joseph can't remember what gave him the harebrained idea to begin with, except that Sofia had loved books. He is surprised that Birdie showed up. Joseph notices Birdie. He thinks she's hard to miss because of the brightly colored scarves she wears every day. Sometimes in her hair or around her shoulders, once around her waist like a skirt. But that's not why he notices her.

He senses his wife in the dapples of sunshine, the fluttering of a curtain, and in the gossamer blue of Birdie's scarf. His wife beckons him from the shadows, pining for his absolution and seeing its potential in the wake of Birdie's desire for the truth.

But Joseph's wife is not bound as we are. What is left of her is fading as her soul prepares to move on.

As it should be.

We ache for that peace. But it is not ours.

Not yet.

Joseph turns off the TV and sits in his chair in the dark. He wishes he'd left the minute Glen and Birdie sat down. But this is Joseph's path now. It's bright white in its clarity, and we are attracted to it like moths.

Joseph gets ready for bed. He lays his head on the pillow and pulls the sheet to just under his shoulders. His heartbeat slows, his breathing deepens, and right before he drifts away, he sobs. A sharp intake of breath that becomes a moan. It happens every night. His soul's response to what he can't ever change. We hover around him until it stops and Joseph sleeps.

Six

A storm was coming. Birdie knew this because she couldn't turn on the television without some weather guy or gal yapping incessantly about the feet (or inches) of snow (or rain) forecasted for the city. The storm was predicted with near certainty to produce significant wind (maybe) and whiteout conditions (possibly). So much hype. The last storm was supposed to have shut down the airport. It had ended up dusting a white powder that melted by midmorning, and the only thing it canceled was the community van to Santa's Village. Which, of course, in no way affected Birdie, since she refused to ride in the van—a statement that Felix had threatened to turn into a bumper sticker.

She stood in the spare bedroom, peering out the window at the current situation: a cloudless blue sky with temperatures in the fifties and no wind. Birdie zipped her coat, tightened her parrot-green wool scarf around her neck, and gave the pictures on the wall one last look.

She'd promised herself that she'd take everything down, but two weeks had passed since her birthday and she couldn't bring herself to do it. She'd known these women. Had spoken to their families and friends, learned who'd they'd been, what they'd wanted out of life. Barb, his sixth victim, had been walking her dog after a fight with her boyfriend. She wrote poetry, drank tea, and listened almost exclusively to the Grateful Dead. Susan spoke three languages and had nursed her grandfather until he died. Karen, the youngest of the victims at fourteen, was a girl who sang like Madonna and still loved her Cabbage Patch doll. But the press hadn't reported any of these facts. Only the words that classified them: *prostitute, runaway, addict, mentally unwell.*

One question had persisted all these years: If she could have convinced the police that Allison was his first victim, would they have found him? If so, would the others be alive today?

She touched the article about the woman recently found in a dumpster. There had been no updates, and she worried the reporters had moved on. The news cycle was brutally quick.

Her stomach churned. She should take it down, put it all back in the box. Felix had been right all those years ago: this wasn't healthy. She felt drawn into their stories, a tightness in her throat whenever she thought of the bastard who got away with it. She sat a minute longer, taking it all in. The women were already in one kind of box; for the moment, she couldn't bear to put them in another. Birdie stood, her hands gripping the cushioned handles of her walker. She closed the door behind her and headed out. Best to get her walk in now, just in case the storm developed as predicted.

The small lobby was occupied by two women on the couch, both still in their coats, one with a small dog on a leash snoozing at her feet.

"Good morning, Dorothea," Birdie said to the one with the dog. And to the other: "Hello, Nan."

"There's a new camper out there," Nan said, her oxygen tank making a *puff, puff* sound, the plastic tubing tucked behind her diminutive ears. Birdie didn't know much about Nan except for the fact that she seemed to be in the know about most things around the community. She was a tiny woman with pixie-short hair and wrinkled skin that dripped from her jaw. Her small stature was further exacerbated by a curve in her upper back that forced her to bend low over her walker.

Birdie lifted an eyebrow. That was another reason for her walk today. "Yes, Faith mentioned that a young girl lives there," she said. She wondered if Faith had brought over her empanadillas like she'd mentioned the other day.

"Alone?" Nan said.

"I believe so."

Nan was shaking her head. "That doesn't sound safe."

"I agree," Birdie said. "I thought I'd check on her. Make sure she's okay."

Dorothea made a noise in her throat. "You can't do that." Dorothea was Nan's opposite—tall and youthful, with amazingly smooth skin unaffected by her perpetual frown. She had piercing eyes that didn't seem to miss a thing, which included who was and was not present at community functions.

Birdie felt a rise of ire. "In fact, I can," she said. Dorothea liked for old people to do old people things. Like mixers and planned outings, and anything that required they all ride on the van.

"But those people could be dangerous or into drugs." The woman's eyes had rounded. "Why else would they live like that?"

Birdie had to breathe in slowly to stem the angry uptick of her pulse. "Have you met John and Lydia?"

Dorothea shook her head. "Do they live on the third floor?"

"No, they live in the camper van that parks here every few days. They lost everything trying to help their daughter fight cancer. So now they have to live out of their van until they can save enough to pay rent again."

Dorothea's lips pursed. "Are you coming to the mixer?"

Eating pie, drinking coffee, and chatting wasn't her idea of a good time. "Did I mention that I'm going for a walk?" She held on to her walker and did a little jig with her legs. "Gotta keep these legs moving while my heart's still pumping."

Nan's face lit up and she barked a laugh.

Dorothea's face scrunched like she smelled something bad. But she recovered quickly and said, "You walk alone?"

Birdie sighed. A big part of her wanted to tell Dorothea to mind her own beeswax. "I do."

"It's dangerous, you know. Glenna . . ." She paused to study Birdie and seemed to decide something. "You probably don't know her, because she lives in the cottages instead of the apartments. But she found a dead rabbit outside her patio door." She sat back, hands folded in her lap, evidently pleased with herself for being the bearer of such horrific news.

Birdie held in a groan. "Rabbits do die, especially with all the coyotes around." Her feet itched with impatience, and the sun already seemed thinner than when she'd set out moments ago. She made to leave. "Thanks for the warn—"

"Glenna said the rabbit had been skinned and it looked like other things had been done to it." Dorothea's eyes narrowed.

Birdie hesitated, a memory sending prickles down her shoulder blades. Of Allison home late one night from the club. Birdie reading a bedtime story to Felix. After she had tucked Felix in for the night, she found Allison pacing the kitchen and chewing on a nail. *What's wrong?* Birdie had asked. Allison, normally so even-keeled, stared at her with wide, troubled eyes.

I ran into Sasha on my way up, Allison said. *You know how her puppy went missing last week?* Birdie nodded. *Well, they found him.* Allison sat down, bouncing her knee up and down. *In the alley by the dumpsters*—a sick feeling fingered its way into Birdie's throat—*with his belly cut open and . . .* She stopped, swallowed, eyes wet. *I can't say what else.* Allison pulled at the ends of her hair. *What sicko could do that, Bird? It's so awful.* Birdie had leaned forward and placed her hand on Allison's knee to stem the shaking. Allison grabbed her hand, squeezed like Birdie could solve the cruelness of the world.

"It's probably someone on drugs." Dorothea sniffed. "Maybe even someone from one of those RVs."

"Did anyone call the police?" Birdie asked, immediately thinking about the safety of the young girl in the camper.

Dorothea seemed surprised. "About the rabbit? I don't know. I doubt it, though." She seemed unsure of herself now, like she'd only meant to spread gossip, not take action. "It's just a rabbit—and like you said, coyotes could have done it."

Years after that night with Allison, when Birdie was deep into her research, she'd learned about the link between animal violence and serial killers and informed the police working on the murders about that early mutilation. Nobody had followed up with her.

Birdie shook off the memory, but with Geneva Smith's murder on her mind, she said, "Have you heard about the young girl who was murdered at the Paragon?" She sucked in the side of her cheek.

Nan's face lit up. "The one they think was murdered by the Vampire Killer?"

Birdie breathed out. "Yes, that's the one."

"I read on a forum that her throat was slashed," Nan said.

"Oh, that's horrible." Birdie fought a flash of disappointment. "But that doesn't fit the Vampire Killer's MO."

"Very true." Nan was nodding. "He was precise and methodical when he drained their blood."

"Nan!" Dorothea said, sounding aghast.

Nan laughed and popped the oxygen tubing from her ear. She slid it back on. "I'm a true crime junkie; you know that, Dorothea." She pointed a finger at Birdie. "But he is a lot older now. Maybe he got sloppy?"

"Could we please talk about something else?" Dorothea asked.

One of Nan's eyebrows shot up. "What about the prowler?"

"What prowler?" Birdie said.

Dorothea's nostrils flared. "He was outside the cottages."

Birdie hadn't heard about that. She squeezed her forearm. Animal mutilations, a Vampire Killer–like death, a prowler. "Doing what?"

"Eileen said he was looking into her windows," Nan said.

"You're on the first floor, too, aren't you?" Dorothea said. "Make sure you lock your windows."

"And keep 'em closed." Nan's oxygen tank puffed. "Fresh air makes for dead people."

"Nan . . . ," Dorothea said in a disapproving tone.

Nan made a face. Her eyes had the rheumy kind of brightness that sometimes comes with age. She smiled and two little dimples formed on either side of her mouth. "I heard something like it on *Morbid*."

"On what?" Dorothea was looking at Nan like she'd never seen her before.

"A true crime podcast with two very funny young gals." Nan sighed and shook her head, looking beleaguered. "You need to get out more, Dorothea."

Birdie decided that Nan was a whole lot more interesting than she'd first thought, but her back hurt from standing in one spot for so long, and she felt a little defeated too. The mystery of the Vampire Killer was a cold case that would never be solved by three gossiping old ladies. But talk of the prowler had turned her thoughts back to the young girl in the camper. "Well, I'm off for my walk."

"I'd give you some company," Nan said, swinging her short legs, the soles of her feet just missing the floor, "but I don't think I could keep up."

Birdie smiled. "It's okay, I don't mind being alone."

"At our age, being alone is bad for our health." Dorothea's eyebrows (drawn on a tad too high above the brow bone, by the way—just an observation, not a judgment!) wiggled. "Spending time with our grandchildren, having a pet, getting *involved*—those are all ways to stay healthier longer."

Nan shook her head so vigorously it knocked the oxygen tubing loose again. She pushed it back in. "My grandkids are all teenagers," she said; then she cupped a hand by her mouth like the next bit was a secret she didn't think was out of the bag yet. "They're kind of little jerks, if I'm being honest. I'm not so sure they're particularly good for my health."

Dorothea's eyes opened wide.

Birdie barked a laugh, surprised but quite pleased with Nan. "Oh yes, *teenagers*." And nodded like she agreed, because Birdie supported a little bit of rebellion in all its forms. Even though she didn't agree at all, at least in her experience. Felix's twins were teenagers now, and perhaps they were the exception, because they were kind and thoughtful, if a tad self-absorbed. What teenager wasn't, though?

Dorothea turned her attention back to Birdie. "You never said if you were coming to the mixer."

Like a dog with a bone. Right now she was wishing she'd gone out her patio door instead. She shrugged. "Oh, you know, maybe."

"It would be good for you," Dorothea said, and Nan smiled, nodding her agreement.

"I bring a glass of wine," Nan said.

Birdie sighed—*Traitor*—and pulled on a pair of thin gloves before taking hold of her walker. "Nice to see you both. Be careful out there. Big storm coming!"

Nan and Dorothea mumbled about the cold coming with the storm. The weather was always an accepted change of topic.

As the two women talked about the snow and, by the way, would the staff fix the ice problem in the parking lot before someone broke a hip, Birdie walked away into a bright and warm afternoon. She angled toward the sidewalk and walked in the direction of the campers. Exercise always felt good and reminded her of evening walks with Felix. After a long day of bending over bathtubs and toilets or on her knees scrubbing floors, she'd take him after dinner or before, depending on the time of year, and in almost any weather condition. During those walks together, she'd tell him stories about Allison. A few where she flew like Superman. But those were just for fun. Birdie told him of Allison's strength, her tenacity, how she would have made an excellent teacher if she'd had the chance. How she'd been an incredible mom.

Once, when Felix was fifteen, he'd interrupted her: *I've heard all these stories about Al—I mean, Mom.* At some point since her death. Felix had stopped referring to Allison as *Mom*; it had pierced Birdie's heart, and now he corrected himself but only out of respect for Birdie.

Don't you have other stories? he'd asked.

Her chest had tightened with the truth. Felix had only known Allison through Birdie's stories, and she didn't have any more. The four and a half years she'd been in Birdie's life had been made up of quiet moments—sitting on the couch sipping coffee on a rare lazy afternoon, watching newborn Felix sleep—and life-changing ones—holding her hand in the delivery room when she pushed, Felix's lusty cry. Enough time to grow so close Birdie felt like she'd known Allison inside and out, but not enough to build an arsenal of stories. Silence had followed her for the rest of that walk with Felix, and soon after, he got his first girlfriend and his walks with Birdie lessened.

Birdie stuttered to a stop, hand to her chest, surprised by a sudden longing. "I miss you, Al." The memories dusted off old yearnings, remembered love.

Sometimes she pretended Allison was there with her now, and she'd say all the things she never had the guts to say when her friend was alive. *I love you too. I'm sorry I was such a coward. We could have had a beautiful life together. You would have hated this place as much as me.*

Allison's throaty laugh in her head. *Maybe.* Sometimes she talked back. *Or we could teach 'em how to dance.*

These old biddies? For a moment, Birdie didn't feel the sun on her face or the breeze tugging at the ends of her scarf.

Absolutely.

She held her breath, closed her eyes, wished with her entire soul that the voice she heard was real. Birdie's eyes flew open, and she started walking again. She was spending too much time in a past she couldn't change. Maybe Felix was right: she did need to get involved and meet more people.

Her feet shuffled forward, the tips of her walker scudding the pavement, and warm air feathered across her cheeks, a cruel but lovely spring tease. She was so focused on her steps that she didn't see the man whose brown shoes appeared on the concrete in front of her.

"Ah, it's you! The beautiful Bird!"

Glen stood in front of her, smiling, thumbs hooked into his leather belt. Birdie hadn't seen Glen or Joseph since the book club two weeks before, and while only seconds ago she'd told herself she needed to meet more people, she scrunched her nose, wishing for just a few minutes to adjust to the idea. "Hello, Glen."

He wore trousers and a plaid sweater-vest with a bow tie. His stomach strained against the vest; the pants hung from his skinny legs. Glen tipped his herringbone flatcap to her. "'Faith is a bird that feels the light when the dawn is dark,'" he said with obvious pleasure.

"I'm sorry?"

"Rabindranath Tagore, of course." Birdie thought Glen's eyes actually twinkled when he said the words.

"Okay." She moved forward, hoping he'd step to the side. "Nice to see you, Glen, but I've got to get my walk in before the storm." Weather. Always such a good excuse.

"Excellent!" He turned to stand beside her. "I'll join you."

Not a question. A statement. Birdie sucked in her upper lip and kept moving.

"Tagore was a great poet and philosopher—Indian, you know, and a painter, too, among other things. I do admire men who don't limit themselves."

What was he going on about? If she didn't know better, she'd think he was trying to impress her with random knowledge. "That's interesting." He seemed a bit on the desperate side. "How'd the move go?"

"Oh, fine, fine."

She'd seen a man who resembled Glen lugging a few boxes down the hallway. "Was that your brother helping you?"

"It was."

"Does he live close by?" She wished Felix lived closer.

They walked a few beats in silence.

"My brother is the reason I am here."

Birdie paused to look up at him. He stood with his hands behind his back. An ascot and pipe would have completed the whole look. "My son is the reason I'm here too."

Glen looked surprised. "Then you understand. We are but autumn leaves at the whim of a breeze."

Birdie didn't quite know how to respond to Glen's histrionics, but she did feel the need to defend Felix. "I don't feel 'at his whim'; he's just worried about me."

Glen nodded. "Ah, well, see here, Bird, that's the difference. My brother only wanted my house for himself."

"Greedy bastard, huh?"

"Indeed." His forehead crinkled, and he leaned down as though telling her a secret. "He tells people he's worried about me, too, but he's a liar. He thinks I'm incompetent."

Abruptly, Glen started walking again, and Birdie followed suit. Poor Glen. It was painful to be doubted.

They arrived at the end of the sidewalk: to the left, it continued along the front of the Sunny Pines community; to the right was the empty stretch of road where the RVs parked. She turned right.

Glen prattled on. "I've always admired the great artists. Art elevates, does it not?"

"Sure, unless it's pretentious, which I think most art is." Her answer seemed to disappoint him, and she felt a little bad about it.

"Perhaps you haven't seen the right kind of—"

"There it is," she interrupted when she saw the small camper Faith had mentioned. The kind that sat on the back of a truck with a bed that fit over the cab. Dented white and brown metal siding. Windows dark, opaque against the bright sun. At her pace, it took Birdie some time to reach it, but Glen didn't seem to mind. The man hadn't stopped talking about paint and canvases and the collapse of society when art was not integral to its advancement.

Glen seemed to be the type who was most amused by his own company, and Birdie found it tiresome until a realization washed over her—he was lonely like her. It recaptured the earlier tenderness she'd felt for him, and her shoulders relaxed. "Do you like to go to the art museum?"

Glen nodded. "Oh, yes I do! I'm a member."

Birdie laughed. "'Course you are. And are you an artist too?"

At that, Glen took off his hat, squeezed it between his hands. "I am," he said with such earnest sincerity that it stopped Birdie's next unkind thought, which had something to do with a gnawing suspicion that he'd started this entire conversation in the hopes that she would ask him that very question.

"Well, that's just great, Glen. Maybe you can show me your art sometime?"

The smile dropped from Glen's face, and he returned the hat to his head. "Oh, but you might not like it. My wife never cared for it."

Birdie laughed. "How old are you?"

Glen looked genuinely confused. "Eighty-four."

"Too old to worry about what people think, right?"

"I think I'm going to head back. Good afternoon, Birdie." With that, he walked away, leaving Birdie staring at his skinny backside before she turned in the direction of the camper.

~

She stood in front of the camper door, feeling short and ineffective. It was unreachable, up a steep stair that she had no hope or business of climbing. She looked down the empty road. A white van was parked a few hundred feet away, and past that was a larger RV with the hood of the engine propped open. The camper that belonged to John and Lydia was gone, and she realized she hadn't seen it for some time. She'd only met them once, when she was going the long way around last fall and they'd been sitting in lawn chairs, enjoying the warm day. They had flowers in clay pots on their metal stairs and a wreath hung on the door. Homey. They'd offered her a cup of hot chocolate. Without John and

Lydia, the lonely road looked different. Less welcoming. Goose bumps pricked the skin along Birdie's spine.

She turned back to face the camper. "Hello!" she called. A soft growl from inside. "I just wanted to . . . well now, welcome you to the neighborhood, I suppose." The response was a cacophony of barking, and the camper shook slightly. When it died down, nothing. Yet Birdie had the sense that someone was inside besides the four-legged kind. Hovering just on the other side of the door, waiting for her to leave. Birdie looked around. This wasn't that far from her apartment, but out here, on this empty stretch of road, it seemed miles from anyone who could help if the young woman needed it. Birdie's heart pushed against her ribs. Why had this one chosen to live here? "My name is Birdie." She tried to speak louder, but more volume turned her voice hoarse, breathy sounding. She cleared her throat. "I think Faith stopped by the other day? Did she bring you her empanadillas?" The dog or dogs had finally stopped their yapping.

A rattling, and then the door opened and two of the ugliest dogs Birdie had ever seen smushed their drooly faces against the mesh of the screen, eye level with Birdie. Pugs, she thought, but not the kind that made it into the fancy dog shows. One had a flattened socket where an eye had once been and a lower jaw that was pushed so far forward it couldn't close it right. Its tongue squished through the open space. The other was smaller and might have been cute but for its swollen, yellow-crusted eyes.

Above the two mutts stood a girl, so young it snagged something in her chest, and for a second, she saw Allison on that day in Kmart. Bulging belly, spine straight, playing tug-of-war with her dignity and the pompous store manager. She blinked and Allison disappeared. The girl stood with her arms crossed, shoulders bowed, white-blond hair in very short braids on either side of her head. A small nose piercing caught the sunlight.

The dogs pressed their wet noses against the screen, huffing like they had colds.

"You know Faith?" the girl said.

"I do." Birdie rolled out her neck; it ached from looking up. "Those sandwich things were really good."

"Yes indeed, they're delicious." Silence, broken only by the labored breathing of the dogs. "Your dogs sound like my neighbor. His snores could wake the dead."

The girl shifted her weight, pulling farther inside the camper. The dogs—bored with little old Birdie, she supposed—disappeared behind her.

"I wanted to check on you and make sure you're okay. If you need anything." Wind kicked up, pushing gray-studded clouds over the sun, giving the air a frosty bite. Birdie shivered. "I just wanted to check on—" Did she sound nosy like Nan? Expectant like Dorothea? "People die here all the time, you know." She didn't know what else to say, but she couldn't leave without letting this girl know she wasn't alone.

The girl made a sound. "What?"

"Well, I mean, of course we do; it's what happens at this stage of life. What I mean is, most of us live alone here, like you, so if you ever need anything at all . . ." Standing there with a death grip on her walker, the wind buffeting her side, probably whipping her thin hair around, exposing patches of her scalp, she knew what she looked like. An old woman who couldn't possibly do a thing to help. "All you have to do is ask. I'm right over there, apartment 106—the ones with the little patios."

The girl stood mostly shadowed by the dark interior of her camper. "Okay." A pause, and Birdie couldn't be sure, but she thought the girl's voice vibrated with nerves. Abruptly, she disappeared, then returned quickly and opened the door. She knelt, holding out a small round platter that shook in her grasp. "Can you give that to Faith?"

Birdie took the plate and slid it into her bag. "I'll give it to her the next time I see her."

The girl gave her a small nod, and Birdie noticed a sheen across her forehead, like she was sweating. "Um, I'm Everly." She scrambled to her feet and closed the door before Birdie could say another word.

Birdie stared at the closed door, surprised by the girl's abrupt exit but not upset by it. The world was full of all kinds of people. She made a plan to check on her again in a few days and turned her walker in the direction of Sunny Pines. It was downright cold now. Perhaps the weather people were right about this storm.

Seven

ALLISON

I feel Everly's heart pounding. It's fast, panicked, and turns her underarms soupy with sweat. She is twenty years old and has already given up on everything she once dreamed of for herself.

She watches Birdie walk away between the slits of the curtains. She presses a hand to her chest. I taste the salt from the tears that linger in the corners of her eyes. Her father's love pulsates in the air around her, and I gravitate toward it, touch its warmth. There's the quicksand of shame, too, but I avoid that.

Everly shuts the curtains tight and turns from the window. She sits at the small table, the dogs snuggled to each side of her. She wakes up her computer, connects to an unsecured Wi-Fi, and finishes reading the email from her college.

. . . dropped from the music program . . .

She's not surprised, but the tears slide down her cheeks nonetheless. She's just like her father. The man who composed a symphony that made him the sweetheart of the classical music world. Who had everything he'd ever wanted at his fingertips. But it wasn't enough to stop the voices that told him otherwise.

And now she hears those same voices. The doubt. The fear. So Everly makes her world so small she thinks she's safe. People set her hands shaking. Performing is a crushing weight on her chest. Her father closed all the blinds in their house. Kept it so dark Everly had to use a flashlight to see the music when she practiced her cello. Food was delivered. School was online, until she won an argument to go to high school in person. Before bed she'd drink decaf coffee with him in the darkened family room and talk. She loved her father despite his faults. But that's love, isn't it?

I drown in her fear, feel the darkness of her home in a heaviness that perches on her back. Her father is here, too, but despite his earthly struggles, he is not chained to her as I am to Birdie. Still, he will not leave her side. Not yet.

She never told him that she applied to colleges. Not until the day before she left.

Everly closes her computer, pulls the dogs onto her lap, and hugs them to her. She doesn't mind the goopy eyes or the constant slobber. She loves them with all her heart.

I soak in her humanness, her potential to affect change a golden hue that shimmers around her. The sun slides down past the buildings. The wind picks up. Everly sits in the dark, holding her dogs. In her mind, she's holding her cello between her knees, the neck resting against her shoulder. She's playing "Cello Suite No. 1," her fingers flying across the strings, the bow gliding elegantly along the bridge. It calms her. I feel the wispy edges of sorrow, of something lost before it can bloom. I remember those sensations.

But we don't feel them the same way.

No, we don't, do we? Yet I remember. And I want for these fragile souls to live in the messy wilderness that comes with each breath. Much is learned in death. But that knowledge waits for the last beat of a heart, and there is no sense in hastening what comes to us all.

I do not envy the living.

But we ache for what is lost.

And that is why we gather for the truth, is it not, my loves?

A dog sneezes. Everly grabs a paper towel and carefully wipes its mouth and nose. She sighs and scoots out from behind the table. Cold air slides through tiny cracks, tickles the tip of her nose. It will be a long night. She checks the lock on the door, then lifts each dog up to the bed that stretches over the cab of the truck and climbs up after them. The dogs burrow under the sheets, and she pulls the blanket up to her eyebrows, breathing in warm air tinged with sour dog breath and eye goop.

Just before she falls asleep Everly thinks about Birdie and the thing she said about people dying here all the time. Everly isn't afraid of death. Everybody dies. It's the living part that is hard for her. Besides the free Wi-Fi, one of the reasons she likes to park her camper here is because of the old people. She likes to watch them. They walk to the community center with yoga mats, take their dogs out even when it's cold and dark, or get dressed up in brightly colored scarves and plaid hats and get on the van to go to a show or shopping or wherever they go. Everly admires them. They aren't afraid of living.

She tosses in her sleep, restless, too young for so many regrets. I sit on the bed, rest my hand across her ankle. One of the dogs whines. They know I'm here. Everly stills, her breathing deepens, and she falls asleep, feeling safe in her small space with her small dogs.

But something is coming for her that only we can see.

I linger in her camper and listen to her even breaths. I am close to her age when I die. With years stretching ahead of me, experiences to have, bills to pay, a son to raise. I do not ruminate on death. Her youth is a tangible thing that takes up space, emanates from her very center. Beautiful for its naivete and terrifying for its fragility. Everly thinks death is her father in a dark house, dying in his sleep having never lived.

She does not know how horrific it can be.

The women gather around me, surging like one.

We know.

Yes, we do.

They are all together.

It's time.

We need their help.

But first, we need Faith.

Eight

Birdie reached the door to her apartment, chilled from her walk, grateful for the warmth of the hallway. Faith would be coming first thing in the morning. She looked forward to comparing notes about the girl, Everly, and she knew Faith would be on board about helping her. They were kindred spirits in that way.

"Hello, Birdie." Joseph was coming out of his apartment. "I'm reading *The Hunger Games*." He held himself straight like a board with broad, squared shoulders, a lean hollow in his jaw. Almost too lean, like the man forgot to eat sometimes. "I like that Katniss character. She's, ah, bold."

"Yes indeed. A badass, don't you think?"

Joseph's lips pressed together, but the ends lifted as if pulled by strings. Like he didn't allow himself to smile. "That's a good descriptive word."

"Faith used it the other day, so I thought I'd give it a try. Figured it might impress the teenagers."

Joseph was nodding. "Who's Faith?"

That soured her just a bit. "She cleans our building." Her voice was harder than before. Was Joseph the kind of man who didn't remember the names of people he didn't deem important?

The creases in his forehead relaxed. "Oh, you mean Sofia."

She met his gaze. Blue eyes, slightly red-rimmed and puffy but no hint of guile. "Excuse me?"

"Sofia Faith Perez. That's her name. But you're right, she does go by Faith. I forgot about that."

It took her a moment to readjust. Seemed she was perhaps a bit too quick to judge. It was possible Birdie had a chip on her shoulder from having been a cleaner herself. "How did you know her full name?" she said.

He shrugged. "I asked."

"But why don't you call her Faith?"

Joseph rubbed his chin. "I told her that my wife's name had been Sofia and that I still thought it was the most beautiful name in the world." He blinked a few times. "She said, 'Then you must call me Sofia.'"

"Oh, that's lovely." Birdie felt like a real jerk. "Did your wife . . ." She hated this kind of question: redundant, thoughtless, pedestrian. "Is your spouse dead" encompassed nothing more than a trite curiosity. Most of them had lost their spouses or, like her, had never been married. Birdie hadn't set out to be single at her age. There'd been a few relationships over the years, but they could never compete for her attention when it came to her son and her business. The one that might have lasted, Cheryl, had grown frustrated by what she called Birdie's "fear of commitment." But Cheryl had been wrong. What held her back was a nagging sense of guilt, that she was living a life she didn't deserve. Fueled by a growing unease that the truth about Allison's death might be the thing she feared most.

She changed course. "How long were you together?"

Joseph looked at her; his eyes were soft. "Sixty-five years."

She raised an eyebrow, thinking he was closer to her age. "You seem too young to have been married that long."

He folded his arms, rocked on his feet. "She moved to my school when we were both twelve, and as soon as I worked up the nerve, I told her I was going to marry her one day." He gave her that smile of his, tight across the middle, a soft lift at either end. "Eight years later we tied the knot, but I started counting the moment I'd met her."

Birdie warmed to his story. "I didn't figure you for a romantic, Joseph."

He ducked his head. "For the next book club, I was thinking that maybe I'd bring, well . . . candy or cookies?" He seemed unsure, his voice petering out like he wished he hadn't even suggested the idea. "Sofia, my wife, she was in a book club, and she used to make food for it."

The idea of joining another book club meeting sounded like a good way to keep the ghosts at bay. "That sounds nice. I could bring some lemonade and iced tea."

He bobbed his head in a relieved sort of way. "Were you out for a walk?"

"I was, and I ran into Glen."

Joseph wiggled his eyebrows in what might have been an attempt to be comical. "He's an artist, you know."

She nodded conspiratorially. "A modest one, it seems."

"Didn't want to show you either?"

"No, he did not." She winked. "Something tells me he'll find a way eventually—probably with a bit more flair."

"He does seem to be a fan of flair."

She laughed. There was something familiar and comforting about Joseph. Like an old, fuzzy blanket.

"Want to make a bet on this storm?"

She blew air out between her lips. "Ha! What storm?"

Joseph tipped his head. "My thoughts exactly." He backed away. "Good evening, Birdie."

"Same to you, Joseph."

~

Before bed, in her nightgown and slippers, Birdie opened the door to the spare room, lured inside by the imagined voices of the women. As though they collected around their pictures, their stories, waiting for her to join them. A deep sadness clung to the room; these women and their families had never gotten the peace that would come with answers. Allison's picture beckoned to her, the one among the others that never quite fit because of a fact that more than one detective had pointed out to her: the blood was missing from the other crime scenes. Not Allison's. Hers had been everywhere. Her death, they said, had been a suicide.

She blinked, touched the edge of Allison's photograph. Tried to exhume the words Allison had spoken decades before: *I love you.* Once a living echo in her head, now an old recording on scratched vinyl. But words she'd wrapped around herself like a shield to ward off the doubts that woke her in the night.

Birdie swallowed past a lump and sat on the guest bed, but she couldn't stop thinking about Everly, out there in her tiny camper, two ugly dogs her only company. The rumors of the tortured rabbit danced around her, poking at the old fear that came for women like Everly and Faith. Anyone alone and vulnerable.

Tomorrow, she'd invite Everly over for coffee or tea. She tightened her robe, chilled by a sudden coolness in the room. Cold air from the impending storm seeped in through the thin windowpanes. Everly and Faith reminded Birdie of the kind of women she would have hired. She'd sought out the ones who needed a chance, a leg up, and felt a deep satisfaction whenever she could offer that to someone. It hadn't come easy for her. A year after Allison had died, Birdie worked out a deal with the manager of Sid King's to clean the club on her days off. Dancing and cleaning: unlikely bedfellows that worked to her benefit. A few years later, when the Women's Bank opened its doors, Birdie was able to get her very first loan, and from there Allison's Maids was born.

The room felt crowded, with the queen-size bed taking up much of the space. There in case the twins came to visit or for Felix and Sharon. But there was a denseness in the air that hinted at something she could not see. She pressed a hand to her cheek; she was exhausted.

The bed welcomed her, and sleep crept around her consciousness, despite the feeling that she wasn't alone. But that was something she experienced more and more. Like a thinning of the veil between this world and the next. A sensation that if she opened her eyes at just the right time, she'd see everything.

Birdie slept hard. So hard that the screech of the fire alarm through the cotton balls in her head was nothing more than a soft beeping. It pulled her from the velvety depths and into utter chaos.

She squinted into the flashing white light from the alarm above her head, covering her ears to the penetrating squeal of the bell. Someone was pounding on her window.

"Birdie! Are you in there? Birdie!"

She pushed herself to sitting, set her feet on the floor, and pulled her robe from where she laid it across the foot of her bed every night, quickly sliding her arms into it. Her head spun from the noise and the flashing light, and Birdie reminded herself to take deep breaths. Her heart pounded in her chest. Fear, turmoil, accidents—anything that reminded her of how fragile each moment was created a direct link to the horror of that afternoon, when Birdie was standing in the bathroom, staring into Allison's sightless eyes. She gripped the mattress. Her screams from all those years ago funneled back into her in a tightening band around her lungs.

Another knock on her bedroom window. "Birdie! Do you need help?" Air rushed into her lungs, dissolving the grip of the past, and Birdie pulled her walker closer, slid her feet into her slippers, and stood. Her leg muscles didn't respond right away, and her progress to the patio was slow. With no acrid stink of smoke burning her throat or eyes, Birdie pushed her panic down and eventually made it to the door. She opened it to a rush of freezing-cold air that stole the breaths she'd just managed to store. Joseph rounded the corner, nose red in the early-dawn glow. "You'll need a coat," he said, calm and composed despite the alarms howling throughout the building. She'd started to turn her walker around—deliberate, because with her, there was no *fast*—when Joseph hurried past her and to the closet by the front door.

He produced her long, puffy black coat, held it out for her to see across the apartment. "Will this work?"

She nodded and he rushed to her side, helping her into it. Outside, the sun was rising fast, illuminating the parking lot and all the sadly underdressed and in-various-stages-of-disarray inhabitants of Sunny Pines who had congregated in the middle of it. There was something odd about the way they stood, some with their arms straight out, unmoving like they'd been caught in a game of red light, green light.

"It's icy. Treacherous." He pointed to a figure prone on the ground. "Looks like Paul was the first one out and fell right away. A few others right after him, before they realized how slippery it is."

Birdie breathed in sharply. Paul was ninety-two, but healthy and capable. Still, he couldn't afford a fall. None of them could. She noticed the other bodies on the ground, their moans drifting to her. "Oh, good grief," she said, her heart twisting for the unlucky few who'd hurried outside first. She smelled the air—frostbitten; crisp; a hint of smoke, but the kind that came from a wood-burning fireplace, not one that would necessitate the evacuation of an entire building. "Where's the fire?"

"I'm not sure there is one," Joseph said, and Birdie felt his hand on her forearm to stop her from moving any farther. "Let's just stand on your patio."

Birdie was grateful not to join the others on the skating rink.

"The hero of the morning! Helping our little bird out of her cage." Glen stood on his porch, too, bundled in a thick wool coat that brushed the tops of his boots, a trapper hat pulled low, thick gloves. Drinking a mug of coffee and looking for all the world like he was prepared to go ice fishing. "Guess the storm was a flop," he announced.

Birdie took in his winter gear; he seemed far more prepared than anyone else. "Were you going for a walk this early?"

Glen looked into his coffee cup, his jaw tightening. "My brother spent the night." He tossed the remains of his coffee onto the ground; it splattered brown across the ice. "He was supposed to leave this morning for a work trip, but his flight was canceled. I needed space. The man's ego knows no bounds."

"Oh," Birdie said, shivering now from the cold. Glen really didn't like his brother if he was willing to take a walk in this. "I'm sorry."

"Yes, indeed," Glen agreed.

Hearing sirens in the distance, Birdie shivered next to Joseph. "Do you know what's going on?"

"No idea."

The storm had moved out, leaving the sky a translucent blue. There was no snow, Glen was correct, but the branches were crystallized, the pavement a dangerous glistening black and everything else white with ice. Flashing lights of first-responder trucks sparkled in the crystals. Birdie watched the residents being tended to; others had been helped to a safer spot. She was grateful that Joseph had prevented her from walking on the ice.

"Cider?"

Birdie jumped. She hadn't noticed Glen make his way down the sidewalk to her patio. He wore big rubber-soled boots that seemed to suction cup his tall frame to the ice, and held out three white packets of cider powder. The parking lot was almost empty of their neighbors now, most of them having been escorted inside the not-on-fire building. A deeper chill had taken hold, spreading from her belly outward, and she was shivering so hard her walker rattled. "Sure, but maybe later?" She wasn't ready to entertain guests at this hour.

"I think we can go back inside," Joseph said, and moved to open her patio door. "Birdie?"

She walked inside, teeth chattering from the cold. "Thank you, Joseph. See you later, fellas." She went immediately to her bedroom, where she closed the door and pulled on thick sweatpants, wool socks, and a sweater. Part of her wanted to crawl back into bed, but once the day got started, there was no going back.

When she slid in her hearing aids, she realized the voices she thought were coming from outside were from her living room. She stepped out of her bedroom and had a shock. Glen sat in the chair by her window, coat off, boots on the tile, gloves stacked on the end table. Joseph hovered by the interior door that led into the apartment hallway, still in his coat and squinting at Glen. "You're still here?" she said, trying not to sound rude, but she'd assumed they would just cross through her apartment and exit into the hallway. At least it seemed Joseph had meant to go. He looked a little miserable, actually, like he'd stayed because Glen had and now he wished he'd left.

Glen patted his shirt and pulled out the three square packets. "Thought we could warm up and chat a little bit." He looked from Birdie to Joseph and then to the floor. "Oh. I think I misunderstood." He shoved the packets back into his pocket. "My wife used to say that I don't know how to read people." He stood, and as she looked at him standing there in his socks and rumpled hair, Birdie had a twinge of conscience.

"It's okay, Glen. Something warm would be nice." She moved to the kitchen, where she pushed the button on her electric kettle.

Glen shuffled over from the living room, setting the packets on the counter. Joseph laid his coat over the back of the sofa. "Can I help?" he asked. The apartment felt small with the two men taking up so much space.

She shook her head and put three mugs on the counter. Then, from a cabinet beside the sink, she pulled out a container of mints, the soft peppermint kind that dissolved in her mouth. "I like to put one of these in the mug with cider. Want one too?"

Glen rubbed his hands together. "Oh, yes, please! My wife used to put Fireball in hers." His face darkened. "She had a drinking problem, of course."

Birdie's hand with the peppermint candy froze above the mug. "I'm sorry to hear that. You sure you want this in yours, then?"

Glen gave her a look. "Well, now, I wasn't the one with the drinking problem."

She shook her head and dropped in the mint, filled his mug with hot water, and did the same with the other two mugs. Glen sat down in the chair he'd been in before—her chair, typically—so Birdie and Joseph took the sofa. Joseph held his mug with one hand, the other gripping in and out of a fist, like he'd rather be anywhere else.

Birdie yawned. What she needed was some peace and quiet after such a brutal wake-up, not a social call.

Glen held his mug between both hands and inhaled. "Mmm." Took a sip. "Delicious!" he proclaimed. Then he set his mug on the end table and looked around her apartment, smiling. "Lovely place, Birdie. Same layout as mine, except flipped, of course."

"Is that so?" she said.

"Yes, but much better decorated. My place needs a woman's touch, I'm afraid."

"Mine too," Joseph said.

Glen's jovial mood dampened. "My wife passed a couple of years ago."

"I'm sorry for your loss." Joseph spoke with such sincerity Birdie felt it like a hug.

"I'm sorry, too, Glen," she said, loss a string that bound them together.

Glen sighed. "It was never going to be easy to lose the love of my life." He picked up his mug, took another sip. "I'm sorry about barging in on you like this. I guess I'm a little lonely. I left my home for this small apartment because my brother is a selfish, greedy bastard who wanted my house."

"Is he living there now?" Birdie asked, figuring that since he brought it up again, there was room for questions.

"Richard sold it like he did our father's business because the man has no soul." Glen fiddled with his beard, agitated. "But he tells everyone he made me leave because he was worried about me falling down the stairs." The edge to his voice didn't surprise Birdie. Glen was in his eighties, and his brother looked considerably younger. Glen sighed. "I just feel a little lost, I guess."

Birdie tightened her jaw. "It's always about the damn stairs."

At that, Joseph laughed, and Birdie liked the sound of it. "Not for me. I moved here for the transportation. My vision's not the best anymore. Had one fender bender too many, and now I'm not supposed to drive."

They sat in companionable silence.

Glen cleared his throat, his darker mood cleared. "This cider is delicious. Where'd you get it, Birdie?"

Birdie and Joseph shared a look. "You brought it, Glen," Joseph said kindly. "And you're right . . ." He took a sip. "It is delicious."

Glen's hands fluttered around him as though speaking for him, then settled on his lap, where his eyes followed.

"Glen—" Birdie started, hoping to comfort the man, when someone knocked on her patio door.

"I'll get it," Joseph offered, and opened it to a tall man in similar boots to Glen and a long, thick coat.

He stepped inside and slid off his winter hat, looking sheepish. "I'm sorry to interrupt." Up close, she recognized him. A much younger version of Glen. "I'm his brother, Richard." He stared down at Glen, imposing with his height and broad shoulders. "I didn't know where you went."

Glen refused to look up from his lap, chewing on his bottom lip. Suddenly feeble and acting five years older. Birdie swallowed hard, saddened by the transformation. "Nice to meet you, Richard. Glen's told us all about you."

"Has he?" Richard looked surprised.

"I'm Birdie, and that's Joseph."

The man nodded but his eyes remained on Glen. "You can't run away when something bad happens." Richard spoke loudly, like his brother was hard of hearing. Birdie hated it for him.

"He was just going for a walk," she said.

Richard finally looked at her, taking in her walker first, then meeting her eyes. A quick assessment that stung her pride. "He set off the fire alarm."

"What?" Joseph said.

"He burnt eggs on the stove, and instead of letting anyone know what happened, he just left." Richard rubbed the back of his neck, not hiding his exasperation. "With the stove on and the eggs still burning."

"A mistake, of course," Birdie said, put off by the man's demeanor. No wonder Glen didn't like his brother. Felix worried about her, too, but he'd never treat her like she was a child.

"Was it a mistake, Glen?" Richard said.

Birdie had had enough. "Of course it was. Now, we were enjoying our cider, and as it looks like we don't have enough for a fourth, I'll thank you to let us finish."

Glen's head jerked up, and a straightening of his shoulders returned his usual air of confidence. "Yes, Richard. Don't you have a business trip to go on?"

"My flight was canceled, remember, Glen?"

Glen's smile faltered. "Right, of course."

Richard replaced his hat. "I'm hoping to catch another flight out this afternoon. Nice to, uh, meet you." The door closed behind him, and they sat in a collective silence.

Joseph was the first to speak. "Your brother's quite—"

"The sanctimonious prick?" Glen said. "I couldn't agree more."

That made Birdie chuckle, then Joseph broke out in his quiet smile, and finally Glen let loose with a too-loud laugh.

When they had finished their cider, Glen stood. "I must go and make sure my brother isn't over there packing up my things."

"Why would he do that?" Birdie said.

"He thinks I do these things on purpose or he thinks I'm forgetful—I don't really know. The man's never liked me, and he'll put me into a nursing home the first chance he gets."

Birdie felt a stab of anger at his situation. How terrible to be treated that way by family. It made her grateful for Felix and Sharon and the twins. They were a wonderful support system for her, encouraging her to move here out of concern and love. Not greed. Not hatred. Poor Glen. "We won't say a word," Birdie promised. "Right, Joseph?"

"You bet," he said.

A brightness returned to Glen's eyes. "Thank you, friends. And thank you, Birdie, for defending me like that."

Birdie smiled. It had felt good to stand up for someone, even if she'd been sitting the entire time. "Getting old isn't for the faint of heart, is it?" she said.

"It is not," Glen agreed. "Birds of feather, right, Bird?"

"Right, Glen."

Nine

ALLISON

Glen thanks Birdie with such effusive praise she looks like she's swallowed something sour. He doesn't register how his exuberance can sound disingenuous, because Glen hears his own thoughts first and foremost; it's impossible for him not to. They crowd inside his head, competing for space, like greedy children at an all-you-can-eat buffet.

Death gives us insight into the complexities of human thought. A confusing mix of the beautiful and the grotesque, the pure and the abominable. Glen remembers the sweet taste of his grandmother's homemade vanilla ice cream, the salt he licked off his fingers when she wasn't looking. The heated sweat under his armpits from turning the metal hand crank as fast as he could. His grandmother's arms around him. Golden, sunshiny thoughts that he keeps hidden in the dark room where he cradled his baby brother.

The living are not one or another. They are all, and I am thrust into the muddied waters of that truth. Glen hates his brother like he hates his father. He does not understand the simplicity of these feelings and never will, until he dies.

But we don't want him to die.

No, we don't.

Glen's nightmare is a dark room, his memories splintered, rushing around in circles of past and present. Right now he's thinking he knows the old woman from some other life. He feels like that a lot these days. Every wrinkled face a ghost of someone he might have known. Confusion worms through his thoughts, and his heart responds with rapid beats. His panic smells sour, metallic. Glen feels confused too much these days, and it scares him.

Inside his apartment, I am suffocated by the staleness. The others stay with Birdie, some follow Joseph, one goes to Everly, but I am drawn to Glen. A widening hole in his mind sucks pieces of his past, details that mean something. At night, he feels our breaths across his thinning scalp. He wakes, terrified, angry, haunted. Glen panics, a new feeling that comes with age and a controlling brother he once protected. He fears sleep, where regret is a night hag sitting on his chest.

His grandparents die in their beds, side by side, at eighty-four years old, burned to a crisp by a wildfire that razes their family cabin to the charred earth. Glen is eighty-four, and he doesn't want to die. As children, he and his brother spent summers with their grandparents. He remembers the lazy, tranquil days scouring the woods for treasure. Glen's brother is just like their father. Beady-eyed and dull. Neither of them is like their grandparents, salt-of-the-earth folks who believed the Good Lord would provide until the end.

But Glen believes he is different. His mind is a complicated forest of desire and ambition that drives him to want more. It's his failures that haunt him.

He stands in the bathroom and brushes his teeth. I am behind him, staring at his reflection in the mirror. His toothbrush stops, foam white in the corners of his mouth, and he looks right at me. His Adam's apple slides up and then down his throat, and his soul squirms just under the surface of his thinning, translucent flesh.

I am restless.

We all are.

I am left with questions, compassion, and a soul-bending desire for what is true.

Glen likes the friends he's made at Sunny Pines, even if he is forced to live here because of his greedy, spoiled brother, who is just like their simpleminded father. Richard is younger than him, and his youth makes him overconfident and cruel. Thanks to Glen, he doesn't have to remember the suffocating heat of the attic room.

The people here are not as sophisticated as Glen, but at this stage of life, beggars can't be choosers. Where once he was important, now he is a shell. He won't tell Richard that he thinks it's good to be around people again. They inspire him, make him feel alive, and it's been too long since he's felt like this. He won't give his spiteful brother the chance to gloat.

Glen wants to make a good impression. He tells himself to ask more questions, because his wife told him that's what he is supposed to do. He falls asleep wondering if the old man who fell in the parking lot this morning will survive the surgery they say he will need. Glen doubts it. He shivers. Glen is not ready to die.

He falls asleep too easily for someone with such heavy burdens.

Ten

Faith never came yesterday. At first, Birdie thought it was because of the ice that had, in fact, shut down the airport. Not the predicted big winter storm, mind you, but the weather people had still been gleeful that some form of disturbance had occurred. The sun poked through this morning, warming things up just enough to melt the remaining ice that clung to the streets and sidewalks and now, midafternoon, it was like it had never happened.

Except for that whole fire alarm business. And poor Paul, whose fall had broken his hip and required surgery. So unfair, and all because of burnt eggs.

She didn't blame Glen, not really, except she couldn't help wondering if his mistake was one of the reasons his brother might be worried about him living on his own. He did seem preoccupied at times—detached, even, like there was more going on inside his head than he let on.

But the biggest thing that had her worried today was Faith. Birdie hadn't seen her cleaning cart around the building, and Joseph said she hadn't been by his place either. So Birdie had decided to go to the office and ask. After a full day in her apartment, it felt good to push her walker outside. Still cold, but not bitter like yesterday. The office was just across the parking lot, and when she reached it, she hit the silver button with the blue stick figure in a wheelchair, and the doors swung open to the lobby.

Jonie sat in her office with her back to the door. She was the Sunny Pines director and always seemed to have a smile, chatting with the residents whenever time allowed, attending community-wide events like the Saint Patrick's Day party.

"Good morning, Jonie," she said from the doorway.

Jonie spun around in her chair. "Birdie! Yes, it is, and a much, much better one than yesterday." She pushed her thin blond hair—always a little unkempt—out of her face and beamed at Birdie. "I'm so glad you weren't caught up in that mess in the parking lot."

"I had the good sense to sleep through the fire alarm."

Her eyes widened behind purple eyeglasses, the kind with a beaded chain that hung around her neck. Birdie guessed Jonie to be in her upper forties, but the woman's style fit in more with the Sunny Pines crowd than other women her age. "Oh dear, that's not good, either, now, is it?" Jonie pulled a file from under a stack of files, checked the tab, and, satisfied, opened it. A bouquet of multicolored sticky notes stuck to the inside cover. "Was it working properly?" She flipped up a yellow square, pulled out a sheet of paper, eyeing it front and back. "Yes, there it is. You see? We just had them checked six months ago. It should have been working."

Birdie leaned into her walker. "It was, but you might have missed the part where I was sleeping."

Jonie blinked.

"I'm a heavy sleeper," she explained. "Especially without my hearing aids. It wasn't the fault of the alarms."

Jonie relaxed into her chair, abandoning the file among the others on her desk and looking rather relieved. "Terrible business yesterday."

"It was," Birdie agreed.

"Did you know Paul went skydiving for his ninetieth birthday?" Jonie said.

"I did not." She knew Paul in passing. He had a cat he walked on a leash, but she really didn't *know* him.

"And now he's laid up with a broken hip from an ice storm. Anyway . . ." She shook her head like she was trying to dislodge a bad dream. "What can I do for you, Birdie?"

"Faith didn't come by yesterday, and I just wanted to make sure everything's okay." Birdie wished the words back the minute they left her mouth. From the squint in Jonie's right eye, it struck her that maybe Jonie didn't know about Faith's missed day. Which made Birdie a big rat. *Dumb Birdie.* "Or maybe with all the excitement yesterday I didn't notice her . . ." She trailed off.

Jonie's spine straightened, a skosh more professional than a moment ago. "I'll check with housekeeping to see what happened. I'm sorry to hear you didn't get your scheduled clean, Birdie." She scanned her cluttered desk, shoulders dipping minutely, but enough for Birdie to see the defeat of an unorganized person. "Anything else?"

Birdie pushed the corners of her mouth upward. While she was here . . . "There is the thing about the newsletter." After watching how Glen's brother had spoken to him, she felt motivated to right a wrong.

"What thing?" Jonie sounded tired.

"The excessive use of capitals and exclamation points? It comes across as, well, condescending."

Jonie searched her desk, miraculously came up with a newsletter. She scanned it, nodding. "Right, I'll speak with Ann." She took off her glasses, rubbed her eyes.

Birdie almost felt bad, but not about the newsletter. Just that the woman was obviously overworked.

"Anything else?"

Birdie smiled. It was a small win. "Nope. Not a thing." Outside, one of the Sunny Pines vans had pulled into the circle, and from the lobby drifted voices. A community outing.

"I haven't seen you on any of our outings, Birdie." Jonie stood, and a few papers fluttered to the floor. "You know, here at Sunny Pines, we pride ourselves on meaningful engagement for all of our residents. Getting involved is the surest path to staying mentally healthy and physically strong." She smiled, and it was sincere, Birdie sensed that, but it was also downright annoying to be told what was good for her. She wanted to remind Jonie that she'd once employed more people than Sunny Pines, and not a single one of her employees had missed a day without calling.

Instead, she smiled back, hoping it came off as genuine. "Isn't that something. Well—" To her relief, her phone rang, the tone indicating FaceTime. Felix! "Better get this," she said, and shuffled out of the office and into the crowded lobby, doing her best to sidle past the bodies bundled in winter coats and thick scarves, some carrying oxygen tanks, wielding canes, or pushing walkers. The ringing stopped, and her heart skipped a beat. Sometimes Felix called when he had only a few minutes between surgeries or patients, and if she missed the call, it might be hours or days before they connected next.

"Birdie?" Nan's voice. Birdie sighed into her scarf. "You're going to Village Inn with us?"

Birdie stopped. Nan was even shorter than her, and curved over her walker in a way that made Birdie's back hurt for her. "Oh, heavens no, just stopped in to have a chat with Jonie."

"About the ice in the parking lot?"

"I don't suppose Sunny Pines controls Mother Nature."

Nan snorted. "Tell that to Dorothea." She wore a cherry-red winter hat that read Best Grandma in white letters around the brim. It was hideous and made Birdie smile.

"Your grandkids give you that hat?" she asked, and immediately wished she'd kept her sarcasm to herself. Not everyone appreciated her sense of humor.

But to her surprise, Nan laughed. "They did! Although I believe it was a Goodwill find. Given their recent behavior, I don't take it literally. And their mother hates the hat." Her voice was breathy, small like her. "I like to wear it anytime we take a family photo."

Birdie warmed to Nan.

The woman moved closer to Birdie. "Hey, did you hear they identified a person of interest in the Geneva Smith case?"

Birdie widened her eyes. "I have not."

Nan's shoulders dropped. "Oh, me either."

Birdie scratched under her chin, confused but also mildly amused. "Enjoy the outing."

Nan shook her head. "I only go for the pie." She nodded toward a man in line behind her wearing earmuffs that didn't quite cover the tips of his elongated ears. "And for the good-looking view."

She laughed. "Bye, Nan." Another ring from her phone, and she pressed a button on her hearing aid. Felix's voice filled her ears. "Mom? I'm on FaceTime."

"I know that, Felix." She made her way across the parking lot with her phone in her bag. "I'm walking back to my apartment."

"Oh, sorry. How's it going?"

"You'll be happy to know that I joined a book club."

"I'm sorry, what? I don't think I heard you right."

She pushed the button to open the doors to her apartment building, then walked as quickly as she could to her apartment. "You heard me. And I just walked past a group getting on the van for an outing and spoke to a new friend. I'm a social butterfly."

"But surely you're not getting *on* the van." Amusement in his voice.

She was glad her peccadilloes were so funny to him. "They herd everyone on like schoolchildren, Felix. Besides, I still drive so what's the point?" Finally at her apartment, she pushed open the door and walked straight to her chair, not even bothering to take off her coat or hat. From her bag, she pulled out her phone, and there on the screen was Felix. She smiled, warmed all the way through. Handsome like his mother, older than she'd ever had the chance to be.

"How's Sharon?" Sharon's mother had passed the month prior, a loss complicated by their estranged relationship. Sharon had once said that she'd married Felix because he was a package deal—she wanted someone warm and loving like Birdie in her life. In return, Birdie had gained a daughter. Sharon was smart and funny, kind, and one hell of a mother and a surgeon. Sometimes Birdie was overcome by their unearned love.

Felix sighed. "It's been tough. Actually, it's kind of brought up a few things in my own life."

"Really?" She knew he was seeing a therapist, understood from Sharon that some things from the past were creeping up on him. Birdie assumed it had to do with Allison; she'd felt that he never fully grieved his mother the way she believed he should. While Birdie had searched for answers in the Vampire Killer's murders, Felix had grown increasingly restless. It all came to a head when he was twenty. Birdie had zeroed in on a suspect when Felicity, the tenth victim, was found. After speaking with her family, Birdie had discovered that Felicity had dated a man who'd lived at the Paragon at the same time that she and Allison had lived there. Birdie had located his current address, found his apartment unlocked, and let herself inside. But his girlfriend had come home and, startled to find her there, called the cops. Felix had had to leave college to come and bail her out. She still remembered how angry he'd been, and it had surprised her. *Please, Mom, you have to stop this. It's insane. You're not a cop. You're not even close.*

She'd tried to make him understand. *You were so young when she died, Felix, so you just can't understand. I need to do this.*

Why? After all this time? Why can't you move on?

His vehemence had shocked her. *Because I loved her.*

I know that. His tone had been dismissive. Like Allison had been an acquaintance. A friend.

She'd swallowed, met his gaze with a firm lift of her chin. *No, Felix. I loved her and she loved me.* It wasn't something she'd kept from him on purpose, but it had never seemed the right time to tell him either. Now it was the only answer that made sense to give him.

There had been a shift in his eyes, like her words had been the final piece of a puzzle for him, and his arms hung limply by his sides. *Oh. I didn't—I mean . . . Oh.*

She'd touched his arm, searched for something more to say that might satisfy him. *And because she deserved more than an end like that. Because she deserves the truth and so do you.*

"Yeah." He cleared his throat, bringing her out of the past. "We only have you now—"

She shook her head, confused. "You've always had me."

"Right, but you're so far away, and I still worry about you."

She tried for playful. "You've worried about me since you were a little boy."

"Well . . . ," he said. "And the twins—"

Relieved to change the subject, she rushed in, "How are the boys? Tell me what they're up to?"

Felix paused long enough for Birdie to think he was going to ignore her question. "A handful, as usual." His face changed when he spoke about his boys. Softer, younger, similar to the way Allison looked when she'd sung Felix lullabies, kissed his tiny nose. Now Felix had a full head of salt-and-pepper hair and a smile that flashed white, even teeth. Braces had given him those teeth. And the money to make it happen had been worth every extra hour Birdie had had to work. By then she'd hired two other cleaners, but Birdie worked right alongside them. Always taking care of the business and her employees first. Making sure she'd never be one of those bosses who sat on her success. She'd worked as hard as her employees, until, at seventy-two, she sold the company to the daughter of her very first hire. They'd given her a wonderful retirement party: Felix and the twins had flown in, there'd been cake and a band. If she'd known then how her body would break down so completely afterward, maybe she would have made a different decision. But the truth was that it was time; she'd grown tired of the work, and retirement seemed like the next logical step.

"You know, there was a woman in our building who had twins," she said. "Your mom always said that if she could have had two of you, she'd have done so without hesitation."

Something shifted in Felix's eyes. It wasn't new; she remembered seeing it when he was a boy. And it happened whenever Birdie brought

Allison into their conversations, which she always had with Felix. Because these were Allison's moments, Allison's pride erupting in her heart. And it only seemed right to share them with her.

Felix's Adam's apple moved up and down, like he was swallowing whatever he might have said in reply. "Cody made the honor roll again."

Birdie smiled. Cody was Felix all over again. Driven, conscientious, sure to be a surgeon just like his parents.

"And he's the starting striker on his club team."

He'd played soccer since kindergarten.

"Apparently, he's got a girlfriend he hasn't told his mother about yet." She chuckled. "You tried that once, but I found out when you dropped your love letter on the kitchen floor."

"Oh God, was that the time you came to school to give it back to me?"

She shrugged. "It seemed time-sensitive." His letter had all the passion of a teenage boy with zero Shakespearean eloquence. But it had been sweet beyond measure, and Birdie couldn't stand thinking of him worried about where he'd lost it. She'd been reminded of her own adolescent letter: *Run away with me.* Birdie was ashamed to recall that at the time, she'd been relieved that his infatuation had been with a girl. She'd wanted an easier life for Felix.

So she'd waited for him outside the lunchroom, and as soon as she saw him, she slipped it to him, wrapped inside a napkin with a cookie. He'd been so embarrassed the tips of his ears had turned pink. When he came home that day, he didn't say a word, except his hug was a little bit tighter and lasted a moment longer than normal.

"And how's our delightful Tyler doing?" she said.

Felix rubbed his chin, a lightness to his tone when he spoke. "Tyler's directing his own horror film." He chuckled. "He does the makeup for it himself. Lots of blood and gore, but actually pretty good, especially considering he's learned everything he knows from YouTube. No girl- or boyfriend that we know of. But the thing about Tyler—he knows exactly who he is."

Birdie shook her head, smiling. "Just like his grandmother."

They shared a quiet moment.

"Mom," Felix said, "how are you? I mean, are you keeping busy?"

He wanted to know if she was depressed again. Birdie tried to redirect the conversation. "You know the campers we have on the side street from time to time?"

"Yes." Felix sounded hesitant.

"There's a young girl who moved her camper there recently, and Faith and I have been checking in on her."

"Faith?"

"The woman who cleans my apartment, Felix."

A long pause, and Birdie felt something shift in him even through the phone. "Mom, I was hoping you'd get to know other people there."

"I am."

"People your own age. You can't keep yourself isolated. It's what happened at the house."

Flashes of her home when Felix made his surprise visit: drawn and dusty blinds, an ant problem in the kitchen because of unwashed dishes, counters and table cluttered with unread mail, unpaid bills.

"I *have* been getting to know people *my own age*, Felix." She ran through anything that might appease him. "My friends Glen and Joseph came over for tea. Glen's brother thinks he's having memory issues, but personally, I think Glen's brother is a bit of jerk," she said, her voice brittle. "And my new and dear friend Nan is a true crime aficionado, and we've had long chats about the Geneva Smith case." The second it was out, she wished she could grab the words from the air and eat them.

"Who's Geneva Smith?"

"Nobody." Her eyes slid to the spare bedroom; guilt crawled up her spine, doubt tugged at her stomach. If he knew about that, Felix would be at her door before bedtime. She tried to pivot. "I told you about the book club, didn't I?"

He stared at her through the screen like he wanted to say something else. Then he sighed. "Yeah, you did, it sounds great." A longer pause. "But are you happy?"

So much hinged on her answer. Felix needed her to be happy. When he was in fifth grade and some horrible kid had told him his mother had killed herself because she was a whore and he was a bastard, Felix had been inconsolable. All he'd known before was that his mother had died and his grandparents had too. It wasn't cruel to hold back the truth, she'd reasoned. Cruel was the police insisting Allison had taken her own life. Cruel was Felix's grandparents refusing to acknowledge him, even after Allison had died. So she'd had to tell him everything. He'd taken it all in, and instead of being angry with Birdie for lying to him, he only clung to her more tightly. Afterward, he grew anxious, worry for Birdie his constant companion. *Are you happy, Mom?*

She was, she'd assured him every time he'd asked. *Because I have you.*

"You don't have to worry about me, Felix. I'm better, I promise."

As he grew older, her investigations, her research into each new death, the wall of women who preoccupied her, had become a source of frustration and sometimes even anger for Felix. He used to say that she never allowed herself peace, as if she believed she didn't deserve it. *It's like you're one of them.* He'd said it when he was a teenager. After the Vampire Killer had taken young Karen and single mother Jan within a year of each other. Between cleaning and speaking to their families and friends, she'd grown ragged—weight loss that accentuated the bags under her eyes, a hollowness in her cheeks. It woke her up at night, these deaths, one after another, going unanswered.

"Are you taking the antidepressants?"

She gritted her teeth. "The doctor said it was my choice."

"Yeah, I know." He sounded exasperated.

She tried to lighten the mood. "Oh, the twins' birthday presents are in the mail. Would you let me know when you get them?" The years piled up carelessly, one on top of the other. Hard to believe the boys would be sixteen years old next month.

That look again in Felix's eyes. Like he saw right through her. She wasn't lying, she reminded herself. She was fine, and maybe even a little bit happy.

"Mom."

She breathed in. "I'm trying, Felix. I promise. I know it got bad at the house, but retirement is hard. You go from being important and needed to . . ." She swallowed. "Adrift." She gave him a gentle smile. "You'll understand one day. Anyway, if the boys don't like what I got, please return them. I don't always know what to—"

"You didn't sign the card from Allison, too, did you?"

Her face stiffened. It was a point of contention between them. But while it had bothered him, he'd never explicitly asked her to stop. "You know why I do that, Felix."

Felix's sigh was beleaguered, and combined with his hand squeezing his temple, Birdie felt his old frustrations build up. "She's not here." He looked tired. "*You* are."

She hung her head. "What's going on, Felix?"

"Sharon's mom passing has made me—made *us*—realize how valuable you are to us. I need you."

"What on earth are you talking about?"

"I've always felt like you held a piece of yourself back. And when I was a boy, it made me feel like I wasn't enough."

"What?" Her mind spun. How could he say these things? "I've loved you with my whole heart." His childhood worry echoed in her head: *Are you happy, Mom?*

"I know you love me."

"Is this coming from your therapist?"

He paused, and she felt a pang; that was unfair of her.

"What I've come to realize is that your obsession with the Vampire Killer is really you searching for some kind of absolution."

She sat, stunned into silence and hurt because it was true. The broken lock. Her lost chance to express her feelings. Still, it felt like he wasn't dealing with what was really bothering him. "Felix, honey, don't you think you've never fully grieved losing your mom?"

Felix rubbed his eyes. "You're not listening to me. I've been struggling lately, but not from anything to do with Allison."

"Your mother." She sounded curt—she knew it—yet she couldn't stop herself.

He sighed. "That's what you don't understand. I never knew her like you did, Mom."

Pain on the underside of her heart, the place she felt her grief now. Like the years had allowed it to settle at the very bottom. "She knew you. Goodness, Felix, why is this coming up now?" But it wasn't new. He'd never been this direct, but he'd said as much over the years.

"I keep dreaming about her."

A flare of hope. "Your mother? That's good, sweetheart. You're connecting with her."

There was something dark in his eyes that she didn't like. "But it's not her. It's you in the tub. You with your wrists cut." He ran his fingers through his hair, left the ends standing up, and Birdie wished she could reach through the screen and take his hand in hers. "I need closure."

A faint ringing in her ears. She didn't understand what he was saying. "Closure for what? How can there be closure when the truth is still buried?"

He was silent.

"I swore that you'd never forget her, Felix."

More silence, and Birdie chewed on the inside of her lip, suddenly unsure how deep the waters had become. His nostrils flared when he breathed in. "Sharon emailed you the name of a therapist she found not far from you. Did you get the email?"

Birdie sniffed, her finger curling above the red button that would end this conversation. "I got it." Sharon had called Birdie after she sent the email, and Birdie had thanked her and said she'd think about it. Truthfully, Birdie didn't see the point. "I'm doing good, Felix." She thought about Joseph and Glen, even Nan. She was trying here, and that's all Felix had asked of her.

He stared straight through the camera, his eyes ringed with dark lashes, thick eyebrows. The George Clooney of the hospital, she knew, love for him an ache in her chest. "This half life you've lived, Mom—it's not normal and it makes me sad."

"Excuse me? Half life? What's going on Felix?" His brutal honesty, his evident frustration, was new. "I ran a business that put you through med school. I employed single mothers; provided health insurance, day care." Her chest hurt, and she felt her true feelings leak out. "And now I'm stuck in this in-between land where I'm spoken to in all caps and exclamation points." It was a trivial thing to bring up, she knew—out of context. But she was grasping for anything, any way to change the direction of this conversation.

His eyes were bright even through the fingerprints clouding her phone screen. "Are you unhappy there?" he said. "I feel like you're regressing. You've talked about her even more since you moved there. Even since you retired. You know we'd still love for you to move in with us." A lilt in his voice like he'd solved the problem. "I read this study about aging adults—"

"Felix, please." Her voice sounded ragged to her own ears. "No more studies."

"Mom, I know you loved her, and I wish none of it had happened, but it did and I want you to let it go. I think I *need* you to let it go."

"But I did let it go." She swallowed air.

Felix's words shook the phone in her hand, and she had to balance her elbow on the arm of the chair to stop it from wobbling. "I'm trying, Felix. I am." Heart thumped against bone. "But getting closer to the end shines a pretty glaring light on all the things I haven't done."

"Like proving Allison was murdered?"

She lifted her chin. "Yes."

Something fully snapped in Felix then; she saw it in the slight tremble of his upper lip, and it reverberated back to her, a blow to the stomach. "Allison *made* her choice. I've read the police report."

Her hand flew to her chest. "You did?" He'd never told her that before.

"Many years ago. It was an open-and-shut case. And there are no similarities to the serial killer's murders. You must know that by now.

Except for the fact that the first two victims were found near or in that complex. She left me. And you. And Cody and Tyler, for that matter. You never did. But you live like you did. Like you don't deserve what she left behind. Like we're not enough." His chin trembled. "I know how fiercely you loved her, Mom, but the only truth is that she's gone." He paused, and then his next words lacked his earlier volume. "And the rest of us have been forced to live in that shadow." He breathed in. "I don't mean to hurt you. But you're different. You seem more distant, like your thoughts are somewhere else most of the time. And the way you're focusing on that girl in the camper and whatever the hell this Geneva Smith thing is—it's a pattern I'm familiar with, and it worries me, Mom."

It was more than he'd said since the time when he bailed her out of jail. She felt blindsided, mute by his feelings laid bare over FaceTime. Miles apart, connected by this thread of technology that provided everything but physical touch. Her mouth opened; nothing came out, and despite her best efforts, Birdie felt tears heating the corners of her eyes. A weakness rushed through her body, lighting up the ache in her back, the gnawing arthritic pain in her joints. It made her feel the frailty of her aging body all at once. She steeled herself. "I'm okay, Felix. Please believe that. I—I think this therapy is good for you, I really do." She smiled like the words Felix had spoken were ghosts, transparent, disappearing with the seconds. And she looked at the man in the phone, hundreds of miles away, who held all the love she had to give.

His face clouded, defeated, hurt—and she hated that he felt that way, she really did.

"Please do let me know when the packages arrive. Give my love to Sharon and the boys. Love to you, too, Felix." And this time she pushed the red button.

Eleven

ALLISON

Funny thing about promises and the dead: we don't have the same attachment to them as the living.

I remember Birdie's promise, but it's not what stays with me after my lungs harden around a final breath. What seems so important to her, like her promise to keep me alive for my son, just isn't. She sits with me until the police show up, talking to me, her hands hovering over me, barely touching me like she's afraid of hurting my dead body.

Death is the forever now. I am always here. Both in the bathroom on the day I died and in the back of the car with Tommy, who pushes up my skirt and tells me I am beautiful. I am the child with brown ringlets and pudgy knees. I am the teenager frantically counting squares on a calendar.

I am a mother.

I am a woman in love.

And while her promise isn't the same for me, the love she pours into it cradles me, permeates the veil between us. Birdie's promise was a foolish thing, and one day she will understand that. The dead do not care about promises, but we do care about truth.

Will the truth set her free?

I do not know, my loves. But she can be caged no longer.

Birdie puts her phone face down on the coffee table. She sits in the chair, with her coat and hat on, staring at her lap. Then she stands and goes to the spare room, opens the door, and crawls on top of the bed. She lies on her side, staring at the wall. I lie down, too, curl my body around her, and remember the way she smells. A woodsy kind of floral. We stay like that until the sun falls behind the building.

Twelve

Since her conversation with Felix, Birdie had sunk a little too deep, staying inside, only going out for groceries or prescription refills. The talk had left her deeply saddened; she'd never meant to hurt Felix like that. To make matters worse, someone else had shown up that morning instead of Faith. Ashley, with curly hair and no personality, was her new cleaner, she informed her.

Where's Faith?

Ashley had shrugged her sloped shoulders. *Quit, I guess? She never showed up for work, so it's basically the same thing.*

Birdie had tried to make small talk, but Ashley gave one-word responses or none at all. After she left, Birdie returned to her bed, a sense of helplessness draining her of energy and direction. Faith had quit? Without a word even to Birdie?

She tried to sleep, couldn't. *Get up. Do something.* Except she didn't know what to do. Outside her window, voices, laughter, and then, through the closed blinds, a large shadow moved past. Another community event on the van.

She turned on her television, started flipping through the newest streaming shows when one slid by that stopped her cold.

Portrait of a Vampire: The Serial Killer That Got Away.

Birdie's mouth went dry. A documentary promising a review of his crimes, interviews with the victims' families, a deep dive into what might have happened to him in the thirty-five years since his last murder. She tried to flip past it. The show would only stir up painful memories; her finger pressed Play.

Two hours later, Birdie brushed a tear from her eye, her mind awash with images of the women she'd never met. Of their families, who'd opened up to her about their daughters, sisters, cousins, mothers. Who'd believed Birdie when she swore to them that their killer would be found. Back when Birdie believed it herself.

She pushed herself up in bed and opened her computer, typed *Geneva Smith* into the search bar. A few links to articles popped up but not much, and not enough to indicate that the police were doing all they could to find answers. A few still speculating that it was the Vampire Killer trying to make a return thirty-five years later. A deep sadness softened the bed beneath her, tugged heavily at her eyes. She should stay here, try to ignore it all.

Her pulse quickened. Or she could sniff around like she used to. Go back to the Paragon and ask some questions. The thing about her, people opened up to her. A fact she used to believe might give her information the police didn't have. She pushed out of bed. Felix thought doing nothing was better. But he didn't understand how destructive it was to feel aimless. How it nibbled away at pieces of her over time.

Asking questions was harmless. She got dressed, and within the hour, she was in her car and driving to her old apartment. There was a vape store across the street from the Paragon, and she parked in the lot, her car facing the apartment building. The years had not been kind: dirty windows, chipped brick, a loaded shopping cart beside bundled forms huddled on the sidewalk.

The decline of the building mirrored herself, and Birdie felt a stab of pity for her old home. It held a conflicting mess of emotions for her. After Allison's death, Birdie couldn't afford to move immediately, forced to stay in the apartment where Allison had died, reliving the nightmare of finding her every time she opened the bathroom door. But then, there were the neighbors. Bringing her meals, watching Felix in the early days when she couldn't get out of bed. A rotating neighborhood watch that held her, then prodded her, then dragged her forward until she was doing it all on her own.

She got out of the car and carefully made her way across the street to the front door, which someone had propped open with a brick. Her leg muscles tingled with nerves. She stepped inside, frowned, suddenly unsure. A tattered piece of paper was taped to the elevator: OUT OF SERVICE. The stairwell door pushed open, and a woman walked out, hair pulled into a greasy bun, puffy circles under her eyes, moving past Birdie without a glance.

Birdie leaned on old habits. "Excuse me."

The woman stopped. "Yeah?"

Birdie breathed in. "Did you happen to know Geneva Smith?"

She checked her watch, head shaking no. "I'm late for work." She was at the door, pushing aside the brick with a disgusted look.

Birdie was losing her. "Wait! They found her body in the dumpster a few weeks ago."

Her face hardened. "I don't know nothing about that."

"I'm not with the police." Birdie sounded desperate. "I—I'm just looking for anyone who might have known her."

A minute softening along the woman's jaw. She jerked her head down the hallway. "Talk to Loretta in 1B."

"Mrs. Dempsey?"

The woman shrugged. "She knows everyone." The door closed firmly behind her, filthy window obscuring the light and giving the lobby a yellowish hue that deepened the acidic stink of urine. Birdie made her way down the hallway until she came to 1B. It couldn't be the same woman. Mrs. Dempsey would have to be a hundred years old by now.

She knocked. No answer. Knocked again, and just as she was about to leave, the door opened to a woman who, apart from her golden-brown skin, looked much like Birdie with her gray hair, stooped back, and walker.

"Mrs. Dempsey?" The woman had been at least twenty years older than Birdie when she'd watched Felix all those years ago. "It's me, Birdie Allen. I used to live next door to you. You watched Felix for us?" A tightness in her chest. The years pinballing, one against the other.

"Oh, heavens, girl, call me Loretta." She squinted one eye. Despite her age, Loretta's skin was remarkably smooth and her voice strong and sure. "Of course I remember that sweet boy of yours, but I wouldn't have known you from Eve. You got old."

Birdie laughed and splayed her elbows above the walker. "All the way through. And you moved to the first floor."

Loretta made a face. "My daughter was worried I'd never make it down the stairs in case of a fire."

Birdie shook her head. "It's always about the stairs."

Loretta laughed. "That's for damn sure." She moved back from the doorway. "Come in, I just brewed some coffee. I hope you take it black, because I'm out of cream."

Birdie followed her inside and joined her at a square kitchen table. Her kitchen smelled like cinnamon and sugar. "Are you still making homemade cinnamon rolls?" Every Sunday, Loretta would bring over three buttery rolls piping hot from her oven. The familiar aroma turned back the clock, made her believe that if she reached out, she might grab ahold of Allison's hand.

Loretta winked. "It's the secret to a long life."

Birdie smiled. "I believe it."

Between sips of coffee and warm cinnamon rolls, they talked— Birdie filling her in on Felix and his family; Loretta updating her about other neighbors who'd lived in the building, her own family, grand- and great- and great-great-grandchildren until eventually she sat back in her chair and gave Birdie a pointed look. "Now, tell me why you're really here, because I know it's not to catch up on old times."

Birdie set her mug down, her stomach twisting. "I'm sure you heard about the young woman found in the dumpster?"

Loretta's lips pressed tight. "You still acting like you're Perry Mason? After all this time?"

"I'm just wondering if you knew her. Did she live here?"

"She did not." The old woman's eyes dampened. "But she was a nice girl."

That didn't surprise Birdie. Loretta had been like the building mother when Birdie had lived there. Kind to all the single women, dispensing sage advice, protective. If there was a woman in need, Loretta would reach out.

"She liked to work this side of the street so we could have coffee sometimes. I watched her baby once."

Birdie wasn't surprised by that either. Despite her age, Loretta seemed agile and mentally sharp.

Loretta narrowed her eyes. "Oh lord, you've been listening to that nonsense about the Vampire Killer? It was her boyfriend who did it. He was a horrible man, and I know she was scared of him." She put her hand over Birdie's. It was warm, comforting, and Birdie's throat tightened. "I always believed you; you know that. Allison loved that boy, and you. I don't know if it was that serial killer like you believed, but there's no doubt in my mind that you were right. Something bad happened to Allison and it wasn't by her own hand."

Birdie felt the floor fall away, and she braced herself in her seat. Loretta's words hit their mark—right in the center of her heart. Birdie put her other hand on top of Loretta's and squeezed. "Thank you," she said.

They talked for a few more minutes; then Birdie stood to go, and when she hugged the old woman goodbye, it felt like she squeezed a bundle of sticks.

～

Later, she sat in her living room, holding the picture of Allison, the visit with Loretta giving life to the past. The phone was in her hand. She found a number for the local police department. A man answered. "I'm calling about the Geneva Smith murder case."

"Yes, ma'am. Do you have information?"

A twist in her chest. "Uh, no, but I have a source who knew the victim and has knowledge that she was scared of her boyfriend."

"'A source,' ma'am? Are you a reporter?"

"No, I—I'm just a concerned citizen." Her face burned, uncertainty thinning her voice. "Just because she was a prostitute doesn't make her less valuable." She was saying too much, sounding desperate. They wouldn't take her seriously. They never did. "Or if it is the Vampire Killer"—grasping at straws, the present melting away—"have you ever considered that he might have once lived or even still lives at the Paragon? That maybe that's why so many of his murders were close to that building? Have you interviewed everyone who lives there?"

There was no reply, and then came a sigh. "Thank you for calling. We appreciate your support."

Birdie stared at the phone in her hand, breathing too fast, Felix first and foremost in her thoughts. She'd done what she'd promised him she would never do again. Still, it had felt good to do something. *Something* was infinitely better than doing nothing.

Her eyes caught the unopened envelope she'd set out yesterday to give to Faith, thoughts ping-ponging from one vulnerable woman to another. This wasn't like Faith. Birdie had employed hundreds of women throughout the years, and she believed she had a sense for people. Faith was a hard worker, conscientious and thoughtful, and not the type to stop showing up without giving her employers a warning. In Birdie's experience, when a woman disappeared, it wasn't good. Now all she could think about was Faith, even as a quieter voice pleaded with her to consider how her latching on to another mystery might affect Felix. But her talk with Loretta had shortened the distance to her past, and Birdie was certain that something bad must have happened to Faith.

A soft rap on her door, and Birdie rose from the chair. Another rap, so soft it seemed the person on the other side had given up. Birdie looked through the peephole. Joseph's face filled the fish-eye lens, nose cartoonishly big and pointy, chin small. Same stoic look in his eyes. He turned to walk back to his apartment, and Birdie tugged on her bottom lip. She should let him go, and yet a distraction seemed better than stewing in her own thoughts.

"Hello, Joseph. Another fire alarm you've come to warn me about?"

His forehead wrinkled. "No, nothing like that." He stood with his hands in his pockets, a gesture that pulled back the gauze of age, giving her a glimpse of the boy he'd once been. "I haven't seen you around since the ice storm, and I wanted to apologize for intruding on you for as long as we did. It wasn't my intention to barge in on you like that. Glen . . . well, he's—"

"A bit presumptuous?"

He smiled. There was an earnestness about him that Birdie liked. "That's one word for it." He shuffled his feet like he meant to leave. "But it was a nice thing you did, standing up for him like that. His brother seems—"

"Like a jerk?"

"Exactly."

"I'm glad you both stayed. I think Glen needed to talk, anyway," she said.

Joseph rounded his shoulders. "I was wondering, Birdie, if you'd like to go and get some coffee or come over for coffee, or tea, or lemonade." One side of his mouth lifted. "I also have whiskey."

Birdie hesitated, flattered by the offer and also, ridiculously, wondering at his intentions. As a businesswoman—and as a single woman, in general—she'd learned to be skeptical of any offer of friendship from a man. In her experience, it often implied a hope for something more.

Joseph cleared his throat. "I know you're not a social person. I'm not either. My wife was the social chair of our family." His chin wobbled the tiniest fraction, and the love it hinted at, the grief it masked, softened Birdie's doubts.

"Sofia made me promise I wouldn't become a hermit after she died, and I'm afraid that's exactly what's happened."

He was being honest, that much she could tell. The man exuded it. And for God's sake, she was too old to shoulder the worries of a young woman.

The greedy darkness of her bedroom tickled the backs of her heels. It would be good for her to leave the apartment. Plus, if she was right about Faith, it might benefit Birdie to be more social in case she needed help in finding out what happened her.

"You know, Joseph, that sounds nice." She grabbed her keys from the hook by the door and stepped into the hallway.

Joseph's eyes widened. "Oh, right now? Weren't you on your way out?"

"Wha— Oh." She still wore her coat and hat. Birdie shook her head. "No, that's from earlier, but my apartment is always so cold that sometimes I leave my coat on till I warm up."

They stood in the hallway, Joseph looking like he'd grown roots.

"Your place?" she said.

"Yes, okay, sure." He turned, slowly, like she'd said the very last thing he expected. "Come on in." Holding his door open for her, the space awkward with her walker and the narrow entryway. "Can I—" He squeezed himself between the door and the wall, trying to be polite and hold it open, instead making it much worse by getting caught behind it. "Oof." A bang, probably his head hitting the wall, his body disappearing behind the door. "Sorry about that." Only his voice now.

It struck her as the funniest thing she'd seen in a long, long time, and she laughed. "What are you sorry about? You're the one being attacked by your own door." She moved farther inside until he was released.

Freed at last, he wiped off his sleeves, straightened his button-down shirt, and met her gaze. "Coffee?"

Birdie grinned. She liked this guy. "Whiskey."

At that, the creases in his forehead eased. "It's five o'clock somewhere."

Thirteen

Joseph's apartment was barren in a way that touched on her gloominess from moments ago. A La-Z-Boy had been pushed into a corner, with one of those arching gold lamps from the seventies hovering over it like an alien spacecraft. A small television sat on a dusty metal stand a few feet from the chair. The kicker was the punching bag hanging dead center in the middle of the room. Pictures hung haphazardly at different heights and in no cohesive order that she could figure out. A studio portrait of his wife and a son and daughter from the eighties, based on his wife's perm and his daughter's upside-down glasses. Beside that, a photo of the two of them from what looked like a church directory.

Birdie looked around for another chair, saw a wooden stool at the small kitchen bar. That'd do. Took a seat, and for the moment appreciated its elevated height. Sometimes sitting down and getting up from sitting were the hardest parts of her day.

Joseph stood by his boxing bag, hands at his side and looking utterly helpless.

"Did you lure me in here for a training session?"

"Wha—" As if on cue, his shoulder touched the bag; he looked at it, his chair, the bare kitchen, like he was seeing his own apartment for the first time. "Oh."

"Let me guess: Sofia was the decorator of the family too?"

He nodded. "She loved red pillows."

Birdie looked around. Not a pillow in sight. "You should get you some, then. Maybe a couch to put them on. No time like the present."

That seemed to jump-start him, and he moved to the kitchen, opened up the pantry door, and pulled out a bottle of Blanton's.

"Bringing out the good stuff, huh? I'm honored."

He pulled two coffee mugs from the cabinet: a green one that read ESTES PARK and another one with Sasquatch walking across it. "I don't drink alone."

"I don't drink much at all, so just a dribble for me."

He poured a little into the Sasquatch mug, then a little more into the Estes Park mug and held it aloft. "Cheers."

She raised hers. "Right back at you." And quickly swallowed the amber liquid. It burned going down and she coughed, hand to her mouth. Immediately, the alcohol warmed and tingled its way to her fingertips and toes. Relaxation sank deep into her core, and for a moment, Birdie thought she might cry. She slid her mug closer to Joseph. "One more for luck, and this time I'll sip it."

He obliged, and with the second drink, she sipped, her tears swept away by its relaxing fire. She smiled, hands around her mug, elbows on the counter, and they finished their drinks in a silence that Birdie found comfortable, even with the incessant ticking of a small round clock on the wall beside them. "How do you stand that?" she said.

He raised his eyebrows. "What's that?"

She waved a hand at his clock. "That ticking. A little on the nose, don't you think?"

He smiled. "I never thought of it that way." He studied the clock. "It keeps me moving."

"Your metronome."

"In a way."

She set her mug on the counter. "I'll take that coffee now."

"Good idea." He pulled out an orange-and-white bag of Dunkin' Donuts coffee from his pantry and used a big spoon to scoop the grounds into the coffee maker. It tapped and sputtered before brown water spurted into the carafe. Conversation stalled again while the coffee brewed, but Birdie didn't mind. When it was done, he poured coffee right on top of the Blanton's dregs, and she inhaled a not-unpleasant aroma of citrus, smoke, and spice.

"So you're not a joiner, either, huh? But you started a book club?" Birdie said.

He stood across the counter, drinking his coffee. "I can relate to Glen in that way," he said. "Not lonely so much as too much time with my own damn thoughts."

"The ghosts?"

He gave her a look, the likes of which he'd certainly given quirky Glen at some point or another.

"Come on, now, not the literal kind," she said. "But the ones that haunt us."

He was already nodding. "I never thought I'd be the one left behind." His honesty brightened the blue of his eyes.

Birdie let that sink in, a twinge in her chest for his pain. She didn't offer him empty platitudes or motivational sayings about death and grief. Listening seemed to her to be the best thing she could do. Sometimes a person just needed to put into words the things that ate pieces of his heart. And for someone to hear them. The other dancers at the club had been sympathetic like that. They weren't immune to loss or tragedy, and they knew more than most how to listen. But when it came to understanding her drive for answers, many of them backed away. *Leave it alone,* she'd heard more than once. *You want to lose your baby? The last thing you need is the cops sniffing around.* They were right. She didn't have legal custody, but she did have every important document Felix needed, had been in his life since birth; and with no father or grandparents willing to take him, Felix was her son, even if the law might not agree. Looking back, Birdie was grateful for one thing: that all of it had happened in the seventies, when times were different and regulations weren't quite so strict.

Joseph sipped his drink. Silent pauses didn't seem to bother him, and for that, she liked him even more.

"I think Felix wanted me to move here partly because he'd hoped I'd find common ground with other people my age." She shrugged. "Like I'm in grade school."

Joseph grunted. "My kids are hoping I'll make friends too. You're right: it's like we're in kindergarten again." He lifted his mug and gave her his one-sided smile. "I never drank whiskey in kindergarten, so joke's on them."

Birdie laughed and clinked her mug to his. "Cheers to that." Something opened up in her then, and she inhaled. "You know, Joseph, I worked my entire life, from the time I left home at seventeen until I retired at seventy-two. And now I'm finding this stage of life a little disappointing." Her voice wobbled with her honesty.

"My feelings exactly," he said.

"Which is why I'm glad I joined your book club. Like you, I might be a bit of a recluse myself."

He gave her that small smile of his, the one that felt like a secret. She liked it. "Thank you, Birdie," he said. "Sofia would be happy to know she's brought two loners together."

"That's a nice thought." Birdie studied the chipped edge of her mug. "Maybe our greatest loves never leave us." She didn't meet his eyes. Birdie had been a churchgoer most of her life, finding communities that accepted her as she was, not pining for her to change her ways. Acceptance had come far too late for her and Allison, but Birdie had been determined to live her life truthfully. She'd wanted to fall in love again, but it never happened for her. Perhaps Cheryl had been right—she'd held back, afraid to commit. She sighed. Most of her life she'd been fulfilled by her business and Felix, anyway. "Who's to say that Sofia's not watching over you now, whispering encouragement and rooting you on?"

Joseph seemed paler than before, and his hand trembled when he sipped his coffee. "Do you have someone who watches over you?" He seemed eager to keep the conversation flowing in her direction.

"I think so. She was my first love—my only love, really—and it ended much too soon."

"What happened?"

Birdie hesitated, her earlier honesty withering. This was the part where most people got that look in their eye, a mixture of pity and condescension. They heard *suicide*; they saw a woman who just couldn't face the truth, and she hated it. Had spent most of her life evading that look.

Joseph was watching her, head tilted slightly as though he heard her thoughts. All she could bring herself to say was, "She died."

His hand slid across the counter, not touching her arm but close, fingers grazing and enough to get the point across. "I'm sorry," he said.

Thoughts of Allison lingered, and suddenly Birdie remembered her present concern: Faith. And the way Joseph sat there, relaxed, not filling the air with thoughtless words and platitudes, made Birdie say, "Actually, more to the point, I'm concerned about Faith."

He leaned his hip against the counter, arms folded. "Sounds like she quit, from what the new girl said."

Birdie felt a frustrated tickle in her throat. "Without giving notice? That doesn't sound like Faith."

Joseph rubbed the back of his neck. "Maybe it couldn't be helped?"

"Or something happened to her."

He shifted his weight, a confused slant to his eyebrows. "Isn't it a little premature to think that?"

Birdie filled her lungs; she was used to the doubt but had hoped Joseph might give her a little more runway. "No one here has seen her since before the ice storm—what was that, a month ago?" Birdie sucked in her bottom lip. To her it was obvious, but based on the crinkle in Joseph's forehead, he hadn't put the pieces of the puzzle together yet. "Who'd notice if she'd disappeared or was hurt, other than people like us who see her regularly? I don't buy that she quit without a word. We— She was my friend."

Joseph was quiet for a moment. "I really didn't know her as well as you. What do you think happened?"

Birdie pushed her fingers into her thighs, preparing herself to be ridiculed. "I don't know. But I have this feeling." She heard how weak it sounded. "I think something's happened to her."

Joseph leaned back like he was taking it in, his stoicism giving away nothing of what he thought. His chest was flat, taut, and his posture was straight as a board even leaning against the counter. A military by-product, she guessed. "Like what?" he said.

Irritation flared her nostrils. "Oh, I don't know, Mr. Man, what could possibly happen to a single woman whose entire support system is thousands of miles away?"

Joseph had the good sense to look abashed. "How about we give her a call?"

Birdie's cheeks warmed. While she'd considered Faith one of her only friends at Sunny Pines, they did not, in fact, talk outside of Faith's work hours. A fact that held a mirror up to Birdie. "I don't have her number."

"Do you know where she lives?"

"No." She pulled at the loose cotton of her pants, hearing herself— an afraid and alarmist old lady. Still, her gut held tight to her instinct. Just because something looked one way didn't make it the only possibility. Hadn't she learned that with Allison?

Joseph took her empty mug and his, and washed them out using a soapy rag before setting them on a rack in the sink to dry. He wiped his hands and turned to her. "Okay, then, how can we find her phone number? Or address?"

His pivot took her aback. She was ready for his dismissal, not an openness to join her in her search. "You want to help?"

"Sofia—I mean, Faith is a good woman. She deserves to have people worried about her."

Birdie blinked, swallowing down a stubborn lump. She wasn't used to someone making space for her concerns. "Maybe we check the internet?"

At that, he frowned and shook his head. "I might not be much help in that area."

Birdie grunted. "Me either." She took out her phone, touched the screen, and brought it close to her eyes for the face scan. It opened and she brought up the internet, typed out *Sofia Faith Perez*. A few links popped up, but nothing that looked like Faith.

Joseph had come around the island and was looking over her shoulder. "Try her name and then type *phone number* and *home address*."

Birdie did; still nothing that looked promising, until something came to her. "She told me she started an Etsy store." She added *Etsy* and then *Clean Faith* after her name. "There!" She pointed. No picture, but a link to Etsy. She clicked, and it opened to a page with *Clean Faith* across the top. "That's her company!"

"Good sleuthing, Birdie."

She scrolled down, disappointed. All that was listed was an email. She clicked on it, and another window popped open with her email.

Subject line: Are you okay?

Dear Faith,

This is Birdie. I haven't seen you since before the storm. Sunny Pines thinks you quit. Would you please email me back to let me know that you're safe?

Sincerely,
Birdie

She hit Send.
"Feel better?"

"Not particularly," she said. If anything, she felt let down. If something had truly happened to Faith—an intruder, a carjacking, kidnapping, or worse—would she be able to answer an email? She pictured Allison in the tub, crying out for help and nobody coming. Birdie's heart beat faster. "I need to find her phone number."

"Okay." Joseph seemed hesitant. "Maybe the office has it in their files?"

"Of course!" She patted Joseph's arm. If he thought she was sad—crazy, even—at least he didn't say it. "Thanks for the whiskey. It was just what I needed to put a little hair on my chest." She stood and moved her walker toward the front door.

Joseph slid into his coat and followed.

"What are you doing?" she said.

He looked surprised. "Coming with you, if you don't mind."

Birdie swallowed, touched. "You know they won't give me her number, so I might have to lie, or sneak in there when Jonie steps out."

Joseph shrugged. "I've decided that I might need a little excitement in my life."

Birdie squinted at him. "What you need is red pillows, but this is a start."

∽

With the cloudless sky and full sun of early spring, Birdie felt almost too warm in her thick coat. The bright rays had pulled people outside of their apartments. Some walked their dogs, others were headed for the community center. Birdie and Joseph made their way down the sidewalk toward the office. Two women stood in the grassy area to the left of the entrance holding leashes, matching white dogs attached to each. One of the dogs shot across the grass toward Birdie, colliding with her walker.

Birdie muttered under her breath and kept moving like it didn't annoy the heck out of her. She'd never had a dog, something alien to most of Colorado. Felix had begged for one when he was in elementary school, and Birdie had said no, they were both too busy to care for one. It had broken his heart, but in time he'd adjusted, and when he had a family of his own, he'd gotten the biggest, hairiest, most slobbery dog he could find. Birdie didn't think she'd missed out on anything.

"Sorry!" The woman with the blue leash and silky white hair tried to pull her dog back. "He's just a puppy."

The other dog followed, pummeling its tiny body into the first, both of them getting tangled in the legs of Birdie's walker and bringing her to a stop. That woman—also with equally shiny white hair—said, "So is Rosemary, but we have them in training, so don't let them jump on you."

"Come, Thor!"

"Down, Rosemary!"

Neither dog obeyed, and Birdie bit her tongue to keep from pointing out that training had failed. The two women finally pulled their dogs away from her walker, the dogs and the women both panting from the effort. It would have been funny—this puppy exuberance in contrast to the retirees. But she was preoccupied with how she and Joseph would get Jonie to share Faith's phone number. She gave them a half wave and started walking again, expecting Joseph to follow, but he had knelt, pure delight etched into his normally stoic countenance. The littlest of the dogs jumped up, its paws balanced on Joseph's knee. The other one, slightly bigger, backed away before carefully joining its friend.

"Bichons, right?" Joseph asked. "Are they from the same litter?"

"No, but they are about the same age," said the woman with the bigger bichon, whatever that was. "It's how we met. Jean and I are the only ones here crazy enough to get a puppy."

Between the swing of their hair and their able-bodied selves, this woman and Jean looked like model ads for retirement living. Birdie pushed into the handles of her walker, trying to straighten the curve of her spine.

"We had a pair when my kids were little." Joseph played with the dogs, looking truly happy. Like they brought back all his good family memories.

She felt a pang. Good memories were the kind you stopped for, and this man deserved a moment of joy. So for Joseph's sake, she stopped trying to find an excuse to leave and settled in.

"They are such characters," he said.

The first woman smiled at Birdie. "You're new around here, right?"

"Six months new." Birdie tensed, expecting the question that always came next: *Why haven't I seen you at any of the community functions? It's good for you. You'll feel younger, smarter, prettier, it's what Sunny Pines is all about, blah, blah, blah.* Birdie pressed her lips together.

But the woman said none of that. "I'm Louise. I've been here two years and I still feel new."

"That's because you refused to go to any of the functions until recently," Jean said.

And there it is, Birdie thought.

"Some of us like to take our time, Jean," Louise said with an easy laugh.

Birdie smiled. Maybe the senior models weren't so bad after all. "I'm Birdie, and the dog lover here is Joseph." Joseph was on his knees now, the dogs standing on their hind legs to try to lick at his face.

"Do you like dogs, Birdie?" Louise asked.

"God, no," she said before she could stop herself.

Joseph stood, smiling wide, and Birdie liked how it made his crooked nose more crooked.

"Are you going to the choir concert?" Jean nodded toward the community center. "They sang here last year." She made a face. "They're not very good."

"No, I'm—" Birdie was struck by a sudden thought. "Do you know Faith? She cleans our building."

"Yes, but someone else came today—and if I'm being honest, she wasn't as friendly as Faith." Jean frowned. "Or good."

"The last time I saw Faith was right before all that mess with the fire alarm," Louise said.

Birdie's stomach did a flip-flop. "The day of the ice storm? You saw her?"

Louise nodded. She had eyes the color of storm clouds. "From my window. She was by the road, leaning over and talking to someone through their car window." Louise pulled the leash and her dog bounded to her side, a cotton ball on legs.

The dogs were cute, Birdie quietly ceded. Like little stuffed animals.

"So I was surprised when she didn't show up that day," Louise added. "But it was such a mess with the ice, I figured she'd gone home."

Birdie's suspicions stacked higher. "They say she stopped showing up to work."

Louise frowned. "That doesn't sound like something Faith would do."

"Exactly my thinking." She glanced toward the office windows. Jonie sat with her head bowed over her desk. "I wanted to check up on her. You know, make sure she's okay. Joseph and I were going to ask Jonie for her phone number."

Louise made a face. "I worked in HR. I doubt she'll give out her number—or shouldn't, anyway."

Birdie nodded. "But it must be in a file somewhere, don't you think?"

"Isn't everything on a computer these days?" Joseph had been so preoccupied with the dogs that Birdie had nearly forgotten he was there.

"Have you seen Jonie's office?" Louise opened her eyes wide like she was sharing a secret. "It's covered in file folders. She's not very organized and doesn't seem particularly tech savvy."

Birdie smiled; Louise wasn't half-bad. "So maybe she still keeps good old paper files?"

Louise shrugged. "It's possible."

"Okay." Birdie looked back at the office window. "Do you think Jonie's attending the choir concert?"

"Doubtful. Rosemary, no!" Jean's little Rosemary was eating something off the ground. "I think the soprano is someone's granddaughter, and a soprano she is not. Did I mention they aren't very good?"

Birdie felt discouraged. It would be helpful if Jonie wasn't in her office. She just wanted to do a little snooping.

"Were you thinking of sneaking into her office and finding Faith's number yourself?" Louise put into words exactly what Birdie was thinking.

"Maybe," she said, testing the waters, but Louise didn't seem appalled or surprised by her response.

Joseph smiled at the dogs. "Don't you think we should ask first?"

Birdie craned her neck to look up at him. "No. Jonie's already made up her mind that Faith quit."

"Sounds like you need some help." Louise sounded casual, like this was a normal Sunny Pines conversation. Maybe it was, for all Birdie knew. A place like this? There had to be a crook or two in the bunch.

A flare of excitement burned through her chest. "Maybe just a small distraction?"

Jean and Louise looked at each other. The dogs had settled down, sitting side by side like bookends. "I think we could come up with something," Louise said. "What do you think, Jean?"

A warm camaraderie laced itself among their small group, pulling Birdie in.

"I've got nothing better to do." Jean squinted. "Except to go to Costco before it gets dark. I got the best bananas there last week."

Louise smiled. "Loose dogs in the building?"

"Like that day Thor ran out into the hallway after Rosemary?"

"Exactly."

Their exchange was that of friends, and for the first time in a long time, Birdie felt envious of it.

Jean tugged on her leash, Louise did the same, and the dogs bolted back to their sides. "This is going to be fun," Louise said.

"Just as long as I make it to Costco."

They started to walk inside, the dogs straining at their leashes. Louise turned. "Once she leaves her office, you've got fifteen minutes," she said. "That's how long it takes for them to wear themselves out long enough for someone to hook a collar."

Five minutes later, with the bichons barking and running rampant inside the building and Louise and Jean crying out for help, Jonie sprinted from her office.

Fourteen

Birdie moved as fast as she could, which wasn't very. "Go ahead of me!" she hissed to Joseph, who was trying to stay by her side. He did, and by the time she got to the office, he had done nothing more than open a filing cabinet drawer.

"What are you waiting for? Start looking." She sat down in Jonie's chair, taking stock of the woman's desk.

Joseph made noises behind her. "What am I looking for?" he said.

Their lack of planning was painfully evident, but now that it was happening, Birdie felt prickles of excitement across her scalp. "Maybe a file with her name? Or an HR-related one? Housekeeping? People who quit? I really don't know, just keep looking for anything that might work."

She leaned down and pulled open the desk drawers, none of which made sense. Packaged food in one, combined with extra staples and Post-it notes. One drawer full of pens and small packages of Kleenex. She picked through the mess that was the top of Jonie's desk. Minutes ticked away, and a rising sense of defeat pickled the air. Her hand hit the mouse, and Jonie's monitor sprang to life. Birdie squinted at the home screen and saw the Contacts icon. She clicked on it, and when it opened, she found the magnifying glass thing and typed in *Sofia Faith*. Even before she was finished, a box populated with matches, and there it was: Sofia Faith Perez, with her email, mailing address, and phone number.

Birdie squawked, too excited to form words, but it was enough to get Joseph's attention. She grabbed one of the sticky notes and jotted down the information.

"Look at that, Birdie. You found her!"

"Found who?"

Joseph shot straight up, and Birdie squawked again. Jonie stood in the doorway to her office, hair askew, a redness in her cheeks, confusion twisting through her thin eyebrows.

"What are you doing in my office?"

"Um," Joseph said. "Well, um . . ." He scratched his head and picked up a stapler. "We, uh, needed—" Then a pair of scissors. "And these too—"

Birdie craned her neck to look up at him; she'd brought a knife to a gunfight. "What Joseph is trying to say is that I lost my balance . . ." She swallowed and tried to look her most delicate. "And quick-thinking Joseph here helped me to sit down."

"And go through my office?"

Birdie gave her a pointed look. "Well, your office is a mess, dear. I thought you might appreciate some help." She raised her eyebrows and gave the top of her desk the kind of look that said it all. She was good at those, according to Felix.

The sharpness of suspicion softened, and Jonie entered her office, contrite. Like Birdie had spoken directly to the woman's deepest fear: she was unorganized and everyone knew it. Behind Jonie, Louise and Jean walked by the door, dogs in tow, giving a question mark of a thumbs-up. Birdie nodded, and the two women air high-fived each other.

Birdie coughed to cover a laugh and pushed up from Jonie's chair, wincing as she did for dramatic effect, which effected quite well, as Jonie hurried to her side, arm out. "Oh, don't rush! Stay seated until you feel better. Please!"

Birdie gave her a grateful smile, pocketing the sticky note as she did and winking at Joseph when Jonie wasn't looking. "I feel much better."

She stood again and pushed her walker out from behind the desk. "That was quite a commotion out there. Is everything okay?"

Jonie collapsed into her chair, surveying her desk with a frown, like she was seeing it for the first time. "It was the bichons again. Dogs are good for the soul, and we here at Sunny Pines know how important that can be in our later years—" She stopped, seemed to hear herself slipping into company talk. "They're cute, but they're kind of little pests." She rubbed her cheeks. "Maybe they should have them in training."

"Oh, they do," Birdie offered. "I just don't think it's taking."

Jonie snorted, and for a moment, Birdie felt a little bad for the woman. Was she married? Did she have children? Birdie saw no ring on her finger and had noticed her working well past when other staff went home. It seemed that work was her anchor, and it reminded Birdie a little of herself.

Joseph stood by her side. "Guess we'll be going," he said, still clutching the stapler. Birdie tapped his arm and he looked down, surprised. "Oh, here." He set it on Jonie's desk, wiped a hand across his shirt. Small beads of sweat had popped out across his hairline.

"Are you headed to the choir concert?" Jonie said.

Birdie pasted on a smile. "Oh, no, not today, although I've heard everyone just raving about them."

Jonie's eyes narrowed. "Really? Okay, then. I feel better about that. I heard they weren't very good."

"I'm told that's just the soprano."

Jonie smiled at that, and Birdie turned her walker around and moved toward the door. An ache in her lower back had spread down the backs of her thighs. She'd had enough of undercover work for one day.

~

In the hallway, Joseph waited until Birdie had opened her door. Ever the gentleman. "You would have made a good criminal," he said.

Birdie laughed. "Who says I wasn't?"

He shoved his hands in his pockets. "That was exciting."

"It was."

Joseph rocked on his heels, like he didn't want to go just yet. "Oh, I meant to tell you earlier, but I heard from Dorothea that there's been another report of that prowler around, and I guess someone at the cottages found a dead cat beside their trash."

Birdie felt the hair on her arms raise. "What happened to the cat?"

Joseph shrugged. "Not sure, but I think they've notified the police." His forehead wrinkled. "You look pale, Birdie. I'm sure it's nothing to worry about. Coyotes probably got the cat."

The news bothered her, especially when she thought about the young girl in the camper. She'd go tomorrow, make sure that Everly was aware of the prowler. "Thanks for the heads-up," she said, and pulled the sticky note from her pocket. "I'll give her a call today and let you know what I find out."

That tight smile again. "I'm sure she's okay, but, Birdie . . ." He folded his arms across his chest. "I think it's nice that you're worried. I'm sure she'll appreciate you checking up on her."

Birdie felt a pang thinking of Joseph without his Sofia to decorate his apartment or make plans. "Book club tomorrow?"

The serious crease between his eyes eased. "I have to be honest, I'm already almost done with *Mockingjay*. I couldn't wait."

"I knew you'd like it." She opened her door. "See you tomorrow." She moved inside, her walker turning every exit she made clunky and inelegant.

Birdie stood for a moment in the coolness of her apartment, a chill snaking up her spine. The air felt stirred, like someone had just left. She waited a moment, listening. Nothing but the click of the thermostat, followed by the blast of warm air through the vents. The rapid beat of her heart. She shook it off and moved across the room to check the lock on her patio door. When her fingers touched the metal knob, her apartment faded around her and she was back to the day she found Allison. For years afterward, Birdie checked her locks obsessively, installing an extra bolt on every door, putting a wooden block in the runner of sliding glass ones. Checking the locks before bed, checking again before she fell asleep, then once more when she woke up in the middle of the night. Making sure Felix was never alone, even when he was a teenager. He'd been annoyed at her for that, especially when it prevented him from having alone time with a girlfriend.

Her hand twisted the knob, and when she pulled the door open, she gasped. Her vigilance might have lessened, but she always locked her doors. She peered outside; her porch—winterized with covers over the two chairs, her orange-and-green outdoor rug rolled up and in storage—was empty. She closed the door, turned the lock. Her lip caught between her teeth. She typically used the main door, especially in winter, preferring the carpeted floors to the slippery and uneven rocky path leading from her patio to the sidewalk. Hadn't she last been out this way the morning of the ice storm? That had been weeks ago.

A pulsing in her neck tightened her windpipe, and Birdie had to sit down, breathing deep to push away lightheadedness. Nothing had happened, obviously, but the oversight bothered her. She slid out of her coat, rubbing her forehead. Allison had noticed the lock was broken a week before she'd died. Birdie had dragged her feet. Their landlord was the kind of man whose hand lingered uncomfortably on an arm, shoulder, the small of her back. His lips wet from licking. The air thick with expectation. She'd put off calling him, wanting to fix it herself, needing to find the time to ask the owner of the hardware store or find a how-to book. Would Allison have died if she'd fixed the lock?

She collapsed onto the sofa, exhausted by the day and a sudden swell of emotion. Regret over what she hadn't done, hadn't said, catching up to her, keeping pace even now. Birdie looked through the pictures scattered around her apartment, picked up one of Allison taken on Felix's third birthday. His chubby legs straddled the red plastic Big Wheel Birdie had given him, and his arms extended upward, gripping the handlebars like he'd waited his entire three years to ride a chopper. Allison sat on her knees beside him, hands out, ready to catch him should he fall off the low-slung seat. Her mouth spread wide, frozen between a smile and a laugh. She'd cut bangs into her hair that year and taken off length in the shag style that had been so popular then. Birdie smiled. With her impish nose and delicate jawline, Allison had made even that god-awful hairstyle look good.

"Oh, Al," she sighed. "You were supposed to be here too." They would have lasted; she believed it with all her heart. Sometimes she remembered Allison into their lives. Working beside her to build Allison's Maids; celebrating Felix's birthdays, his high school graduation, his wedding, the birth of the twins. Her arms ached with remembered longing, the emptiness of what they never said combined with an unanswered yearning to have held her, loved her, lived alongside her. She put the picture down.

Her thoughts immediately went to Faith. Thinking about someone else was an anchor to her present. Was the young woman missing, or was Birdie overreacting? There was only one way to find out. She pulled out her phone and carefully punched in the number from the sticky note. It rang once before an automated voice came on, informing her that it was not a working number. She tried again with the same result. "Okay," Birdie mumbled, and picked up her computer from the coffee table, setting it onto her lap. Into the search bar, she typed *Sofia Faith Perez*, along with the address from the sticky note. An ad populated first, asking for money to find out if Faith had a criminal past. Birdie scrolled past that, annoyed. Scammers roamed through the internet, lions on the hunt for aging wildebeest like her. One link looked promising: a Sofia Perez, thirty-one, same address but no phone number listed.

After a few more minutes of searching and nearly losing herself down a few rabbit holes, Birdie closed the computer, tapping her fingers across the cool metal. At least she had an address. Tomorrow she'd drive over to Faith's house and knock on the woman's door herself, ending her worry once and for all. She thought of Joseph helping her today, inviting her over for coffee, confiding in her. Maybe he'd like to go with her. It might be nice to have someone along for the ride.

Fifteen

We all have our stories.

Felicity works a street corner.

Jan cooks dinner.

Karen is only fourteen.

Tonia has it coming.

Judy is perfect in every way.

Barb walks her dog.

Susan begs.

Carol isn't supposed to be here.

Freida gets in the way.

Cora is too easy.

And I am the mistake.

We all have our stories.

Mine is that I didn't kill myself. Birdie is right. She's always been right. Except for the lock. That would never have made a difference.

Sixteen

Birdie tossed and turned, the excitement and activity from the day running laps up and down her legs in pricks of electricity that made it impossible to sleep. "Restless legs," the doctor called it. She checked the alarm clock—12:30 a.m.—and groaned, pushing the covers off and scooching herself to sitting with her back against the headboard. She turned on the small television that sat on her dresser, pushed Play on *Suits*, and tightened and released her leg muscles. But the restlessness continued, and she couldn't concentrate on the show. She sat on the edge of her bed and turned on the light, studying her bare feet on the carpet. Her toenails needed to be trimmed. She sighed, giving her pillow a look of longing. It would be no use trying to sleep until she worked out the ants in her pants. She slid into her slippers and robe, tied the robe closed, and made her way to the kitchen.

The faucet spat water against the stainless steel sink, and she filled a cup, drank a full glass. She was thirsty. And wide awake. Yet her mind felt gummed. Had she gotten her mail today? The basket where she stored it was empty; she'd forgotten to pick it up. A walk down the hallway to the mailboxes would be a nice excuse to stretch her legs. She went back to her room, put on a long sweater and shoes, and gave herself a quick glance in the mirror. Still looked like she was in her pajamas, but who could she possibly run into this time of night? This place was a ghost town after 7:30.

After opting for her cane, Birdie grabbed her keys and headed into the quiet and empty hallway. Yep, ghost town. She kept one hand on the wall; the walker helped her with balance, but Birdie thought a little extra exercise might tire her legs enough to kick the restlessness out. Eventually, she made it to the small cubicle that held the mailboxes and pulled out the usual—a statement from her bank, the newest health care options, and catalogs for Eunice James, former tenant of her apartment. Eunice had either stepped up in care, as often happened here, or moved on in the spiritual sense. Birdie was learning that one was as likely to happen as the other.

She shook her head. *C'mon now, Birdie. Don't let yourself slide back into that place.* She remembered Felix's words: *I think you're depressed.*

No kidding, had been her reply.

He'd found Sunny Pines, given her the brochures. On another trip, he'd brought the boys and set up an appointment so they could tour the place together. With the boys there, Birdie was forced to wear her game face. Secretly, she'd agreed with Felix. The house was too big for her, its crevices deep, the steps too many, the basement full of things she didn't want anymore.

But selling it had been the end of something, and it had left her diminished, her independence a quantifiable thing that could be contained in a brochure for senior living at Sunny Pines and catalogs for the (dearly?) departed Eunice James.

She slid the bank statement into her sweater pocket, tossed the rest of the mail into the recycling bin, and yawned. A wasted trip, but worth it if it let her sleep tonight. She started back toward her apartment, crossing the lobby. To her left were the main doors; to her right, the small living room they used for gatherings. It was dark and empty now. Except for a small light cutting across the furniture from the direction of the kitchenette. And a sound.

She froze.

What was that sound?

A moan.

Scratching.

Something heavy falling.

She stood in the middle of the open hallway, no wall for her hand, legs wobbly. Footsteps across the carpet. *Move, Birdie!* There stood a man, sweatshirt hoodie over his head, long hair poking out. Not a resident of Sunny Pines. A stink in the air, something burning that should not be. He moved slow like he walked through water, and his eyes, two black holes, chilled her all the way through.

He was coming at her now, and Birdie stumbled backward but didn't fall. Her scream stuck in her throat. A firm hand on her back gave her enough leverage to find her balance. Then Glen was in front of her, hands out like he could ward off the intruder with the power of his mind. "No, you, stay back!" he yelled. "Call 9-1-1, Birdie!"

The man seemed momentarily surprised, but it was obvious who held the power, and it was not Birdie or Glen.

Her lungs opened up and she cried out, "I don't have my phone." They looked at each other; then Birdie yelled, "Help! Help!"

Glen carried an air of authority. "You do not live here, sir. You need to leave. The police are on their way."

Birdie saw the fire alarm on the wall by the mail cubicle. Miles away, but she had to do something. The man hadn't moved, staring, head tilted like they were creatures from another planet who'd been dropped into his galaxy. High, she thought, so high he probably had no idea where he was. She turned and hurried toward the alarm, agonizingly slow without her walker, heart throbbing in her chest. In any other situation, this would have been comical.

Glen was talking: "You stay where you are, buddy. I mean it. I hate to ask, Birdie, but could you move any faster?"

Birdie groaned. Her fingers finally touched the alarm, and she pulled. Immediately, the lights strobed and the alarm screeched. She leaned against the wall, lungs tight, and turned to see the man back himself into the living room and slide through a window he must have broken to get inside.

Glen was by her side, supporting her with one arm and carefully leading her to one of the sofas. She sat down, despite the noise and the lights, and wrapped her arms across her stomach. People started filling the lobby, in various stages of undress—rumpled hair, disgruntled looks.

"Not again," a woman mumbled, her white nightgown flowing underneath a floral robe. They filed outside, and already Birdie heard sirens in the distance, relief softening the ache in her back.

"Guess we should join them," she said, and Glen offered his arm again, and together they walked over to one of the benches outside.

Joseph hurried through the doors, eyes wide, normally tidy hair sticking out on the sides. "Birdie!" He noticed Glen hovering beside her like a mother hen. "Glen! Are you okay? What's happening?"

"A man broke in, he—" Birdie yawned, the kind of tired she'd wished for earlier, but this one brought on by shock. "Glen here stood up to him like the cop he was." She touched Glen's arm. "Thank you."

Glen smiled, standing a little taller. "We are chivalrous men, are we not, Joseph?"

Joseph offered a tight smile. Birdie felt a tenderness growing for the awkward man.

"Do you know what he wanted?" Joseph said.

Glen shook his head. "The man was high as a kite, with eyes like black saucers. I don't think even he knew what he wanted."

"He was in the kitchen, and I—I think he was smoking something," Birdie said, her voice wobbly. "Where did you come from, Glen?"

Glen's face darkened. "I was with my brother."

"Oh," Birdie said.

Police cars pulled into the parking lot, along with a fire truck and ambulance, their lights and sirens competing with the fire alarms still going off inside the building. Birdie's head hurt, and she wrapped her arms around herself, preparing to tell the police what had happened. A bad taste expanded inside her mouth. Interacting with law enforcement did that to her, touched on the shame of being dismissed, the frustration of being ignored. Joseph and Glen had taken up a position on either side of her. Nothing like that would happen tonight, of course, but their presence was nice.

When it was her time to speak, she told them everything that had happened. The officer had sandy-blond hair pulled into a ponytail, her eyes slightly narrowed while Birdie described what the intruder had looked like, the way he had smelled, and anything else she could remember. Her name tag read HAYES, and she wrote everything down in a small notebook with a purple pen. "And did he say anything to you?"

Birdie shook her head. "No, nothing." Her stomach turned. She could tell the interview was coming to an end.

The officer closed her little notebook, pocketed it. "We'll be in touch if we have any more ques—"

"There's more," Birdie said quickly.

Officer Hayes raised an eyebrow, notebook open once again.

Birdie pulled at her fingers. "There's a woman who works here, Sofia Faith Perez, and she's missing."

The officer was writing, then lifted her pen from the page. "How long?"

"One month. They think she quit, but I'm sure something is wrong."

Lines hardened around the officer's mouth. She closed the notebook and slid it back into her pocket.

Birdie's stomach cramped. "And you've heard about the mutilated animals they keep finding here?" The officer had stopped listening; Birdie knew the look. Once, it had been because she was a stripper, now it was because of her age. She was losing her case, and she should stop. "Do you think any of this might be connected to the Geneva Smith case? Or the Vampire Killer?"

Joseph made a noise. Glen's smile looked frozen in place.

Officer Hayes cleared her throat and stood to her full height. Birdie hadn't realized how far she'd bent down to speak to her. It made her feel small, like a child. "The animals are likely being killed by coyotes—a fox, maybe. This intruder's been linked to a number of break-ins around this area. He's an addict, Ms. Allen, looking for drugs or money or both." An upturn on one side of her mouth. "And based on your own description, he's much too young to be the Vampire Killer."

The tips of Birdie's ears burned. She lowered her gaze.

"I'm sorry for your troubles tonight, ma'am, but that's all the questions I have. Why don't you go on home and get some sleep?" The officer attempted warmth in her voice, but Birdie heard the effort.

She knew it had been rash to bring it up, could feel how paranoid she must have sounded. Her fingers kneaded her sweater. Joseph and Glen had been quiet, but they hadn't left her side.

"Well, fellas," she said, pushing herself to standing, "I think I'll head on home." She didn't meet their gazes, did not want to face their pity.

They both stood. "That was very brave, Birdie," Joseph said.

"Indeed," Glen agreed.

"Brave or stupid?"

Joseph shrugged. "Sometimes it's the same thing."

Birdie tapped him on the arm and then made her way back to her apartment. Despite the dismissiveness of the officer, she felt herself stand a little taller. At least she'd done something for Faith, and her friends hadn't thought she was a complete looney.

Seventeen

Birdie woke up late the next day—not as late as she'd have liked, but the few hours of sleep she did get had been deep and dreamless. The bright sun outside her blinds was disorienting, and for a moment, she couldn't remember a thing. Then it flooded back, and her first thought was of Everly outside, with that man on the loose.

Birdie wasted no time getting dressed, then opened the door to find a paper bag on the floor. Inside was a bunch of bananas with a note:

Heard you stood up to a crazy person!

Jean

The bananas are from Costco. They're on sale right now.

She picked up the bag, warmth brushing her cheeks. Joseph was right: it felt nice to be thought about. She put the bananas into the basket clipped to her walker and headed out. After the late-night fiasco, the lobby was quiet, and she wondered how Nan was doing. When the fire alarms went off, the elevators stopped working. From her third-floor apartment, little Nan would have had to take the stairs to get outside, and with her walker and oxygen tank, that seemed an impossible feat.

It was another spring day, chilly in the shade but a promising warmth from the sun. Birdie took her time walking down the sidewalk, enjoying the brightness on her face, letting it push away the worry that had built up like plaque inside her heart. The world was a dangerous place, and sometimes the bad seemed insurmountable and she felt the impossibility of it all at once.

She stood in front of the girl's camper. "Hi, Everly! It's me, Birdie. I stopped by a few weeks ago." The dogs started up their barking, sounding much bigger than she knew them to be. "I brought some bananas." A slight movement in the curtain, and Birdie pictured the young woman sneaking a peek. "They're from Costco," Birdie offered. "Jean says they're really good."

The door opened, and immediately two little wet noses smooshed up against the screen door. Everly stood back like she had before. "Who's Jean?"

"Oh." Birdie's neck protested the angle it took to look up. "She's Louise's friend. They both have these little puppies, if you can believe it, at their age. A bish–something or other."

The girl moved closer to the screen. "The two little white dogs? They're adorable."

"I guess, like cotton balls with teeth—if you think that's adorable."

Everly laughed, so softly it might have been a sigh. "I do."

Birdie looked down, rubbed the back of her neck to remove the crick.

Everly softly whistled, and the dogs retreated from the door. She opened the screen and climbed down, standing opposite Birdie. She was tall, with long, thin arms and legs and fingers to match. Her platinum-blond hair was cut short to her chin, pale white skin the translucent kind that almost looked blue. Birdie handed her the bananas and Everly hesitated, then cradled them to her stomach.

"They're still green, so you might want to give them a day or two."

"Thanks. It's Birdie, right?"

Birdie nodded.

"That's really nice of you." Everly's teeth pulled at her bottom lip and she shuffled her feet, looking quietly miserable. "I heard all the sirens last night." Her voice was soft, like she didn't want to disturb the air around them with her breath. "Is everyone okay?"

"That's why I stopped by, actually—well, one of the reasons."

"Oh?"

Birdie didn't want to scare the girl right away. She'd only just gotten her to talk. "Have you seen Faith? You know the woman who gave you the empanadillas? She cleans our apartments."

Everly's eyebrows crinkled over ice-blue eyes. "No, not since she stopped by the one time. What happened?"

Birdie shrugged. "Nothing that I know of, but she just stopped showing up for work." She thought of what Louise had said about Faith and the car. "On the morning of the ice storm, did you see her talking to someone in a car?"

Everly shook her head and glanced at her camper like she'd rather be inside than out here in the sunshine.

Sadness for the girl tugged at Birdie. "And she hasn't stopped by since then?"

"No, I'm sorry. She's really nice, though. Do you think she's okay?"

"I don't know." A breeze lifted the ends of Birdie's hair, cooling her sun-warmed skin, and she shivered. Beyond Everly's camper, the road was bordered by an open field on either side. A broken-down RV and curtained van turned the vacant lot ominous. An uneasiness spread into her fingertips. Did the man from last night live in one of those? "Do you know your neighbors?"

"Not really." She'd moved closer to the stairs, one hand touching the side of her camper.

"Something happened last night," Birdie said quickly, afraid she was losing the girl to the allure of her camper. "A man broke into our apartment building, but he ran off before the police got here."

Everly had wrapped her arms across her chest, but she didn't seem worried—or not enough to satisfy Birdie.

"According to the police, he's broken into a few houses around the area. They think he's looking for money, that he's an addict or something. Anyway, do you lock your door? You should. Maybe even put something in front of it like a chair or"—she looked at the face smushed into the screen door—"a dog. You're pretty vulnerable out here." The girl's lack of response baffled her. "And there seems to be something or somebody killing small animals."

That did it. Everly's hand went to her mouth, and her eyes flew to the camper with her little dogs inside. "Oh no! That's terrible. I have seen coyotes."

Birdie breathed out, frustrated that the girl was more concerned for animals than for herself. She wanted to worry the girl enough that she went back to whatever home she'd left in favor of this. "If you don't mind my asking, what are you doing out here, anyway? Don't you have a better living situation?"

Everly, still cradling the bananas like a baby, looked at Birdie. "No." Her eyes were bright with whatever she kept inside. "I have to go. Bye, Birdie." The deep wrinkle between her eyes eased with a tiny smile. "I played in the pit when my high school put on *Bye Bye Birdie*."

The girl's words were an offering. "What do you play?"

"The cello."

"Well, now, that's something."

Silence grew, and Birdie watched as Everly inched closer to the camper, first her hand on the railing, then one foot on the bottom stair. An octopus sliding away. It widened the pit in Birdie's stomach. "I worry about you out here."

"Why?"

Birdie shrugged. "It's just what I do." She noticed tiny beads of sweat across Everly's hairline. "Are you okay?"

Everly's expression didn't change, but for the first time, her eyes met Birdie's straight on. "Not really, but that's just how I am."

When Birdie was younger, she'd been more persuasive. Maybe it was the confidence that comes naturally with youth and the feeling that she still had a purpose. Standing here in front of Everly, who seemed both frail and stubborn, Birdie felt ineffective and small, the differences in their life experiences somehow taking Birdie out of step with her generation. Birdie pushed against her walker and straightened up as much as she could. *You know you aren't responsible for all the young women out there, right, Mom?* She shook off Felix's voice. "Sometimes life's a bitch, isn't it, Everly?"

A smile etched itself into Everly's lips, and she brought her foot off the stair and set it back on the ground. "A real bitch."

"Okay, then." She looked down the street, heard the angry bark of a dog coming from the direction of one of the campers. Noticed its rusted metal, a fabric-covered chair on the sidewalk beside it. And thought of the man's eyes, black and vacant, too high to care about who he might have hurt. Turned back to Everly—pale, thin, young, scared of a little old lady—and couldn't stand the thought of her facing that man on her own. Birdie's concern filled her chest like a helium balloon. "Would you like to come over for coffee?"

Everly sucked in her lip, hugging the bananas so tight Birdie knew they'd bruise before they went ripe. "Um—"

"Great, how about tomorrow morning?" She shifted her weight. What would it take to make this girl understand the kind of danger she was in? "Eight o'clock?" Birdie flexed her fingers, testing the strength of her own stubbornness. She had a sixth sense for those in need, and this girl radiated it. "I've got chocolate scones"—she didn't, but she'd get some from the grocery store—"and coffee or tea. You can tell me all about playing the cello."

Everly had climbed the stairs and was backing into her camper, the dogs tumbling over themselves to welcome her back. "Thanks for the bananas," she said.

"Sure, sure. So I'll see you tomorrow." Birdie smiled, the wide kind that piled smile lines up her cheeks and made her look more grandmotherly. She knew this because Tyler had told her when he was eight. "Bye, Everly!" She turned her walker around and started back. She'd given it her all. If the girl didn't show up tomorrow, she'd just bring the coffee to her.

And from the camper: "Bye-bye, Birdie."

Birdie smiled. Get the little mole out of her hole—check! Next she'd drive over to check on Faith.

~

When she returned, the living room sofas were full of people, including Joseph and Glen. The smell of freshly brewed coffee wafted from the kitchenette, where plates of chocolate chip cookies and thick brownies had been laid out on the counter. *Book club.* Birdie ducked her head and tried to sidle past. In all the excitement, she'd forgotten, and it was the last thing she felt like doing now, especially with that whole crew.

"Birdie!" Glen called.

"Hi, Birdie!" Nan waved at her.

Birdie slumped over her walker. *Rats.*

Glen moved farther into the lobby. "Don't worry, we've got a seat for you! Come on in."

No way out now. She made her way into the living room and took the seat Glen pointed to. He pulled over a chair from the desk in the corner for himself, then handed her a napkin with a brownie on top. "I made those," he said with a wink. "Sea salt caramel."

"Oh, thanks." With no coffee table within arm's distance, she set the napkin on her lap, wishing he'd asked if she'd wanted one first.

In the middle of one sofa, Joseph was bookended by Jean and Louise. Nan puffed away on her oxygen in a chair opposite Birdie; Dorothea sat on the other couch.

Her face stiffened, and she felt like Everly when Birdie had invited her to coffee: surprised and a bit annoyed at having to be there. "So you all read *The Hunger Games* too?"

"Of course not," Dorothea said, in that plucked way of hers that pressed Birdie's teeth together. "We want to hear about what happened last night."

Birdie straightened her sweater, a light perspiration in her armpits. She didn't care for being the center of attention. "I'm sure you've heard it all from Glen."

"We've heard from Glen," Nan said. "But we want to hear what it was like for you too."

"It must have been very frightening," Louise said, giving Birdie an encouraging nod.

Birdie relaxed. It was the most exciting thing to happen since the ice storm. "I couldn't sleep, so I went to get my mail, and when I turned around there he was." A wave of goose bumps down her arms; he'd appeared so quickly she'd frozen. "I was lucky that Glen happened to be there too."

Glen chortled, eyes bright above a smile. "My pleasure, my pleasure."

Ever the interrogator, Dorothea trained her gaze on Glen. "Where were you coming from so late at night?"

Birdie wrinkled her nose. "Seems that's Glen's business, don't you think?"

Dorothea sniffed. "Maybe he saw something that's important. I wasn't being nosy."

Birdie doubted that.

"My brother dropped me off."

"Your brother lives close by?" Jean asked.

"Yes, but he travels a lot."

"I have one sister in Utah and another in Oregon," Jean shared.

"My sister lives in Florida, but I'd love it if she lived here," Louise added, then laughed. "Or maybe I should move to Florida."

"Florida wouldn't be far enough," Glen said rather forcefully. "Richard lives in my house and thinks he's better than me because he's younger." Glen's voice had lost its typical pomposity, making him sound elderly. "I don't care for his company."

"I thought he sold your house." It was out before Birdie could stop herself.

128

Glen's eyebrows lowered, a look of genuine confusion in his eyes. "Oh, yes, he did. I just, well—"

"Forgot?" Jean said. "We all do. Don't think anything of it."

The group fell silent.

"Is your brother handsome?" Nan piped up.

Birdie smiled; so did Louise, followed by Jean, and then Joseph did his subtle lip-quirk thing. It lightened the mood.

"Nan," Dorothea said with obvious disapproval.

"Actually, Nan," Birdie said, "he's a real jerk."

Glen settled his hands on the arms of his chair and straightened his shoulders, which had become uncharacteristically rounded. He smiled at Birdie. "I concur."

"And I'm glad you were there last night," she added.

"If I may." He tapped his fingers on the wooden arms of his chair and his chest rose with an inhaled breath.

Birdie felt a soliloquy coming on.

"'The strong man is the one who is able to intercept at will the communication between the senses and the mind.'"

Bingo. She caught Joseph's nostrils flaring, and her stomach clenched around a giggle. She took a bite of the brownie to push it down, and her eyes went wide. It was delicious. At least the man could bake.

"Napoleon Bonaparte." He drew out the *ar-te*, looking quite pleased with himself, and glanced around the room as though waiting for a response.

Birdie shoved another bite of brownie into her mouth.

Dorothea's forehead wrinkled. "Napoleon?"

Glen tapped the side of his head. "He was a man of high intelligence and a keen memory. I, of course, am no Napoleon, but I do believe that had I not been there to stop the man, Birdie might have been hurt, or worse."

Nan raised her hand, and when nobody said anything, she raised it higher.

"Nan?" Birdie said, amused.

"What does that have to do with anything?"

Glen's smile faltered and his eyes narrowed. Nan stared back, nonplussed. "Well," he said, speaking slower as though to a child, "the man who broke in here was *out* of his mind, and one had to have the *presence* of mind to talk him down—"

"I don't think that's what that quote means," Nan said. She barely took up the chair, her shoulders small, hunched, the tips of her shoes on the ground.

"Me either," Jean agreed.

Glen fell silent, and Birdie felt a little sorry for him. "This brownie is delicious!" she said.

"Divine," Dorothea agreed. "You said you made these, Glen?"

The upbeat affirmations seemed to shake him out of his glumness, and he briefly bowed his head. "I did."

Nan raised her hand.

"Yes, Nan?" Birdie said, hoping Nan had let the Napoleon thing go.

"Is it true that his eyes glowed red?"

"Who?"

"The intruder."

"What? No, of course not."

Nan raised her hand again.

"Yes?" Birdie said.

"Was his name Bill Banichek?"

Everyone looked at Nan.

"I have no idea what his name was," Birdie said, perplexed by Nan's line of questioning. "Do you think you know him?"

Nan rehooked the tubing that had loosened over one ear, shrugged. "Well, I know Bill Banichek."

The corners of Joseph's lips moved up.

Dorothea was shaking her head. "It's the homeless and the addicts in the RVs that are the problem. We need to get the police to clear them out."

Thinking of Everly, Birdie couldn't help herself. "Not so homeless if they have a home. And just because it's on wheels doesn't make them nefarious people." Even though she'd wondered the same thing, damned if she was going to side with Dorothea.

"Or addicts," Louise added.

"My great-nephew and his wife sold everything they owned and live in a tiny home," Jean said. "It's on wheels too."

Dorothea looked surprised to be contradicted by more than just Birdie. She sniffed.

With all of them gathered, Birdie realized it was a good time to bring up Faith again. The more people who were concerned about her absence, the more chance she had to actually make something happen. "I'm still very concerned about Faith."

All eyes on her.

"The cleaning woman?" Dorothea sniffed. "She quit. Just up and stopped coming to work. That's the problem with this generation: no work ethic."

"I don't think that's true," Birdie said.

Dorothea made a face. "So you think management is lying to us?"

Birdie sat up straighter. "No, I think that Faith is a woman who lives alone with no relatives close by, supports her mother in Puerto Rico, works her fingers to the bone trying to start a new business, and has two day jobs." She glared at Dorothea. "Missing a work ethic is not her problem. But missing a support system of people who care is."

"Oh," Louise said.

Nan grunted. "You're right to be worried."

With their interest spiked, Birdie went on. "And someone is hurting animals around here too. We've all heard about it or seen it for ourselves," Birdie said. "I don't know if it's the intruder or someone else entirely, but we don't need management to tell us what we already know."

"I heard a dead cat was found out back by the garages," Louise said.

Birdie swallowed. "Another one?" That made it three so far. A vibration ran just under her skin.

Everyone seemed to take it in. Then Louise leaned forward, meeting Birdie's eyes with her pretty gray ones. "So what should we do?"

Birdie was taken aback, even if it was exactly what she was hoping for. "Keep a lookout for one. And record anything suspicious."

"Glen, you were a cop, right?" Dorothea said. "Can't you talk to the police for us?"

Birdie had not expected Dorothea to be on board.

Glen straightened, hand on his sternum like he was sitting at attention. "I was," he said solemnly. "Good idea. Perhaps coming from one police officer to another, they'll be more apt to listen."

Nan raised her hand, and from where she was sitting, Dorothea swatted it down. "Oh, for heaven's sake, we're not in school, Nan."

Nan bit into a cookie, chewed, and swallowed while everyone waited. "Did you ever work on any cases I might know about, Glen? Like disappearances or murders or stolen money?"

Glen looked pleased to be asked, and Birdie didn't begrudge him. Who they'd been before Sunny Pines was a piece of all of them, and it occurred to her that she knew very little about her neighbors.

"A few cases here and there," Glen said. "Nothing too sensational, except for maybe one or two."

Nan's face lit up. "Tell us!"

"Oh, well, the biggest one was probably the v—"

"I know you," Jean said, interrupting Glen.

Birdie noticed Jean staring intently at Joseph. Uncomfortably so, she could tell by the way Joseph had retreated as far back into the seat cushion as he could, arms tight to his side, hands palm-side-down on his thighs.

"I live here," Joseph said.

"I don't mean that. I mean, I know you from somewhere," Jean insisted.

Joseph breathed in through his mouth.

Jean snapped her fingers. "Boxing! My husband lived and breathed it. You look different—older, smaller, but remarkably the same too. You were . . ." She scrunched her eyes like she was trying to see into the past; then she smiled. "Joe 'the Killer' Callaghan! Featherweight, right?"

Murmurs spread among the group. Joseph nodded. "That was a long time ago."

It made perfect sense to Birdie. His lean physique, the way he held himself, the lone punching bag in his apartment.

Jean's smile was watery, like the memory had set her firmly in the past, sitting on the couch with her husband in front of the television. "You lost quite a few fights, but I recall Frank saying it was a skill and that you were one of the best."

"Not such a killer, then," Nan said around a mouthful of brownie.

Birdie chewed on the side of her cheek, wishing she could save Joseph from the women dissecting his career.

"Oh, what did Frank call you?"

Joseph cleared his throat. "A journeyman—"

She snapped her fingers. "That's it! He said you made the other boxers look good on purpose, and losing like that took someone who truly understood the sport." She pulled a receipt and a pen from the bag at her feet. "Would you sign this for me? Frank would have been so tickled." She tripped over the last word, her eyes bright. Louise patted Jean's shoulder.

Joseph blinked, and from the way his face softened, Birdie knew he was touched. He took the pen and signed the back of her Costco receipt.

"Thank you," Jean said, holding the signed paper to her chest. "It was a big to-do when you left. My husband said you were throwing it all away to be a family man." She elbowed him. "How'd that work out for you?"

Joseph's hands tapped his thighs, and Birdie knew he'd rather be anywhere but here. "Fine, just fine."

"My grandson's a boxer too," Nan said.

"Oh really?" Louise said.

"So far he's punched three kids at school."

"Oh no," Louise amended.

"I was an officer, Joseph here a renowned boxer . . . Who else do we have among our exclusive gang?" Glen said.

The group chattered, sharing past lives. There was Louise, who'd been in HR and had seventeen grandchildren; Jean, a former catalog model (Birdie had been half-right about the pair); Nan had written a syndicated advice column; and Dorothea had been a principal, which Birdie thought fit quite well.

"And what about you, our little Bird?" Sometimes, Birdie wished Glen would just talk like a normal person.

"I ran my own cleaning company," she said.

"Residential or commercial?" Nan said in between puffs.

"Both, but mostly residential." Birdie didn't like talking about herself, although she was proud of her company. "Allison's Maids."

Louise's face lit up. "Your employees cleaned my office for years! The best company out there."

Birdie dipped her head, pleased. "Thank you." She felt oddly warmed by the conversation, lulled by the ease with which everyone shared a piece of themselves.

"Is everyone from this neighborhood?" Louise said.

Sunny Pines was located in a suburb of Denver and was one of the largest and most well-regarded senior-living communities on this side of the city.

Most of them nodded. Jean and Nan realized they had grandkids who went to the same high school. Dorothea had lived most of her life in the foothills, Louise and Joseph on the other side of town; Birdie's house had been ten minutes from Sunny Pines, and Glen had lived on the north side of town. "Although my father owned many buildings around Denver when I was younger, so we lived there for many years too."

"He was a landlord?" Nan said.

Glen patted his legs and chortled. "A proprietor, dear Nan, who provided occupancy for many dwellers along Colfax."

"So, a landlord," Nan said.

Birdie's ears perked up. What would be the chances? "Did he own the Paragon on West Colfax?"

"Indeed he did."

The thing about Denver was that paths tended to cross in unexpected ways to those who'd lived there for most of their lives. "No kidding," Birdie said. She thought about the landlord, the one she had avoided calling about the lock because of his wandering hands and licked lips. She shuddered. Had that been Glen's father? She didn't like the connection one bit, yet her own parents had rejected their only daughter when they could have chosen to love her as she was. Apples could fall very far from the tree. "Did you ever live at the Paragon, Glen?"

"No, only for a visit or two—but my brother did." Glen's distaste came through in his clipped speech. "And he sold it as soon as my father died. Did I see any of that damn money?" Glen held up his hands. "Who's to say?" He breathed faster, eyes open wide, like he was ready for someone to disagree.

They were all quiet for a minute, letting Glen's outburst subside. The dislike for his brother was a heavy burden; Birdie could feel the way it played in the background of Glen's thoughts. Still, the coincidence crept around her, a nagging voice in her ear to ask him more questions, get more details. Rusted wheels starting to turn. Could Glen or his brother know something important?

"That's where Geneva Smith was found," Nan said, interrupting her thoughts.

Jean leaned forward. "Who?"

"Young gal found murdered a month or so ago and left in the dumpster."

Louise wrapped her arms across her body. "That's terrible."

Nan peered up at Glen. "Do you know anything about that?"

Birdie noticed Glen's face had mottled, and he rubbed his hands repeatedly up and down his thighs. The building had been a magnet for horrible deaths. It would be hard to be connected to a place like that.

"Ask Richard what he knows."

Birdie perked up, and she searched her memory. Could she have spoken to Richard back then?

"He sold that place without even speaking to me about it," he said, rubbing repetitively at his beard.

Birdie held her tongue. There was no sense in upsetting Glen more with questions he couldn't answer. Especially since his family didn't even own the building anymore.

After a beat of silence, Dorothea cleared her throat. "So, about that intruder . . . ," she said, ending the awkwardness, her eyes on Birdie. "How did you fight him off last night?" A suspicious lilt to her voice, like Birdie might have made the whole thing up.

"With my cane," Birdie said.

"There was no fighting, dear Dorothea." Glen laughed, his sudden gloom clearing as quickly as it had gathered. "Birdie was a field mouse frozen to the spot with that man advancing on her like a hawk. Who knows what would have happened had I not stumbled upon them?"

Dorothea pressed a hand to her chest, her eyes wide, enthralled. "Terrifying." She turned to look at the window the intruder had broken, now boarded up with plywood.

Birdie shivered. "Hopefully, they'll catch him soon," she said.

"Do you think he might be the one doing those horrible things to the animals too?" Louise asked.

Birdie shook her head. "I don't know, but we all need to be vigilant."

Glen lifted his lemonade. "Hear! Hear!"

Dorothea gave Birdie a pointed look. "Or we should leave it to Glen and the other professionals." She stood, looking toward the front door. "There's my daughter. Let us know what the *police* say, Glen."

Glen nodded. "Will do."

Everyone else dispersed soon after, leaving Birdie, Glen, and Joseph. "I guess that was book club for this month," Joseph said. "Seems like you convinced a lot of folks to be concerned about Faith. That's good, huh?"

Birdie nodded, touched and a little overwhelmed by how quickly they all seemed to support her. Except Dorothea, of course.

Joseph pulled *The Hunger Games* from the side table. "I finished the series. Any other suggestions, Birdie?"

"Do you like dystopian?"

"If that's what this is, then yes, I do."

"Try *The 5th Wave*. Another of my favorites. I like anything that takes me completely out of reality." She turned to Glen, thinking of his sad and angry tone when he spoke about his brother. He seemed as lost as she felt at times, and that hit a chord in her. "Would you like to join Joseph and me on a little drive?" Her worry for Faith was eating at her, and she wanted more than anything to know that she was okay.

Glen's eyebrows shot skyward. "I would. May I chauffeur our merry gang?"

Birdie tugged on her lower lip. "Sure, as long as you don't call us a 'merry gang' again."

Glen laughed. "Of course, of course. I get carried away sometimes, you know."

"I do."

Joseph stood with his arms folded, his face tightened against what Birdie guessed was a smile. Glen could be absurd, but he was also quite charming, she'd decided.

"So, where will this adventure take us?" Glen asked.

"To check on Faith."

"Faith . . . Hmm, the cleaning woman you mentioned? May I inquire as to why you are so worried about her?"

Birdie sighed. Had she not already explained it herself? But with Glen, she was learning that perhaps he wasn't always the best listener and was caught up in his thoughts much of the time. "Ever heard of a woman's intuition?"

Glen seemed to consider her words. "Ah, yes, women and their intuition." He smiled, nodding. "Well, then, let's go."

Eighteen

Glen was a terrible driver. Birdie should have asked to check the expiration date on his license. When they pulled into Faith's apartment complex, his tire rolled over the curb, bouncing Birdie so hard her shoulder hit the door. She rubbed at the ache and stared up at the buildings, looking for number three.

"There." She pointed. "That's hers."

Glen swung his boat of a sedan toward a row in front of the building, straddling two parking spots. "Don't mind if you do," she said under her breath.

Glen turned in his seat. "Pardon me?"

Joseph scooted forward. "You're taking up two spots."

Glen turned off the engine, ran a loving hand over the expansive dash. "That's to keep this old girl in pristine condition. Most people are terrible drivers; the rest of them can't park."

Birdie opened her door and was quickly met by Joseph, who had taken her walker from the back and was unfolding it for her. "Thank you, Killer." She smiled. Joseph grimaced back.

"Still can't believe she recognized me. That was over fifty years ago," he mumbled.

Birdie put her hands on the walker and pushed to standing. "Must mean you're a memorable guy."

Glen joined them. "I wish I could say I remember your boxing career, Joseph, but I'm afraid that my years as a detective narrowed my pursuits." Glen wore a tweed blazer with a black wool scarf, and he slid his hands into the front pockets.

"You didn't miss anything, Glen," Joseph said. "A few years in the ring after the navy. Had one or two notable fights and then Sofia had our first child and I took over the family business from my father." Birdie sensed there was more to the story, but she didn't pester him.

"What kind of business?" she asked.

"A furniture store."

Birdie laughed.

"What's so funny?"

"The irony."

Joseph raised an eyebrow. Glen looked on, smiling.

"The only furniture you have is a punching bag."

Glen laughed and clapped Joseph on the back. "Are we men not allowed our bachelor pads, dear Bird?"

Birdie shook her head. "Bachelor pads." She started moving toward the apartments and was soon flanked by the men.

"Did you say Faith lived on the first floor?" Glen asked.

Birdie looked up at the building, nodding. On the one hand, she hated the thought of Faith living in a ground-floor apartment; on the other, she was relieved she didn't have to climb any stairs, because, from the looks of the apartment building, there was no elevator. "Apartment 154."

They followed the signs and eventually, with Birdie slowing the two more able-bodied men, found Faith's door tucked behind an outdoor staircase.

Glen knocked.

They waited.

Glen knocked again.

Nobody answered.

Birdie pulled at her fingers. She reached for the door handle, turned. It didn't budge. She'd noticed that every apartment had a back patio with a sliding glass door. "Let's check the slider."

"Good idea, Birdie," Glen said. "Did you know that most people forget to lock their sliders? I always tell my daughter to check hers twice." He shook his head. "It's a shame how many robberies and worse would have been prevented by the simple twist of a lock."

Her heart absorbed the sentiment like an electric shock, and Birdie squeezed the handles of her walker until it evaporated. "That's not really helping, Glen," she said a bit too sharply.

"Oh, my apologies." He made a zipping gesture at his lips, then clasped his hands behind his back.

They made their way to the side of the apartment that faced the parking lot. Birdie was grateful that there weren't many people around because otherwise their trio might have appeared to be casing the place. Joseph reached for the handle, and Birdie held her breath. She wanted to be wrong, would give anything to be an irrational worrier, but when the door slid open, her heart dropped to her knees.

"Faith!" she called. A cloud passed over the sun, and its shadows prickled her skin with goose bumps. "It's me, Birdie." She wanted to feel foolish, to see Faith's dark eyebrows meet in confusion and then maybe in anger at Birdie's disregard for her privacy. But the past lapped at her heels: the unlocked door, an emptiness inside the apartment hinting at more, the air thick and undisturbed. Her head filled with the rising peal of an alarm bell.

Cream-colored curtains flapped out the open slider. "Faith?"

The silence was concerning, but it was the smell that sucked the blood from Birdie's veins. Staleness laced with a sour decay and something else. Something . . . animal. Joseph went in first, followed by Birdie and Glen in the rear. Her eyes were still adjusting to the darkness inside when Glen flipped a switch and a fluorescent bulb in the kitchen flared to life. Birdie tensed, ready to be faced with the bad.

She blinked. Nothing looked to be out of the ordinary. A clean kitchen, coffee mug and cereal bowl washed and set to dry on a cloth by the sink. Glass containers of flour and sugar on one side of the stovetop, stack of cookbooks on the other. Tidy counters, wiped down and gleaming. A sense that she'd recently stepped out. Birdie opened, then closed her mouth. Her racing heartbeat told a different story. Something was off, something was wrong. It lingered in the air, pungent in its truth. The same sensation she'd had when she'd found Allison flooded her chest, and Birdie moved deeper into the apartment, down a hallway with a closed door at the end.

"Faith," she called again, her voice a whisper. An acrid stink tickled her nostril hairs.

"Um, Birdie," Joseph whispered, not far behind her. "I think she's okay. I mean, I don't think we should be here."

"Shhh," she said. "Do you hear that?" A mewling whine from behind the door.

"I didn't wear my hearing aids," Glen said a little too loudly.

The carpet was a thick pile that made pushing her walker harder than normal. She tried to move as fast as she could, which felt like a snail. But then she was there, in front of the door, hand on the knob, pulse racing. Flashes of Allison's sightless stare, the bluish pallor of her skin, her life in puddles in the tub. A heavy press against Birdie's chest compressed the air in her lungs, and she couldn't speak. She wished for younger limbs, a more able body, to be someone who could help if her friend needed it. The door swung open, and Birdie screamed.

Nineteen

ALLISON

A stranger in my room wakes me with a cloth to my face, pressing harder and harder. I fight. My hands flail, my fingernails gain purchase on strong arms. But I inhale deep, ragged breaths, and my eyes grow heavy, my throat sticks. When I wake up, there is less of me and they win.

The way Birdie finds me in the bathtub plays over and over in her mind. The truth of my murder is an open wound that only lightly heals. She thinks of me now while she stands in a different woman's apartment, her fear for Faith ripping the scar at its seams and floating all her memories to the surface. She inhales buttery frosting, sees blue and yellow birds against a white backdrop. Her stomach heaves at the cloying sweetness exploding into the air when her birthday cake hits the wall. I am there with her then as I am now. Young Birdie swims beneath the surface, her cries ringing in both of our ears.

My sightless eyes are Faith's, and there, standing in the doorway to Faith's bedroom, the distance between Birdie and my essence narrows. The beat of her heart pulses in my palms. She feels me there. My breath on her neck, my fingers brushing her hair.

The beginning of death is filled with a rage that bloats and expands before it empties into an awareness of everything. I see the others that will join me, and I mourn for them. We are linked then and now. This hallway. Faith's bedroom. And the cat that is half-starved and finally free.

Twenty

A furball hurtled from the bedroom, darting between Birdie's legs, past Joseph and Glen, and into the small living room, where it crawled its way up a rope pole and to a small bed on top. From there, it meowed again, and as they watched, it crawled back down and slunk over to a pair of ceramic food and water bowls. With another look at them, it started crunching dry food, reluctantly, like it would rather be hiding but had no choice in the matter.

"Poor thing is starving," Joseph said.

Birdie walked into Faith's bedroom, neat and orderly like the rest of the small apartment. Except for the smell, which she recognized from houses that she'd cleaned. Cat pee. A box in the bathroom was full of clumps, more clumps than litter. Some of it scattered on the floor around it. And that was all she needed to know. Faith would never let the litter get this bad.

Birdie sat on the edge of the bed, her lips numb. Something had happened. This proved it. But there wasn't enough here for her to convince anyone of that. She crossed her arms, felt the familiar weight of helping someone in the curve of her back.

Joseph sat beside her, worry lines creased across his forehead. "Are you okay?"

"Not really."

"I don't think she'd leave her cat."

Birdie met Joseph's gaze, hope scratching at her heart. "I don't either."

Glen had disappeared down the hall, and she heard him talking to himself or the cat.

Joseph sighed. "Well, what should we do?"

We. She took a moment to absorb the sentiment. *We.* Not Birdie alone. We. It was a new feeling, and new feelings at her age were a rare thing to experience.

Birdie inhaled, letting her breath feather its way through her body. She could be quick to jump to conclusions, especially when she was concerned for someone's safety. She knew this about herself; it was what had led to her arrest all those years ago. Her rational mind engaged with alternate explanations. "She could have gone out of town—" she started.

Joseph snapped his fingers. "And the cat sitter never showed." His suggestion wasn't too off base. It was possible.

"Or she has a roommate who left the cat trapped in the room by accident?" Birdie added.

Joseph pushed up, hurried to the hallway. "There is another bedroom, but it's got a bare mattress on the floor and emptied drawers. Looks like someone moved out."

"Okay." Birdie had to work hard to keep her thoughts from landing on the worst possible outcome. "So she went out of town and the cat sitter didn't show—"

"Or she's met with an unfortunate accident," Glen said, wandering back into the room, hands clasped behind his back. "Or crossed paths with a dangerous individual."

Birdie's body jerked—her worst fears said out loud.

Joseph cleared his throat. "Glen, why would you say that?"

Glen looked surprised; then his cheeks reddened. "Oh, I'm sorry. Old habits, I suppose."

"No, it's okay," Birdie said. "Something bad might have happened to her or nothing at all, but that's not the point."

"What's the point, then?" Glen said.

"The girl has no time to build a community of people or friends who might notice if she's gone missing. The point is that I . . ." She looked at Joseph, stroking Faith's cat in his arms, and Glen, both of them standing in the empty apartment of a woman that Birdie had convinced them may need their help. "That *we* do care."

Glen smiled. "Hear, hear."

It calmed her, and she took a moment to think, letting the sharpness of her worry dull. "Okay, I was thinking we should call the police, but maybe we should leave a note here for when she comes back, and if she doesn't call me in the next few days, then I call the police. Maybe they would consider that better evidence?"

Glen and Joseph were both nodding. "Agree, Bird," Glen said.

"And for now, I think we should take the cat."

Joseph raised an eyebrow.

"Let's say she left like everyone says," Birdie said in defense of her plan. "Do you really think she'd abandon her cat to starve to death? At the very least, her cat sitter failed—like you said, Joseph—and Faith doesn't know it. But now we do, and we have to do something about it."

"So you're going to cat-sit?"

Birdie smiled, deciding to test the waters of this new friendship. "No, I hate cats." She shuddered. "And I might be allergic. But you— well, Joseph, your apartment is frankly depressing. You could use a friend, I think."

He gave her a look. "I might be allergic too."

She patted his leg. "Then let's hope Faith returns before the allergy pills wear off."

～

Joseph packed up the cat box and litter, Glen took the food and water bowls, and Birdie wrote a note. *Dear Faith, We stopped by to check on you. Your back door was unlocked, and we found your cat stuck in your bedroom without food. Joseph will watch the cat until you return. I hope you are okay. Birdie*

She balanced the note against a bowl on the kitchen counter, turned to leave, then grabbed the pen and added her phone number, along with, *I'm worried about you. Please call as soon as you can.*

Outside, the clouds had burned off, and she had to shield her eyes against the sun's glare. The cat yowled in Joseph's arms, but it didn't fight him, sensing, Birdie imagined after being trapped for days without food, that they were helping it. Inside the car, the cat's cries scraped Birdie's nerves. Glen sighed in an annoyed kind of way. He kept eyeing the cat. "I hope she doesn't have an accident in here."

"It's a he," Joseph said. "His collar says *Tom.*"

"Tom the cat," Birdie murmured. Time folded itself around her. She saw the kitchen they'd shared: round table, Formica countertops, baby Felix in a metal high chair kicking his chubby legs, and Allison spooning pureed squash into his slobbery mouth. Birdie laughing. *I always thought you'd named him after Felix the Cat.*

Allison had rolled her eyes. *Why would I name my son after a cartoon cat?*

Birdie swatted her shoulder with a kitchen towel. *I love that show! Enough to name a baby after it?*

Well, no, I suppose not. But what do I know? I never planned to have children anyway.

She observed the decades-old memory through the end of a narrow tunnel, cobwebs of time dulling the crisp edges of her kitchen. Allison had paused, spoon in the air, to look at Birdie. Even now, Birdie felt the magnetic pull between them. Her fear back then a ruthless guard, shielding the intensity of her feelings. Felix shook his fists and smacked his lips, excited for his next spoonful. *Guess your plan failed, Bird.*

Allison's frankness kept Birdie's gaze locked on hers, until Felix grabbed for the spoon, shooting an orange blob onto Allison's cheek. The moment was broken, what they hadn't said lingering in faint hopeful sparks between them.

Birdie sniffed, a hand pressed against her mouth. She wondered if the ache of losing Allison had persisted over the decades without more tender moments like these to comfort her. The *if only*s filled all the gaps, deepened her grief.

Glen pulled into the garages behind Sunny Pines, stopping before his narrow bay to let them out. "Thanks for the ride, Glen," she said.

"Do you feel better about your friend now, Birdie?" Glen asked, seemingly indifferent to the fact that they'd taken a cat from a woman's apartment precisely because Birdie did not feel better.

"Not really, no," she said, and he looked at her as though she were an exhibit in a museum, interesting but unrelatable.

"Well, now that you have her cat, I guess"—he tapped the steering wheel, seeming to be at a loss for words—"she'll find you?"

Birdie sighed. "Let's hope so." She picked up the stacked food and water bowls and small bag of food from where Glen had set them on the passenger floor, slid them into the bag on her walker, and pushed to standing.

Glen tipped an imaginary hat and waved. "I'll leave the litter box outside your door, Joseph. You're a better man than I to take in a stray cat."

"It's not a—" Birdie started to correct him and stopped herself, rounding her eyes at Joseph instead. He smiled back. Together they walked inside the building, the cat remarkably calm in Joseph's arms. Birdie followed him inside his apartment and put the bowls and food on his counter. The cat jumped and stood in the middle of the room, tail twitching and meowing. He was small, a velvety brown with big yellow eyes. "You sure are loud, Tom cat," Joseph said, bending down to scratch between the animal's triangle ears.

A gratefulness for Joseph's companionship, his support, melted into the memories that lingered of Allison and Felix, and Birdie found she suddenly wanted to share a piece of herself with him. "My—well, Allison named her son Felix, and I thought it was after—"

Joseph was smiling. "Felix the Cat?"

"Exactly."

"Do you stay in touch with him since she died?"

"Yes, I raised him."

"How about that?" Joseph tilted his head. "You have a son."

Her fingers twitched. "Yes. I mean, he's Allison's son, but I raised him." Even now, she felt that familiar sense of undeserved joy, unearned affection from a little boy who'd freely given his love and trust. Who clung to her after nightmares, drew her into family trees. Who had completed her life in such a profound way it had nearly undone her with its sweet simplicity. But no matter how many stories about Allison she shared, Felix saw only Birdie. All he thought he needed was Birdie.

Joseph stood, and the cat rubbed its head across his shoe, purring loud enough for Birdie to hear. "Does Felix live close by?"

She sank onto one of his kitchen stools. "He's in Virginia with his family. He's a heart surgeon at Johns Hopkins." It was impossible to keep the pride from warming her voice. "His wife is a surgeon, too, and they have twin boys, Tyler and Cody."

Joseph picked up the cat again, stroking underneath its chin. "You must miss them."

"I do." She breathed in, felt the sting of it in her chest. "How about you, Killer? Where are your kids?"

"I have a daughter and a son. My daughter lives in Grand Junction with her husband and a farm full of llamas, and my son's in Chicago. He's divorced, so I don't get to see my grandkids as much as I'd like. Their mom lives in Minnesota. But I FaceTime them every week."

It was like a gate had been opened in both of them. "The FaceTime makes a difference, doesn't it?"

Joseph smiled down at the cat, who purred back at him. "Sure does. My grandson Kirby set it up last week so I could watch a practice match at his boxing gym." Joseph's pride hugged his words.

She sat up taller, leaning an elbow onto the counter. "A boxer like his grandad."

Joseph looked up at her, his blue eyes near sparkling. "Maybe he'll land a few more winning punches than I did."

"From what Jean said, losing like you did was an art form. Besides, who's to say you still don't have a winning punch in you?" The cat jumped from Joseph's arms and started exploring, smelling the chair, standing on its hind legs to bat at the boxing bag, running its body along the stool, and . . . well, that was the entire tour. Birdie studied his apartment, frowning. "Joseph, can I ask you something?"

"Sure."

"Why do you live like you've got one foot in the grave?"

He stepped back like she'd come at him with her fists. For a moment, she wondered if she'd crossed a line; Joseph was shaking his head, rubbing his jaw with one hand. "My wife is the one who should be here."

"I could say the same about Allison." It was more honest than she'd been with someone in a long time.

"Okay." He folded his arms. "Sofia, well, she struggled with her . . ." He looked at the ceiling, then at Birdie. "With depression. Back in those days we didn't really understand it, not the way we do now. First the doctors said it was anxiety, then hormones, then pregnancy, then hormones after pregnancy, then menopause. Eventually, we got her the help she needed."

"I've struggled with it myself." It was becoming easier to share. "Even now, sometimes," she said. "I'm glad your Sofia got the help she needed."

Joseph rubbed his cheek, and Birdie could tell there was more.

"For the last ten years or so of her life, she was at peace." The cat had settled by his feet. "But I'd done something I never told her about." He squeezed his hands in and out of fists. "Because I was a selfish fool."

"Oh." Birdie could guess, and a deep empathy welled in her for his mistake. Especially one that, with his wife gone, couldn't ever be forgiven by her.

"It was only twice—not even an affair, just a stupid, selfish thing for me to do." He looked around his apartment. "I don't deserve this part of my life. This should have been hers. She was a good wife, a wonderful mother, a deeply caring person. I should have been more for her. More compassionate, more kind, more everything," he finished, shoulders stiff, pain raked across his face. "I've never told anyone. I've kept that secret my entire life."

Birdie sat for a moment, taking in his admission, wishing for one of those confessional screens that a priest sits behind to allow Joseph privacy in his heartache. His eyes were soft with uncertainty and shame, and she hated that for him. Hated for anyone to be defined so narrowly because of a mistake. Her stomach churned, a yearning to share her own deep secret bubbling up. "I had a girlfriend in high school—it was a secret, of course. Her father found us kissing and sent her away to some camp." Shame from that time had crusted over, clinging to her like barnacles. She'd never even had the chance to tell Allison this story. She stole a glance at Joseph. He waited with his hands by his sides. "When she came back, well . . . I tried to get her to run away with me. I—I didn't see how deeply she was hurting." Birdie's hand shook as she tucked a strand of hair behind her ear. "Two weeks later she sat in her father's car in the garage when her parents were out to dinner. The only reason she didn't die was because her mother had left her purse at home."

"Oh, goodness," Joseph said.

"Her father came to my house and blamed me." Birdie looked him in the eyes. "My parents never said a word in my defense. When I met Allison, I was too scared to love her because I didn't want to lose her too." She studied her hands. "When I finally had the courage, it was too late." She looked up. Joseph's eyes were bright with compassion.

"We all have our secrets, Joseph. Especially at our age."

He nodded.

She stood, hands on her walker, shoulders as square as she could make them. "But I have more than one secret you know. One that would shock the socks off our prim and proper Dorothea."

"And what would that be?"

She flipped her gray locks. "I used to be a stripper."

His eyes widened; then that smile of his, just at the corners of his mouth. "I— Oh, I mean—"

"What's the matter, Joseph?" She gave a delicate swing of her hips, mindful of her limited range of movement, and smiled back. "Cat got your tongue?"

At that, he laughed—a deep, cleansing boom that lightened the soles of her feet until she was laughing too.

Twenty-One

The next morning, Birdie sat in her chair waiting for Everly to knock on her door, her knee jiggling up and down. She checked the clock again. Birdie had planned to give her exactly fifteen minutes before she packed up the chocolate scones and headed over there herself. She checked her watch. 8:14. Watched the minute change, went to the kitchen, and slid the scones into a bag. She turned and gasped. A figure stood on her porch, fingers cupped to the glass and peering inside. Hand to her chest, Birdie breathed out. Everly, of course. She made her way across the apartment and opened the door.

Everly wore denim overalls with a long-sleeve shirt and a baseball hat over her white-blond locks. She stood away from the door, holding one arm to her body.

"You came," Birdie said, oddly proud of the girl, and relieved. If they got to know each other, the girl wasn't alone. And if the girl wasn't alone, Birdie could make sure she stayed safe.

"Yeah." She didn't move, eyes lowered, feet already backing up.

Birdie opened the door wider and stepped to the side. "Oh, no you don't," she said. "You got this far; might as well commit."

Everly looked up, eyes just visible under the large brim of her hat. "Okay." She walked inside.

Birdie closed the door, feeling like she'd caught a fly with honey. Everly stood awkwardly in the middle of the room, looking around, one arm still holding the other, like she was afraid of taking up too much space. Birdie moved past her and into the kitchen. "Cream? Sugar?"

Everly nodded, and Birdie took that as both, making the coffee sweeter than normal. Like her grandmother had done for her: more milk than coffee, more sugar than necessary. Everly took the cup and slid a scone onto a napkin.

"Come on, let's sit."

Everly balanced on the very edge of the sofa while Birdie took her chair. They sipped in silence until Birdie realized there would be no conversation if she didn't speak. "So, you play the cello."

"I used to." She rubbed her hands up and down her thighs.

"Oh? Did you get tired of it?"

Everly picked at her scone. "No, I love the cello."

Birdie had at first thought the girl was shy, but she was beginning to think it was far deeper than that. "I'm sorry if I'm making you uncomfortable," she said, shooting for honesty over coyness. "I'm just interested, and you seem, well, maybe a little lonely? I can relate. I know what it feels like to be lonely."

"Really? Everyone here seems so full of life."

The idea surprised Birdie. "Have you seen us? Half of us on oxygen, the others using walkers or canes?"

Everly shrugged. "The ladies with the two dogs. Do you know how much they laugh? They seem so happy to be themselves. And then there's this tiny woman who wears this bright red hat that says 'Best Grandma.' The hat's really ugly, but you can tell that she wears it for her grandkids, you know?"

Birdie bit her tongue to keep from mentioning that Nan might also wear it out of spite. It was refreshing to hear a young person see the value of her peers.

As she spoke, Everly seemed to grow smaller, and Birdie had to fight the urge to tell her to sit up straight or the girl's back would curve like her own one day. "Nobody here is afraid of anything," Everly said.

Birdie raised an eyebrow. "You don't think so?"

"Not like I am." Her voice had shrunk to a whisper.

"What are you afraid of, Everly?" The conversation had turned very real, very fast, but one thing Birdie knew about herself—people confided in her easily. Felix used to call it her *Dear Abby* gift.

"What am I afraid of?" She tapped her fingers across the top of her knee. "People, life, everything."

"That's quite a list."

Everly nodded. She pulled on the strap of her overalls. "I lost my scholarship."

"A music one, I'm guessing."

"Yeah. I couldn't get up in front of people anymore."

"That would make performing nearly impossible, I imagine." Birdie set her cup down. "Has this always been difficult for you or . . . well, did something happen to make it worse?" The girl had a story, and Birdie knew this was only the tip of the iceberg.

"My dad died."

"I'm so sorry."

"And he was this brilliant musician and composer but he, um . . . he stopped leaving the house when I was ten."

"Oh." It wasn't a lot, but it said everything. Birdie could imagine how that had impacted her childhood. Everly studied her feet on the floor, lapsing back into silence. Birdie understood that if there was to be a conversation, she needed to ask the questions. "And your mom?"

"She left us."

"Oh." Birdie pulled at the fabric of her pants. *Poor kid.* "But with all the cards stacked against you, you went to college, with a music scholarship no less. Good for you."

Everly sat up a little straighter, like Birdie's words had inflated her the tiniest bit. "Yeah, I guess, but I thought I was different from him, and now I feel . . ."

"Guilty?" It had been Birdie's lifelong demon that entangled in her moments of joy, eroding her peace.

Everly's head shot up. "Yeah. I couldn't take it anymore, living like that. I thought maybe I could be strong like my mom."

"Sounds like your mom was a coward."

The girl's mouth twitched, as though the unkindness of Birdie's comment surprised her in a good way. "I guess she was. Dad never blamed her, though, so we just accepted it."

"Because you were a team."

"Exactly. But I wasn't like him. I wanted to go to college. I wanted to—" She stopped, studied the scone on its napkin.

"Escape the prison he'd made for himself?" Birdie filled in.

"Yeah." Everly's back rose and fell. "So I left him in that house alone, and when he died, I don't know . . . it's like I inherited all of it."

Birdie sat back in her chair, breathed out. "Well, that is a lot."

"Yeah."

"So now you live in your camper to save money, I'm guessing, and what else?"

"It feels safer."

"To be alone?"

"Yeah."

Everly's words sifted the air, tugging at Birdie's chest. "Guilt's a heavy burden to bear alone," she said, feeling a connection to this girl that touched on her own pain.

Everly finally took a bite of her scone.

"Listen, I'm sure you don't want to be living in a camper for the rest of your life, and something tells me you love playing the cello way too much to give it up forever." The girl sat so still that Birdie questioned if she was even listening. "But it's not safe out there."

She ducked her head. "Nowhere feels safe."

Birdie's fingertips felt cold when she thought about Allison. Everly was right: even a home could be dangerous. She rubbed her arms, anxious. An invitation sat on the tip of her tongue. *Live here.* Birdie could offer Everly a safe place. It was better than her flimsy camper. Better than being alone. She pressed her fingernails into her palm and swallowed the ridiculous thought. She changed course. "Since you think we have it all here at Sunny Pines, why don't you start with us? We're an easy crowd." Birdie frowned. "Except for Dorothea, but she'd make anyone want to hide."

"Start what?"

"Getting out again, making friends—whatever it is you need to work through what's holding you back."

"Don't you think I've tried?" An edge of defensiveness, and Birdie was relieved to hear it. It meant the girl had at least a small fire brewing inside.

Instead of answering, Birdie said, "I've only just started making friends myself." She winked. "And I've had a whole lifetime to try."

Everly seemed to consider her words. Birdie noticed that the girl acted more comfortable than before, less fidgety. She took it as a win. But a knock on her door ruined the moment; Everly sprang up like a startled cat.

"Now, hang on a minute," Birdie said, getting to her feet too. "Let me just see who it is."

Joseph was in the peephole, and Birdie considered her next move. She turned back to Everly to find the girl's face splotched in pink, arm held against her chest. "It's Joseph. He's the first real friend I've made here apart from Faith. You'll like him." She waited, her hand on the door. "There's no time like the present. And you picked the right place to start your personal-improvement journey. We're about as harmless as they come." Birdie held her breath, hoping she wasn't coming on too strong.

When Everly didn't turn and flee the way she'd come in, Birdie opened the door.

"I can't find the cat!" Joseph was frantic, rubbing his head, shifting his weight from foot to foot.

"What?" A pit opened up in her stomach. "You didn't let him outside, did you?"

"Of course not." It was the first time she'd heard anything close to annoyance in his voice. His eyes widened. "Oh, hi," he said over Birdie's shoulder.

She twisted around. Everly stood right behind her.

"Cats love to hide," she said. "I can help look for him."

"Okay, yes, thank you." He turned back to his apartment, and Everly sidled past Birdie, following Joseph and leaving Birdie in her doorway with her mouth hanging open. Either she'd missed her calling as a motivational speaker, or the girl's love for animals outweighed her fear of people.

She was walking across the hallway to help look for the cat when Glen's door opened. "Birdie! I heard a commotion. Is everything okay?"

"The cat's gone missing."

"Oh dear."

She knocked on Joseph's door, and it took a moment for him to answer. "Any luck?" she said.

"Not yet. Come in."

Glen followed her inside, and they stood in the middle of Joseph's empty living room. "A bachelor pad, indeed," Glen said, giving the punching bag a soft one-two.

Everly hurried from the back room, so focused on Joseph she didn't even blink at Glen's presence. "He's not under the bed," she said to Joseph, who rubbed his head like it was a crystal ball with all the answers.

Birdie felt a rise of panic. They couldn't lose Faith's cat. "Could he have gotten out, Joseph?"

"I don't think so, but how else could he just up and disappear?"

In typical obtuse-Glen fashion, he stepped forward, arm across his waist, and gave a little bow toward Everly. "Hello there, dear. I'm Glen, the third member of our little clique." As if this was the reason they'd come together. "And you are . . . ?"

Everly ignored him, and her eyes scanned the room. When she spotted Joseph's chair, she hurried over, kneeling on the floor and putting her cheek to the carpet to peer underneath. Her voice pitched higher. "Hey there, sweet kitty." Birdie pushed into her walker, knees weak with relief. Joseph made a noise that was a half gulp, half sigh. Everly reached under and carefully pulled out the small, sleepy cat, cradling it to her chest. "Aw, little buddy. Taking a snooze, huh?" She stood, stroking its sable fur and smiling. Birdie liked her smile.

"A heroine in our midst," Glen said. "How did you know to look there?"

"I had a cat growing up who liked to hide inside furniture," she offered, and the ease with which she did surprised Birdie.

Glen's eyes bounced from Joseph to Birdie. "Is this your granddaughter, Joseph?"

Joseph looked at Everly as though just realizing he had no clue who she was. "No, actually. I'm sorry, I don't know your name."

"This is Everly," Birdie said, measuring the girl's level of comfort. "I invited her over for coffee this morning."

It seemed she drew solace from holding the cat, because Everly shrugged a wave at them. "I live in one of the campers."

Glen moved closer, tilting his head toward her. "You don't say! A Jack Kerouac fan? Going where the road takes you?"

Everly made a sound that could have been a laugh. "I don't know who that is."

Glen pressed a hand to his chest as though he'd been shot. "What do they teach you in school these days?"

"Well, I was a music—"

"You seem far too young to be living out there on your own. Does anyone know where you are?" Glen kept talking like his questions were rhetorical. "What do your parents—"

Everly seemed okay, and Birdie was grateful for Glen's interest in the girl, but she didn't want to scare her off. Everly was like a cat herself, skittish and shy. "I think that's enough twenty questions for now, don't you, Glen?"

Glen closed his mouth, nodding. "We don't see many young people around here. You're so full of life."

Birdie sighed at Glen's exuberance. "Ready to finish our coffee?" she said to Everly.

Everly gave the cat to Joseph and went to stand by Birdie.

Birdie waved. "See you around, fellas."

"Bye," Everly said.

Everly followed so close behind her that Birdie thought she might trip on the back of her heels. She hoped it meant Everly had decided to trust her.

Twenty-Two

Allison

Everly loves the feel of an animal in her arms. She's a natural caretaker, and an animal's vulnerability touches on her inner desire to protect. She wonders if that's why she breathes easier around Birdie. I tell her it's because Birdie has that effect on everyone. On some level, she hears me; I know, because she sways closer to where I am.

We spend our time with them. The present *is*. The future is split into many paths, and we see them all. Young Karen does not leave Everly's side, because at fourteen Karen's heart never had the chance to feel all the shapes of love. She wants for Everly to have all that she was robbed of even if it means leaving the safety of her camper. Even if it ends with her in darkness. We can't decide the future, but we can be there for the one that is.

Everly walks just behind Birdie. She studies her thinning gray hair, the frail slope of her shoulders, and her labored progress with the walker, and she feels a lump in her throat for the brittleness of age. She extends her long arm past Birdie to the door, holds it open for her, and Birdie smiles up at her. Everly wonders what she looked like as a young woman.

She enters the cinnamon warmth of Birdie's apartment and feels content. Her camper is cold, and inside Everly's nose runs so much her nostrils are dried out and sore. This place feels like a home.

Birdie's apartment is the brightness that strains against terrible shadows.

We are the shadows.

And we are the light in the beautiful dark.

I fill the air, push my fingers into the space between molecules, my fists into the thickness that separates us, but I can't make them hear me. Can't feel Birdie's hand in my own.

It is right for Everly and Birdie to know one another, and a future possibility materializes because of it. But another possibility deepens in shadows, and all I can do is watch and hope that when the time comes, it is not Everly's soul we escort away.

Twenty-Three

After Everly left, Birdie's heart felt oddly full and tender from worry, all at the same time. She liked the young woman and believed she could help her find a way to go back to her regular life, where she wouldn't be so alone.

Birdie watched the sun slide behind the building, the light dimming rapidly. She tugged at her lip. She couldn't do anything more for Everly now. But between the animals, the intruder, and everything else, Birdie couldn't shut her mind off to all the variables in play. She checked her email: no message from Faith. Then took to the internet, searching for any updates on the Geneva Smith case. Nothing. If the boyfriend was a suspect like Loretta thought, wouldn't they have reported something on that by now? She pulled at a fingernail. Did it mean there was another suspect on the loose?

From outside, an animal cry set her pulse racing. She hurried to her patio door, cracked it open. Two tabby cats slunk under her patio fencing and into the garden area, slipping under the bushes. Not Faith's cat, escaped from Joseph's. She breathed out and closed and locked the door, twisting shut the blinds. Her fingers tingled; Birdie was on edge.

She opened the door to the spare bedroom and sat on the bed, surrounded by the pictures of Allison and the women. Somehow they brought her comfort and at the same time intensified her need to do something more. She located the community directory and found Louise's number.

"Hello?" Her voice was deep and friendly.

"Hi, Louise. It's Birdie."

"Hello, Birdie. What an unexpected call."

Suddenly, Birdie was nervous. "Yes, well, I was wondering if you could do me a favor."

"Anything." Without hesitation.

"Do you know about the girl who lives in that truck camper?"

"Nan told me about her. Said you had gone to check up on her one day. You're such a thoughtful person, Birdie."

Birdie's face warmed. "Her name's Everly, and she's all alone out there. And with the intruder and the animals—"

"And with Faith missing, of course."

"Exactly. I just want to make sure she's okay. You can see her camper from your window, right?"

A rustling on the phone. "I'm looking at it right now."

"Oh, good. Would you mind texting me when she turns her lights off for the night?" Birdie scrunched her nose, hearing how paranoid and intrusive she sounded. Like Dorothea.

A ping on her phone, and Birdie took it away from her face to see the message: Lights are still on for now. Will let you know when they go off.

Birdie smiled, a tingle in her stomach. "Oh, that's nice. Thank you."

Another ping. You're welcome. And Birdie giggled. Like a girl.

"Good night, Birdie," Louise said.

"Good night, thanks again, Louise." She pushed End, tried to ignore the somersaults in her stomach, felt the women watching her, Allison's frozen smile somehow knowing. "Oh, please," she said, imagining she heard their soft laughter.

She wrapped her robe tighter against a sudden chill. "So what do you think, ladies?" Young Karen looked at her from under thick bangs and heavy eye shadow. "Am I right to be worried about Faith? And Everly?" An arthritic ache in her fingers; she rubbed her hands together to ease it.

Back then, Birdie had sent the police letters, and when she didn't hear from them, she called, stopped by in person. She'd scoured the newspapers, looking for other deaths, murders—anything that might create suspicion around Allison's death. When she found something, she'd put it in an envelope and mail it to the police. Or she'd drop it off. At first, they'd take her envelopes, her leads. One uniformed man after another with a patronizing smile.

She never let their bloated pity stop her. But a year later, an officer showed up at her apartment. His firm knock had startled Felix from falling asleep. The boy slept fitfully, still crying out for his mama until he'd give up from exhaustion, usually with Birdie spooning his small body, singing softly into his hair. The officer had been grim, and when she saw what was in his arms, it ripped open a hole inside her chest. Her envelopes—all of them, from the looks of it; a few opened, most of them not. He dumped them on her kitchen table. *Case closed,* he'd told her. There had been a shade of kindness in his tone when he said, *Nothing will bring your friend back. Best you get on with your own life.*

Birdie had sat in the bathroom and cried. But she didn't stop searching. Years later, when the serial killer was terrorizing Denver neighborhoods, Birdie collected the stories of the murdered women, their manner of deaths, and reached out to the police yet again. Most of the women were throwaways. The type who went missing too easily. The ones no one thought to look for until it was too late. Like Allison. Like Faith. Nothing ever happened, but they never sent her envelopes back either.

She stood from the bed—the dead couldn't give her answers—and returned to her room. Checked her phone: no new message from Louise. Stretched her fingers across the screen . . . *No, don't text so soon. You'll look like a crazy person.* Slid under the covers—bed felt so good tonight—and rolled onto her side, television on and an episode of *Suits* playing. She'd wait until Louise texted her that Everly was tucked in for the night. She turned out the lights, the room flashing blue and white from the television. Wide awake, her bones on edge from a nervous vibration. Maybe tomorrow she'd drive back to Faith's apartment. Maybe this time Faith would be there.

~

Birdie woke up clawing at her throat, pulling her nightgown away from her neck. She couldn't breathe.

Birdie!

Her whispered name woke her fully, and she inhaled a sob. It had been Allison calling to her. She leaned against the headboard, an ache emanating from her heart and leaking into the rest of her body. Birdie wrapped her arms across her chest, shaking and wide awake. *Everly.* Her fingers searched the bedsheets, located her phone. She'd fallen asleep, missed the message waiting for her, sent at 10:28 p.m.

Lights out. All tucked in for the night.

And another one from this morning.

She's up and just took her dogs out. Cute pups but a little ugly too. ☺

Birdie pressed a hand to her cheek and laid back against her pillow, touched by Louise's diligence. She hadn't expected that. Still shaking from Allison's voice that lingered in her ear, she FaceTimed Felix, needing to hear his voice, see his face.

Cody answered, Allison in the delicate sweep of his cheekbones, his eyes the same dark brown. "Igbird!" The name the twins had settled on when they were three had started as *Big Bird*, but over time their young tongues and silly natures had whittled it into *Igbird*. And because it made them laugh like crazy every time they said it, Igbird had stuck.

She smiled, the shock of Allison's voice disappearing in his warmth. "Hi, Cody. I heard you made honor roll again, you smart kid."

"Yeah, but my GPA went down from a 4.6 to a 4.5 because of my stupid chemistry teacher."

"Sounds like your stupid chemistry teacher needs to be fired."

Cody smiled. "Exactly! I knew you'd agree with me. Dad tries to be all reasonable, and sometimes—"

"You just want to say the thing," she finished for him.

"Exactly! How do you like your new digs?"

"Just fine."

"Do you miss your house?"

She smiled. Cody had always been deeply empathetic. "I miss *you*," she said. She hadn't seen them in months.

"Same. Hey, Tyler!"

The video jiggled and then Tyler's face appeared, and Birdie jumped at the sight. He smiled, despite a jagged wound that sliced through his right eye and split open his cheek down to teeth and bone. "That's incredible, Tyler. Is this for the movie you're making?"

"Yeah, but I'm thinking of entering a special effects contest, too, except I have to be eighteen, which is dumb."

She nodded. "Very dumb. Maybe you can just lie about your age."

"I know!" He sighed. "You have to come out and see my movie when I screen it."

"I wouldn't miss it."

Tyler's gruesome smile widened. From another room came his mother's voice, and the smile disappeared. "Mom's making me take off the makeup before I go hang out at the mall. Can you believe that?"

"I can, actually." She laughed at his bloody frown. "I love you, Tyler."

The frown didn't last long. "Love you, Igbird. Here's Dad."

Felix came on the screen. They hadn't spoken since the last time, and Birdie was surprised to feel a little nervous.

He seemed preoccupied. "Hi, Mom."

"Hi, Felix." A weak timbre in her voice.

His face softened. "You okay?"

"I'm fine. I just wanted to hear your voice." She searched for more to say. Something benign that wouldn't cause him concern. Certainly not anything about the intruder. That would have him on the next plane to Denver. Her worries about Faith danced on her tongue; she tried to hold them in, but the remnants of the dream tingled cold in her fingertips. If she mentioned it, Felix might think she was going down old paths. Birdie thought of how supportive everyone here had been, how it had even made her a few friends. Felix would like that. She thought of Louise keeping an eye on Everly, not questioning Birdie's motives, just helping in any way she could. It warmed Birdie. "I thought you'd like to know that I'm on a roll here, making new friends left and right."

"Really?" A note of yearning in his voice that reminded her of the boy he'd been. *Are you happy, Mom?* How desperately he needed that, even now.

She pressed a palm to her heart. "Yes, really. One of them is Louise. She's got this little white dog who's actually kind of cute but also very ill-mannered."

Felix smiled broadly, nodding, encouraging her to go on. "So you like dogs now?"

Birdie gave him a look. "I've never disliked dogs. They're just hairy. It's cats I don't care for."

He shook his head, still smiling, still clearly happy. Birdie breathed in. "How'd you meet?" he said.

"Oh, she helped me get Faith's number from the office." She said it without thinking, having let her guard down in the glow of his contentment.

"Who's Faith?"

She froze, then tried to sound casual. "You remember Faith? The woman who cleans my apartment?" Searched for something else to say that would redirect the conversation.

Confusion knitted into his forehead. "Why would you need her number?"

"Oh, well, Faith's mother lives in Puerto Rico, and she doesn't have a lot of friends here, so I just wanted to check up on her. Make sure she's doing okay since I hadn't seen her in a while. You know, if she's in trouble, no one would know." She spoke too quickly; a familiar wrinkle deepened between Felix's eyebrows. "Hey, so Tyler's really serious about this movie, huh?"

One side of his cheek sucked in. Birdie held her breath, hoping the moment would pass.

"Yeah, he is. He wants to take a film class at the community college this summer." He shook his head. "It's nice to see him so determined, you know?"

She breathed out, relieved that the conversation had moved on, and smiled, thinking about Felix as a boy. "You were like that, you know." Starting in elementary school, he'd come home from school and sit at their table, books spread open in front of him, making up work to do if he wasn't satisfied with the amount of homework his teachers had assigned. Determined to learn all that he could. "Do you remember the time you took apart our television to see what was inside?" she said.

Felix snorted. "The one we had to pay that repair guy to put back together?"

She laughed. "That's the one."

"Did I ever repay you for that mistake?"

"Nonsense. You were curious. Who punishes curiosity?"

Felix laughed and the moment was nice, especially in the wake of their last conversation.

"Are you okay, Mom?"

She tilted her head. "I am, Felix. Truly. I just needed to see some friendly faces. You and the boys have perked me right up. Now, make sure you reserve me a ticket or two for the premiere. Maybe I'll bring a friend."

Twenty-Four

After she hung up, her phone buzzed. Louise.

The bird has flown the coop.

She squinted at the text. What?

☺ Everly has left her camper. Looks like she's taking the dogs for another walk.

She smiled at her phone and got dressed as quickly as she could. With no answers about Faith's whereabouts, Birdie was restless. Maybe she could catch Everly on her way back.

In the early morning, the sidewalk was empty, and she walked to Everly's camper without running into anyone. After a few minutes, she saw Everly and the dogs coming from the direction of the lake. The dogs strained at their leashes as they approached, excited, it seemed, to sniff Birdie's shoes.

"Good morning, dogs," Birdie said. "And Everly."

Everly ducked her head. "Hey." The dogs hopped around her legs. "I need to feed them."

Birdie smiled. "By all means. I just stopped by to say hello."

"Oh, hi." She tied their leashes to a metal loop on the side of her camper and climbed inside, came out a few minutes later with two small bowls full of mushy food.

The silence was punctured by the dogs slurping their food. Everly leaned against the camper, arm held against her side, watching the animals.

"Thanks again for helping to find the cat," Birdie said.

She seemed to relax. "Yeah, of course. Joseph's cat is so cute."

"Actually, the cat belongs to Faith."

"Really? He's cat-sitting for her?"

"Not really."

Everly raised an eyebrow.

"The truth is that I—I mean, Joseph and I are a little worried about Faith."

Everly hugged her arm tighter. "Why?"

"She didn't show up for work, and I can't seem to get a hold of her. So we went to her apartment to check on her and found her cat trapped in her bedroom. It looked like he'd been in there for days."

Everly's eyes rounded. "You think something happened to her?"

Birdie hesitated. Everly was meeting her gaze straight on now, clearly concerned. "I'm not sure—but yes, I'm worried that if she needs help, there's not a lot of people around who care enough to find out."

The girl tilted her head. "That's really nice of you."

She grunted. "Is it? Most people tend to think I'm a little nuts."

Everly laughed, and the unguardedness of it surprised Birdie. "Some people think the same of me."

Birdie laughed too. "Aren't we a pair?"

"Yeah." The dogs lapped their water noisily, food bowls licked clean. "Thanks for having me over yesterday. It was really nice."

Birdie raised an eyebrow. "We didn't scare you off, then?"

Everly shook her head.

Birdie sniffed, satisfied. "You are welcome anytime."

Pink blushed across her cheeks, and she leaned down to pet her dogs. "Okay. Thanks, Birdie."

~

A few days later there was a tentative knock on Birdie's patio door. Everly gave a small wave through the window and Birdie opened the door, surprised but pleased to see her.

"Good morning, Everly," Birdie said. "Come in."

Everly held three small woven baskets, each filled with paper grass and what looked like a boxed chocolate rabbit. The girl's wide smile sharpened her cheekbones in a pleasing way. She came inside smelling of lemon and fresh air.

Everly offered her one of the baskets. "What's this?" Birdie said.

"It's Easter." She held an awkward stance, like she might bolt at any second. But there was something more solid about her today. "I weave the baskets myself, and since I moved into the camper, I've had a lot of time on my hands to weave." She sucked in her top lip. "It's an Easter basket."

Birdie smiled. "I gathered that. Thank you, Everly."

"My dad didn't do a lot of things well, but one thing he made certain of—we always celebrated holidays. And, I don't know, I figured you might not have anyone to give you an Easter basket, so, well . . . It's just a chocolate bunny I got from the dollar section. And you can use the basket for napkins or hand towels or whatever you want."

Birdie was taken aback by the girl's gift. "Why, thank you, Everly." She took out the bunny and bit half its head off, relishing the taste of milk chocolate in the morning. "The best dollar-section bunny I've ever had."

"I made one for Joseph and Glen too." She held the other two baskets tight to her chest, seemed unsure of herself. "Um, Birdie, what you said the other day about doing this for the rest of my life . . . I—I don't want to live like this forever." She seemed to shrink, shoulders rounding over the baskets. "I'm just really lost."

Birdie nodded, letting her admission sink in. "You know what, Everly? Me too."

A moment of silence passed between them, and to Birdie it felt like a pact. "Would you like some assistance, Easter Bunny?"

She smiled. "Yes, please."

"Follow me."

~

Glen wasn't home, so they left the basket by his door with a note from the Easter Bunny. Same with Joseph, but just as they had returned to Birdie's door, he poked his head out, and since Birdie felt that some company might keep the bleakness from coming back, she invited him to lunch.

She made three microwave dinners—spaghetti and meatballs, lasagna, and steak and mashed potatoes—and the three of them sat at her little round table to eat.

"Well, this is a first." Birdie scooted her chair close, wondering why she'd ordered the pub height and not a normal table where her feet could rest on the ground.

"Having guests for lunch?" Joseph said.

"Eating at my table."

"This is really good." Everly had nearly finished her steak.

"You should taste my microwave popcorn."

Everly ducked her head, grinning.

"So, you play the cello?" Joseph asked.

"Yeah." Everly had some conversation skills to work on, but this was progress.

"My wife loved to go to the symphony. I enjoyed it, too, but I didn't know the music the way she did."

"Oh." She poked at small hills of mashed potatoes with her fork. "My dad played his whole life, and when I was a baby he composed this really beautiful piece. The Cleveland Orchestra debuted it. It was a big deal." She laid her fork down, and her shoulders rose and fell. "He was really talented."

Birdie swallowed her last piece of lasagna. "Are you talented too?"

Joseph looked at her like it was the wrong question, but it didn't seem to bother Everly.

"I am."

Birdie looked her in the eye, appreciating her honesty. "Good. I like your confidence. Your father's, uh, condition . . . was it always a challenge for him?"

Joseph squirmed in his seat.

Again, Everly seemed okay, and that was where Birdie took her cue. Maybe the girl needed to talk about him. "When I was really little, he was fun and creative—even spontaneous. He bought me my first cello." She held up a hand to her thigh. "It wasn't much bigger than a violin." She smiled at the memory. "We played the *Barney* song together and other silly things that I loved. I had no idea how well known he was in the music world at that time. It was just me and him and our cellos."

"That sounds nice," Joseph offered.

"Yeah." She pushed a piece of steak around the tray. "Then he stopped leaving the house when I was in fourth grade, banned electricity or anything to do with wireless when I was in sixth grade. Something about how it affected his brain."

Birdie had an image of a dark house, Everly's pale skin and white-blond hair the only brightness inside.

"My mom left that year too. She didn't even ask me if I wanted to go with her." It seemed the floodgates had opened.

"Did you want to go with her?"

"Birdie," Joseph whispered.

Again, Everly seemed almost relieved to have the question asked. "No."

Birdie sat back in her chair, feet balanced on the footrest under the table. "I was close to my father too. My mother used to say I was the son he never had." It was funny now, after all these years; she could laugh at it, even if it was tinged with pain. "He taught me how to change the oil in our car and worked on teaching me knots he'd learned as a Boy Scout. He could be strict, though, like many fathers were back then. My mother sewed my dresses—and once, she snuck me out to a dance without my father knowing." A warm glow built around her at the thought of her mother's handmade lemon-yellow tea-length silk dress with the crinoline skirt and white lace gloves. It had been so beautiful, and her mother had teared up as soon as Birdie put it on. "My date was a boy from church—Tommy something or other—and I think my mother was sure he was the one."

"Was he?" Everly sat with her chin in her hands, eating it up.

Birdie smiled. "If his name had been Sarah and his suit a dress, then maybe. Who knows?" Joseph watched her while she spoke, a softening in his jaw that let her know he was thinking of the whole story she'd shared with him.

"Oh." Everly seemed surprised but pleasantly so.

Birdie leaned forward. "They weren't perfect, but I loved them anyway. Like you love your dad. The thing is, Everly, we don't have to be like them. We get to be our own versions."

"Yeah, I hear you." She said it like she did, like maybe it had been something she'd told herself a million times before.

Joseph cleared his throat, and both of them turned to look at him. He opened his mouth, closed it, used his napkin to wipe the corners. "My wife, Sofia—she had depression."

He'd told Birdie, but she realized that he likely hadn't spoken about it much. Birdie wanted to tell him that she understood his wife's struggles. From her bedroom, a bleakness spread like black vines, reaching for her, waiting to wrap itself around her waist, pull her inside. Mocking voices. *Allison's death was your fault. Your fault. Your fault.* Birdie shook her head to dislodge the voices, focused on Joseph.

"I don't know what all you're struggling with, Everly, but I do know that it's worth getting help now," he said. "No sense in waiting. Sofia, well . . ." Joseph looked down at his plate before continuing. "Eventually, she got what she needed, counseling and medication that helped, but I wish we'd reached out—er, found help much earlier." Joseph's mouth moved like he was chewing on something. "Everly, do you—or I mean, *have* you gone to therapy?"

Birdie's eyes burned at Joseph's openness. She knew how much it took, and it seemed Everly understood, too, with the way she sat, hand pressed to her chest, eyes glued to Joseph's face. "No, I have not."

Birdie had gone to therapy once. After she'd been arrested, it had been one of Felix's requests. And it had been exactly what she'd expected: a man who knew nothing about women and even less about murder. It had lasted a few sessions.

"Okay," Joseph said. "Do you think you would be open to it, Everly?"

His measured way of speaking—so kind, so patient. Birdie blinked several times. She couldn't help but be reminded of Felix and Sharon's most recent offer. Of Felix's own need to see a therapist because of the pain Birdie had caused. She hadn't meant to hurt him. Nothing she'd done had ever been meant to do anything but give him answers.

Everly shifted in her chair, her shoulders slumped, looking unsure of herself. "Yeah, I'm open to it, I think. I—I don't want to be like this. But I lost my way and I don't know how to get back." There were tears on her face, and Joseph shot to his feet, looking both uncomfortable and touched. He put a tentative arm around Everly, squeezed her shoulder with his hand.

"Okay, it's okay," he said. "You have us. Me and Birdie here—and she's a firecracker. So you're not alone, okay, Everly?" Birdie squeezed her neck, moved by his words.

Everly nodded, head bent and just touching Joseph's shoulder.

"Do you have a job? We could, uh, help you find one? To get back on your feet?" He sounded like the TV dad everyone wanted.

Everly lifted her head. "I give cello lessons over Zoom." Teeth caught her bottom lip. "But I'm using an unsecured Wi-Fi from this building."

"Unsecured?" Joseph said.

Birdie waved him away. "Never mind that."

Everly stood. "Can I use your bathroom?"

"Of course." She pointed toward the small hallway with the bedrooms. "Just that way."

Everly walked across the apartment, and Birdie gathered the plastic microwave plates, using one hand on the chair, then the counter to carefully make her way to the kitchen. Joseph followed with the glasses and silverware. "You're a good person, Birdie," he said quietly. "Your Allison was lucky to have you, even for the short time she did."

Birdie stopped what she was doing. She wished she believed that too. "Thank you, Joseph."

Their eyes met; Joseph's crinkled in the corners.

"Birdie?"

Birdie turned. The spare bedroom door was wide open, light on, with Everly standing just inside. "I'm sorry, I thought this was your bathroom, but . . ." She stopped and stared at the walls.

Joseph got to the room before slow-moving Birdie, and her fists grasped for the tail end of the control she normally felt. But there they stood, her friend and the girl she wanted to help, looking into the room and back at her like she was the one who needed a therapist.

"Oh," Joseph said, surveying the walls, and Birdie saw it through his eyes. A spiderweb of news articles, research notes, and pictures of women. There were handwritten notes in her heavy chicken-scratch on yellow legal paper, decades old; pictures Birdie had taken herself of victims' childhood homes, best friends, siblings, parents. Even in some cases a beloved dog. A vortex of the lives lost and their grieving families that Birdie had spent hours, weeks, years collecting.

Everly went from picture to picture, touching the notes, reading through some, one arm tightly bound to her body by the other, and occasionally looking over her shoulder at Birdie. "Are these women, um, all dead?"

Birdie leaned against the wall. Seeing the room now, in the dusty afternoon light, with Everly and Joseph studying the walls like it was an exhibition in a museum of the weird, Birdie felt sick. "They're unsolved murders."

"Are you a detective or something?"

Joseph turned from a picture of Felicity, the killer's last known victim, to Birdie, his eyes giving nothing of how he felt away.

"No, not a detective. Just a cleaner." Anxiety unfurled, brushing across Birdie's back and sending goose bumps down her arms.

"Is this Allison?" Joseph stood by the wall with the window where she'd closed the blinds to affix everything she had on Allison's life and death. It flowed from the wall to a narrow table below—a shrine, Birdie realized, or at least that might be how it looked to them. To her, it was every scrap of information that led to answers. He held Felix's baby album, opened to a blank page in the middle of the book. Proof, to Birdie at least, that Allison had a future she wanted to be a part of. In her mind's eye, there was Allison, on the floor of their apartment, legs folded to the side, pictures and tape scattered around her. *I should have done this before his first birthday*, Allison said, flipping through pictures to decide which one went next.

He's still a baby. Birdie had just put Felix down for the night, singing quietly to him until he released his hold, cheeks ruddy from sleep, lips suction-cupped to his thumb.

He's three!

And still sucks his thumb.

Allison had laughed. *Okay, he's still a baby.* She'd taped in the next photo. *I just want him to know how happy he makes me. How much I love him.* She'd seemed frantic, like time was slipping away. Birdie had figured that was how children made their parents feel with how quickly they grew.

Birdie had knelt beside her. *He'll know.* She handed her a photo of Felix eating his very first piece of cake.

How?

Because he'll have you to remind him.

Allison had peered up at her from under her bangs. *And you.*

They'd held each other's gazes, Allison's intense, expectant, and Birdie had withered; she looked away. She could not promise Allison what she couldn't give. Allison and Felix deserved to be loved and accepted their entire lives, and with her, that would never happen. *He'll always have you,* Birdie had said.

So many moments Birdie wished she could take back. But death was final, and mistakes lasted forever.

"Birdie?" Everly had moved closer to where Birdie stood, her face unguarded like she recognized something in her. "Did you know all these women?"

Shame tickled her throat, and Birdie swallowed. She had nothing to be ashamed of. She tried to straighten her shoulders. "No, I did not."

Joseph held tight to the baby album, staring at her. She held out her hands, impatient now. "Give that to me."

He moved around the bed and handed it to her, then stepped back until his legs hit the edge of the mattress.

"Who's Allison?" Everly asked, studying a picture of Felix when he was two, sitting on Santa's knee, a look of sheer terror in his widened eyes, and Allison on Santa's other knee, a loving and amused smile trained on her boy.

"She was . . ." Birdie paused. "The love of my life, and she died when her son was a little boy."

Everly's face fell. "Oh."

"Allison was murdered?" Joseph said, his stoic facade slipping on the words, settling into the faintest twitch of his jaw.

"Yes." She didn't owe him the full story, because with it would come the looks, the disbelief, the pity that after so many years, Birdie refused to accept her friend's suicide. That it had festered into an obsession to prove what even the cops could not, and into a belief that she alone could. Their faces were mirrors, and in them she saw her reflection: an old woman with nothing to show for all that work but pictures of dead women on her walls.

"Oh, Birdie," Joseph said.

"That's horrible." Everly turned a shade whiter than her normal pale. "I'm so sorry." She gave the walls another glance. "So you're like a vigilante or something?"

"No," she said a little too sharply. "I'm a cleaner." She could tell them everything. For a second, she thought she might. But she knew how that went. Her fingers pressed into her thighs, anger spiking at their intrusion. "I used to think I could find the person who did it, but it never happened."

Joseph rubbed the back of his neck. "But why are you . . ." He cleared his throat. "I mean, you're still trying to find the person who killed her all these years later? That seems—"

"The police never believed me." Birdie's voice squeaked with frustration. They weren't there. They couldn't possibly understand. "They thought she committed suicide."

"Oh, that's so awful," Everly whispered.

Once she started, Birdie found it hard to stop. "So when Geneva Smith was found—"

"Who?" Everly asked.

Birdie hesitated. "She was murdered a few weeks ago, and her body was found in a dumpster at the same apartment complex where Allison and two other victims died, and I think they're connected, that maybe they were murdered by the same person, or—"

"But that doesn't seem possible, does it?" Joseph stood with his feet planted wide. "Wouldn't whoever have killed Allison be at least as old as us? And you think they're still murdering young women?"

"Yes, I do," she snapped. Suddenly, Birdie heard herself the way Felix and the police had: desperate, delusional.

"I'm so sorry, Birdie," Everly said.

Birdie's skin itched with irritation. This was exactly why she avoided people and close friendships—because of this look, this tone of voice that alluded to their pity. Above most things, Birdie hated to be pitied. She pushed air through her teeth. "The police were wrong about Allison." The pair of them were silent, driving Birdie to do the thing she hated most: explain herself. "She loved Felix too much to leave him. I knew it then and I believe it now. That has never changed." A rush of weakness down her legs, doubt keeping pace with her certainty. That Allison had found it all to be too much and, like Sarah, had found her own way out. Birdie shook her head. *No, no, no.*

The room turned claustrophobic. She stood back, arm held out. "Please," she whispered. They took the hint and left the room; she shut the door. The three of them stood awkwardly in the middle of her living room, Birdie wishing for her walker to lean on but not wanting anything to make her look older than she already felt.

Everly had taken what Birdie thought of as her protective stance— one arm across her body, the other holding it. Her eyes took in the photographs spread all over Birdie's apartment of Felix as a boy, a man, and then as a husband and father. Of the boys and Sharon. "So you raised her son?"

"I did."

"And you did all of this for him?"

"Exactly." Birdie was weary now, vulnerable in a way she'd only felt with Felix. "I think you both should go," she said as gently as she could.

It hurt the girl anyway; Birdie saw it in the way she pulled back inside of herself. "Okay, thanks for lunch. Bye, Joseph." And she was out the patio door before either one of them had a chance to respond.

Joseph watched Everly flee, then turned to look at Birdie, and there was a frankness there that made her uncomfortable. Like he'd understood something. "It's a little shocking to see—you know, Birdie?"

Anger prickled hot across her cheeks, fighting with the coolness of disappointment. Joseph was like all the others. She fought an urge to leave her apartment herself. "To you, maybe."

He rubbed his cheek. "You said something to me once. About living like I've got one foot in the grave."

She struggled against an urge to look away. "And?"

"Do you think you might be living with both feet in the grave? I know I didn't know Allison or all the terrible things you must have lived through afterwards, and I'm sorry for being presumptuous, but I'm certain that anyone who loved you wouldn't want you living with all of that on your heart."

Birdie tried to rouse her anger, but it had wilted with the truth. She'd always thought that her search for answers was the only thing that was right. Now it seemed that all she'd done was hurt the one person who meant the most to her in this world.

The heavy door thunked closed when Joseph left, and in the quiet that followed, Birdie felt more alone than ever.

～

Half an hour later, Birdie sat with her hands in her lap, staring at the closed bedroom door, startled by the sound of her phone ringing. Felix. Her shoulders slumped with relief. It was like he'd known how much she needed to hear his voice.

"Hi, Felix." She smiled into the camera and tried to keep her voice from wobbling.

"Hi, Mom. Are you okay?"

Her eyes burned. She pressed a hand to her chest and waited a few seconds. "You know, sweetheart, it's just been one of those days."

He cleared his throat. "Are you thinking about her a lot?"

Part of her wanted to deny it, to spare him from worrying more than he already did, but after what had happened with Joseph and Everly, she just couldn't lie. "Yes, actually, I am."

He opened his mouth to say something, then seemed to reconsider. "I'm sorry."

It was said with such warmth that Birdie could only nod.

"That's kind of why I called. The other day you mentioned Faith."

Her pulse picked up speed. She nodded.

"Well, do you think that you might be digging up old feelings? You know, with how you're worried something bad has happened to her? It felt . . . I don't know, like something you might have done before with Allison and the women."

Birdie opened her mouth to deny it but couldn't because he wasn't wrong. And a part of her was tired of pretending. "Faith is missing, Felix. I know it. She's the kind of person I would have hired. Reliable, hardworking, with big dreams. She's not the kind of person who quits without a word to anyone."

His mouth pursed like he'd tasted something sour. "Who thinks that?"

"The management here."

Felix rubbed his forehead.

Birdie's heart beat loud in her ears. This wasn't the kind of thing Felix wanted to hear. "You know what? I'm sorry I brought it up. She's just the kind of person who could be overlooked. Like—"

"Allison?" The screen dipped away from Felix's face; then he was back, rubbing his face with one hand. "Mom . . ."

"Only in how everyone is making assumptions about her." Birdie tasted something bitter. "I'm worried about her, Felix. That's all. I mentioned it to the police after the man broke into our building, but they aren't taking it seriously—"

"What?"

Birdie slumped. What had gotten into her? "Nothing, it was nothing." She tried to smile; it felt stretched out. "I know you don't believe me, but something has happened to my friend, and I can't just sit by and do nothing." Her breaths were ragged, her face flushed.

His lips flattened, deepening the lines around his mouth. "I can't believe this."

She needed to fix this. "Listen, don't mind me. I'm fine."

His anger was palpable, familiar, and it turned her skin clammy. "There was a time I understood this part of you, or thought I did."

"What part of me?"

"This obsession of yours. For Allison, then for the victims of that serial killer, then for any woman who worked for you and seemed the least bit vulnerable. Like this Faith person. I've let so many things go—"

Time felt suspended. "What things?"

"You pretending that Allison was my mom—"

"*Is* your mom."

He rubbed his temple, a brief tremble in his chin. "Why do you fight so hard for everyone else?"

Indignation boiled in her chest. "I fight for others; you know that about me. I always have."

"Why don't you fight for me, then?"

That shocked her cold. "What?"

"Everything is about Allison for you. Everything. You think you can save her by saving everyone else? What about me? I've begged you to let it go. To be my mother. To be the boys' grandmother."

"I am." Where was this coming from? She'd never been anything but those things.

"No, Mom, you haven't, not fully. Not when you continue to do the things that I've told you hurts me. Allison was *not* murdered. She killed herself because I wasn't enough for her." His voice had risen now, and in the background she could just make out the edge of Sharon, her hand on his shoulder. Felix reached up and gripped it like it was his lifeline. "*You* weren't enough for her."

She couldn't speak, his anger a palpable force, his words arrows sinking deep into her flesh.

He cleared his throat, eyes on her through the screen, and Birdie felt his anger thaw. "I'm concerned about you, Mom. It's like you've regressed. I worry about your mental health. You refuse to see that therapist."

She curled her toes inside her shoes until they cramped, needing to feel something other than the hurt inflicted by his words. "I haven't refused."

"With absolutely zero evidence, you've convinced yourself that a woman you hardly know has been harmed." He rubbed his forehead.

Her throat tightened.

"I worry about you living on your own."

"Excuse me?" Thoughts of Glen's brother making those same accusations inundated her. It was unfair, this belief of the young that a cognitive decline was a slippery slope where all the elderly balanced. "I'm fine, Felix." A lump in her throat. Felix would never understand, because he'd never known his mother the way Birdie had. And as a man, he couldn't truly understand what life was like for some women. Love for him softened her heart. "Just forget I said anything, okay? I love you." She pressed End, heart pounding, and when the screen went dark, Birdie lay down on the couch and curled into a ball.

Twenty-Five

ALLISON

Birdie is alone, but that's how she prefers it. She is strong and independent, even before I arrive in her life. She defines herself this way because she is not like her parents, who can't love their daughter as she is. She is self-sufficient, capable, tough. It is what draws me so strongly to her. As the young pregnant woman I am and as the bodiless soul waiting for closure. Perhaps I know that my life is to be cut short and my instinct is to find Felix a person who loves him as I do and keeps him safe.

She does all of that.

My death cages her, and I want to set her free. One future is for Birdie to pull away from these new friends, the way she does whenever anyone pushes against her confining ways. If that happens, the moment will dissolve and nothing will be discovered.

I cannot change the present. And the present is everything.

I sit beside Birdie on the couch; the others are around me. The need for truth feeds our souls, and we are one. I close my eyes and let the air take me in, harness the energy of our combined being, and fling out an arm, our hands rushing through a picture frame by the couch. There is no feeling of contact, nothing more than a disturbance in the stratosphere, and it wobbles. The sound it makes is but a whisper.

But Birdie sees it move. Picks it up and makes a sound that is a sob. It is the picture of Felix holding his newborn twin sons.

Birdie sits up on the couch, and her back shakes. She is lost, like Everly; regretful, like Joseph; and for the first time since my death, she wants more. We collapse inward, scattering like leaves, and when it is time we will offer what we have and retreat.

Twenty-Six

Gloom wrapped itself around her, and hours passed with Birdie on the couch, her mind a jumble of the conversation with Felix and the one with Everly and Joseph. Felix's words nudged her deeper: *You weren't enough for her.* Her deepest fear ping-ponged inside her head, sucking on her longing to do something. As long as she was *doing* something to occupy her mind, she could keep out from under this melancholy. With each new Vampire Killer murder, Birdie had felt a spike of adrenaline lacing the sadness, a fresh opportunity to discover a mistake, a link— anything that might show the killer's hand. But her failure to bring peace to the families, to connect Allison's death to those horrific crimes, became a mocking presence chained to her side, whispering to her at night. About the time she'd wasted, the relationships she'd avoided out of some perverse guilt, some irrational need to prove Allison's murder.

Her old doubts swam around her like water snakes. A detective had once told her she was making something out of nothing. Felix had said the same thing. Was she? About Faith? About Allison? Birdie's head fell into her hands. Was it just too hard for her to face the truth? Images spread behind her eyelids of Allison taking the blade to her own wrist. She wrenched her head up, air tangled in her lungs. *No!* She didn't care how unstable, how obsessive, she might seem to others, even to Felix, because that was a truth she could never accept.

Restless, Birdie pushed herself up from the couch, painfully aware of the blackness that tiptoed out from her bedroom, beckoned her. She walked to the spare room, opened the door. Joseph's words on repeat: *It's a little shocking to see.* It was, but it was what Allison deserved. Someone to fight for her, because on the day that she'd died, Birdie had not.

What nobody knew, not even Felix, was that Birdie had almost gone home early. She'd been slipping out of her bra, letting her focus drift over the slick bald spot on a customer's head, away from his hungry eyes, when she'd caught the glint of the necklace on her chest. She'd stopped undressing, slowed the sway of her hips to touch the tips of the bird's golden wings. *I love you, too, Allison.* It had hit her full force on the stage, breasts pressing into her forearm, the stink of cheap alcohol and cigarette smoke redolent in the air. Her heart had ticked several beats faster. What was she waiting for? She'd knelt, shaking, smiling, and picked up her bra, fumbling with the straps, trying to slide in her arms.

Hey, what're you doin'? The balding guy stood, gestured to the bartender. *What's she doin'?*

The manager had appeared from the back, speared her with a look and a pointed finger. *You leave and you ain't coming back. You hear me?*

She'd stood frozen to the spot, bra pressed against her chest, the most naked she'd ever felt. The manager would fire them both, and they couldn't afford it. But Allison wasn't going anywhere, and Birdie, still smiling, believed she had all the time in the world to be in love. She let the bra slip from her fingers, a soft thump when it hit the stage, and she refocused her gaze past the bald spot and to the wall beyond.

The moment she could never take back. Would it have changed anything if Birdie had gotten home in time? There was no answer because the past was the past and nothing would change it.

Birdie couldn't help but wonder if finding Faith was her do-over. Faith's words from the last time she saw her rang in her ears: *We're all facing the end, Birdie. Some of us get there sooner than others.* Had it been a premonition? Birdie's mouth turned dry. Just because she'd never been proven right about Allison didn't make her wrong. And her instincts were just as strong about Faith. Maybe it wasn't too late to help her. She got her coat, grabbed her keys, and headed out the door.

Nan was walkering past with her red hat firmly in place.

"Going to see your grandchildren today?" Birdie said, speaking fast. She didn't have time for niceties.

Nan's smile put dimples on her pixie face. "How'd you know?" Birdie tapped her head, and Nan laughed. "My grandson is picking me up. He just got his license, so I told him he could take me to the Village Inn for pie."

Nan walked beside her, and Birdie couldn't bring herself to out-walk the older woman, so she slowed down to accommodate her pace. "I'm not sure which is worse: being driven by a new teenage driver or being driven around in that van."

Nan cackled. "It's about the same—but hey, both times I get pie, so I'm not complaining." She looked up at Birdie. "Where are you off to?"

Birdie didn't hesitate. Nan had been on board from the beginning. "I'm going to Faith's apartment."

Nan's mouth parted in delight. "You're a real-life Jessica Fletcher."

"Only if I solve a crime." Her throat tightened. "But I want her to be okay. And if she's not, then I want to convince the police to look for her."

They arrived at the front door. "Let me know what I can do to help," Nan said.

The electric doors opened for them, and in the roundabout, Birdie saw a shiny BMW in the circle. "Is your grandson a tech guru?"

Nan laughed again. "He's a spoiled brat, but there's a chance he might grow out of it."

"Well, he's got you." They walked outside to a warm breeze.

Nan made her way toward the car, and her grandson hopped out of the driver's side and opened the passenger door.

Birdie waved and headed toward the garages behind the building. She remembered the short drive to Faith's apartment and parked in the same spot Glen had, except this time between the designated white lines. A knock on Faith's door brought no answer. Another knock and still no answer. A neighboring door opened, and a man with long hair and a yellow-and-brown flannel popped his head out. "You looking for Faith?"

A flare of hope. "Yes, I am."

"Yeah, me too. I'm kinda tired of keeping all her packages in here. She could have told me she was going out of town." He raised his eyebrows. "You have a key? I could just dump this stuff in there." He ducked inside, came back with a large cardboard box. "There's three more in my apartment."

She gripped the walker, suddenly anxious. "Does she usually leave without telling anyone?"

"Look, I'm just trying to be nice and all. Things get stolen all the time, and I noticed her stuff was sitting out here." He set the box by the door. It was addressed to Clean Faith. Probably supplies for her products. "So if you have a key, then I'll leave this stuff inside."

"When was the last time you saw her?"

He ran a hand through his hair; it got stuck in tangles. He sighed. "I don't know—weeks ago, maybe?" He toed the box. "So, about that key?"

"I don't have one." And she wasn't about to tell him about the unlocked patio door.

"Damn."

Birdie started to back away.

"I don't suppose you can take the boxes?"

"Young man . . ." Birdie made a show of rattling her walker.

He folded his arms. "Yeah, okay. Maybe I'll dump them at the office."

"Maybe you should be more worried about your neighbor," Birdie mumbled, walking away.

"What's that?"

"Maybe I'll see you later," she amended.

"Oh, yeah, see you later," he called back, sounding confused.

$\sim$

Birdie made her way around to the patio; she tried the door and it opened easily. "Faith?" She poked her head inside. Dim, musty, cat pee rancid in the air. Her heart caught in her throat. On the counter, untouched, her note.

Back inside her car, phone in hand with her stomach churning, she dialed 9-1-1.

"9-1-1, what's the address of your emergency?"

"Well, I don't know that. My friend is missing, has been missing for several weeks now, and I think something's happened to her."

"Are you calling to report a crime in progress?"

"No, I don't know what happened. It's just a feeling . . ." She trailed off, wincing at the weakness of her own words.

"Ma'am, you need to contact your local law enforcement agency and file a report with them."

The call unearthed echoes from the past that set her hands shaking. "I need to do what?" She sounded feeble, and she hated it.

"To file a missing persons report, you need to contact your local law enforcement agency."

"Oh, okay. Thanks." She hung up. The police had never listened to her. Birdie felt the wobble of skin under her jaw, stared at the blue veins crisscrossing the tops of her hands. What made her believe anything had changed?

She sat with the heat blasting from the vents, chilled to the bone. If she didn't report Faith missing, who would? This was something concrete that Birdie could do for Faith and her mother. She located the number for the police and held her breath as it rang, pulse thumping in her ears. Before anyone answered, she cleared her throat to scatter the frogs that collected there from time to time. This time she didn't mince words. A woman answered the phone.

"I'd like to report a missing person," Birdie said before the female officer could finish her greeting.

"Okay, let me just get some information first," the officer said.

Birdie gave as much as she could, but it quickly became obvious how little she knew about Faith. The officer's helpful tone shifted. "Ma'am, I have to be honest with you. It doesn't sound like your friend is technically 'missing.'"

Birdie's cheeks flushed, and heat spread from the back of her head down her spine. "You also don't know that she's not."

A sigh came across the line. "Fair point. But this woman has her own life both here and in Puerto Rico, correct?"

"Yes."

"So maybe it's possible she went home? An emergency of some kind, maybe? And"—the woman's voice softened—"maybe it had nothing to do with you or her job and, no offense here, wasn't any of your business to begin with?"

It knocked the wind right out of her, and Birdie slumped in her seat. Nobody believed her. Nobody ever believed her. "Thank you for your help." She ended the call and drove slowly back to Sunny Pines, the sun drifting down to the horizon and washing everything in a cold spring pink. Doubts pecked away at her like vultures, pulling back flesh to expose her deepest fear: that she was wrong about everything.

It took a few minutes to park, the garages being narrow and at the most difficult of angles, and several turns of her car to get it straight enough so she didn't scratch the side. Before she got out, her phone buzzed. Louise.

I stopped by Everly's camper to introduce myself. She's over here having coffee with me. You're welcome to join us too.

A rush of warmth diluted the failure of her two phone calls. Knowing that others were looking out for Everly helped her to relax.

Once she had sidled out of her narrow garage space, she used a small key to close the door. While she waited for it to lower, she noticed a grouping of crows in the grass to the side of the garages. On any other day she would have ignored them, but something caught her attention.

Her walker scraped across the pavement. The birds paid her no heed, beaks like knives, pecking tentatively at the grass. There was something there, small colorful blobs like round pieces of candy combined with a decaying stench that churned her stomach.

When she got close enough, the birds scattered. And as she bent lower, squinting to see in the bluish light of dusk, Birdie struggled to understand what she was looking at. Heads, she realized, and pulled back, repulsed. Small green, blue, and yellow bird heads—ten or twelve, from what she could count—that had once belonged to parakeets. A scattering of their bodies in a sickening bouquet around their heads. The crows hopped on the pavement not far from her, waiting to feast. Had they done this? Beheaded the birds? She'd never heard of such a thing. Except this looked too precise, cookie-cutter in its exactness.

"Birdie?"

She backed away, her mouth souring. This was the work of someone unhinged. Her thoughts rolled back to their neighbors' puppy. The trembling of Allison's voice when she relayed the story. She turned to see Nan, with her hat a brighter red in the evening dusk, making her way down the sidewalk, a tiny graying dog no bigger than a squirrel on a leash beside her.

Nan squinted up at her. "You're white as a sheet. You okay?"

Birdie pointed to the bird massacre, her body numb. "It's horrible, Nan." She pushed into her walker, her knees wobbly.

Nan moved closer, making a clicking sound with her tongue when she saw the birds. "Well, now, that's downright macabre, isn't it?"

Birdie took another glance, winced. "Doesn't look like something a coyote would do, right?"

Nan shook her head. "No, it does not." The dog inched forward, and she yanked on its leash to pull it back. "You think a person did this?"

A sprinkle of relief for not being the first to suggest it. She looked again at the birds. "I do." Her pulse thundered in her neck. "The cuts seem too precise to be made by an animal."

"My thoughts exactly. Oh, hang on a minute . . ." Nan pulled a phone out of her pocket and started snapping pictures of the dead birds.

Birdie watched in disbelief. "What are you doing?"

Nan paused. "Evidence of foul play." She narrowed one eye. "You always need evidence. We can give this to the police."

Birdie cleared her throat, touched by Nan's support. The woman hadn't doubted her or questioned her sanity. Instead, Nan agreed with her. And she was right: they needed proof.

Nan, surprisingly quick with her phone, clicked on the pictures. "I'm sending these to Dorothea. She'll definitely reach out to them," Nan said. "She's like that, you know."

"Like what?"

"A busybody with her nose in everyone's business." Nan shrugged. "But when it comes to someone murdering animals, I think she's a good friend to have, don't you think?"

Birdie could only nod. For once she wasn't the only one sounding the alarm. A crack inside her heart; she wished Felix believed her so easily.

Nan slid her phone into her pocket. "They never caught the intruder you stopped." She eyed Birdie. "Think he could have done it?"

Birdie gave her a look. "I didn't have a chance to get to know him well."

Nan snorted a laugh. "You're a funny gal."

Birdie shook her head. "But I don't know. It could be. Or it could also be—"

"The Vampire Killer?"

Birdie swallowed, unused to someone else confirming her deepest fears.

Nan continued to study the birds, even bent down to get a better look. "Maybe after he botched killing Geneva Smith, he realized he couldn't kill women anymore the way he used to, so he's regressed to slaughtering animals?"

It was as wild a theory as Birdie might have come up with. "Maybe." A crow hopped closer to the bird parts, not scared anymore by old ladies and their walkers. The little dog backed away, hiding behind Nan. Birdie shivered. "But you know, it's what I think may have happened to Faith."

Nan's eyes popped open. "That the Vampire Killer got her too?" Did Nan sound skeptical? Birdie couldn't tell.

"She's still not home, and the note I left her hasn't been touched. Her neighbor says she's been gone for weeks, and her cat was trapped inside a bedroom."

Nan's face lit up. "You broke into her apartment?"

Birdie tried to backtrack. "No, her sliding glass door was open the first time I went over there with Glen and Joseph."

Nan tapped a finger to her chin. "The Gainesville Ripper broke in through a sliding glass door to murder one of his victims. Dangerous business, leaving it unlocked."

Birdie opened and closed her mouth, sickened. It was all adding up to be exactly what she feared most. "And most people don't quit their jobs without saying something to someone, right?"

Nan seemed to consider her words. "My granddaughter left her job as a produce stocker at Safeway in the middle of her first shift because, and I quote, she doesn't like vegetables and that job was stupid anyway."

"Oh." Birdie deflated a bit, hoping Nan would see her point. A chill had crept in with the evening shadows. She glanced at Everly's camper, the windows dark. At least for the moment she was safe with Louise. "Maybe we should go inside."

"Good idea."

Together they walked, not exactly side by side, with their walkers and the narrow sidewalk. Birdie was happy to leave the mutilated birds behind. Before they got far, the dog stopped, back hunched, and pooped.

"Did you get a dog?" She'd never seen her with one before.

"Oh, heavens no. Henry is Delilah's dog, but you know with her vision deteriorating, she can't take him out when it gets dark."

Birdie did not know Delilah, but watching delicate Nan carefully stoop to pick up the dog's poop in a bag made her wonder if dog walking was the right pastime for Nan. "Can I help?" Birdie asked.

Nan pushed to standing, sucking in oxygen through her tubing before tying a knot in the plastic bag. "We must keep doing until we can't, don't you think?"

Birdie breathed out. It was exactly how she felt. Nan's determination was like sunshine, and in its glow, Birdie's earlier gloom receded. When Nan was finished, they started walking again. "How was pie with your grandson?"

Nan sighed. "He takes after his mother these days." She twisted her neck to glance back at Birdie. "But I'm hoping he'll outgrow it."

Birdie tried to smile, but she couldn't stop thinking about the birds.

"What are you doing for lunch on Thursday?" Nan said.

"I haven't even thought about it."

"The van is going to the Village Inn for lunch. We could talk more about the case."

Like they were a team. Birdie blinked back a sudden wetness in her eyes. "Thanks for the offer, but I don't ride on the van."

"Why not?"

Birdie opted for the truth. "It makes me feel old."

Nan laughed, and the loop of tubing flew off her ear. She put it back. "You're hilarious. Then why don't you come over for lunch tomorrow? My daughter-in-law keeps my freezer stocked with meals."

"That's nice of her."

Nan pushed the button to open the doors to the apartment building. "It's the one nice thing she does. Sometimes I wonder if she's trying to poison me so I'll stop ruining her perfect family photos."

"She sounds like a piece of work."

"She is." Nan pushed the button again. "I'll invite the whole gang over for lunch." She sounded firm, like it was a done deal.

"The gang?"

"Exactly!" Nan spoke with her eyes trained on the floor, watching where she walked. "I'll send those pictures to Dorothea. Since the meth head broke in, the police have a car coming through here from time to time, thanks to Glen. I bet he can let them know about the birds too."

Birdie made a decision and joined her on the elevator. "I think I'll go speak to Dorothea myself."

Nan narrowed one eye. "That's a good idea."

"It is?"

"The more of us that work on this, the better. Besides, you and Dorothea need to figure out how to be friends. Your bad vibes are ruining the gang."

The doors opened to the second floor and Birdie got off.

"Good luck!" Nan said.

"I think I'll need it," Birdie muttered.

"Nah, she's not as bad as you think." The doors were closing on Nan's smiling face. "See you tomorrow!"

Twenty-Seven

Birdie knocked, and Dorothea opened her door as if she'd been expecting her.

"Oh, hello," she said in her slightly flat, slightly accusatory tone. "Come in."

Birdie crinkled her nose but followed the woman inside. Dorothea's apartment was smaller but with much nicer furnishings. A white leather couch, expensive-looking paintings on the wall, a fancy espresso machine in the kitchen.

Birdie sat on the couch; Dorothea sank into her Dutch-looking leather swivel chair that might have cost more than Birdie's first house.

"I've already left a message with Glen," Dorothea said. "I'm hoping they can up their patrols to twice a day." Her mouth twisted, a slight crease in the skin giving her age away.

Nan had been right about Dorothea; she was a busybody. But at least she channeled it into doing something that might help put a stop to whoever was hurting animals.

"I think we should talk to the police too." If they wanted the cops to take them seriously, it seemed important to get as many of them together as possible. Birdie on her own wasn't enough to tip the scales. There was power in numbers. But Dorothea looked skeptical. Birdie pressed on. "We can support what Glen is telling them by giving them statements of all the things we've witnessed."

Dorothea shook her head. "I think we'll be muddying the waters. Glen is our voice, and he's one of us." She sniffed. "Plus, I'm of the belief that the police have our best interests at heart."

Birdie bristled at her tone. "And you think I don't?"

"You just seem to have your own agenda. Like with those campers."

Birdie narrowed her eyes. "What are you saying?"

The woman blinked, shifting in her chair. "I know you won't like this, but Glen's going to speak to the police about clearing out the campers. It's illegal to park there, anyway. And you might not see it, Birdie, but they're dangerous."

Anger closed her throat, and Birdie quickly rose. Everly wasn't safe from intruders or serial killers or the police. "Thank you, Dorothea."

She looked surprised. "For what?"

"For encouraging me to help a friend even if you didn't mean to." Birdie walked as fast as she could to Louise's apartment, which was just down the hall, and knocked firmly.

Louise answered in a pale pink cotton robe, frowning. "You missed her!"

Birdie's shoulders fell. "I'll go check up on her before I turn in."

"No, wait, she was headed out to a campsite for the night so she could use the showers and dump station. I think she'll be back tomorrow." Louise tilted her head. "Are you okay, Birdie?"

The truth was that she was exhausted—mentally, emotionally, physically—and she felt it all in the wobble of her hips. "Be careful, Louise. Nan and I found more mutilated animals—birds, this time. Lock your doors, okay?" She didn't have the energy to go into details. It had been a long day. "Glen's working with the police on it, but we need to keep an eye out."

"Of course." She leaned into the doorway, resting her head on the frame. "If you ever need anything, help or someone to talk to, I'm here, okay?"

The sincerity of her offer hit Birdie square in the chest. "Thanks, Louise, but I'll be just fine."

When Birdie walked away, she noticed Louise standing in her doorway, watching until Birdie rounded the corner to the elevator.

~

Before she got to her apartment, Birdie ran into Glen's brother. Literally. He walked with his head down, eyes focused on the phone in his hand and not watching where he was going until his computer bag was tangled up with Birdie's walker.

"Oh no, I'm so sorry." He pulled until the strap came loose, brushing a hand through his thinning hair. "I wasn't looking where I was going— Oh, wait . . ." One eye narrowed. "Bird, right?"

"Birdie, actually."

"Right. I'm Richard. Nice to see you again. Glen talks a lot about his 'gang.'" His demeanor was different from the man she'd met the morning of the ice storm. Less taciturn, more friendly. She wondered what had caused the change.

"Is everything okay with Glen?" she said, wondering if his appearance meant something.

Richard rubbed his chin, looked behind him toward Glen's apartment. "Not really, Bird."

She pressed her lips together. Seemed nicknames were a thing for the brothers.

"He cut himself slicing onions for a sandwich. Nearly took his finger off. Jonie called me; I guess he'd gone for a walk afterward and left a trail of blood on the sidewalk that alarmed the staff. All he had on his finger was a regular Band-Aid, and it had soaked clear through." Richard shook his head, hints of exasperation bruising the skin under his eyes. "He needed stitches."

There was a twist in her stomach for Glen, and even for Richard, who seemed genuinely concerned. "That's terrible," she said.

Richard nodded. "He blames me."

"For cutting his finger?"

He shook his head. "For everything that didn't go well in his life. For living here. For getting old. For being a shitty brother. Everything."

Birdie hesitated. His oversharing had caught her off guard. Too intimate, too cozy for someone she didn't know.

Richard rubbed the back of his neck. "Has he been different lately?"

"I haven't known him for long."

"I know. I mean, forgetful? Emotional? Not stable?"

Birdie heard the toll of a warning bell. Was Richard fishing for something negative to use in his plan to move Glen to a nursing home? His concern rubbed her the wrong way, coming off as forced, insincere. Reminding her of Felix's own hurtful words. She pasted on a smile. This wasn't her fight, but she sure as hell wasn't going to tell on Glen, even if she had noticed a few lapses in his memory. It was nothing that should send him to a nursing home or be of concern to Richard. "Nothing at all. Glen is just a delight."

"Really?" Richard's forehead rolled into lines. "Okay. But if you do notice anything"—he handed her a card—"mind letting me know? If anything, I don't know, major happens?" He finished off with a smile that showed yellowing teeth, the front one chipped, the rest in need of a good brushing.

She took the card. "Of course."

When he left, she went inside her apartment and tossed the business card into one of her junk drawers. If she was worried about Glen, she'd speak to Glen first, not rat him out to his brother.

Twenty-Eight

She didn't sleep well that night, but not because of back pain or restless legs or any of the normal reasons. Instead, she tossed and turned, her dreams haunted by dead parakeets and nursing homes and Faith screaming for help. She woke up late, sweaty from fractured sleep, with one arm pinned beneath her. A message from Louise on her phone:

She came back this morning.

Thank you, Birdie typed. Do you ever sleep?

Not much, but I can sleep when I'm dead. ☺

Birdie laughed at her phone. Bubbles appeared, then disappeared. Birdie waited, but nothing more came through. She put the phone down, disappointed.

Cobwebs of her dream trailed around her, tangling together with Faith's cries, Everly's face, and Dorothea's words from last night. She pushed up out of bed and got dressed. She didn't care how crazy she sounded—that girl was coming to live with her today.

〜

As soon as she stepped into the hallway, Birdie heard the beautiful chords of a cello coming from inside Joseph's apartment. It took her a moment to realize that the music was not a recording and to remember that the only cellist she knew was Everly. She felt mostly happy that the young woman was inside and safe, but a small part of her stung at being left out. It was an unfamiliar and juvenile feeling.

She breathed in and knocked. Glen answered, a wide smile pushing up his rosy cheeks. She noticed his ring finger, bandaged and splinted. "Our little Bird is here! Come in, come in!"

It vexed her that they would invite Glen and not her, but she walked inside like none of it mattered. Another jolt of surprise to see a couch with two fluffy red pillows and a coffee table had been added to Joseph's spare decor. Everly sat on the edge of the coffee table with a cello between her knees. She made a beautiful sight: her long arms elegantly splayed, the bow clasped delicately between her fingers, the paleness of her skin and hair in stark contrast to the dark, glossy wood of her instrument.

Joseph sat on one of his kitchen stools, but when he saw Birdie he hopped to his feet—looking a little guilty, Birdie liked to think. Everly, too, she imagined, with the way she fidgeted around the cello. The small satisfaction it gave her was enough to clear away the other feelings. Could she blame them, after how she'd acted when she saw them last?

She looked around at the new furniture. "Looks like a grown man's apartment now."

"I ordered this after our heist in Jonie's office. They were delivered yesterday. What do you think?"

"They're perfect," she said, and shared a look with Everly. It was a small moment, but it felt normal, like all had been forgiven, and Birdie relaxed, deciding she didn't have to bombard the girl with her invitation right that minute.

"The lovely Everly was just giving us a private concert!" Glen said, taking a seat on the sofa.

"Carry on, please." Birdie leaned back into the stool beside Joseph. "It sounded beautiful."

String music flooded the apartment—beautiful, haunting, at some points moving Birdie to tears. When Everly was done, the four of them sat in silence, soaking up the last half hour.

Birdie was the first to speak. "I'm sorry about yesterday. I know that you were both just being honest. I'm . . . I guess I'm a little embarrassed about it. It was just a really bad day."

Everly carefully laid her cello on its side and walked over to Birdie, her hand holding one arm. "I don't think you have anything to be embarrassed about. It just shows how much you care about Allison and so many others. I'm sorry too."

Joseph cleared his throat. "I was out of line."

Birdie shook her head, relieved. "You weren't. I do understand how, well, *crazy* it must have looked to you. But that room, all those women . . . I just believe they deserve answers. Like Faith. I need you to know that I still believe something happened to her and I don't intend to back down about it."

Joseph nodded. "Okay, then."

A rush of warm relief swept across Birdie's back.

"If I may"—Glen stood—"what on earth are we talking about?"

Everly and Joseph said nothing, leaving Birdie to choose how much she wanted to share with Glen. *In for a penny.* "Well, Glen, my dear friend was murdered, and I suppose I've never gotten over it. Partly because the police said she took her own life and I know she'd never do that, and partly because I was in love with her and I was too chicken to say it. And these two called me out on it yesterday, so I threw them out."

Everly's eyes bugged, and Joseph's mouth did that thing that was a smile but not. Birdie felt stronger for having said it out loud like that.

"*Throw* is strong language," Joseph said.

"Yeah," Everly said. "It was more like *politely asked.*"

Birdie waved a hand. "However it happened, I'm sorry."

Glen brightened. "Secrets abound among our little group. Everly, with her musical prowess, and you, Birdie, with an unrequited love."

Birdie gritted her teeth, and she noticed that Everly's lips had whitened from holding in a laugh.

Glen seemed not to notice. "But oh, I am sorry about the death of your friend. Tragic, I'm sure." He folded and unfolded his arms across his round belly, looking uncomfortable.

"Thank you, Glen." She straightened her shoulders. "Yesterday, I found parakeets out by the garages that had been . . ." She swallowed, remembering. "Cut into pieces."

Everly's hand flew to her mouth.

"This isn't a coyote," she said. "It's a person, and—"

"Dorothea sent me the photos." Glen held one hand out like he had some profound news. "I have been in touch with the police, and they are in agreement that with our local madman and this new development, something sinister is afoot here at Sunny Pines."

Birdie faltered, a mixture of relief that the police were finally taking this seriously and annoyance that it had had to come from Glen. She shook her head. Did it matter? The important thing was that they were finally concerned. "Are they taking Faith's disappearance seriously now too?"

A grave look passed over Glen's face. "I must warn you, Birdie, she has been missing for some time, and they aren't confident it's because of foul play."

A lump in her throat, and all Birdie could do was nod. "I know." She turned to Everly. "Which is why I want to ask you something."

Everly, paler than normal. "Those poor parakeets," she murmured.

"And because of that and other things, I don't think it's safe out there for you."

Everly sat down and picked up her cello, holding it like it brought her comfort. "I don't have anywhere else to go."

Birdie straightened her shoulders. "That's not entirely true." She breathed in. "Move in with me."

Joseph made a noise. Everly's head popped up. "With you?"

"It might seem like I'm overreacting, but I'm not." Nerves thinned her voice. "I know what can hap—"

"Um, what about my dogs?"

Birdie breathed out. "Bring them, of course."

"Really?"

"Absolutely. They need as much protection as you. No offense, but those two are the real coyote meat."

Everly's eyes widened above a smile. "Birdie!" she said. She put the cello on the ground and stood. "When should I move in?"

At first, Birdie couldn't speak, overcome by everything: Nan's support, Louise's vigilance, Dorothea looping Glen in to be a bridge to the police, Joseph just being his steadfast self. It had never happened this easily. All those years trying to find Allison's killer, she'd been so alone. Her chin wobbled. "This afternoon?"

Glen clapped his hands, being careful with his injured finger. "It's settled, then. As Albert Einstein famously said, 'We'"—he chortled—"here at Sunny Pines, of course, 'live in that solitude which is painful in youth, but delicious in the years of maturity.' It will be good for us to have you here."

Joseph caught Birdie's gaze, his eyebrows wrinkling close together. Glen's misuse of quotes had become an amusing quirk.

After a pause, Glen said, "I do believe Nan has invited the gang over for lunch. Now that you are one of us, would you like to come, too, Everly dear?"

Everly pulled at her lip with the tips of her fingers, shifted her weight back and forth. "Um." Nobody spoke, all of them seeming to sense that the girl needed to make her own decisions. Eventually, she said very quietly, "Yeah, okay, but I don't want to play for them or anything like that."

Joseph stood. "No, of course not." He grabbed his bottle of whiskey from the cabinet. "Ladies?"

"Don't mind if we do." Birdie led the way to Nan's apartment, smiling the entire time.

~

Nan's place was the same size as Birdie's, and with two walkers and eight people, it was crowded. A smorgasbord of home-cooked dishes covered the small counter space. Birdie left her walker by the door. "Did you defrost *all* of them, Nan?" she said.

Nan winked. "My daughter-in-law will have it restocked by Friday. It's my community service to give the dragon lady something to do."

"Whose granddaughter are you?" Jean called from where she sat across the room in a wooden chair next to Louise.

"That's Everly," Louise said, and both of the women waved, their white bobs glossy and bouncing.

Everly gave a small wave back, her face turning a beet red that looked almost like a tan against her white-blond hair.

"You know Louise, and that's Jean, Sunny Pines' resident senior models." Jean and Louise both laughed. "Everly is, uh, my friend." With Dorothea there, Birdie didn't want to put the girl under a microscope any more than she already was by adding that she lived in one of the campers. The place was too crowded and the noise level too high for follow-up questions; Birdie was relieved.

"What on earth did you do to your finger, Glen?" Jean said above the din of conversation.

"Oh, that. Nothing of consequence." Glen studied his hand. "My brother slammed the car door shut on it."

Jean winced. Birdie stood frozen by the food, unsure if she should say something or leave it be. Was Richard telling the truth or Glen?

She filled a plate and found a seat, surprised to see that with the addition of a few folding chairs, there was a place for everyone. Everly sat next to her, and for the most part, they listened to Glen tell stories about his time as a cop, with Nan pestering him for any gory details. As it turned out, Nan was a fan of horror as well as true crime.

"Glen, did you inform the police about the birds?" Dorothea said.

"I sure did. They think it might be that prowler." Glen shook his head, clearly disturbed. "A sick, sick man. We need to be very careful."

Dorothea raised an eyebrow. "Jonie told me just this morning that the police finally apprehended the prowler. Turns out his family in Fort Collins had reported him missing a few months ago. Left rehab and poof—up and disappeared." Her mouth twisted. "You didn't know about that, Glen? It happened a few days ago."

Glen blew air into his reddened cheeks, and he rubbed hard at his thinning hair. "I suppose they didn't tell me," he spluttered, seeming at a loss for words. "I am retired and maybe not so important as I once was."

Birdie's heart cinched, and Jean clucked her tongue. They all understood what it felt like to be dismissed. As though the more years they accumulated, the less their experiences mattered.

"The important thing is that they got the guy," Nan said.

Louise held up her plastic cup of water. "Hear, hear."

"And that's one suspect we can cross off our list," Nan added.

"There's more?" Jean spoke around a bite of chicken salad.

Nan looked around the room. "Birdie and I think the Vampire Killer is back."

Birdie froze. Nan had tossed the idea out so nonchalantly. She ate a piece of buttered bread, waiting for their skepticism.

Dorothea's face soured. "Don't be ridiculous."

"Who's the Vampire Killer?" Everly's voice was barely above a whisper.

"A Denver serial killer from back in the eighties," Louise offered.

Glen made a little humming noise in his throat. "He terrorized the city, dear girl."

Jean was shaking her head. "Never heard of him. I didn't live here then, but I've heard of Bundy and Rader and that Dahmer guy, and I didn't live where they were either."

"Rader." Nan stuck her fork in the air. "A real psychopath, that one."

"I never heard of a serial killer in Denver, and I grew up here," Everly said. "What did he . . . you know, do?"

Nan opened her eyes wide, pushing her eyebrows into the soft wrinkles of her forehead. She put her plate on the coffee table and scooted forward, then told it like a bedtime story. "He kidnapped, tortured, then drained his victims of their blood."

Dorothea's upper lip curled in distaste.

"There was a real panic," Louise said. "Remember how people started carrying crucifixes and wearing garlic?"

Birdie remembered, but all of that had been nonsense when there had been a cold-blooded *mortal* man murdering innocent women.

Joseph, always so quiet in a group, said, "Everyone speculated about what he did with the blood."

"Drink it?" Jean guessed.

Joseph shrugged. "Or used it in some kind of ritual?"

"Nobody knows," Nan said. "But he only had one kind of victim—women."

"Forgettable women," Birdie murmured.

Glen craned his neck to look at Birdie. "What did you say?"

Birdie wiped her mouth, set her plate aside, her stomach soured. "They were addicts, prostitutes, runaways, immigrants, women of color—people who could be easily written off because they didn't matter to polite society." Her bitter tone shifted the joviality of the room into something darker, and a few of them looked down at their laps. They knew it was true. And Birdie couldn't help her thoughts drifting to Faith. "It still happens today. Young girls, women, going missing, authorities assuming they ran away, discovering much later they'd been kidnapped, murdered, sold into the sex trade. You name it. My . . ." She swallowed, a familiar fire stoked inside of her that, once lit, she found hard to quench. "Allison was like that. A single mom—"

"It's why you're so worried about Faith," Joseph said gently.

"And me." Everly touched Birdie's arm; the two of them like supportive bookends.

Nan's oxygen tank hummed. "Who's Allison?"

"Birdie's greatest love," Glen said, and Dorothea's shocked inhale, combined with Glen's unexpected share, turned Birdie's fingers into talons. Birdie had lived her life openly ever since she'd learned that hiding was her biggest regret of all. But something about Dorothea's old-fashioned gasp reminded her of her parents, and that struck a nerve.

"Come now, Dorothea," she couldn't help but say. "It's the twenty-first century, for God's sake. You have a problem with who I choose to love? Who anyone chooses to love? At this stage of your life?" Birdie's gaze was locked on the woman.

Dorothea wiped at something on her jeans. "I don't have to accept what I don't think is right . . ." The woman's words were strong, but the fact that her eyes remained on her own lap wasn't lost on Birdie.

"Oh no." Nan pushed up from her seat and grabbed for her walker, her slender shoulders hunched up by her ears. "I'm leaving before a fight breaks out."

That broke the tension, and Birdie and the others laughed. Even Dorothea managed a smile. "Nan!" Louise said. "You can't leave, you live here."

"But before you go, can I have some of the dragon lady's apple-crumb pie?" Jean said.

Birdie decided to let Dorothea's comments go; as long as the woman kept her opinions to herself, then things would be fine. Birdie had learned that sometimes, that was just how things worked.

A few minutes later, with the pie dished up, Nan asked, "So, what happened to Allison?"

The food Birdie was chewing turned to dust; she took a sip of water to wash it down. Nan was a ruthless and tiny detective, a Chihuahua with a bone.

Joseph coughed. "Well now, Nan. That's a bit private, I think." Coming to Birdie's rescue like he was wont to do. She liked that about him—not the rescue part, as Birdie was no damsel in distress, but the loyal part of him that was always willing to stick his neck out for a friend.

She looked around. They were quiet, for once, everyone—even Dorothea—waiting for her to answer. She settled herself with an inhale. "I met Allison when she was nineteen, pregnant, and all alone."

The room was quiet, a united held breath.

"She moved in with me, and later, when Felix was born, well, we became a little family." She pinched the fabric of her pants, the bones of her chest vibrating from the thumping of her heart. The next part she didn't have to say, but she'd come this far and she figured, well, *In for another penny.* "Good money was hard to make as a single woman back then, and my landlord . . ." She hesitated and chanced a look at Glen; she hadn't mentioned that she'd known his father when he'd been their landlord. She shuddered. The man had been a slimy parasite who sniffed out women with their backs against a wall and used it to his advantage. Glen looked nothing and acted nothing like the landlord she remembered. "He had a friend who owned a place where women danced for money. You might not be able to tell now . . ." She'd always kept a sense of humor about it all, choosing that over shame. "But I was quite the dish."

Nan barked a laugh that blew the oxygen tubing from her nose. "You're still a dish, Birdie," she said.

"Quite," Louise agreed, smiling at Birdie.

Birdie loosened her scarf, suddenly warm. "I loved Allison, but I never told her how much. It was much harder to be ourselves back then, you know." A few nods around the room. Everly's arm had found its way around Birdie's shoulders, and the contact calmed her. She straightened her spine and lifted her chin, meeting the eyes of everyone there: Jean and Louise were encouraging; Joseph, supportive, of course; Glen, surprised; Nan, fascinated; and Dorothea . . . well, look at that, she seemed contrite. "I came home from work and Allison was—" Fifty-two years later and the clarity of that moment in the bathroom was seared into her brain. A porcelain pedestal sink under an oval mirror that reflected the dim lights of the chandelier, white hexagon floor tiles that stretched under the claw-foot bathtub where Allison's body lay slumped, one arm draped over the side. And the blood. In the tub, soaking into the grout on the floor, smeared on her skin. "The police only ever saw Allison for what she was not, and they rushed to judgment by calling it a suicide." Again, Birdie met the eyes of everyone there. "But I knew Allison from her heart out and she would never—I mean, *never*—leave her son behind."

Birdie found her hands were shaking with remembered anger, and she clasped them in her lap.

"Glen, there's something I wanted to tell you." She hadn't brought up the fact that she lived in one of his father's properties, because anything to do with his family seemed to bother him. But now it felt odd not to.

"Whatever is it?" He leaned forward.

"I was living at the Paragon when Allison died."

Someone murmured, "Small world."

Glen looked at her with a deep interest. "You and Allison?"

"And Felix too."

"You don't say." He rubbed his chin.

"Do you remember it? I mean, did you happen to live there at that time?" A spike of hope. Could Glen know something that might give her answers? Her tongue pressed into the roof of her mouth as she waited.

Glen shook his head slowly. "I'm afraid not. My father's buildings were piss pots even then, and I would not have wanted to live there."

Birdie twitched at the harshness of his words. Scattered gasps around the room mirrored her reaction.

"Glen . . ." Dorothea's censorious tone didn't bother Birdie this time.

Glen seemed to have surprised himself, and he leaned forward, eyes warmer with remorse. "I'm sorry, Bird. I didn't mean to be so frank. But, well, as you might have picked up, I have little love lost for my family, I'm afraid, and my father was not someone I wanted to be around."

"It's okay, Glen." And she meant it.

"The police didn't believe you?" Dorothea said, and she sounded surprised and maybe a little fired up about it too.

"I tried to convince them . . ." She shrugged. "But no, they didn't. Years later, when they realized what the Vampire Killer was doing, I wrote to the police again, begged them to reopen Allison's case. We'd lived in that same neighborhood where the first murders happened. Cora, a dancer at the club where I worked, and Freida, a woman with mental health issues who lived in my building."

Everyone leaned in. "You know their names?" Dorothea said.

"I know *everything* about them," Birdie said. "Before Allison died, my neighbor's puppy was found mutilated in the alley behind our building."

Nan's eyebrows shot up. "Animal mutilations? So you think Allison was one of his victims?"

Birdie nodded. "His very first. His mistake."

"Oh my," Louise murmured, and Birdie met Louise's eyes, gray like storm clouds, pretty like the rest of her. "And you never told her how you feel?"

Birdie shook her head. "And the police didn't believe me. Much like they don't believe me about Faith—and from what Glen says, they aren't concerned. They assume she disappeared because she wanted to."

Glen gave a slow, sad nod.

"Oh, that's terrible," Everly said.

There was a sting in Birdie's eyes. Telling everyone had brought it all back with breathtaking clarity. And sharing it with a group of people who genuinely seemed interested and sympathetic felt therapeutic. She sucked air in through her nose. "But the thing that's been the hardest for me to face is that nothing I say or do, no truth I uncover, will ever change the fact that Allison's gone and I never returned her love." She looked down at her hands, the truth of it all sinking deep into her bones. Kind words echoed around the room. Telling them had carved away some of the gunk inside her heart.

Nan's oxygen tank puffed. "My husband gambled all our money away," she said with a shrug. "We lost our house before he walked out on me for my son's fifth-grade teacher." Her voice wobbled. "I wasn't the best mother for a few years after that."

"I left my husband's side to get a bowl of soup from the hospital cafeteria, and when I came back, he'd died." Louise rolled her neck and shoulders like the memory had been wedged there. "I hate soup now."

"I wish I'd been a better husband," Joseph said.

Birdie's honesty was contagious.

"I was offered a modeling contract in New York that I didn't find out about until years later on my mother's deathbed. She'd told them no on my behalf because she'd wanted me to be a proper housewife." Jean stood and did a short walk to the kitchen for more pie. "I might have been the original Twiggy, but now we'll never know. I was a terrible housewife."

Everly laughed.

"I longed to be an artist of some renown," Glen said.

Joseph's secret smile mirrored around the room. Glen's most endearing quality had become the narcissistic thoughts he shared with clueless abandon.

Birdie braced herself when Dorothea opened her mouth to speak. "I saw a girl being bullied by my classmates every day when I was in high school and I did nothing about it." Gone was her typical high-minded demeanor. In a much quieter voice: "She jumped off a bridge when we were juniors."

A respectful silence followed until Everly said, "Ever since my dad died, my anxiety about being around people has debilitated me. Now I live in one of the campers on the empty street because I lost my scholarship, my housing—everything."

And it was Dorothea who spoke first. "You're here with us. That seems like a good first step."

Birdie widened her eyes, surprised at the woman's kind sentiment.

Everly shrugged. "Yeah, I don't know why, but you're all easy to be around."

"It's the gray hair," Louise said. "Makes everyone think we're harmless."

Nan piped up. "And the walkers and oxygen tanks too."

Everly smiled. "Yeah, maybe."

Something new bound the group, their honesty softening and opening them up to each other.

Birdie thought about what Felix had said, about her searching for absolution. The truth of it tapped her on the back.

"So you think Faith might be the Vampire Killer's newest victim?" Jean said. "Because you haven't spoken to her?"

"With her mother in Puerto Rico and not much of a support group here," Joseph said, echoing Birdie, "there's really no way to know if she's okay."

"And she left her sliding glass door unlocked," Glen pointed out.

"You've called her?" Dorothea said.

Birdie nodded.

"And emailed her?" Jean added.

"And googled her and her mother, went to her apartment—"

"Rescued her cat," Joseph said.

"And talked to her neighbor, sent her a message through her Etsy account. No response." Birdie did not sense doubt, only a keen interest. She clasped her hands and squeezed. "But it's all come to nothing."

"Maybe we can help," Louise said.

Birdie's heart skipped a beat. "You want to help?"

"If Faith is missing, she deserves to be looked for," Dorothea said quietly.

"Okay, yes, whatever you can do." Birdie's entire body buzzed. "Thank you."

They finished their desserts, fully decimating the dragon lady's frozen-food section of Nan's freezer.

Nan brought the entire conversation full circle. "I read in the paper that this week marks the thirty-fifth anniversary of the Vampire Killer's last murder before he went poof!" She looked around at everyone, nodding like they all knew this fact.

"I think I saw something about that on the news," Joseph said.

"There's a documentary on Netflix," Louise said.

Nan brightened and her oxygen tank puffed along with her breathing. "So what do you all think happened to him?"

Everly wrapped her arms across her body. "Wasn't he caught?"

Nan shook her head, smiling like it was the greatest story ever. "No, he was not. He killed ten women." Here, she paused and her face softened when she caught Birdie's eye. "I mean, eleven . . . And then poof! He stopped and nobody ever heard from him again."

Birdie pressed a palm to her chest. It meant more than Nan knew to have Allison's murder acknowledged by someone.

Jean smirked. "Maybe he found God."

Louise snorted.

"Maybe he was arrested for something else?" Dorothea suggested.

Joseph leaned forward in his chair. "Or moved?"

"Or he got married, had a family and a career, and got too busy," Jean said.

Nan clicked her tongue and gestured at Jean with her pointer finger and thumb cocked. "That's more feasible than you may realize, Jean," she said. "They've speculated that the Vampire Killer may be more like Rader: a true psychopath who's been able to fit in with the rest of us." She seemed delighted to share her knowledge, and Birdie decided that the conversation would go equally well around a campfire, with Nan holding a flashlight underneath her chin.

"Maybe he goes to church like us," Nan said. "At this point, maybe he's got grandchildren too." She looked around the room, her eyes narrowed, suspicious. "Maybe he was a she? Although that's statistically unlikely. Maybe he's retired like us, with our same aches and pains and bad vision."

"Hey!" Jean piped up. "Speak for yourself. I hardly need correction."

Joseph, who sat ramrod straight with his arms folded tightly across his chest, grunted. "A retired serial killer. Well, there's a thought. I guess age catches even the devil, eventually."

That lightened the mood yet again, and somebody chuckled. Birdie wiped crumbs from her lap.

"There's one possibility that none of you guessed," Glen said.

Everyone turned to him expectantly.

"That he's dead."

Birdie felt herself grow smaller. With each passing year of the Vampire Killer's silence, it had become a possibility. In most ways, his silence was a relief. Women were safe—at least from him. In other ways that she could never admit to anyone, it swept the ground out from under her. How could she prove Allison's murder without more evidence? More proof? More chance of a connection? These thoughts haunted her, and she hated herself for them.

"The best possibility, if you ask me," Louise said.

"Can we stop talking about serial killers?" Dorothea's words were void of her usual firmness. "At least for now."

For once, Birdie agreed with Dorothea. Speculating about why the serial killer stopped so suddenly always left her vaguely depressed because it reminded her of the women who'd never gotten the answers they deserved.

Joseph picked up his bottle of whiskey. "A digestif?"

Louise patted her hair. "Fancy."

Dorothea looked at her watch. "Isn't it a bit early?"

"It's five o'clock somewhere," Jean said.

Nan pushed to standing; it took a few seconds after sitting for so long. Birdie understood—heck, they all did. "I'll get the shot glasses."

Twenty-Nine

ALLISON

Karen screams. It vibrates the room with Birdie's friends, worms around them, through them, but they do not hear her. We take her in our arms. Her soul is young, and she is the girl who runs away from one monster only to be taken by another. When Birdie speaks about Karen, she holds the girl's name in her heart, and Karen is soothed.

Freida stands behind the couch and circles her arms around Birdie's neck in a loose hug. Protecting her. Maybe that is why Birdie shares her truth with the others. A future is decided because of it. One where her friends stand by her.

They shimmer, a reflection of their long lives and their souls poking through skin thinned by age. It is hard for us to be with them like this. They sense pieces of us in the quickening of their pulses and the glow of memories that cluster around them. Nan thinks of her youthful days, when her body moves as she wants it to and her husband is faithful. After he left, Nan was angry most of the time and forgot that she was a mother first. She believes that's why her son married someone more like his father.

Joseph's wife would have loved it here. Louise tastes Italian wedding soup hot on her tongue and thinks she might be sick. Glen wants to tell Birdie what he knows. Jean imagines herself walking down a runway. And Dorothea is silenced by thoughts of the girl she did nothing to help.

It whips us into a frenzy, and when they disperse, it is a relief.

I am left holding Karen and whispering peace.

Thirty

It had been a long afternoon, yet Birdie wasn't depleted the way she normally would be after social gatherings. It seemed they'd all left with slightly different perspectives about each other. After saying goodbye to Everly and Joseph, who'd been kind enough to walk Everly back to her camper and help her gather her things, Birdie waved to Glen, who had stopped outside his door. It wasn't her business, but Birdie wanted to ask about his finger again. She was worried for her friend.

"I saw your brother yesterday." She bit the inside of her cheek. "He said you cut your finger slicing onions."

Glen's eyes dimmed until they were almost black. "My brother's a liar."

Birdie studied him for a beat. He looked angry but also vulnerable. "I'm sorry, Glen." She wished she could do something for him.

A smile tugged the edges of his mouth. "I find myself inspired by our little gang."

"Oh?"

"Indeed. Enough to think about painting again."

"That's wonderful, Glen."

"Indeed. *Buonanotte*, Bird."

Inside her apartment, warmed by the intimacy of friendship, Birdie realized that, like Glen, she was inspired, too, and felt a rush of optimism thinking about Felix. He was just worried about her, like he always had been. And it wasn't fair of her to expect so much of him.

With all the support from the people here, Birdie realized how unfair she'd been to Felix. With a palm against her chest, she recalled the grieving little boy she'd held until, sweaty and exhausted, he'd cried himself to sleep. She dialed Felix's number.

"Hi, Mom." He sounded reserved, and her confidence deflated.

"Hello, sweetheart." She tensed, unsure what to say next, nervous that it would be wrong. The anger and the hurt that had saturated his voice when they last spoke punctured her nerves. She wanted this call to go better.

"How are you?" he said.

"I'm good, I really am. In fact, today I had a lovely lunch with a few of my new friends. It was very nice."

"Great. You do sound good, Mom." A note of hopefulness in his voice.

"I do, don't I?" She was riding a high; she could feel the way it inflated the air around her. She breathed in, struck by sudden clarity. "You were right, you know, encouraging me to move here. That house was too much. If I haven't thanked you for that, well . . . thank you." Another pause. She tugged at her bottom lip.

"You're welcome, Mom. I just want you to be happy." A thickness to his words.

"I know you do, sweetheart." His childhood voice: *Are you happy, Mom?*

"I'm sorry about our last call. I—I did hear what you said last time, and you're right. I have felt so much guilt about your mom."

"Mom—"

"No, let me finish. You know what I've held on to. I should have gotten the lock fixed. I should have returned her love when I had the chance." She rode the tail end of the high she'd felt from the support of her friends. "And you're right about whatever your therapist helped you understand. I have wanted absolution. I have believed that if I can prove her murder, I'll gain her forgiveness. You're right about all of it." She inhaled, fingertips tingling. Time was running out to find this murderer, but in some ways it felt like the clock had just started ticking. "I can't change the past or the ways that I've hurt you, but I can try to be more present." She sighed. "And I want you to know . . ." She thought of Louise stepping out for soup when the love of her life died. No time like the present. "You are the son of my heart and I love you, Felix."

A few deep breaths came over the line. "I love you, too, Mom."

"Oh, and I have good news! The intruder I told you about has been caught."

"That's great." Hesitant, like he was afraid she'd say something he didn't want to hear.

She wanted to tell him so much more, but she held back. It wasn't the time.

"Did you schedule a follow-up with your primary care? Want me to come with you?"

She froze. His question was intrusive, hinting at the concerns he'd mentioned yesterday. That Birdie was losing pieces of her faculties.

"That won't be necessary." Her heart ached at the emotional distance between them.

"And are you still worried about that cleaner friend of yours?"

She knew the answer he wanted to hear; still, it was hard to lie to him, so she opted for mostly true. "Of course I'm still worried, but I'm hoping for the best." She bit her tongue to keep from adding that her friends were as concerned as she was. And she stayed absolutely silent about Everly moving in with her. That would only add to the worry Felix wore like a second skin.

"Give my love to Sharon and the boys."

"I will. Love you, Mom."

They hung up, and Birdie sat with her phone in her hand, staring at the black screen and wishing she didn't have to lie to her son.

~

Something cold touched her arm, and Birdie awoke with a scream, staring into the single black eye of Everly's ugliest pug. Its tongue lolled through the hole in the space between its misaligned jaws and licked her again.

"Allegro!" Everly ran into Birdie's bedroom and grabbed the dog from her bed. "I'm sorry, Birdie. He likes you."

Birdie sat up in bed, a little disgusted by the wet tongue. "How did he get up here?"

Everly held the dog in her arms and flipped him up to kiss his stomach. He grunted, legs sticking straight out. "He might not look athletic, but this dog can jump. Can't you, Allegro?"

"You're up early." It was Everly's first morning here.

"Some of my students live in different time zones, so we meet early. I made coffee."

Everly took the dog from the room, but as soon as she set him down, he shot back through the crack in the door and, by some feat of strength, popped straight up and onto her bed. He scurried his little legs across the mattress and resumed his spot, nestling into her side. Birdie couldn't help but smile at his lolling tongue and soft eye. "That was something, Allegro—but joke's on you, buddy, I'm getting up."

Everly had turned on the fireplace and a few lamps, so the apartment was already warm and cozy when Birdie left her bedroom.

She sat in her chair with a cup of coffee. The door to the spare room stood ajar, and Birdie caught a glimpse of Everly's few possessions, including her cello, among the photos of women that papered the walls. "Oh," she said, and set her coffee down. She'd meant to take it all down before Everly arrived but had forgotten. "Do you mind all that in there?"

Everly looked up from her tablet. "Your research?"

Birdie made her way to the room.

Everly joined her, staring at the pictures. "You did a lot of work learning about all these women, Birdie. I loved reading all their stories.

Like how Carol played the violin and she was really good, and that Barb's dog was a little pug like Allegro and Adagio."

Birdie turned to her, hand to her chest. "You read all this?"

Everly's eyebrows scrunched closer. "Yeah, of course I did. I thought that was the point of hanging it up. To remind people that they were women with hopes and dreams first, before they were victims."

Birdie leaned against the doorway, heart in her throat. Across the room, Allison looked at her from a photo Birdie had taken one fall afternoon. Behind her, the trees flamed gold and red, making her hair darker, her eyes a chocolate brown. Allison stared straight into the camera, caught in a moment of candor, just before a smile, a perfect moment. "Yeah, that's exactly what this is."

There was a knock on her door, and Birdie hurried to answer it: Louise, with her cheeks lightly pink, like she'd just been outside. "I think you're onto something with Faith. So I made some phone calls."

A squeeze around her heart. "You did that for me?"

Louise's smile deepened the elegant lines of her cheekbones. "I've spent most of my life wishing I'd done more. But you, well—you're such a go-getter and determined. You inspire me, and I figured I could do something to help." She held out a file folder. "I put together a timeline from just before the ice storm to now. It includes your two visits to her apartment, the conversation with the neighbor, and then a phone call I had with the apartment manager." Louise tugged at her lip. "They did say she was late on her rent."

Birdie's stomach dropped; she didn't want to be right. "Late?"

Louise nodded. "That can't be good, right?"

"Not at all."

"Maybe this will help with convincing the police to take it more seriously?"

Birdie had another idea. "Or convincing the news stations."

"Even better." Louise cocked an eyebrow. "Let me know if you need any help with that. A cute bichon or two might get more viewers."

Birdie smiled. "I will."

That afternoon, Birdie left messages and sent emails to the local news and radio stations, and had sent a few more emails to Faith's inbox. She was antsy; this was a treadmill she'd been on before. This time, emboldened by the support of her friends, Birdie had no intention of getting off until someone listened to her. But with nothing happening right away, she needed a distraction.

"Everly, I was thinking of going to the library today. Would you like to come with me?"

Everly held one arm to her body, and Birdie could tell by the reddened tips of her ears that she wasn't being rude, just avoiding the prospect of being around people. Birdie went on. "There's a local author talking about her book—some steamy fantasy with dragons. I'm a fan of dragons, apocalypse woes, and the occasional zombie love story. What do you like?"

Everly shrugged. "I'm not much of a reader."

Birdie let the silence draw out. "You know, I don't want to tell you how to feel, but I find that when the world's upheavals are affecting my sense of peace, reading settles me."

Everly laid the tablet screen down on her lap. "My mom loved to read too. On the beach, especially."

"Ah." Birdie sipped her coffee. "Is that a good memory?"

Everly crossed an ankle over her thigh, pulled at the hem of her pants. "After she left, I imagined her on a beach somewhere, under an umbrella, with tan skin and pretty saltwater waves in her hair, the ocean making perfect little whooshing sounds in the background."

"Mmm." Birdie pictured the girl left behind like that, in a dark house with a father who was slowly losing his mind. A different thought stung her heart. What had it been like for Felix to grow up with her dark research displayed on the walls of their home?

"My dad didn't read books—or not that I remember. He wrote music, or tried to, but in the end it was just notes."

Birdie didn't know what to say; the compactness of Everly's life gathered in her chest. "The talk starts at one, but if that seems like too much, we could just go now and peruse the books. Maybe there's one about a young cellist who learns that her music gives her magical powers and—oh, I don't know, a pet dragon."

That put a smile on Everly's face. "You have a thing for dragons?"

"Nah, just a thing for good stories that let me forget about the world for an hour or two."

Everly's chest moved in and out, and she nodded. "Okay, Birdie. I think I can go to the library with you."

~

They left the library, each with a book in hand. For a weekday morning, the library had been busy: story time in one corner with a class of preschoolers; what might have been a homeschool group of elementary kids on the computers; and the usual folks like Birdie, quietly sifting through the shelves.

It had been hard to watch Everly struggle in the public setting, see the light sheen of sweat across her forehead, and Birdie felt certain she heard the rapid beat of the girl's own heart. She wondered if it had been a mistake to encourage her to come along. Was it too much? Everly stayed close to Birdie's side, and without knowing, most people probably assumed she was a thoughtful and perhaps overly attentive granddaughter, and not that she was using Birdie's physical presence as a shield.

They left within an hour, Everly with *The Violin Conspiracy*, a mystery about a stolen Stradivarius that the librarian had expertly recommended, and Birdie with a Patrick Rothfuss novella.

She waited for her garage door to lower, Everly holding both their books. "Thanks, Birdie."

The door thunked to a close. "Not as bad as you thought?"

"Not quite, no."

Birdie smiled. "Well, that's a win, if you ask me."

A few doors down the aisle of garages, Birdie saw Glen opening his door to leave. He waved and made his way over to where they stood. "Good morning!" His eyes lighted on Everly. "I heard you'd been captured by a bird." He laughed, always a fan of his own jokes.

A warm breeze tickled the skin on Birdie's neck, and she shivered. "Any news, Glen?"

"Not yet, I'm afraid."

"I've called news and radio stations to help spread the word."

Glen looked troubled. "Bird, don't you think some matters are best left to law enforcement?"

She rolled her shoulders, disappointed in Glen. He sounded like Dorothea. "I'm sorry, Glen, but no, not always."

He dipped his head, perturbed, she could tell, and it curled her fingers. "Good day, ladies."

They left Glen, and when they reached her apartment, Birdie saw Joseph power-walking toward them from the direction of the front door, alarm in the firm set of his lips. "Jonie's heard about Everly staying with you," he said, so fast the words jumbled together.

"What?"

Before he could repeat himself, Jonie strode around the corner. When she stopped, her hair fluttered limply. She took in Everly. "Um, Birdie . . . Well, I've heard you had a guest." She smiled, her lipstick a tad too dark, bringing out the fine lines around her lips.

Sunny Pines was advertised as independent living, but the rules sometimes felt like the exact opposite. Like the business about preapproval of guests and guests being only family and family only allowed to stay for X amount of days in a row and other nonsense like that. Birdie pasted on a smile and straightened her shoulders, wishing for the youthful swing of Louise's hair, the strong spine of Joseph's back. "This is my great-niece, Everly."

Jonie's nose scrunched. "But don't you live in one of the campers?" she asked Everly.

Everly held one arm across her body. Joseph stepped in so that he partially blocked her.

"She's a traveling soul, Jonie, but she's decided to stay put for a bit, and with all this murderer-on-the-loose business, I asked her to stay with me for a few days." A bit of truth mixed with a white lie. "I'm sure you'd do the same thing for your family."

Jonie was already nodding, head ducked and looking abashed. "Yes, of course, of course." She gave an uncomfortable wave. "Oh, in case any of you were planning on going to the concert this weekend, they had to cancel because of some family issue."

"Was that the string ensemble?" Joseph asked.

Jonie nodded, then started to back away. "Bye, then—and sorry for the misunderstanding, Birdie." Her smile was warm. "And, Everly, welcome, of course."

When she was gone, Birdie mumbled, "Dorothea." The rule follower had gotten wind of Everly staying with her and said something to Jonie.

Joseph turned and was staring at Everly. "Do you think you could play a small concert here?"

Pink streaks crawled up Everly's cheeks. "This weekend?"

"No, no, of course not. Just sometime. Like a goal."

Everly sucked in one cheek. "I don't know."

From inside, the dogs, having heard them standing outside the door, started barking. Birdie quickly unlocked the door. "Good thing they didn't do that when Jonie was here. I don't think she'd be thrilled about dogs without deposits staying here."

Joseph followed them both inside. The smaller of the two jumped up onto Joseph's shins; Allegro sniffed his feet. Without looking up from the dog, Joseph said, "So, Everly, my wife's therapist . . . well, I started going to her after Sofia died. I hope it's okay, but I talked about you at my last session and she's given me a referral for another therapist for you, for therapy, if, well—if that's something you think you want."

There was a brief silence in which Birdie, surprised at Joseph for making such a bold move, wondered how his presumption might affect Everly.

"I lost my health insurance when I dropped out of school," she said.

Joseph gently rubbed behind the pug's ears. "You know, we save all this money so we can retire, and then when we're retired, we keep saving it for fear that we'll run out." He looked up at Everly, and a lump hardened in Birdie's throat. Whatever his flaws had been, Joseph was a deeply good man. "If you think therapy is something you'd like to try, I can't think of a better investment."

A shy smile played around the corners of her mouth. "Yes, okay." Then she hugged him. "Thank you," Birdie heard her whisper.

Birdie caught Joseph's eyes over Everly's shoulder. He patted her back, blinking fast and clearly surprised by the girl's reaction. Birdie hugged her arms across her body. Felix wanted her to go to therapy. Maybe after they found Faith, she'd think about it. If Everly could do it, so could she.

Thirty-One

It had only been a few days, but Everly was a bright spot that Birdie hadn't realized she needed, infusing her apartment with a quiet peacefulness, even with her two yappy dogs. One afternoon, Louise stopped by and the three of them looked over the information they had collected and added to the timeline everything they knew about Faith's disappearance. Later that day, Everly was busy typing on her computer, a deep concentration line between her eyes while she worked. Finally, she pulled a piece of paper off the printer and handed it to Birdie. "Is this okay?"

Faith's face was in a square at the top of the page above the line *Have You Seen Me?* Below that were a few lines describing her height, possible weight, and other details.

"I asked Louise what she was wearing when she saw her that day of the ice storm, and I pulled her picture off her Etsy page." Everly stood with one arm trapping the other. "I thought we could have copies made and hang them up around the area."

A lump hardened in Birdie's throat. "You did this for her?"

"And for you."

Birdie patted Everly's arm. "This is perfect." She stood. "Let's go."

In the hallway outside, they ran into Glen. "Just the ladies I was hoping to see!" he said, and then, with a rather dramatic bow: "Everly, could I ask something of you?"

She smiled. "Sure."

"Would you mind performing another concert for me?"

"Yeah." She looked at Birdie. "Can we do it at your place this time?"

"Yes, of course," Birdie said. "We'll invite Joseph too."

Glen bowed again. "Wonderful, wonderful. I'll bring a pie."

Later, with Allegro curled up on her lap on the sofa, Joseph to her right, and Glen once again in her chair, Everly played. Birdie didn't know the cello well, apart from having heard about Yo-Yo Ma, and while she considered herself to be a discerning audience regardless, she thought Everly was exceptional. When she played, it was effortless—her limbs, the cello, each an extension of the other that created a beautiful flow with the music.

Everly switched to a different piece that reverberated through Birdie's body. "Hallelujah" touched on something deep inside of her and brought to mind a particular night with Allison. As a Christmas and early-birthday present, Birdie had bought tickets to see The Who at the Coliseum. They never splurged, but that night they had a babysitter for Felix and dinner plans at the Cherry Cricket before the concert.

At the restaurant, Allison turned heads in her embroidered peasant blouse and bell-bottom jeans. She was stunning. When they were shown to a booth in back, Allison slid in right beside Birdie, the way couples did. They'd giggled about it, but when Allison's leg touched hers under the table, Birdie's throat turned dry. She drank several cups of water and an entire pint of beer; nothing quenched it. Allison leaned an elbow onto the table and had turned to face Birdie, her back to the restaurant so that it felt like it was only the two of them in the dim light of the table lamp. Her long fingers toyed with a sugar packet. *I've decided I don't want to get married.*

It wasn't the first time she'd said it, but something in her voice made it seem different. Like she was trying on the idea.

What about Felix? It was a challenge to support him on what they alone could make. A man's income would make the difference for Allison.

Allison finished her beer and smiled. The blush she'd swept up her cheekbones glimmered in the glow of the small lamp, and Birdie's stomach danced. *You know what I'm saying.* A soft slur to her words—they didn't often drink—and under the table her hand on Birdie's thigh, lightly caressing.

Birdie stiffened, immediately looking over Allison's shoulder to see who might be watching. *He needs a father,* she'd said. She didn't believe that—not really. But to let her feelings override reality was foolish. They danced for money, got naked for strangers. Who was she to want more? Especially when it wasn't available to them in the first place.

He's got two moms. I think that's more than enough.

Longing tied her tongue. Allison's fingers played around her thigh, stirring up images, desires Birdie couldn't own. *Blasphemy,* her father had said, with a look of disgust that had burned into Birdie's soul. Through clenched teeth and with a willpower she didn't own, Birdie said the thing that ruined the rest of their evening.

Think of your son. She was a chorus for judgment in those few words.

Allison had dropped her hand, lips in a frown, disappointment in the downward slope of her eyes. She'd stood and the space between them turned cold and cavernous. *I'm going to the bathroom.* They'd never spoken of it again, until that day outside Sid King's when Allison tried and Birdie stopped her one final time, and the chance to feel her love was gone forever.

Everly pulled her bow through the final chord, and the memory settled low in her stomach.

"Beautiful," Birdie said, her eyes wet, her rejection of Allison a palpable thing that squeezed its arms around her.

Joseph cleared his throat. "Very."

Glen, who had listened to the entire song with his elbows on his knees, fingers steepled under his chin, said, "Enchanting."

Everly spoke to her cello. "My dad loved that song."

"Thank you for sharing it with us." Birdie settled herself with a breath. For a moment, she'd felt Allison there on the couch beside her, fingers entwined with her own.

"Joseph?" Everly said.

"Yes?" Joseph acted like a proud grandfather whenever she played.

"I think I'd like to do that concert." As she spoke, her hair closed like curtains in front of her eyes. She pushed them out of the way, visibly straightened, and looked at Joseph. "I mean, I'd like to do that concert you talked about for Sunny Pines."

Joseph's face lit up. "You would?"

"Yes," she said with a little less confidence.

Glen clapped. "Brava, Everly!"

"I'll talk to Jonie," Joseph said.

"Okay."

"Your upcoming recital puts me in mind of my beloved art." Glen's voice was wistful.

"Do you still have your paintings?" Everly asked, clearly interested. She'd mentioned to Birdie how she felt sorry for Glen. *He seems so full of regret, like he meant to be a lot of things he never was. It makes me sad for him.*

Glen tilted his head. "I would never part with them." Like it was a promise, his Scout's Honor.

"So, not the type of artist who ever wanted to make money, then," Birdie said. Joseph's lips curled at the ends.

Glen seemed annoyed, but he kept his attention on Everly.

"That's kind of like hiding them away, don't you think?" Everly said. "Like what I'm doing too."

Glen touched his beard. "A parallel, yes, of course. We are similar. You hide yourself away because you are afraid, and I let my beautiful art diminish."

Birdie nearly piped up to say she didn't see the parallel in that example, but glued her lips shut. The sharing was therapeutic.

Everly delicately put her cello into its case. "Can I see them sometime?"

Glen smiled, looking thoughtful and a little excited. He rubbed his hands together. Birdie knew that he had a daughter who didn't live close and hardly visited. He must miss her.

"My brother has put them into storage. I'll have to get the key from him."

"Let me know if you need help talking to him, Glen," Birdie said. She felt protective, worried that Richard might trip Glen up, confuse him.

He gave her a quizzical look. "I can handle my brother on my own, Bird."

Birdie hoped he could. "Of course you can."

Thirty-Two

Allison

When Birdie remembers me, I am there with her. In the booth, with my hand on her thigh, my lips tingle, my heart bursts with want. She believes we can't ever be together, not when we put our son first. I do not agree with her.

Louise stands outside Birdie's door, hand raised to knock. Her fluttering heart mimics my own. I like her silky hair and nervous confidence. Her husband is her best friend, and his death leaves her without someone to share the new feelings vibrating against her ribs. His love drapes around her in folds of soft cotton: dependable, safe, what she wants all her life. But not all she wants. He knows that. They are each other's confidants, secret keepers, vaults. Hers, he takes with him to the grave.

Birdie lives as she is, unapologetic and bold, and Louise is drawn to her.

She lets her hand fall to her side, straightens her cardigan, and feels the heat build in her cheeks. Louise is southern and proper—or at least, that's how her mother raised her. She looks at her hands, crisscrossed in blue veins, pimpled with age spots, paper-thin on the palms. With eight decades behind her, what right does she have to such youthful feelings?

These are her thoughts, not my own.

We have substance when they feel alive. And Louise hasn't felt this alive in years.

Louise turns from the door, allowing her illusions of what is and is not allowed at her age to speak for her heart.

I am nothing but a whisper, a disturbance of the air, and I cannot convince Louise that now is the time to live. But there are things bigger even than me. Purpose. Free will. Choice. And right at that moment, Birdie thinks she hears someone and opens the door.

Thirty-Three

"Louise!"

Louise turned, holding something behind her back. "Oh! Birdie, how nice to run into you." She seemed off—nervous, even.

"I thought I heard a knock." Birdie shook her head. "Do you want to come in and listen to Everly?"

Louise ran a hand through her hair and seemed to regroup with a smile. "I would love that sometime, but not now. I'm meeting my daughter for dinner." She wore a pink cardigan over boot-cut jeans, looking as stylish as ever. "How's she doing?"

"Good. I mean, it's only been a couple of days, but it's nice to know she's safe." Birdie inhaled warm apple pie. "Do you bake too?"

"Oh, heavens no, but I have a candle that smells just like I do. My husband was the cook." Louise seemed suddenly insecure.

"Is everything okay?" Birdie had only known Louise for her sunny confidence, not this person who looked unsure of herself.

"Yes, everything's fine. Here." She held out a file folder like the one she'd had the other day.

Birdie smiled. "Another file folder?"

"Old habits from my corporate days." She sounded sheepish. "Nothing seems more official than paperwork in a file folder."

Before Birdie could open it, Louise's hand shot out and her fingers stayed her wrist.

"I hope I haven't overstepped my bounds here, but I know how worried you are about Faith, and for Faith's sake, I sure hope you're wrong."

It felt like a punch to the stomach to hear Louise say it out loud. Of course Birdie wanted Faith to be okay. She wrapped her arms across her chest, shamed. "I hope so, too, Louise."

"I've always told my girls to listen to their intuition, and it seems to me you've lived by it. If you're right about Allison, you could be right about Faith, too, and I don't want to sit here and be part of the problem by doing nothing. I know Glen is trying to get the police to listen, but I had a better idea." She breathed in through her nose like her words had been a sprint. Louise raised her eyebrows at the folder. "You can open it now."

Inside was a single sheet of paper, and on the paper was a name, with a date, time, and web address. "What's this?"

"My granddaughter has a podcast—and a TikTok, too, I think. Anyway, I guess in some circles she's well known. She's a bit like Nan, minus the red hat and with more of an audience. Her show highlights cold cases, and this week she's doing a series on the Vampire Killer, which is why she wants to interview you."

"Me?"

Louise nodded, and this time Birdie was sure the woman was nervous. "I told her all about you and Allison."

Birdie looked at the paper again. "This is for tomorrow."

"It's a video call." She pointed at the web address. "So you just go to that website and plug in the security code when it's time." She tugged at the onyx stone hanging from a chain around her neck. "I thought this might give you a chance to share everything you know about the victims on a somewhat-bigger stage than Sunny Pines. And I didn't mention Faith, but I figured you'd find a way to bring her up too. Maybe we can get people interested enough to look into it, especially since the police don't seem to be getting anywhere."

It was a big gesture, one of trust and respect and the deepest empathy, and Birdie was speechless.

"Are you upset? Should I have minded my own business?"

Birdie took Louise's hand in her own and squeezed, meeting the woman's rainy-day eyes. "This is the kindest thing anyone has ever, ever done for me."

Louise stilled, her shoulders softening with a smile that wove its way across her lips. They stood like that, holding each other's hands, and Birdie felt the air shift and saw something reveal itself from behind Louise's eyes that surprised her. Birdie dropped her hand, heat creeping up her neck at the schoolgirl feelings erupting from her stomach. "Thank you."

"You're welcome." Louise's easy confidence returned, like she'd gotten something heavy off her back. "Oh, and Birdie?"

"Yes?"

"Just remember to be yourself." She started to walk away, stopped to look over her shoulder. "Allison was lucky to have you."

Birdie's heart beat a little faster; Louise's honesty hinted at something more. "I was the lucky one," she said.

~

Everly set up Birdie's computer on her kitchen table, raising it with books so that it was slightly above her. According to Everly, it was a better angle for all ages. Then she moved the small lamp from her hallway and set it behind Birdie's computer, wishing out loud that Birdie had a ring light.

"Would it make me look twenty again?"

"No."

Birdie primped her hair. "Then this will do just fine. Besides, Natasha said the video piece is just for promotional clips." When Birdie looked up the podcast, she realized she'd listened to one or two herself at some point. Louise's granddaughter was funny and down to earth, with a youthful way of putting grisly crimes into perspective and always focusing on the victim. Birdie liked her style and wasn't surprised her podcast was so popular. With over a million true crime junkies tuning in to each episode, Birdie knew Allison's story—and in turn, Faith's—would be heard. Beads of nervous sweat formed on her upper lip, and for the first time in ages, her apartment felt too warm.

Joseph sat in the big chair, squirming in his seat, wiping at his forehead, a bundle of nerves himself. She pursed her lips at him. "I invited you for moral support, Joseph."

"I know. I'm sorry, Birdie. It's just a big deal." The dogs snuggled up on either side of him, their radar for anxiety preternatural.

She fanned herself with a picture from a pile in front of her. She'd brought a few to share if the time seemed right. "I'm aware."

"Time!" Everly said, and Birdie clicked on the Connect button, an excited rush of adrenaline racing down her legs.

A young woman appeared on the screen, hair in a messy bun, glasses framing expressive eyes, and wearing a crewneck sweatshirt. Like a college girl going to the library on a Sunday. In her navy blue blazer and jewelry, Birdie felt overdressed.

"Hi, Birdie!" She waved with a smile, big headphones over her ears and a professional-looking microphone hanging by her face. "I'm Natasha. Thanks for being on the show. Grammy has spoken so highly of you."

"Thanks for having me, Natasha. Louise is a special lady."

"Yes, she is." Natasha squinted through the computer. "And your apartment looks just like hers! I wish we could have recorded there."

"Ah, yes, that would have been nice." Birdie's stiffness had spread to her lips. She breathed and remembered Louise's words: *Be yourself.* She rolled her shoulders and smiled. "I read that many of your listeners are internet sleuths. What's the chance they can unmask the Vampire Killer?"

Natasha grinned. "Well, Birdie, probably about as likely as you and Grammy finding him, but we like a challenge."

Birdie nodded. "Me too." With that, she relaxed, and the rest of the conversation flowed more naturally. She talked about Allison's death, pointed out inconsistencies that she felt had been ignored. Like how sick Allison had been with the flu, how weak and likely unable to make the fatal incision to begin with. They talked about his victims, and how when Birdie had realized the first two had been found at the Paragon, she'd begun doing research of her own that she had shared with the police. Like the mutilated puppy found in the alley behind the building. Or how Cora had worked at the same club as Allison.

In the background, Joseph and Everly watched, emphasizing her points by quietly nodding.

"I mean, Natasha, think about it: we lived in the same neighborhood as those early murders—hell, the same apartment building as one of them. The other victims were purposefully bled out for reasons I've never wanted to guess. Allison's wrist was slit, and studies show that most wrist-cutting attempts have a low mortality rate. Allison's did not because I believe—and I've always believed—that someone else did that to her."

Natasha seemed to take that in, even taking notes on a small notepad beside her.

"But, Birdie, all ten victims were missing significant amounts of blood, enough for the police to suspect he was collecting it. Forgive me for being blunt, but Allison's blood was found mostly at the scene, correct?"

A humming in her ears made Birdie pause. Doubts wormed through her ribs. Her rejection as painful to Allison as her passion had been overwhelming to Sarah. Sarah had tried to end it in a car, Allison in the bath—Birdie made a fist with her hand and tapped it against her thigh. *No.* She *knew* what had happened to Allison.

"They didn't investigate, Natasha. It was a different time back then; women weren't as free as they are now. It wasn't until two years later that the Equal Credit Opportunity Act was passed, guaranteeing that a woman could open up a bank account without a signature from her husband."

Natasha's upper lip curled. "Gross."

"Exactly." It was hard to go into all the details, but Natasha chewed on the facts, weighing the possibilities like they were legitimate options. "Allison was an unwed mother, and we were both dancing to bring in enough money to pay the bills and take care of our son. They made their assumptions, and that was that."

Natasha had leaned forward onto her elbows, her eyes piercing the screen. "So what's your theory, Birdie?"

"She was his first. Maybe he wasn't prepared or he got interrupted, but he made a mistake and he had to leave before it was done." She swallowed, her throat suddenly dry. She picked up a picture of Allison. In it, Felix was asleep in her arms, head on her shoulder, little arms around her neck, and Allison was looking past the camera, her mouth upturned in a drowsy smile. "Allison was smart and kind. She loved everything about being a mother. She was the kind of person who released a spider outside instead of killing it and the kind of friend who celebrated every birthday. She had dreams and she deserved to live them." Her voice had grown ragged at the end, her breath too shallow to say more. Cotton-ball silence filled the apartment and the video feed. Joseph wiped at one eye. Natasha slid a finger under her glasses.

Birdie tilted her head. "Has your grandmother told you about the animal carcasses that have been discarded around Sunny Pines?"

Natasha shook her head.

"Mutilated cats, a couple of rabbits, and a small flock of beheaded parakeets." She paused, realizing she might have gotten her friend in hot water. "I'm sure Louise didn't tell you because she didn't want to worry you."

Natasha's lips pressed together. "Yep, that sounds like Grammy." All of Natasha's youthful sweetness evaporated; she turned serious, edgy. A couple of seconds ticked by. "Are you saying you think the Vampire Killer has been tormenting these poor animals around a retirement community where my grammy lives?" Notes of incredulity spiced with anger.

Cool air filled her lungs. She couldn't stop now. "And then there's the Geneva Smith case."

Natasha's eyebrows raised. "Who?"

"A young mother who was working as a prostitute—"

"Sex worker."

Birdie tugged at her ear. "Right, sex worker. Her body was discovered in the same dumpster where Cora was found bled to death, behind the same building where both Freida and Allison died from blood loss." She got close to the screen. "Rader went silent for years before resurfacing."

The scratch of pen on paper as Natasha took notes. "And you think this asshole's another Dennis Rader psychopath?"

Birdie shrugged. "I think it's foolish—dangerous, even—to assume that he's dead or in jail."

Natasha slumped over her desk, glasses in one hand, the other pressed into her face. "Wow. I mean, wow. The Vampire Killer is a serious asshole, and he hardly deserves more airtime than he's already gotten. But, crew"—she was speaking to her listeners, Birdie guessed—"if he's alive and Birdie's right, we have *got* to find this douchebag. He has to be old as fuck—" Her eyes widened and she clapped a hand to her mouth. "I'm sorry!"

"For cussing or for saying he's old?"

Natasha laughed. "Both, I think."

"Gray hair doesn't make me a prude, you know. Did you miss the part where I used to be a stripper?"

Natasha replaced her glasses and tilted her head to the side. "You've got a wicked sense of humor, Birdie. I can see why you and Grammy are friends." She readjusted her headphones and leaned into the mic. "Crew, do your magic. There is evidence out there still, and we can find this sick motherfucker and give these beautiful women"—here she took an audible breath and said each name slowly, softly—"Felicity,

Jan, Karen, Tonia, Judy, Barb, Susan, Carol, Freida, Cora"—her voice rasped—"and Allison, the peace they deserve."

Another moment of silence that filled Birdie from her toes all the way to the tip of her heart. Her next breath felt wild and unbound.

"Birdie, thank—"

"And one more."

"What?"

"There's someone else, Natasha. If he's still alive, and if he's victimizing women yet again, there's another potential victim. Faith Perez—or rather, Sofia Faith Perez. She went missing from this area a month ago, right around the time the animal mutilations started here and right after Geneva Smith was murdered, and nobody's asking the right questions." Birdie's heart hammered against her ribs.

Natasha's mouth opened and closed. She flipped through her notes, then found Birdie's eyes through the screen.

Birdie kept going. "She worked on the cleaning staff here at Sunny Pines but had also developed a line of her own cleaning products. On March fourteenth, she didn't show up for work and nobody has seen or heard from her since. Just like Allison, she's a single woman working to make ends meet—and just like Allison, the police are not looking into it." Birdie felt the quick rise and fall of her chest.

Natasha was quiet for a few moments, and Birdie wondered if she'd gone too far. "And you think she might be one of his victims?"

"I hope she's still alive, Natasha. I hope we're not too late. But here's what I do know: a serial killer is still out there, animals are being mutilated, a woman is missing, and no one seems to care enough to find her. Is this really the time to play it safe?" She leaned back in her chair, puffing for air, heart pounding. "The point is, Faith deserves to be found like anyone else."

Natasha's eyes had narrowed, and when at first she didn't say anything, Birdie felt her hopes plummet to the floor. She tried to keep her gaze level with Natasha's, but it was hard, and when her chin trembled, Birdie grabbed hold of it.

Natasha removed her glasses and leaned back in her chair, hands behind her head. "You heard it here first, crew. Is Sofia Faith Perez the Vampire Killer's latest victim? Is the Vampire Killer a threat to my grammy? Who is slaughtering innocent animals around Sunny Pines? What really happened to Geneva Smith? We might be the only ones who can answer these questions. With our resources pooled together, I think we can find Sofia Faith Perez and nab this asshole. What do you say?"

Relief brushed over her skin, and Birdie released her chin.

"Whew! What a show. Thank you, Birdie, for joining us today. Thank you, crew, for being badass champions for those without voices. Check out the show notes for all details related to today's episode, including any new information on the Vampire Killer's first victim and on this breaking missing person case."

After a few more pleasantries were exchanged, Birdie pushed End on the video connection and sat back in her chair, unable to move, stunned, like a bird after it had flown into a window.

Everly closed her computer and moved it out of the way. She put a cup of coffee on the table in front of Birdie. Beside it, Joseph set down a shot glass, filled it with an amber liquid.

Birdie raised an eyebrow. "Tequila?"

Joseph shrugged. "I thought a chaser might be in order after that."

Birdie lifted the shot glass, tears pressing into her eyes. "To Faith. Let's bring her home."

"To Faith," Joseph and Everly echoed.

Thirty-Four

Louise had shared early clips of the podcast with Birdie and their gang. It was hard to listen to her own voice, but Birdie thought she sounded okay. The show aired that morning, and Natasha had emailed her twice with follow-up questions; it seemed her "crew" was busy looking for Faith.

A million listeners had heard about Allison and Faith. Birdie had spent so much of her life being doubted—sometimes even doubting herself—that to have been heard like that, to have been taken seriously for once by people who might be able to do something to help, came at her in waves of disbelief.

On her way back from the pharmacy, she ran into Glen outside by her garage bay, pacing. Dressed in his uniform of white button-down, sweater-vest, and khaki pants, stomach straining over his brown leather belt. "Ah, Bird, I've been waiting for you."

Her stomach somersaulted. "Do you have news?"

"I heard the podcast." He clasped his hands behind his back. Birdie noticed his eyebrow hair had grown long and his beard, usually trimmed and neat, looked a bit neglected. "There's something I need to talk with you about." There was a grayish sheen to his forehead. "Could you come over right now?"

She was a bit taken aback by his demeanor; he seemed almost ill. "Sure, Glen, of course. Are you okay?"

He swatted at something in the air. "I'm fine, just fine. But come on, let's go."

She followed him inside, slightly alarmed and wondering if she should text his brother. Glen seemed a little off.

He opened his door. "Come in, come in."

His apartment was the one-bed/one-bath variety that opened immediately into the living room, no hallway to contend with. And it was decorated . . . well, nice, she supposed, with a vase of bright yellow flowers on the counter, a sofa and a love seat with fluffed matching pillows, twin end tables and lamps that glowed a warm yellow. Yet it all felt just a little too perfect, stale in a model-home kind of way. And there was an unpleasant odor that she couldn't quite put her finger on. "Lovely," she said, hoping her true opinion wasn't plastered all over her face.

"Thank you. I think my late wife would have hated it, but she was closed-minded when it came to most things." He stood close to Birdie, arms crossed, rocking on his heels.

She felt observed, and when he didn't sit, she did, perching on the edge of his couch. There was a neat row of books, spines facing her on the coffee table, a metal bookend on each side to hold them up. She glanced at the odd display, then back at Glen, whose eyebrows had arched expectantly.

"So, you have something to tell me? Is it about Faith?" She squeezed her hands together in her lap. *Please be okay, please be alive.*

"No, no news on Faith."

Her relief was punctured with dread. No news was not good news. "What is it, Glen?"

His eyes shifted away, then back to her, then to the books on the coffee table. She slid one from the row. The title, *On The Trail of a Vampire*, gave her chills. She looked up, and Glen nodded encouragingly. She pulled out another book: *The Vampire Killer: What We Know So Far.*

"So you're a true crime buff like Nan?"

He looked confused. "What's that?"

She held up the book. "You like crime too?"

He sat on the edge of the sofa, smiling. "Ah, no, dear Nan is a couch enthusiast. This was my work."

Things started to click into place. "You worked on this case?" Her skin itched. "Why didn't you tell me?" She'd been so open and he'd said nothing.

The way he looked at her now was different, intimate. "I remember you."

That gave her a jolt. "From the Paragon?"

His eyes were dark and serious. "From when I worked on the case. You were right all along, Bird." Glen hung his head; he looked flushed. "I think of them often. They've haunted me for years."

She gripped the side of the couch, her world spinning; she was flung back in time to those long nights feverishly collecting information on the murders, keeping a file on the women, and subjecting herself to the details of their gory deaths. At night, it would wake her in a panicked sweat, and she'd rush to Felix's room, watch him sleep until her heart stopped racing. Glen had just said she'd been *right*. "Nobody ever believed me, Glen. Why—" A flare of anger. "Why didn't you *do* anything about it? I might have known something that could have helped"—her hand turned to a fist—"or something from Allison's murder scene could have held a clue that would have helped you find him before he killed so many women."

Glen was nodding. "I know."

Birdie softened. This wasn't Glen's fault. Or the police, for that matter. The only human at fault was this psycho, who had ruined so many lives for his own sick enjoyment. The same person who might still be out there hurting women today. She pulled at her fingers. "So the police think he's back too?" Sweat across her back. "Do they want to talk to me? I can go right now."

He straightened his once-broad shoulders, and in it she saw ghosts of his younger self—assured, authoritative, a cop. "I've already talked to them on your behalf, Birdie."

"Good. That's so great, Glen." Her body buzzed. With the podcast and now this—her close friend a former detective on the case—the colors around her shimmered, the world alive with possibility. She was overcome by the coincidence—or, more appropriately, fate—that had brought them together. A rush of emotion burned her eyes. "Thank you, Glen." She squeezed his bony forearm. "I mean it."

Glen stared down at her hand like he was taken aback by the contact. He placed his big palm over hers and patted. "Thank *you*, Bird."

She looked at him, perhaps seeing him for the first time. A man full of regret, who, like Everly said, had meant to be a lot of things he never was. "It can't have been easy to work on this case."

Glen scooted forward on the couch. "It was an emotional fuckfest."

His language surprised her. It wasn't typical of the man she'd come to know, but it hinted at the baggage he carried, the burden of his own guilt. "Why haven't you told me before?"

He was quiet, studying her. "It was a long time ago." He looked at his hands. "And I'm ashamed."

They were so similar. Both of them swimming in the wake of a psychopath's gruesome devastation. She sniffed, Glen's strong aftershave tickled her throat.

"Allison should never have died like that," he said.

His words crawled just under her skin, a sentiment she'd echoed a million times herself. She slumped forward. Birdie was not to blame for her death. Years of doubt swept away in a minute. "You're right, Glen. She was supposed to be a mother and a teacher and whatever she dreamed." She straightened up from the couch, feeling the pop in her knees. "I can share all of my research with the police. Something in there might help."

Glen stood, hands clasped around his belly. "Birdie, I beg of you not to say anything yet to the others until it's official."

"Of course," she said.

He ducked his head. "I should have told you before, but I was afraid I'd lose your friendship."

"I get it. But let's be truthful from here on out."

He smiled. "Deal."

"And, Glen?"

"Yes?"

"Let's not let the bastard get away this time."

His eyes narrowed. "Not a chance."

~

Days passed with Birdie on edge, waiting for something to happen now that everything was out in the open. Several times she picked up the phone to call Felix and tell him everything, but she held back. If she said something before the police made a statement, it would only upset him. So she bided her time, and each moment that passed with no updates, no Faith, no call from the police, the walls of her apartment moved in on her. Everly's concert was a good distraction.

A record number had signed up to attend, so much so that Jonie had splurged for appetizers and mocktails. A few classical-music buffs had recognized Everly's last name and learned that she was the daughter of the once-famous musical composer who'd mysteriously vanished from the music world after composing a promising debut piece.

Birdie tied her peacock-blue scarf around her neck and ran a brush through her hair once more before she headed to the community center. Joseph was already there with Everly, having set up the entire event with the administration himself. *You've come a long way from hosting a book club that no one attends,* she'd said to Joseph the other day. He'd smiled and shrugged. *I guess I learned a thing or two from Sofia.*

"You two be good," she told the pugs, who had already settled side by side on their shared pillow.

She opened her door to find Louise, Nan, and Jean about to knock.

Jean held a twelve-pack of paper towels in her arms and peeked over the top. "These were on sale at Costco." She moved past Birdie to put the package on the floor of her hallway.

"Oh, thanks," Birdie said, amused.

Louise smiled. "It'll take you a year to get through all those."

Birdie laughed.

"Looks like you're ready to go," Nan said. "We thought we could walk over together."

Birdie was pleased. "Where's Glen?"

"He can't make it," Jean said. "Something came up with his brother."

"I don't care for his brother." Nan wore a short-sleeve button-down covered in musical notes.

"Me either," Birdie agreed. Her phone rang. Felix. A spike of happiness to see his name on her screen. Birdie pressed Decline; she'd call him back later when she had more time to talk. Together they walked into the community center and found seats among the crowd. When the lights dimmed and Everly took the stage, Birdie relaxed into her chair, nerves for the girl eased by a deep contentment; all of the answers she'd searched for were finally within reach.

Thirty-Five

ALLISON

Everly's racing heart doubles her vision, and when she peers out at the spot where she is to perform, she thinks she sees a group of women around the chair, a young girl running a hand along her cello. She blinks and they are gone. But they are still here, waiting to surround her when she performs. Everly vibrates on a frequency so high I feel her fears as if they are my own. Her old soul strains against the chains that bind her to primal sentiments like doubt and anxiety.

She whispers a quick prayer, and I draw close to listen.

Dad? Are you there? Please help me.

He is there, pieces of him in dust motes floating in sunlight, or bending shadows in the corners. His love reflects in the effervescent white of Everly's hair, the glow of her aura. And in the slowing of her pulse.

Her decision to play is directional, and it is this moment, among others, that moves us all toward a specific conclusion. It is not perfect. She will be hurt. Birdie will be hurt. But pain is the antihero of life, and without it, there is no joy, no peace, no salvation.

Joseph joins Everly, and she smiles at him, immediately relieved. Everly imagines how different her life might have been with a father like him—warm, supportive, unflappable. He squeezes her shoulder, and the act inflates a confidence she hasn't felt in ages. Her fear is not gone, but it is bound, and anticipation stretches into her fingertips, her ears hear the music she will infuse into the room, and she is ready.

Everly takes her place on the chair and begins to play.

Thirty-Six

Birdie hurried inside her apartment after the concert, her phone ringing. Felix again. He hadn't left a voicemail earlier and Birdie felt a tinge of worry. Could something have happened to one of the boys?

She answered quickly. "Hello, Felix? Is everything okay?"

"Birdie, it's Sharon."

A coldness tickled the skin on the back of her neck. "Why are you calling from Felix's phone?"

"He had an accident."

Her grip loosened and the phone wobbled in her hand. "W-what?" She swallowed. "Oh my God. Is he okay?" The room spun.

"Yes, yes, he's fine. He rear-ended someone, and the airbag broke his wrist. He doesn't need surgery, but it will take some time to heal. He's already home and resting."

Irritation flared for her daughter-in-law. "Why didn't you start with that?" She'd thought he'd died.

"Well, Birdie . . ." There was a mirrored irritation in Sharon's voice. "He was listening to that podcast when it happened."

Birdie's knees buckled, and she sank onto the arm of her sofa. She hadn't mentioned the podcast to him because she knew it wasn't something he'd want to hear. "How did he—"

"Tyler heard it and shared it with him."

A sinking feeling in her stomach. "Sharon, I—"

"You went on a show with millions of listeners and made it sound like the Vampire Killer killed Allison first."

"I've always believed that; Felix knows that."

"You're not the police, Birdie. And you made outrageous claims about two women you know nothing about."

Her lips had stiffened. "I know Faith."

"How well? She cleans your apartment."

Birdie's thoughts gummed in her head. "I— Wait! My neighbor, my friend Glen, worked as a detective on the case. The police believe me!"

"We spoke to the police, Birdie. Felix called them. They don't believe any of this is related to the Vampire Killer."

"Yes, I know! Glen said they've not gone public with it yet, but soon—"

A heavy sigh. "And Geneva Smith was murdered by her boyfriend."

Birdie froze. "What?"

"Felix sent you the article."

She fumbled with her computer, opened up her email. An attachment from Felix with no subject or text in the email. An article from yesterday. The boyfriend had confessed. Birdie's right eye twitched. "But Glen said . . ." She tugged at her lip. Glen had never mentioned anything about Geneva.

"Is Glen the one you told Felix about?" She heard a softening in Sharon's voice. "The one with memory problems?"

Birdie's heart sank. "No," she said weakly. "His brother thinks that. Glen's fine, he's just a little eccentric."

Bits and pieces of her conversation with Glen spun around her. *I remember you.* She pressed a hand to her temple; she couldn't recall the exact words, but he'd said that Allison was the first victim. She was sure of it. She heard Sharon take a calming breath, like Birdie was a child. She made fists with her hands. "Allison was killed by the Vampire Killer, and the police aren't ready to announce it yet. You need to believe me."

"This sounds like your tunnel vision, your imagination, your obsession has come back in full force, Birdie, and it's not healthy for you."

"No, Sharon, that's not true. The police want to talk to me—"

Sharon's voice was full of pain, and it shocked Birdie to her core. "And to add this business about the cleaning woman on top of everything . . ." A pause. Sharon inhaled. "Allison has been dead for fifty-two years, Birdie. Do you know who hasn't? Felix. But he's the ghost in your life, always reminding you of what you lost. Why haven't you ever been able to focus on what you gained? A son, Birdie. Felix is your *son*. And he's never felt like he was enough because he wasn't her." Now she was openly crying. "God, Birdie! You're so blind. He's tried to get you to listen, tried to tell you in so many different ways. So many times. And you just—" An audible swallow. "You don't ever listen."

Birdie's spine curved, and the weight of it threatened to drag her forward off the arm of the couch. She couldn't think, couldn't come up with the words that would make this better. The police finally knew about Allison. She'd waited her whole life for this moment. A sharpness in her chest. Richard had concerns about his brother's memory. She'd experienced some of it firsthand with Glen. Had he been confused when he spoke with her? He'd been so convincing. But could he have been mistaken? Or delusional? She moaned, gripping the sofa with her hand. Was Glen's condition more serious than any of them had realized? Allegro jumped onto the couch, paws on the other side of the arm, his little body braced against the low of her back like he could bolster her.

"I know this hurts you, Birdie, and we don't want to hurt you. Felix, me, the boys—we all love you so very much."

She was numb all over, confused, wanting to defend herself but not knowing how.

"I think it's unfair to surprise you."

That turned her cold. "Surprise me with what?"

"Felix and I are flying out to see you. We want to make sure that you're getting all the services you need at Sunny Pines. We're concerned that maybe you need more." Sharon sounded professional, like Birdie was one of her patients having a consultation. She understood suddenly why Felix had not made this call. It was too hard for him, and Birdie knew that Sharon loved him—loved *her*—enough to be the one to say it.

A memory from their wedding of Birdie hugging the bride, so beautiful in her white lace, so steadfast in her love for Felix. *Take care of him,* Birdie had whispered in her ear and lovingly clasped her gold bird necklace around Sharon's neck. *Protect his heart.* At the time she had meant from outside forces or the slow degradation of love; she had meant a million other things, not from herself. But now, feeling the depth of Sharon's love for Felix, both awed and ripped apart by its strength, she felt all her years settle into the space between her joints.

Birdie couldn't feel the phone in her hand. For the first time in her life, she doubted her own mind. "Tell Felix I love him—and you, too, Sharon. And I'm sorry. For everything." Birdie discontinued the phone call. An emptiness in her chest opened into a sucking hole. Her bed called to her, the darkness of her room a cave where she could escape. Richard's words—*Forgetful.* Glen's side of things was always different from his brother's. His finger injury. The burnt eggs. Her arms cradled her stomach. Had she trusted a man who might be suffering memory problems because he was saying exactly what she had wanted to hear?

Felix was worried about Birdie. Perhaps he had a right to be. She pushed into her walker and made her way to the door. If she could straighten things out with Glen, maybe she could find a way to explain it to Felix, help him see that she wasn't sliding back into old habits.

She knocked on Glen's door. Richard answered, wearing a wrinkled white button-down, untucked over navy blue dress slacks. There was a deep, tired rut between his eyebrows. "Hi, Bird."

Something wasn't quite right. "Is everything okay?"

Richard seemed unsure, his eyes a soft brown, worry lines carved into the corners. "Not really." He stepped into the hallway, closing the door behind him.

"Did something happen?"

Richard sighed. "I got a call from the police this afternoon at work. Glen was at the mall and got confused and didn't know where he was.

Climbed into some woman's car thinking it was his own. Scared the woman half to death, and she'd sprayed him with her Mace and hit him with her bag before she realized he was just an old man."

Birdie gasped. A sick feeling unfurled in her stomach. "That's terrible, Richard. I'm so sorry. Is he okay now?"

"Yes, he's fine. We went to the hospital and everything looked good, and Glen was alert and frustrated by then. He didn't remember what happened." Richard rubbed his forehead. "He's sleeping now."

Birdie's head ached. She'd been so blind to Glen's suffering.

"The thing is . . ." Richard sounded pressed. "I have a meeting I can't miss."

"Do you want me to check on him?"

His shoulders rounded. "That would be wonderful. Here." He reached into his pocket and brought out his phone. "What's your phone number? I'll text you when I'm done."

Birdie gave it to him, battling an uneasiness that spread from her gut. She wanted to test Glen's stories with a question that wouldn't alert Richard in case she was wrong. "Glen mentioned that your parents owned the Paragon."

His eyebrows lifted. "Yes, they did. My father owned many buildings, but the Paragon was his very first."

"And you sold it recently, right?"

Richard looked confused. "He told you that?"

She nodded.

He shook his head. "He's lying. Again. He's so hyperfocused on some things, especially when it comes to me." Richard rubbed the back of his neck. "I took over my father's business after he died. I still own the Paragon. But Glen's never been happy about any of it."

Shock rippled cold across her skin. Had everything Glen told her been a lie? "Any of what?"

"Anything to do with me, really. But the fact that I inherited the business has always gotten under his skin. I earned that inheritance.

Our father was a"—Richard's nostrils flared—"dark man, and when Glen left home, he left me to deal with it and never looked back."

There was something under Richard's kind demeanor, an ire that came out in a slight tremble of his voice. He breathed in and, like a curtain pulled to shut out the night, seemed to gather himself. He smiled, and this time Birdie didn't find it so sincere. "Sorry about that. It's a touchy subject, but I'm glad you told me. It helps to know I'm right about this."

Her phone rang and she jumped, forgetting she'd slid it into her pants pocket.

"You should get that. See you later, Bird." He was inside the apartment before she had a chance to remind him that her name was Birdie.

Her phone buzzed again, and she pulled it out. Unknown number. She let it go to voicemail, unsettled by her conversation with Richard. Glen was confused. He'd had a terrible father. He truly did hate his brother. And now Glen was struggling, getting into cars that weren't his own, fighting the invisible nemesis of memory and age, and she'd been pulled right into it with him. Because she'd heard what she wanted to.

By the time she'd reached her apartment, her phone was ringing again. Same number. She let herself in and sat at her kitchen table. It rang again. Same number. Finally, she answered.

"Hello?"

"Birdie?"

The lilt in the caller's voice was familiar and strange at the same time. She felt a compression in her spine that settled into an ache in her lower back. "Who is this?" But she knew, oh God, she knew, and she wanted to feel relieved, to overflow with joy, and she was, but she was also sick to her stomach.

"It's Faith."

Birdie's mouth went dry. "Faith? Are you okay? What happened? I've been so worried—"

"Yeah, I know." There was something off about her voice. "I heard the podcast." She sounded wary.

Birdie pressed a hand into her stomach. This was all she wanted, she reminded herself. To know that Faith was safe. Then why did she think she might throw up? "You went missing and nobody knew what happened to you . . ." She trailed off, hearing herself for perhaps the first time. The way Felix did. "What happened?"

Faith breathed through the phone. "Oh, Birdie." Like she needed a moment to take it all in.

Suddenly, Birdie felt like a very foolish, very old woman.

"My mamá had a stroke."

"Oh no, Faith, I'm so—"

"Didn't you get my note?"

"What note?"

"The one I left with your neighbor. I was supposed to work that morning, but I got the call just as I got to work. I was leaving you a note when I ran into your neighbor, and he offered to give it to you. I know how you worry."

"But Louise saw you talking to someone in a car that morning." She searched for meaning in her mistake, something to make sense of how she'd gotten so far down the wrong path.

"The Uber driver? I had to leave straightaway and I couldn't wait for the bus."

The puzzle pieces didn't match. "Jonie said she'd never heard from you."

Through the phone, Faith sighed. "I was going to call her when I got here. The doctors didn't think Mamá would make it, and I was in such a panic I forgot my phone in the airport bathroom. After that, I did call, but by then they'd already replaced me."

"Jonie knew?" Jonie had said nothing to Birdie—but Birdie hadn't brought it up with Jonie again, and it was likely that the disorganized woman hadn't thought much of it. After all, it had only been Birdie's Sunny Pines friends who knew about her concerns. And now, of course, all of Natasha's listeners. Birdie cupped a hand to her cheek, bent low over the table. She caught her reflection in the mirror hung on the wall across from her. A grayness beneath wrinkles, skin hanging from her jaw, fingers gnarled from arthritis, bent over like a crone. A scared old woman who'd made up an entire story and shared it with the world all because she couldn't take the truth. That she was the reason her friend had died. Her stomach heaved.

Faith's voice broke through a roaring in her ears. "And the job, I know it wasn't responsible of me—but, Birdie, she's my mamá. I had no choice."

"Oh, Faith." Birdie's heart hurt for the woman.

"Once I got here, it was touch and go for a while, and I couldn't leave her side. Everything there just seemed . . . less important, you know?"

"I do." Birdie clutched the phone. "How is she doing?"

"Better, but she needs me."

"But what about your cat?"

"My cat?"

"We found your cat locked in your bedroom. Poor thing was half-starved. Joseph is watching him for you."

Faith let out a string of curses in Spanish. "That's my roommate's cat. Or my ex-roommate. Always late with the rent and such a slob. She'd moved out a few days before I left and was supposed to come back for her things." Another word in Spanish that Birdie didn't have to know to translate. "She didn't take her cat? What a— Sorry, Birdie."

Birdie's head tensed around a headache. Sharon was right: she'd had tunnel vision, making everything fit the way she wanted. Still, she grasped for straws. "Your landlord said you're late on rent."

A bitter laugh. "I am. Between my roommate and this." A heavy sigh came through the speaker, and when she spoke next, her voice was hoarse. "Starting the business was a risk. I knew that. But it put me in a vulnerable position, and now everything's tumbled like a house of cards."

Birdie thought of Allison on the street outside the store—smoking, pregnant, lost. "Send me your information. I'll pay it."

"Birdie, no! I'm not even sure if I'm coming back. I might need to move back here. I just . . . I don't know yet."

Birdie needed to make something right, and this was concrete. This, she could do. "It will give you time to breathe. How about that? And you can pay me back by telling Joseph that he's adopted the wrong cat."

Faith breathed loudly, almost like she was hyperventilating. "I've been so scared."

"I guess I was right about that. I knew something was wrong."

Faith laughed, a lightness in it this time. "You are a warrior for your people, aren't you, Birdie?"

She wished that made her feel better, but all Birdie could think about were the mistakes she'd made, the people she'd hurt because of her single-mindedness. About how deeply her actions had damaged her son. She pressed her forehead into her hand and breathed slowly. Something Faith had said earlier tickled her brain. "You said you gave a note to my neighbor. Who was it?"

"The new one. I can't remember his name, but he looks like a skinny Santa Claus."

Glen? Oh, Glen. They were more alike than she'd ever realized. The difference was that his memory lapses weren't his fault. Her obsession was entirely hers to own.

"I have to go. I'm taking Mamá home today. Thank you, Birdie, for worrying about me when no one else did."

Birdie blinked hard. "You're welcome."

"But can you call off your cold case crew now? They're relentless."

Thirty-Seven

ALLISON

Glen lies in his bed, and he can't feel his toes. Fear drives all the blood from his extremities to warm his heart, but it won't beat as strong as it once did. His brother hands him a cool washcloth, and Glen places it over his eyes. They still burn. I am beside him on the bed, and I caress the length of his carotid artery, feel the blood move wormlike under his skin.

He whimpers.

Richard is fed up with Glen, and if it were his decision, he'd move him into a nursing home, not to this money-suck apartment complex, with no nurses or meal plans or anyone to task with taking care of his brother when he does something stupid.

Glen is afraid of his brother.

"Your friend Bird stopped by. She seems nice."

Glen grunts. He doesn't want his brother to be here.

Richard's lip curls when he looks at Glen's prone form on the bed. They are not close and never have been, but Glen's daughter ran off to Montana years ago and Richard is stuck babysitting. *Hate* is not too strong a word for what Richard feels. *Loathing* works too. They both know that what is broken can't be fixed and the secrets between them are living, breathing beings that suckle on their apathy toward one another. When his parents weren't there, Glen shoved him inside a windowless room and locked the door. He knows how to wield the dark. Richard shivers. Glen's apartment smells like that room. As the older brother, Glen once held all the power, but now it's Richard's turn.

Your brother won't hurt you, I whisper into Glen's ear. He can't hear me. And yet he senses some*thing.* Glen shakes. Richard thinks he hears a woman sigh, feels a cool breath brush across his neck. Gooseflesh prickles his skin. Freida stands behind him. She knows Richard as the handsome young boy with a winning smile and charm.

Glen shifts away from me on the bed and pretends that he doesn't hear anything but the grating voice of his only sibling. He falls asleep and dreams about nothing.

Thirty-Eight

After the phone call, Birdie didn't feel up to welcoming Everly back from the concert. She closed her blinds and slipped under her covers, fully clothed, lost. She wanted to call Felix, explain everything. But even she knew how thin her excuses would sound. She wanted to rejoice that Faith was alive, Louise's words like flashing lights in the dark: *I sure hope you're wrong.* She'd wanted to be wrong about Faith, hadn't she? Even if it meant that she was wrong about everything. Maybe even about Allison. She sank into the blackness, let it sit on her chest, compress her heart until it touched her spine. When Felix was ten, she'd gone to visit the family of Barb, the sixth victim. Their sitter wasn't available, and Birdie, who couldn't bear leaving Felix alone ever, had taken him with her. Tears leaked from her eyes at the memory, shame spreading down her face. She'd done what she always had—asked about Barb, what she was like, who'd she been, tried to find links between her and the other victims. But the family's pain had been raw, her aunt's voice so hoarse she could barely speak.

You bring your boy here to see all this pain? What kind of a mother does that?

Felix had sat beside Birdie, arms binding his stomach, his cheeks whiter than normal, and she'd stared at him, shocked. So tunnel-visioned in her search for the truth that she hadn't even given it a thought. She'd gathered her things, taken his hand, and left.

She rolled onto her side, wishing she could take it all back. To have not hurt the little boy who'd loved her with all his heart. Allegro jumped onto the bed and curled into a ball beside her. She pushed him off. "Go." He jumped to the floor.

When Everly came home later with Joseph, Birdie heard them through her door making microwave dinners, Everly's voice rising and falling, relaxed, freer than Birdie had ever heard her. She pulled the covers up to her chin. The door opened once, closed. Sometime later, it opened again, closed. The third time, light from the hallway spilled across her bed, and Allegro returned to his spot by her side. The bed dipped.

"Birdie?"

Birdie feigned sleep. She couldn't face them.

"Do you want to eat dinner with me and Joseph?"

A lump in Birdie's throat made it hard to swallow. This wasn't her secret to hold on to. "Faith called me."

Everly sucked in air. "Oh my God!"

Birdie turned and saw Joseph's outline in the doorway. "And she's fine, absolutely fine. She went to Puerto Rico because her mother had a stroke." Birdie's cheeks burned. "I was wrong."

Everly touched her shoulder. "But it's good. She's okay. That's all we wanted."

"It is." Heartache pooled inside her chest. A painful truth: she had let Allison down, dragged her son through the mess instead of protecting him from it.

"Are you okay, Birdie?" Joseph's deep, level voice.

"No," she said. "I just need to be alone."

"Okay," Everly said. "But we're here if you need anything." The door clicked shut behind them.

～

The next day, Birdie woke with Allegro tucked close to her side. Pieces of blue sky peeked through her blinds, and the tepid air that leaked through the thin window seals promised a pleasant spring day. Birdie lay in bed and stared up at the ceiling, absentmindedly running her fingers down Allegro's side. The small dog groaned with pleasure.

She started to push the covers off and stopped. The hours stretched long, and the drive she normally felt to get out of bed and start her day had waned.

"Birdie?" Everly called from the other side of her closed door.

"Come in."

Everly stood by the door, worry in the narrowness of her eyes. "Is there anything I can do for you?"

Birdie wanted to throw off the covers and be the strong one, to revel in her mistake because it meant Faith was alive. But her legs were too heavy, the bed a suction cup from which she couldn't move. "No."

"Okay." The door closed again.

Sometime later, another knock that startled Allegro to his feet with a bark. Nan stood above her bed in a wide-brimmed flowered sun hat that in no way coordinated with the cats printed all over her shirt.

"So I heard that Faith is safe and sound. You must feel like a real noob. Is that why you're still in bed?"

Birdie scooted until she was sitting up and eye level with Nan. "A what?"

"A rookie, a novice—you know, a neophyte." She laughed, and both the hat and her oxygen tubing fell off. "Oh, shoot." She carefully bent over to pick up the hat and set it into the basket of her walker. "Bought that at the dollar store. My daughter-in-law wants family pictures for spring."

Birdie was too tired and too sad for this conversation.

"Don't be hard on yourself, Birdie," Nan said. "Sometimes our hunches work out and sometimes they don't. You thought Faith was in trouble and she wasn't, and that's a good thing. Right?"

Birdie leaned against her headboard. "Of course, Nan."

"But you feel like a fool, huh?"

Birdie nodded.

"Well, of course you do."

Birdie raised her eyebrows.

"But that doesn't mean you are one. You took a chance, and you got all of us feeling like we were a part of something."

Birdie tried to smile, but her lips went limp. "And I was wrong about Geneva Smith."

Nan blew air through her lips. "*Many* people were wrong about Geneva, including me." She sighed. "But it's not over, you know."

"It is for me."

"What do you mean?"

"Allison might have killed herself. I—" She pressed a hand to her head; she couldn't bear to mention how misled she'd been by Glen's delusions. "I might have been wrong about that too."

Nan was quiet for a moment, chewing on her lip like she was working something out. "Okay, so maybe you're wrong, but maybe you're right. Here's what we do know: the Vampire Killer may still be out there, Birdie. After your podcast, I got myself hooked up with Natasha's crew. Most exciting thing I've done in decades." Nan's brown eyes widened with delight. "And you know, I think we need to keep our eyes and ears open."

Birdie shook her head; not even Nan's energy could move her. "I don't think I have it in me."

"Well, listen to this—yesterday I visited the campers. I'm not agreeing with Dorothea, but with the animals and all, I figure I should cross them off our list of suspects."

Birdie raised her eyebrows. "Suspects?"

Nan looked at her like she'd grown two heads. "Someone's still killing animals."

"And you went over there on your own?"

Wrinkles piled deep around Nan's smile. "The walk took me a while, but what you might not know about me is that I'm the determined sort."

A flash of good humor. "I think I've picked up on that."

"One of them is a veteran who said he prefers the freedom of living wherever he wants." Nan opened her eyes wide. "I've never seen so many tattoos. He gave me the name of the artist he goes to. Might just get one myself before our family beach vacation. But he's got three dogs, and I don't think he'd be hurting animals. The other one is a younger man and his girlfriend. A bit shifty, you might say, but nice enough. They're new to the road. They said they usually park in the Walmart lot because it's safer, but with the warmer weather, the girlfriend wanted to be close to the pond for all her yoga. Said it was more zen."

Birdie pushed off her covers, feeling bad with Nan standing, hunched deeply over her walker while Birdie lay in bed. "You've been busy."

Nan shuffled her feet in a dance step. "Yes, I have, and it feels good." A small laugh escaped her lips.

"But here's the kicker: the girlfriend said she saw something on the evening when her Taurus moon was rising and something else was setting."

"Excuse me?"

"I have no idea what she was talking about," Nan said. "But it sounds like it was right around Easter, and what she saw is what's important."

Birdie felt a slight uptick in her pulse. "And that is . . . ?"

"A tall figure behind the apartment buildings doing something in the grassy area by the garages."

"Where we found the parakeets?" Birdie had to fight the old urge to try to put the pieces together in a way that fit. She'd thought she'd made connections when all she'd had was a long string of coincidences.

"Bingo. So what we know about our animal killer is that he's tall. I'll be reporting everything I learned to the police."

Birdie warmed to Nan, shifted so that her feet slid from the bed to the ground. "I sure could have used a friend like you when Allison died."

Nan's eyes brightened, and she reached out to touch Birdie's forearm. "Nah, I wasn't half as fun or adventurous back then—and after my husband left me, I was angry for a long time. I'm the best version of me right now."

Birdie gave her a half smile. "Well, you're a good friend—but, Nan, I think I'm retiring from all this crime business."

"You don't say." Nan frowned. "Just when I found a partner."

"At least you have Natasha's crew," Birdie offered.

"Good point." Her usual lightness dampened. "Just because you were wrong about Faith doesn't make you wrong about Allison, you know."

Birdie's shoulders dropped. "I know. But I think maybe it's time I do what's best for my son. It's what Allison would have wanted above everything else."

Nan nodded. "You're a smart one." She patted Birdie's shoulder. "Are you coming to book club tonight?"

Birdie shook her head, the heaviness returning at the prospect of seeing the entire gang. "I don't think so."

～

Birdie never made it out of her room. Everly knocked a few hours later.

"Want to take the dogs on a walk with me?" Before Birdie could say no, Everly added, "I wanted to check on my camper, too, but I'm a little nervous about walking over there by myself."

The girl said it innocently enough, but Birdie knew she'd been played. After she dressed, she took Allegro's leash from Everly; her desire to protect others hadn't dissolved overnight.

Adagio, the smaller of the two, pulled hard on his leash, panting with the effort and straining against Everly's hold. Birdie could grip her walker and Allegro's leash at the same time because he walked calmly by her side. "I don't think either of your dogs lives up to their names."

Everly laughed.

They made their way down the sidewalk and to Everly's camper. She unlocked it and climbed inside. A few minutes later she came out, her forehead wrinkled, and sat down on the edge of the doorway, legs dangling over the stairs, Adagio in her arms.

"Everything okay?"

She scratched the dog's head, looking thoughtful. "Yeah."

"Then why do you look like that."

Everly met Birdie's eyes. "It's dark in there."

With only the one small window and the door, there weren't many places for the light to slip through. "Hasn't it always been?"

Everly twisted around to give the inside another glance. "I guess so, but I didn't notice it before."

"But now you do?"

"Yeah. It feels like the house I grew up in."

"And what do you think about that?"

"Like I don't belong in there anymore."

"Maybe you never did."

Everly was shaking her head. "I think I want to go back to school, Birdie." Her voice shook, but not too much, Birdie noticed.

"That's a big deal."

Everly smiled, and while her lips wobbled a bit, it was a good smile. "It is." Her eyes dropped, then met Birdie's again. "I—I know that you're sad about Faith—er, I mean that you made a big deal about it when she was okay. But, Birdie, you made a big deal about me, and look at me now." She spread her arms wide. "I'm not stuck in the dark anymore."

The back of Birdie's throat tickled. The girl's honesty lightened the load that had been weighing her down. She smiled. "I guess we better tell Joseph that his therapy idea worked."

~

Joseph was beside himself, dabbing at his dry eyes with a handkerchief and beaming at Everly like she was his own granddaughter. They sat in

Birdie's apartment, the dogs snoozing on their bed. Everly had turned shy after sharing her news, head ducked, face reddened.

"I think it's great, Everly, just great." He wanted to say more, Birdie could tell from the way he kept opening and closing his mouth, smiling and shaking his head like Everly had just performed a magic trick and he wanted to understand the mechanics of it. "I'm very proud of you."

Everly stretched her arms in front of her like a cat and grinned. "Thank you, Joseph."

He turned to Birdie. "I'm glad to see you up and about."

Birdie gestured toward Everly. "It's hard to stay down with so much youthful energy prancing about." She checked the clock. "But you two are going to be late for book club."

Joseph made a face. "Actually, I hope you're not mad, but—"

At that, there was a knock on the door, and in walked the gang like a single amoeba. Jean and Louise, who had stopped by to get Glen; and even Dorothea, whom Birdie had tried to avoid since deciding that she had been the one who told Jonie about Everly staying with her. "We almost couldn't get this guy to come, but we weren't taking no for an answer, were we, Glen?" Jean said, tapping him on the arm. Birdie hadn't told anyone yet about the Mace incident or his confusion about his work with the police.

Glen's normal exuberance had diminished—much like Birdie's, she guessed. Like a light had been snuffed out. Birdie felt a pang for her friend and for herself.

Nan came in a few minutes later, sans the sun hat from earlier and sporting a T-shirt that read IT'S NOT STALKING. IT'S CALLED BEING AN INTERNET SLEUTH.

"I like your shirt, Nan," Everly said.

"Me too!" Nan looked down, delighted. "It's merch from Natasha's show. I'm part of the crew now, Louise."

"Oh, goodness, Nan. They're perfect for you."

"Yes, I know," Nan said, utterly serious. "I think they're lucky to have me." She turned to Dorothea, who had sat on the very edge of the sofa. "You're quiet, Dorothea."

Dorothea smoothed out her skirt. "I don't know what you mean."

And Birdie found she couldn't stop herself from speaking. Like her own emotional bottom had drained her of any tolerance she had. Dorothea was a bully, and the best way to handle bullies was to be direct. "You told Jonie about Everly staying with me. What do you have against me giving a girl a safe place to stay?"

Dorothea's eyes shot from Birdie to Everly and then around the circle. She looked like she wanted to say something, but stopped herself and went in an entirely different direction. "Your concert was beautiful, Everly. Thank you for sharing your music with us."

That surprised Birdie enough not to say another word on the matter. She crossed her arms and felt a little smaller.

Nobody brought up Faith, and Birdie was relieved to pretend that everything was normal. They talked about the month's activity schedule and what they each planned to attend, Nan pointing out that Birdie would not attend any event if she had to ride on the damn van.

"I never said the *damn* van," Birdie protested.

"But you wanted to," Nan said, and Birdie shrugged in agreement.

"Why are you so afraid of the van?" Louise said.

Birdie thought about it for a moment. "You know, it's not that I'm afraid. But my body . . ." She touched her walker. "It's weak, it's failed me, and it makes me look older than I am inside."

There were nods of commiseration.

"There's just something about taking that van that seems like one more nail in my coffin," she said.

Everyone was quiet for a moment, until Louise smiled at Birdie. It touched her eyes, turned them silver. "Or it could feel like freedom."

Birdie nodded, a tightness in her throat. For a moment, Louise reminded her of Allison. She would have said the same thing, because Allison was always the brave one. "Or it could be that."

They talked about upcoming surgeries, new grandbabies, and if anyone thought that winter was over yet. That discussion went on for some time because the weather brought out many dissenting opinions.

All of these things, they talked about. What they did not talk about was a single book.

Louise gently switched gears when she turned to Birdie and said, "We were so happy to hear that Faith is alive and well, and sad to hear about her mother." She spoke delicately, kindly, and nobody said anything about how Birdie's obsession sent everyone, including an internationally well-known podcaster and a host of internet sleuths, hurtling down the wrong path. Not even Dorothea.

Birdie's face burned with gratitude for their tactfulness. "Yes, Faith is quite well."

"You were good on that podcast," Dorothea said, surprising everyone—maybe even herself—with the compliment. "I mean, you sounded very professional."

"Thank you." Birdie felt even worse for having called Dorothea out earlier.

The conversation moved on, and Birdie sat up a little straighter. It was a kindness, and perhaps something people learned with time, Birdie thought, to let others have their mistakes, because by her age, everyone had their share.

"So, Glen," Nan said, "what's the latest on the investigation on the mutilated animals?"

Glen, who had been even quieter than Dorothea, raised his head—he might have been sleeping—and blinked. "The what?"

Birdie's heart jumped into her throat. Was any of it real? Or had the police been placating him, making him feel important but not taking him seriously?

He shook his head as though to clear it. "Oh, good—I mean, fine, I think. They certainly aren't moving very quickly, but I'm happy to be of help."

"But you told them about my lead?" Nan said.

His eyes held a dullness Birdie hadn't seen before. "Your lead?"

"About the tall man behind the garages around the time of the dead birds."

He straightened; there was something desperate behind his eyes. "No, I forgot . . . But I'm afraid that's not much of a lead, Nan."

Nan waved a hand at him. "It's okay, I'll stop by the police station myself tomorrow. I'm sure you're tired of being our go-between." Nan tilted her head. "What happened to your head?"

"My head?" Glen touched his temple, lightly bruised like a peach, and winced. "Oh, that. Just being clumsy, I'm afraid. Hit it on an open cabinet door."

Birdie kept her mouth shut. Clucks of empathy around the room. It was as plausible, maybe even more so than Glen getting into the wrong car. Who was Birdie to decide? Eventually, they all moved on to the next non-book-related subject.

An hour later, everyone was saying goodbye, and Joseph and Everly helped the others bring food back to their homes. As her apartment emptied, Birdie started thinking about Felix, his accident, the anger coming from Sharon. Despite her concerns, she felt oddly comforted by her friends. Dorothea hung back, thumbing through the local *Senior's Active!* magazine on her kitchen counter.

When the last person had left, she said, "Birdie, a word, please?"

Birdie sighed. "Yes?"

Dorothea pulled at her fingertips. "I didn't tell Jonie."

Birdie made a face. "That's hard to believe."

"I know, I know, but it's true. And it's not to say I wouldn't have." She bowed her head. "Before I knew the girl, of course. But I'm telling you that I did not."

To her surprise, Birdie believed her. "Okay."

"But I know who did."

"Who?"

Dorothea looked over one shoulder, then the other—quite dramatic, in Birdie's estimation, since they were alone. "It was Glen."

"What?" A heaviness in her heart for Glen. "Are you sure?"

She nodded, smoothed down her short hair. "I was outside of Jonie's office, er—"

"Eavesdropping?" Birdie finished.

Her eyes narrowed. "No, I was waiting for the van. Some of us aren't snobs about it."

Birdie sighed. "Okay, fine, I'm sorry. And then what?"

"I overheard—"

Birdie raised an eyebrow.

Dorothea swatted at the air. "Okay, fine, I was listening. Anyway, Glen was telling Jonie about Everly staying with you."

It came as a genuine shock. "But why would he do that?"

"I have no idea, but I thought you'd want to know. And another thing . . ." Dorothea stepped closer. "On a couple of evenings, I've been seeing a man who looks like Glen out by the garages, coming in and out of Glen's bay."

"Richard?"

Dorothea responded in her normal clipped tone. "I don't know his name."

Birdie thought about Nan's tip: *A tall man.* Richard was tall. Immediately, she shook her head. *Get a grip. Not everything has meaning. Some things are just a coincidence.* The likely story was that his brother was helping Glen put some things in storage. "Richard is Glen's brother. He's around quite a bit. Something happened to Glen the other day, and his brother is worried about him."

Dorothea squinted. "What happened?"

"Just a misunderstanding, I think."

"Well, okay. But just remember, it didn't feel nice to be falsely accused about the Everly thing. I think that girl is just lovely." Dorothea sniffed. "And I thought we were friends."

Birdie softened, amused. "Are we?"

"I'd like to think so."

It was a surprise but not an unwelcome one. Birdie was finding that her friendships had spread like spiderwebs. "If we're friends, I have to warn you—don't go disappearing on me or I might unleash the entirety of the internet to find you."

Dorothea smiled and it was a nice smile, and maybe the first genuine one Birdie had seen on the woman, because it touched her eyes and smoothed the wrinkles on her cheeks. "That's precisely what I like about you."

~

After Dorothea left, Birdie knocked on Glen's door. He answered, his eyes dull like before. He didn't invite her in.

"I heard about what happened at the store from Richard."

"I told you my brother is coming for me." His voice gravelly, angry. "He wants me out of the way." His hair hung in short, greasy strands. He looked disheveled, older. "He's a liar."

"Glen," she said softly, "do the police really believe Allison was his first victim like you said?"

His face darkened. "She was the first."

Hope spiked and she tried to push it down. It was what she wanted to hear. "Do they believe that?"

Glen opened and closed his mouth. "We know it's true." He rubbed the bruise on his head, winced, confusion twisting his features.

Pity hardened into a ball. She didn't know if he was telling the truth, but she realized it didn't matter. The truth had twisted her world around Allison's death. Clarity shone a glaring-white light on her. It didn't matter what had happened to Allison. The only truth was that she had died, and Felix, her grandsons, Sharon were what mattered now.

It was time for her to let it all go.

Thirty-Nine

The next morning Birdie woke up, feeling lighter than she'd felt in decades. She asked Everly to join her in the spare bedroom. She looked at the walls, thought of Everly sleeping in there among the pictures of the women.

"Help me fix this," she said, and started taking everything down one by one.

"You're putting them away?"

"They deserve to be at peace, don't you think? And you deserve a room that's not haunted by their deaths."

It didn't take long, but once Everly slid the box under the bed, Birdie let out a long breath.

Everly sat on the edge of the bed. "Now what?"

Birdie shook her head. It felt like a final goodbye, one that had been a long time coming. She smiled and looked outside. No walk today; the sky was pregnant with dark clouds, and a stiff wind spun rain against the windows. "*Chair Yoga with Gayle*?"

The community had a tiny studio similar to the one at Felix's high school, with occasional community programming hosted by none other than Sunny Pines residents. Like eighty-five-year-old twins Ruth and Mary, who hosted *All About Tea with the Twins*. The show's premise was exactly that—all about tea. Or Susanna, a retired zoo director who must have cashed in on favors for a show featuring exotic animals. Sometimes she had a live studio audience. Her best show by far had been when the sloth escaped. It gave them all hope.

They sat side by side on folding chairs. "This is going to be too easy for you," she said to Everly.

"It's good for me." Everly sat tall. "Musicians need to stretch more."

At nine on the dot, the screenshot of the activity schedule for the following day dissolved, and there was Gayle, gray hair in a braided ponytail, a tie-dyed caftan flowing over black leggings, and sitting in a chair of her own. She started with heavy breathing and a meditation in which she *omm*ed for a very long time. Birdie opened one eye to look at Everly. "I think Gayle likes the sound of her own *om*."

Everly giggled.

The flow was easy: a forward bend, a side angle, and a glorious chair pigeon that made Birdie want to cry from how good it felt in her hips. She decided to call Felix when it was over. To apologize sincerely for everything she'd put him through and share with him that she was ready to leave it all behind once and for all. Gayle ended with more of her guttural *omming* and a prayer for peace in the world that was interrupted by a screech from both of their phones. A news alert.

Vampire Killer Breaks Silence after 35 Years

Birdie froze.

Everly gasped, holding up her phone. "Oh my God. He's alive."

Birdie couldn't feel her face. Her hand shook as she reached for the remote to change the station and found a local one carrying the breaking news.

"The serial killer known as the Vampire Killer—who tortured, murdered, and bled dry ten female victims in the seventies and eighties—breaks his silence. In a letter to KCFR, he shares details of other victims previously unknown to authorities, including a twenty-five-year-old woman from Lakewood who went missing in 1985 and a twenty-three-year-old woman who—"

Her fingers splayed wide. Allison had been twenty-three. She couldn't breathe.

". . . a single mom . . ."

Allison had been a single mom. Everly was staring at her, blue eyes wide, and the room darkened with expectation, the newscaster's voice loud in her ears.

". . . from Denver . . ."

Allison had lived in Denver.

A rush of static, and something tugged at her stomach. She felt her younger self there in the room with them. Everything was coming together all at once. Not a coincidence.

". . . an exotic dancer who was his very first victim in 1972."

Birdie. Voices, not her own.

You knew all along. Whispers of truth caressing her cheek.

She did. Her fingers gripped the seat of the chair. In her mind: Allison, the bathtub, the blood, and Birdie's sworn promise.

"Birdie?" Everly's hand on Birdie's arm, real and warm and solid.

"That one victim. It's Allison. I know it." A familiar conviction embraced her like a well-worn coat.

"Oh!" Everly was nodding, concern etched into the corners of her eyes. "What do we do now?"

A knock on her door, muffled voices, and Everly jumped up to open it. Joseph, followed by Louise and Nan.

"We just heard," Joseph said, and they all joined her in the living room.

Louise touched her hand. "Do you think one of those other victims could be your Allison?"

They waited, her friends, and she blinked several times, so grateful. "I do."

Nan tapped her walker. "He's hurting people all over again!"

Everly sat on the coffee table, facing Birdie. "But maybe now the police will see it too?"

"Maybe." Would this make any difference to Felix? She felt more confused than ever. "Thank you, all of you."

"What for?" Joseph said.

"For believing me all this time."

Nan smiled. "That was the easy part. The hard part is going to be finding this bastard. You ready to jump back in where you left off?"

She sat with her hands in her lap. It was everything she'd ever wanted. But she hesitated, reminded of the hurt in Felix's eyes, in Sharon's voice. "I think I'll hand over everything I have to the police and let them handle it from here."

~

After everyone left, Birdie sat by her phone and waited, Allegro tucked by her side. She knew Felix would call, and she wanted to be ready. His face appeared on her screen, a video call.

"Hi, Felix."

He looked pale white. "I heard."

"It's made quite the splash, hasn't it?" She tried to keep her voice light; it felt too big a moment for the phone. She wished he was sitting beside her. "Did you hear about his first victim?"

Felix rubbed his face. "I did, but he never mentioned her by name."

"No, he did not." She could feel his worry through the heat of the phone.

"It's not enough information to know for sure. Are you able . . . I'm worried this will bring it all back for you, and I just don't know if I can go through it again." His voice broke, and Birdie's heart nearly did too. "That podcast. Why did you hide that from me?"

"I've kept too much from you, Felix, I'm so sorry. But I'm going to give everything I have to the police."

"That's what you did before and—"

"And I never stopped, did I? I know, sweetheart, but this time I'm giving it to them and they can decide what to do. I realize how much it's hurt you, son. And how I've done exactly what I didn't mean to do by defining her entire life by her death. I was terrified that because I had rejected her, that maybe she did take her own life—"

"Oh, Mom, no."

She held up a hand. "It's okay. Let me say it. My biggest fear was that I was the reason you grew up without your mom." The minute the words were out, the hold it had over her slid easily to the floor.

Felix's head bowed and his shoulders shook. She wished she could take him in her arms.

"I'm sorry about all the things Sharon said. She worries about me and—"

"Don't you ever apologize for that woman. Everything she said, everything you've said, is valid. I've hurt you, Felix. Over and over again. You've been the biggest blessing of my life. One I never saw coming and never felt like I deserved. Please hear me, son: I have accepted the only truth there is. Fifty-two years ago Allison died and gave you to me to raise. I will always be sad you didn't know her the way that I did, but you are enough, and I love you with my whole heart." She breathed in. Allegro had woken up, sitting on his haunches and staring at her like he understood every single word. She rubbed his chest.

"I'm going to let the police do their jobs. I'm going to let it go."

There was a heavy quiet on the other end, but Birdie didn't panic. She understood his need for silence.

"I love you, Mom," he said at last.

"I love you, too, Felix."

They hung up, and Birdie pressed a palm to her heart and felt her chest move up and down with each breath. The faded remnants of her brief life with Allison filled the space around her in sunbursts of memory, but this time Birdie didn't feel tormented by what might have been. A deep peace folded itself around her, and Birdie smiled. Then she touched Allegro's tiny nose and sent a text to Louise.

Do you like Marlene Dietrich movies?

Louise's quick reply: a thumbs-up emoji, followed by Movie night? Birdie smiled. It's a date.

Forty

Later, she made cinnamon rolls from a can and took Allegro for a walk. Joseph had gone with Everly to help her clear out her camper. She was hoping to sell it to help pay for her college tuition.

When they returned, Everly inhaled and smiled. "Are those cinnamon rolls?"

Immediately, she was on top of the platter, and Birdie had to swat at her hand to stop her. "Glen's coming over too. You can wait."

Everly pulled back. "Fine, but he'd better get here soon."

As if on cue, there was a knock on the door, and Everly hurried to open it. "Come in quick. Birdie made cinnamon rolls and she's holding them hostage."

They gathered around Birdie's small table, the room filled with the spice of the rolls, the bite of the coffee. Glen had been different since the incident at the mall. Something in him had changed, and Birdie didn't like it. "Are you hanging in there, Glen?"

"What?" He was disheveled, his hair uncombed, his beard unkempt, wrinkles in his normally pressed pants. "Yes, dear Bird, I'm fine. Just fine." A vestige of his old self coming through in his odd, clipped tone.

"How are you doing, Birdie?" Joseph said.

She sat with his question, doing a scan of her heart, looking for places of doubt. Finding nothing, she smiled. "I'm okay. I mean, I'll be okay." She inhaled a light scent. Ginger and grapefruit. How Allison smelled after a shower. "We all die one way or another. If he's not caught, he'll get what's coming to him eventually. And I've decided that I won't waste any more of my life thinking about him or thinking about how Allison died." Joseph, Everly, and Glen sat quietly. "I think it's what she would have wanted. Probably what she's always wanted for me."

She glanced at Everly, who was wiping a spot of icing off her lip. "But I think I still have a lot of work to do. Therapy's done such a fine job with our Everly here, you think you can get a referral for me, too, Joseph?"

Joseph's eyes grew bright. "Am I paying?"

"Um, no . . . Actually, you've already paid."

Half-moon creases around his eyes. "How's that?"

"The cat you're keeping? It didn't belong to Faith." She did her best to look sheepish. "It was abandoned by her roommate, and I think he belongs to you now."

Everly laughed.

Glen patted Birdie's arm, then let his hand rest there. "Brava, Birdie, brava. You are fighting against your birth story."

Birdie had no idea what he was talking about, and it made her smile. The old Glen was back. "How's that, Glen?"

His hand still lingered on her arm. "It's said that those born on a leap day live a life of untold suffering, but you are determined to beat the odds."

Joseph grunted. "You were born on a leap day?"

Everly's eyes opened wide. "That's so cool. Wait . . ." She started counting on her fingers, then got out her phone, and Birdie saw her searching for a leap year calendar. "Doesn't that make you, like, younger than me?"

"Officially, I'm seventeen," Birdie said, wanting to feel more playful but overcome by prickles of uneasiness she didn't understand. She shifted the topic. "How's your finger doing, Glen?" Between the bruise on his head and the bandages on his fingers, Glen looked rather beat up.

He stared at his finger, a flash of anger in his eyes that surprised her. "My brother did this to me."

She stiffened, Joseph stopped chewing, and Everly's lips pressed together. Birdie thought of Faith telling her about the note she'd left with Glen. And Birdie's own suspicions that the police were placating Glen, leading him to believe he was part of their investigations. It seemed Richard had been right this whole time. Birdie tried to be as gentle as possible when she said, "Your brother is really worried about you, Glen."

Glen's face darkened immediately, and he withdrew into himself, a candle blown out. "A little too worried." He crossed his arms above his belly. "Our mother coddled him too much as a baby."

Birdie didn't know what to do with that, but she recognized someone on the defensive, and she softened her voice. "He thinks you're having trouble remembering things. And you know what? I think we all struggle with that sometimes."

Glen rubbed his beard, shifted dramatically in his chair. She'd upset him and she felt bad about it, but she also didn't want to shy away from being his friend. And friends told the truth. "Do you think maybe your brother just wants to help you?"

Glen rocked a little, not meeting her eyes.

Birdie looked from Joseph to Everly, both of them looking uneasy. Oh, for heaven's sake, she was on her own.

"There've been a few things I've noticed, and I'm wondering if you might consider going to the doctor to get their opinion."

Glen's face had reddened from anger or embarrassment, and she didn't begrudge him either feeling.

"We're here for you, Glen," Joseph said.

When Glen met her gaze, it was with a seething anger that stopped her next breath. "You believe my brother's lies? I've told you he's a snake."

"He's worried about you," Birdie said gently.

"You're all sheep."

The cruelness of his words scraped across Birdie's skin. This wasn't like him. "What do you mean?"

Glen's eyes glowed with anger. "He wants me to quit driving and sell my car. He wants to put me in a nursing home. What that bastard wants is revenge."

"Revenge for what?" Joseph said.

But Glen stood abruptly, knocking back his chair until it hit the wall. "I have to go."

"Wait, Glen, we're your friends." A sourness rose in her mouth. Control of the conversation was slipping away, and all she'd succeeded in doing was making him angry. "We just wanted you to know we're here for you."

"Friends wouldn't scheme with someone like Richard." Without another word, Glen walked out of the apartment.

Birdie slumped in her chair and sighed. "That didn't go well," she said.

Joseph grunted. "You might have given us a heads-up that you were going to say something."

"It seemed like the right time."

"Poor Glen," Everly said.

Birdie's back curved a little more. "I thought I was being a good friend."

"You were, Birdie," Joseph said, giving her shoulder a squeeze. "It's the losing control that he's angry with, and we can all understand that."

Everly pulled at the ends of her hair. "I feel so sad for Glen. Maybe we can do something for him the way you did for me, Joseph."

"Teach him how to play the cello?"

She laughed. "No. What if we help him put on an art show at the community center?"

Birdie felt a rush of warmth for the girl. "It does seem to be something he regrets having never pursued. I think that's a wonderful idea. But maybe give him a day or two to take all this in. I'm going to let Richard know I spoke with him."

◠

That evening, Everly and Joseph worked on art show logistics ahead of speaking with Glen, so Birdie had the apartment to herself. She settled in to catch up on *Suits*, but before she hit Play she texted Richard.

> Hi Richard, it's Birdie from Sunny Pines. I spoke with Glen about some concerns I had about his memory and I'm afraid it didn't go well.

She hit Send, and before she could push Play on her show, her phone dinged with a text from Louise.

> I have homemade popcorn with lots of butter and a Red Box selection of her films. Interested in joining me?

A youthful flutter in her stomach. Another ding. This one from Richard.

> That doesn't surprise me. My brother is a proud man.

She liked his message and set the phone down, smiling at Louise's offer. Another ding from Richard.

> Do you mind if I stop over? I'm on my way to speak with Glen about a few things but there's something I'd like to talk to you about in person.

Birdie felt like she was going behind Glen's back when she texted OK, but his brother obviously cared about Glen, and she wanted to help out however she could. She frowned, disappointed at the next text she sent in response to Louise.

> I like the sound of that but tonight won't work. Rain check?

Louise's reply came a few seconds later: I'll hold you to it.

Birdie smiled at the phone. Well, well.

A half hour later there was a knock on her patio door, and she invited Richard inside. Like his brother, he immediately took the big chair. Birdie sat on the sofa. Their likeness was uncanny apart from Richard's salt-and-pepper hair and beardless face.

"Would you like some coffee?" she said. "It's decaf."

"Yes, thanks." He stood, took the mug she filled for him, and returned to his seat. "Do you live alone too?" He seemed to be avoiding his reason for coming.

"Most of us here do." She shrugged. "It comes with the territory."

"Right." His knee bounced up and down.

"Are you all right?"

"Yeah, I'm fine." He stopped surveying her apartment and met her gaze.

She sipped her coffee.

"Glen despises me. I'm fifteen years younger than him, which might account for some of it. And our father—these days he'd be called *abusive*, but back then . . ." He shrugged. "I hardly knew Glen; he left home when I was young. He lived with us briefly when I was a teenager and we almost became friends, but then—" He shook his head. "Glen's different."

Birdie was growing hot; the conversation felt wrong, too intimate for someone she hardly knew. She tried to change course. "Did Glen tell you that I lived at the Paragon in the late sixties and seventies?"

That stopped his knee from bouncing.

"Small world," he said. "I lived there with my parents at that time."

Echoes of the past surrounded her. *Landlord's son.* Birdie felt a tingling in her fingertips. "Do you remember the woman who died in the bathtub?"

The smile vanished. "There were two, if I recall. One committed suicide and the other was that serial killer's victim." He shuddered. "Terrible times."

"The one they thought killed herself was my roommate."

"Oh, Bird, I'm—I'm so sorry. That was horrible." He rubbed his head, eyes traveling the room like he wished he was somewhere else.

A baker of some renown. Facts were adding up inside her head. Richard was the son who did maintenance work around the Paragon. She curled her toes, tried to stop herself. This was how it started, and she'd promised Felix, she'd promised herself. *Let it go.* "Do you bake, Richard?"

He tilted his head, giving her an odd look. "Sometimes. Our mother owned a bakery off Colfax."

Stop it, Birdie. She closed her eyes, imagined holding all her questions in the palm of her hand and squeezing them into a lump. She was going to let the police do what they did best, and she was going to go to therapy, work on herself, and be a mother and grandmother. She'd had fifty-two years to solve this crime and had failed.

Richard slumped forward in the chair, his coffee forgotten on the end table. "I can't do this anymore."

"Do what?" Suddenly, Birdie wanted more than anything for Richard to leave.

"Keep guessing whether he's well or not." He stood and started to pace, and he was so tall and imposing in her small living room that it set her hands shaking. "A few months ago I thought he could use some company because all he did was complain, so I got him a cat. Glen forgot and left a door open, and the thing ran away. And then this last incident—he could have been arrested. I have my own life and I don't have time for his shit."

Glen had never mentioned a cat. Pricks of doubt across her scalp. Facts piling around her. Birdie shook her head to clear them. Sharon's words loud and clear: *You are not a cop.*

"Maybe you should talk to his daughter?" Birdie pulled at her fingers, eyeing the door.

"She's fucking useless. Moved as far away as she could get first chance she got."

Birdie inhaled loudly, and in that moment, Richard seemed to remember himself, and he sat down, looking contrite. "I'm sorry. This is not your problem. Listen"—he spoke softly now—"I'm going to have to move Glen into assisted living. This just isn't working for him."

Birdie cringed. Why was he telling her this? "So soon? Has he been to a doctor yet? There are medications these days that might help. He seems to do okay on his own, don't you think?"

Richard speared her with a look quite similar to his brother's. "He's different lately, like his mind is looser, more pliable, and he says things I don't understand. With how much I travel, I'm worried about him being alone." He reached into his bag and pulled out a handful of pamphlets, laid them on the coffee table. "These are some step-up facilities in the area. I thought maybe you could—since you've already talked to him—maybe give these to him for me? I'm going to mention the idea to him after I leave here so he has some time to adjust to it." He stood like the conversation was over, an expectation that she would do as he said.

Birdie decided she agreed with Glen: she didn't care for Richard either.

"I think hearing it from his friends might help him to accept it," he said.

Glen's deepest fears realized. She felt a pang thinking how right he'd been. "Seems like you're making the choice for him." She didn't mean to say it like that, but it was the truth and she couldn't help it.

Richard slumped. "I know, but I just don't see what options I have."

"Maybe ask your brother what he wants."

"Maybe."

Maybe? She'd talk to Glen in the morning. Be there for him in what would likely be his darkest hour. She was his friend, not Richard's.

Richard rubbed his face like he was washing off the conversation. "Here." He held out a note card. "That's his daughter's name and phone number. I thought maybe you should have it, too, in case anything were to happen to Glen and you can't get ahold of me. She's got your information as well."

She took the card, wondering how she'd become so entrenched in Glen's personal affairs. "Sure."

He walked over to the inside door, where he could access Glen's apartment from the hallway. "Oh . . ." He turned. "I stashed a spare key under the mat on his patio for an emergency. Just in case. But don't tell him, please. He'd kill me if he found out."

Birdie waved her agreement but did not get up from the sofa. The conversation left her wishing she'd chosen to watch the Marlene Dietrich marathon with Louise instead.

~

When Everly returned later from Joseph's, she was bubbling over with excitement. "Joseph is going to talk to Jonie about getting the space reserved, and he's got a friend who used to own a framing store who can probably get us a bunch of easels. I'll talk to Glen tomorrow." She chewed on a nail. "Do you think he'll want to see me after today?"

Birdie thought about Richard's plan for Glen, and a rush of sadness rolled down her back. "I think a visit from you might be exactly what he needs to cheer up."

Everly beamed.

Birdie went to bed early, and despite her exhaustion from the day's events, she tossed and turned for hours thinking about Glen. When she finally did sleep, it was pitted with nightmares of a dark room and her own screams.

~

"Birdie?" Everly poked her head inside the bedroom. "Oh, good, you're awake."

Birdie was sitting up in bed, reading. "Only because I never fell asleep in the first place."

Everly frowned. "That sucks, I'm sorry. But I've got coffee already brewed, and I made some hard-boiled eggs— Oh, and the dogs have been out. I just wanted you to know that I'm heading over to Glen's now. Wish me luck!"

Birdie smiled at the girl. Since the concert, she'd blossomed. Her pale skin glowed like moonlight, and she moved like she was comfortable taking up space instead of trying to shrink herself down to nothing. Thoughts of her conversation with Richard the night before turned her stomach. "You'll make his day."

"I hope so."

Forty-One

Allison

Everly tells Glen about her idea for an art show. She is touched when his eyes get wet and he dabs at them with a handkerchief.

Everly still has heart palpitations when she thinks of going to class and performing, and sometimes she sweats so bad she has to change her shirt, but it's different now. She is supported and she feels strong. The art show is Everly's way of paying it forward.

She shines so bright I look away. Karen tries to hold her hand.

Poor Everly.

Glen invites her inside. His hands shake, and when Everly sees that, she is filled with pity.

Glen is still very angry from his visit with Richard, so he has to pretend to be the same old Glen. Everly does not deserve his acrimony. But it is hard for Glen because Richard thinks he's better than Glen. Richard thinks he's the boss because he's younger and richer. Rage burns, flowing hot just under his skin, and I cannot be too close for it singes the ether.

Everly goes on and on about the art show. Her excitement makes her luminescent. She wants to see the paintings. Glen is prideful, he knows this, but he is honored to show her his paintings. No one else has ever seen them, except for his wife, who never appreciated them. All she sees is trash, not the masterpieces Glen knows them to be.

Poor Glen. He doesn't hear his own lies.

Richard waits for Glen in his car because Glen agrees to look at the assisted-living places as long as he can show Richard something first. Richard agrees because he will do anything to rid himself of his brother.

Poor Richard.

Everly follows Glen to the garage. He walks more stooped than before, his pants hang loose from his waist, and Everly finds it hard to look at him. He is defeated. He is elderly. It tightens into a ball in her throat and glistens in her eyes. Glen uses his key to open the garage door. His shining sedan fills the entire space.

"I can't wait to see your work," Everly says.

Glen smiles back. His heart is full. Everly is perfect in every way, and he is lucky to share his passion with her. He touches the small of her back when she walks inside.

Karen screeches, and it sets off a flock of crows from the trees above.

"Where do you keep your paintings?"

No, Everly, no.

Karen weeps. Tonia's arms are extended, ready to welcome Everly into our fold.

The garage door closes, and Everly and Glen are submerged into a midnight black where shadows harden.

"Lights, please?" Everly says. We sense her waning lightness; we feel the first pricks of fear in the space between her breaths. We are the white-hot pain when a tire iron swings for her head.

Forty-Two

Sometime after Everly left, Allegro raced through the door and hopped up onto the bed. Birdie spent a few moments petting him. Her phone rang and she scrambled across the bed to pick it up, hoping it was Felix or Sharon or one of the boys.

"Hello?"

"Hi, this is Diana. Glen's daughter? Is this Birdie?"

"Yes, hi, Diana. Richard told me he'd given you my number." Birdie cringed; she did not want to be put in the middle of Glen and his family any more than she already was.

"I'm so sorry to bother you. He called me after my uncle stopped by last night, and he was pretty upset and not making a lot of sense. Now this morning I can't get ahold of him. I think Uncle Richard's right about him."

Birdie gritted her teeth. How had she become the confessional for Glen's family?

"But Uncle Richard's mission to get Dad into assisted living is making it so much worse."

Birdie blew air through her nose, not in the mood to dispense advice. "You know, I don't think your dad has been to a doctor yet. This could be from stress too."

"What kind of stress?"

"I don't think that working on this case again has been what he thought it would be. It's probably added quite a bit of stress, don't you think?" She yawned quietly into her hand.

"Case?" Genuine confusion in her voice. "What are you talking about?"

An uptick in Birdie's pulse. "The Vampire Killer?" Her mouth turned dry. Had Glen been more than just confused? Had he made it all up in a desperate desire to feel important again? "He was consulting with the police, wasn't he?"

"Why on earth would they ask that of him?"

"Because he knew so much about the case." The idea seemed suddenly ridiculous. "Didn't he tell you?" she said, sounding weak.

Silence. The woman's breathing. "Oh God." The words seemed to catch in her throat. "He's as bad as Uncle Richard said—even worse."

"What do you mean?"

"My dad was never a cop, Birdie."

Her pulse sped up. "What?"

"Dad was a maintenance guy. Worked most of his career for my grandpa and then for my uncle." Diana breathed heavily into the phone. "I need to call Uncle Richard. I'm really worried now."

Birdie's head was spinning. Glen hadn't been a cop. She smoothed an eyebrow, thinking of all the things he'd said. Birdie shivered, the room suddenly too cold. Voices chattering in her head. Glen wasn't a cop. Glen worked in maintenance at his father's properties. *The landlord's son.* A certainty grew in her stomach.

A thought. A voice. Birdie wasn't sure. *Glen's a liar.*

"Will you check on him for me?"

Glen's a liar. The voice was that of a girl. Birdie looked through the blinds of her window to the empty parking lot, glanced in the family room. Allegro and Adagio were huddled together on their bed.

But a certainty was taking shape, sprouting into something real and true and one that Birdie could not ignore. Felix's face flashed before her.

I was never enough for you. Suspicions building, eroding her promise to him— *No!* She couldn't do that to her son. Not again. She'd promised him. Birdie pressed a hand to her chest, heart racing. Diana was still speaking.

"I'm sorry, are you saying something, Diana?"

"I said"—she increased her volume and slowed down her speed—"will you check on Dad for me?"

The ringing in her ears stopped.

"Birdie?" Diana said.

"I'm here. Yes, yes, I'll go check on him now." She hung up with Diana and hurried over to Joseph's.

Forty-Three

Birdie knocked in rapid succession on Joseph's door. Finally, he opened it, and Birdie said the one thing she shouldn't: "I think Glen's the Vampire Killer!" Hearing it out loud, Birdie doubted herself almost immediately. After everything, she carried no credibility. Even with herself. But she couldn't take it back now, and her suspicions had begun to harden into panic.

"What?" Joseph's expression gave nothing away.

Birdie's breath was shallow. "Glen's not a cop, and Everly's with him and I think she's in danger. Come on, there's a key under the mat."

Joseph didn't hesitate, grabbing a coat on a hook by the door and stepping into the hallway. "Let's go, then."

He might be the best friend Birdie had ever had.

They took a shortcut through Birdie's apartment and out the door to get to Glen's patio. Joseph knocked. He knocked again. Dread tightened around Birdie's throat. With the blinds closed, they couldn't see inside. "His dad managed the apartment where Allison and I lived."

"What?" Joseph sounded shocked.

"And Glen's daughter told me he worked in maintenance for his father's buildings."

She tried to look through the blinds, feeling cold all over. "Everly came over to see him this morning, but she didn't come back. I called her and she's not picking up. We have to get inside."

He bent down, pulled the key out from under the mat, and quickly opened the door. They hurried into the dark apartment, the only light burning above the stove. The place felt off, the air tinged with something chemical, and Birdie's mouth watered unpleasantly.

"Let's look around," Birdie said, and opened Glen's bedroom door. It was bare, just a mattress with a fitted sheet and a blanket thrown across the middle, a lamp on the floor, and not a single picture on the walls. Her stomach sank. Where was Everly?

She turned to the closed bathroom door and felt a sudden rush of vertigo when she touched the knob. The room tilted sideways, and when she grabbed for her walker, her hands were those from her youth. The arthritic curl gone, her fingers long and straight, the skin free of age spots. Her vision doubled, and her old hands materialized. Joseph pushed the door open and Birdie walked inside, her feet dragging.

It was a normal bathroom, just like hers, bare of any decoration except for one: a framed drawing hung on the wall above the toilet. She glanced at it, nearly dismissing it as nothing important, but something turned her head back to the picture and she peered closer. A rust-colored sketch so faded the image blended into the paper in some places. She squinted to see it more clearly and stumbled on the rug, only the grip on her walker to keep her from falling to her knees. She couldn't breathe. The walls of Glen's apartment peeled away, revealing the floral wallpaper, wooden chair rail, and white beadboard of her old apartment. The kitchen with the Formica countertops and yellow appliances; the short, dark hallway to the bedrooms; the closed door to the bathroom. Birdie's hand on the knob turning, turning, turning.

"Joseph," she wheezed.

He was by the shower. "What is that smell?" She heard the shower curtain slide open and Joseph moaned. "Oh my God."

But Birdie was frozen to the spot, staring at the drawing Glen had hung above the toilet. She heard Joseph gagging.

"What in the hell?" he croaked.

"Joseph," Birdie whispered.

"What?"

"It's Allison." The drawing was of a woman in a bathtub, head turned away, arm draped over the side, blood falling from her arm to a pool on the floor. Their bathroom, Allison, exactly as Birdie had found her. The very image that had haunted her all these years. Birdie's tongue thickened, and she couldn't speak or make sense of her thoughts except for what she knew to be true.

"Birdie," Joseph's voice was low and serious.

She turned, and in a different bathtub lay the remains of a small animal. What it had once been, she could not tell, nor did she want to know. She pressed a palm to her mouth, her stomach revolting, and before her legs gave out, Joseph rushed to her side and helped her from the room.

"He's the one killing the animals," Joseph said, breathing hard, his skin a chalky gray.

Panic threatened to overwhelm her, but Birdie put a hand to her stomach and breathed deep.

Joseph's hands turned to fists. "You were right about Allison and you're right about Glen."

Birdie gripped his arms. "And Everly is with him!"

Joseph grabbed her hand and helped her move as fast as she could outside Glen's apartment, where they both pulled in lungfuls of fresh air.

Dorothea stood on the sidewalk with Nan by her side. "So, you're adding breaking and entering to your list of activities you'll do instead of riding on the van?" she said. Nan chuckled.

"Call 9-1—" Birdie didn't have enough air to get the numbers out. It felt like she was drowning.

Dorothea's eyes widened. "What?"

"Glen's the Vampire Killer!" Joseph shouted. "And Everly's with him!"

"I knew it!" Nan said, huffing in her oxygen.

Dorothea sprang ahead of them. "I saw them!" She was gasping now too. "They went into Glen's garage!"

Birdie's heart jumped into her throat. "Oh my God!"

The four of them took the sidewalk that went to the back of the apartment building. Jean and Louise stood in the grassy area by the garages, chatting while their dogs sniffed each other and peed on a tree. They waved and Louise said, "Isn't it beautiful tod—"

"Glen's the Vampire Killer!" Joseph barked. "And he's got Everly in his garage."

"Someone call 9-1-1," Birdie gasped, frustrated by the slowness of her walker speed. Nan beside her, head down and hunched, watching the ground with each step. "The rest of you . . . run!"

Joseph, Louise, Dorothea, and Jean got to Glen's garage door first, with Birdie and then Nan bringing up the rear. Louise put her ear to the garage door. Joseph knocked. Dorothea knocked even harder.

"Everly!" Louise called.

"Are you in there?" Birdie screamed. "Everly?"

"My name is Nan Hart. My location is Sunny Pines Retirement Community—" Nan said into her phone. "And the emergency is that we found the Vampire Killer, and he's an eighty-four-year-old nutcase with a young girl and nothing to lose."

Forty-Four

ALLISON

Glen feeds off vulnerability, is satiated by pain, and when they beg, he wants to do it all over again. He prefers them untouched, beautiful in their perfection. He hates that he hurt her. There is blood matting her hair, which is already drying. If he could do it all over again, he would be kinder, gentler. He is not a monster. But she comes to him, sweet and perfect, with skin that shows the blue of her veins, the salubriousness of her blood, and he knows that she is a gift. His last masterpiece.

The power of his remembered youth flows into the wasted muscles of his arms and legs, gives him strength to see his labor through to its beautiful end. Glen is stronger now. His brother lies motionless underneath the girl in the trunk of his car. Richard is a sanctimonious prick, and last night Glen listened to the final beat of his heart with satisfaction, celebrated the last panicked suck of the plastic bag around his head. He does not want his brother's blood. His medium comes from the supple, untouched veins of women. If he could, he would bathe in it. He draws them instead, honors them with their own viscous plasma. Poetic and beautiful.

But this time is different, and Glen knows it. He feels us more strongly than ever, and it sets an erratic beat to his pulse, thickens his fingers, and makes him fumble. We are silent in this cramped space of pain and fear, not the furies, pulling at our hair, shrieking with delight in the capture of our prey. We are here for the truth. It is all we care about.

We are victims no more.

And Glen knows it.

Glen has a system he developed after me. Clean and neat. First, the chloroform to knock us out, soaked in a handkerchief and tied tightly around our noses and inside our mouths. Followed by the binding of our hands. And then the bloodletting. He leaves us pale and stiff but peaceful, and Glen is proud of that.

Because Glen believes he is smarter than a monster.

But this was too sudden, and Glen finds his hands slippery from sweat and blood. And the trunk where he pushed her body is too low. And the ache in his back is unbearable. And the screams in his head insufferable.

He hits his temple with the flat of his hand, confused and panicking, and he makes mistakes.

Everly comes to, groggy, bewildered, the binding around her mouth tied too loosely to keep the air in her lungs filled with chloroform.

Mistake number one.

I am happy to count his mistakes. They are piling up, and the women giggle at his clumsiness. Glen the brilliant one. Glen the master of those around him. Glen the artist. Is now nothing more than Glen the old. He does not hold command of his body in the same way. It fails him. As does his mind, which unspools like thread.

He is not the smartest in the room.

Or the strongest.

Glen swats at his ears. "What?" he bellows. "Shut up!" He is distracted; he is tired.

Karen is in the trunk with Everly, whispering in her ear.

Get up. Get up. Get up.

Get out. Get out. Get out.

Run. Run. Run.

Everly's head clears to the lilting voice of a girl that disappears into the pounding of her heart. It is too dark to see, but the dark does not scare Everly. She has grown up in its embrace, and it does not own her like it once did. Her arms twist behind her, move freely beneath her, hands free of any bond.

Mistake number two.

She touches something, some*one*, beneath her. Lightheaded from panic, she very nearly passes out. She doesn't need to know that it's the body of Glen's only brother, who stuck his nose where it didn't belong. *She just needs to run.*

Everly frees her arms and removes the bandanna. We flow in between atoms, push aside molecules, and with our screams the trunk cracks open. Glen is busy with his needle and bag and doesn't hear the soft creak because he forgot to put in his hearing aids.

Mistake number three.

Everly pushes against the stiffened body below her to climb out. It makes a sound like an exhaled breath. She swallows a sob.

Glen stands at the front of the car wearing a headlamp and holding a needle and tubing. Everly drops to her knees. She puts a hand over her mouth to keep a growing hysteria inside. Karen crawls beside her. *Open the door.*

Everly jams her fingers under the garage door and pulls up; her nails rip away from her skin. It doesn't budge. Her tears are silent. She crawls to the other side of the car, away from Glen. Small rocks from the hard pavement dig into her kneecaps. Her pain is electric and brushes over us.

Carol weeps.

But Everly will not give up. She knows the grip of fear. It is familiar, comforting in its predictability. Her companion for too long. It took her father, but it will not take her. She sees the garage door opener clipped to the sun visor. Hears voices.

Not our voices.

No, not ours.

Everly slips her hand into the door handle and holds her breath as she pulls it open.

She's so focused on crawling into the car, fingertips touching the plastic opener, that she doesn't notice the headlamp.

Jiggling across the walls.

Moving.

Toward her.

Open the door!

Someone behind her, hands around her neck squeezing with a desperate strength. Everly's fingers drop from the opener, instinctively reach to loosen the grip around her neck. Her vision dims, and with it shadows harden into feminine shapes. Voices deepen in her head.

Karen whispers in her ear.

Push the button. Now!

Everly is built like her father. Tall with long arms and fingers. Perfect for the cello. Or for escaping from a serial killer. She extends one trembling arm, finger scrabbling in the air, until . . .

She pushes the button.

Forty-Five

"I hear someone in there!" Jean yelled.

Birdie banged her fist into the garage door until she couldn't feel it anymore. A cold sweat slimy on her neck. She'd been right. All along, she'd been right. And it would all have been for nothing if she lost Everly.

"Nan!" she screamed.

"Police are on the way!" Nan sounded breathless. They all were from pounding on the metal and yelling for Everly.

Suddenly, the garage door began to lift, and Birdie stepped back, holding her breath and wishing she'd used her cane today so she could slam it over Glen's head. Her vision blurred, her lungs burned, and an old grief twisted through her heart. Were they too late? Inside the garage, all she could see was his boat of a car with its trunk open and nothing else.

"Oh my God, is that a body in the trunk?" Dorothea said, and sour acid rushed into Birdie's mouth. They all hurried forward.

Birdie gasped; relieved and horrified to see Richard's body crammed inside like he hadn't been sitting across from her last night, alive and breathing. Shock turned her skin cold, clammy. Glen was a killer. Capable of such horror, even to his own brother. "Everly," she wheezed.

Joseph bellowed and hurtled around the passenger side of the car, pulling at something, but the garage bay was narrow and with the open trunk she couldn't see anything. Her heart beat against her chest.

"Joseph?" Her voice had grown hoarse. "What is it?"

Grunting, a moan, and a man's scream, and Joseph squeezed out from the narrow space, hauling Glen out by his neck. He pushed him outside the garage. Glen stumbled, then regained his balance, eyes darting around like a reptile. He landed on Birdie, and his smile was sick and twisted. "Ah, Bird. Did you like the cake I made for you?"

Birdie's cry burned her lungs. Revulsion bled through her stomach all the way to the tips of the fingers she wanted to dig into his eyes. "Where is she?" she screamed.

Joseph came up behind Glen, much shorter but fast on his feet, hands in fists by his chin.

"Punch him, Killer!" Jean yelled.

And he did. Two quick punches to the back of his head, then Joseph shuffled around and sank one in the kidney, the stomach, Glen's chin and nose. Blood poured from Glen's face, red smeared across his white teeth. Joseph kept punching until, like an old, rootless tree, Glen tumbled to the ground, where he rolled up, arms over his head. Joseph stood above him, feet apart, hands still in fists, the Rocky Balboa of Sunny Pines.

Birdie couldn't breathe. "Where is she?" she screamed again.

"Car," Joseph wheezed.

She left her walker and used the car as support to move around the driver's side, avoiding eye contact with the body in the trunk. Please, no, she wasn't too late again. Fear ran under her skin, making her itch all over. Louise squeezed in behind her with her hand on Birdie's lower back to support her.

And Birdie felt the strength drain from her legs when she saw Everly crawling over the seat toward her.

Tears streaked the girl's face, whiter than Birdie had ever seen it. Birdie opened the door, and Everly's fingers found her own through the opening and squeezed. "You're safe now, Everly. We've got you."

Birdie let her own tears fall.

~

When the police arrived, Birdie was sitting outside the garages on the grass with her arm tight around Everly. The girl sucked on a little bit of Nan's oxygen to help settle her. A few feet away, the Vampire Killer lay prone on the pavement, Joseph still standing guard. The shock of the last few minutes sat on her shoulders, turning the light outside a bright Technicolor that wasn't normal and made it all seem like a dream. A ringing in her ears. So close—she'd been so close to losing Everly too. Birdie hung her head and pulled Everly closer.

Nan walkered her way to Joseph, took ahold of his forearm, and lifted it as high as she was able. "Winner!"

Joseph, breathing hard, one fist swelling to the size of an orange, the other raised high in the air, stared at Nan like she'd come from a different planet.

Stunned and exhausted, none of the gang said much of anything until police cars screeched into the parking lot, lights flashing, sirens blazing, uniforms surrounding Glen. Birdie kept her arm tight around the shaking girl, gently stroking her hair and making soft, comforting noises deep in her throat.

Nan stopped a young officer. "You fellas can take it from here," she told him. "We're exhausted."

Forty-Six

Allison

We surround Glen on the ground, our hands hovering over his body. He is not dead. Not yet. But that was never the point.

We come to set the truth free.

And it flitters and swoops around us, going wherever it likes.

Now we give him the gift of our memories to hold on to until he draws his very last breath. A floodgate opens, bloating him with vestiges of our fear, our pain, our nightmares. Glen squeezes shut his eyes, but it slips beneath his lashes, illuminates the inside of his lids, where he is tormented even in the dark.

He whimpers, haunted by the lightness of our beings.

Glen is not an artist.

Glen is not a genius.

The police handcuff him, shove him into the back of a car.

Glen can't see well through his swollen eye, and he feels excruciating pain radiating from his hip and lower back. When he looks out the window, he sees the air fold in on itself, mold into forms, into faces he once knew as victims.

Our very last gift is his singular truth.

Glen is only a man.

Forty-Seven

A media frenzy descended on Sunny Pines following the Vampire Killer's unmasking by residents of the retirement community. Birdie gave an exclusive interview to Natasha that went viral but refused all other interviews. She was done with anything to do with murderers and name-clearing for as long as she lived.

When the truth was finally freed, she realized how caged she'd been by it. The families had their answer, but it didn't bring any of the women back and it washed Birdie in a deep sorrow. She focused on what she did have: her family and her friends.

Nan accepted every single interview that came her way, earning the reputation of being Denver's favorite grandma. She wore the red hat to all of them, much to her daughter-in-law's horror. For a while, life at Sunny Pines didn't feel so predictable, and when the excitement died down, Birdie and the gang were all a little bit relieved to go back to their normal lives.

The very best outcome, apart from Glen finally facing the families of the women he'd murdered and life in prison, was the surprise visit she received from Felix, Sharon, and the boys a few days after everything happened.

They'd knocked on her patio door, and when Birdie saw them through the glass, she started to cry. Felix took her in his arms and held her. He was joined by Sharon and Tyler and Cody, who all took a side, put their arms around her, and held on until she'd cried herself out.

"You're a baller, Igbird," Cody said when they'd disentangled themselves.

"I'm making a movie about you," Tyler added. "It's called *Revenge of the Igbird.*"

She smiled at her grandsons, tears springing once again to her eyes, but this time for their nearness and the love for them that nearly shattered her. "Can you make Glen die in your version?"

Tyler's eyes widened. "Can there be lots of blood?"

"Please."

Everly stayed with Joseph so Sharon and Felix could take the spare room, and the boys slept on her pullout couch. For the next four days, her apartment was full to bursting, and it was exactly what Birdie needed to recover. On the last day of their visit, Felix took her for a drive, and to her surprise they went to the Paragon. Rain fell in sheets from a dark gray sky, the windshield wipers working overtime to keep up.

"What are we doing here?" She was inundated with memory, the good rising easily to the surface. Of Allison singing to Felix after a bath. Her laugh that sometimes ended in a snort. Her shoulder lightly touching Birdie's on the couch. Of Felix calling Birdie *Mama* for the first time. His little body curled into her arms where he felt safe.

"I thought it might be the right place to say goodbye to my mom." His voice was thick with emotion. "I figure she's been with you all this time—with us—and maybe now she's okay to move on."

She touched his arm. "Felix—"

"And I just want to tell her I love her." He reached over and took Birdie's hand, and they sat like that, with the rain in rivulets down the windshield, each of them saying their own goodbye.

On their last night, Birdie introduced them to everyone and hosted a very crowded and loud dinner party at her place with a private concert from Everly herself. Her heart hurt to say goodbye to her family at the airport, but with a promise to get out for Tyler's YouTube movie premiere and a family trip to the beach, the distance between them felt the shortest it had ever been.

On a warm spring day, Birdie sat on her patio with Everly and Joseph, sipping an iced coffee Everly had made her and trying to pretend she liked it.

"You don't have to drink it," Everly said, smiling.

"What? I like it."

"Your face says differently."

Birdie groaned and loudly sipped the coffee. "Well, my face is lying. I love it."

Everly laughed. Joseph shook his head.

"So, they accepted me back into the program," Everly said. "I start this fall and I'll be living in the dorms."

Joseph clapped his hands. "I knew it!"

"Congratulations!" Birdie said, thinking about the girl she'd first met in her camper on the empty stretch of road. She tilted her head. "Do they allow dogs in the dorms?"

Everly's shoulders crept up to her ears, and her eyes darted to Joseph, back to Birdie. "I was hoping you might keep them for me? Just until I get my first apartment."

Birdie looked at Joseph, whose smile had a touch of glee to it. "I got a cat out of the deal, and you get two dogs," he said. "Seems fair to me."

Birdie narrowed one eye at Joseph but smiled at Everly. "I guess I'm quite the dog person."

Everly let out a rush of air. "Thank you."

Birdie patted her hand. "You've come a long way, kid."

She nodded. "It turns out that there is something more terrifying than being around people and performing."

Joseph raised his eyebrows. "What's that?"

"Getting kidnapped by a serial killer and nearly having my blood drained so he could paint my portrait with it." She shivered, then smiled at Joseph. "Are you ready?"

He clapped his hands on his thighs and stood. "More than ever."

Birdie looked up. "Where are you going?"

"Joseph's going to introduce me to his wife."

Joseph ducked his head. "I want Sofia to know I've changed."

"And I'm his proof," Everly said.

Birdie reached out and took his hand, squeezed; he squeezed back. "I'm sure she's very proud of you, Joseph."

"Do you want to come with us?" Everly said.

"Not today," she said, and petted Allegro under his chin. "Today I have something planned that's just for me. I'm facing my own serial killer, you might say."

Everly made a face. "The real one wasn't enough?"

Birdie smiled. "Not quite." She shooed them away, and after they left, she finished the rest of the god-awful iced coffee, her heart fuller than it had a right to be.

~

Birdie settled the dogs on their pillow, brushed her hair, and slipped her favorite peacock-blue pashmina around her shoulders. Then she walked outside.

I am beside her, the backs of our hands just touching, I remember the way she smells: a woodsy kind of floral. Her hair—gray now, but still wavy and beautiful—brushes her shoulders. She is Birdie now and the youthful one with auburn locks and hazel eyes. This Birdie I like even better.

Birdie made her way to the circle drive by the office, where a crowd of Sunny Pines residents were hanging about. Some with walkers, others with canes, a few with oxygen tubes, and most of them standing and breathing all on their own. She scanned the crowd, stopping just outside the group, the white-knuckled grip on her walker the only giveaway that she was nervous.

Oh, Birdie.

I am the forever present. A scared pregnant woman with a swollen belly and no place to stay. A mother snuggling her baby. A woman in love.

Birdie inhaled and moved her walker forward. A man in a plaid shirt tucked into jeans turned around. "You're Birdie, right? The famous crime stopper?"

A few other heads turned. One woman, bundled in a winter coat and gloves despite the warm temperatures, nodded vigorously. "That's her!"

Birdie waved them both off. "I'm retired just like everybody else."

"You're a hero," someone said.

A van pulled into the circle, and the group turned toward it and formed into a line. "Are you coming with us?" the man asked.

Out of habit, Birdie hung back, shaking her head, an internal fight that nobody but her could see. The line of people disappeared into the van.

She lifted her chin, felt the warm sun across her skin. "Goodbye, Allison."

I linger beside her for a moment until my heart swells so big it lifts me up. I am free now, too, and the women take me in their arms, and together we dissipate.

Finally, Birdie saw her and she relaxed, a smile spreading slowly across her lips. Louise walked confidently across the emptying parking lot, her white hair hanging in shiny waves to her chin, gray eyes trained on Birdie.

Birdie straightened her shoulders, feeling stronger. "You look exceptionally beautiful today, Louise."

"Do I?" A pale pink blush stole across her cheeks. "Why, thank you."

Birdie bent an elbow, but Louise put her hand on Birdie's walker instead.

"First time?" Louise said, keeping her pace even with Birdie.

"It is."

"So where does this one take us?"

Birdie laughed. "I have no idea."

Together, they got on the van.

Author's Note

The idea for this story began when my mother moved into a senior-living community after my father passed away. What struck me most about this community was the fascinating mix of people who lived there too. Retired teachers, doctors, artists, lawyers, business owners, world travelers, writers, parents, grandparents, athletes, etc. People with decades of lived experiences and stories together navigating the challenges that come with a different phase of life. Some, like my mom, wading through the grief of losing a lifelong partner, others with physical challenges that make independent living a daily feat. Some with families who live close by and others with families states or continents away.

And all of them with stories.

These last few years have not been easy for my mom. In many ways it's been like starting over, redefining and discovering new things about herself in a time of life when change is hard and even a little scary. I have been in awe of the way she has tackled these life changes, the friends she's made along the way, and the support they provide for one another. As Birdie says, getting older is not for the faint of heart, but my mother and her friends are doing it with such grace and humor, showing me how much more there is to learn and experience and do for the very first time, no matter our age.

And this is what sparked the creative fire behind Birdie and her friends at Sunny Pines. Each one has their own story. Some scandalous, some haunting, and some dangerous. While these characters are completely fictional and in no way represent anyone I know, their desire for community, friendships, and adventure are very much inspired by everyday people who often have the very best stories of all.

Acknowledgments

I'm beginning to think that I shouldn't save acknowledgments for the end of books. I should write a new one every week for the people in my life who simply make my world a better place. I could read aloud my thanks at gatherings, dinner parties, family reunions, a girls' weekend. To all the people who matter to me when I'm writing and not writing a book.

But that might get weird.

So I'll dive right in here and make the most of this part of the book where I get to say all the things to all the wonderful people who make writing stories and living life fun.

To the team of folks who take my book and my hand and walk us from Point A (let's make this story better) to Point Z (let's get it into the hands of readers). My editor, Selena James, for being there from the first creative spark to the final word and helping me to deepen Birdie and the gang's story in all the right places. To Tiffany Yates-Martin, who can read an entire manuscript in a record amount of time (future Olympic sport, perhaps?) and then break it down with me as though she had written it herself. Tiffany, you know how to get inside a story with an author and then make space for our creative pen to do the work. You have a gift. To my publicist, Ann-Marie Nieves, who gets my books into all the right hands and knows how to make waves come pub day. To Jessica Faust, for keeping this career going with me. That first phone call seems like yesterday and also decades ago, and I'll always be grateful for it. And finally, thank you to the entire team at Lake Union, who work behind the scenes to make books better and help to get them read.

To my cousin Allison, for asking to be put into a book. I might have only used your name for inspiration, but our brainstorming session on the porch in Pensacola with all the family was some of the best fun. To Christi and Sherri, for putting up with Allison. And to Gwynne, for being the best Nina my kids could ask for.

To my mom, for living the kind of life that inspires me to do better and for patiently working through the many iterations of this story with me. Please stop moving furniture now. To Norma, for your love of Costco and for reading an early version of this and sitting through my barrage of questions. And of course, to Loki and Sage, who are in fact the behind-the-scenes inspiration for the two most important characters of all.

To Ray, we miss your dad jokes and your great laugh, but we are so grateful for your love. To Becca, thank you for being my enthusiastic fan club of one and for your sweet support of my writing dreams for all these years.

To Jen and Scott, for also putting up with Allison (jk jk Allison). But mostly for all our amazing childhood memories together. The older I get, the more appreciative I am of our family and all the stories we have between us. Except for the time Jen shoved you outside in only your towel during an Iowa snowstorm, Scott. That was all her idea.

To Sara Miller: I will never write a book that your eyes don't see first. You are so talented at asking just the right questions. To my Ohio U girls, who used to wake up early after a night out to volunteer at an event I organized and are still supporting me thirty years later by reading manuscripts for me. To my critique partners and fellow authors, Mary Johnson and Elizabeth Richards, for your always insightful feedback. Salem was a blast. Finally, thank you to Brenda Hobgood, Denise Boeding, and Sara Florence for reading my work before it's even had a chance to get dressed.

And to Sean: We've shared heartache and loss, raising kids to adults, and so much more. I can write because you always make sure I have the creative space and emotional support to do it. Thank you for being you. To Ella and Keira, call your brother. He misses you. And to Sawyer, I promise not to make a big deal about you being the only kid still at home. But what would you like for dinner?

Book Club Questions

1. Birdie spent much of her life trying to discover the answers to Allison's death, even when it kept her from truly experiencing and enjoying the life she had built for herself and Felix, and even when it hurt the ones she loved. Did you understand what drove her? Or did it frustrate you? Why?

2. Birdie finds it difficult to adapt to her new life at Sunny Pines and with the challenges of getting older. Do you identify with her frustrations? If so, how? If not, how would you have done things differently if you were in Birdie's shoes?

3. If Birdie had been able to tell Allison that she loved her in the very beginning, do you think her story would have taken a different turn? If so, how?

4. What would Birdie and the others at Sunny Pines say is the best thing about getting older? What would they say is the hardest?

5. At one point, Felix had to make a very tough decision about Birdie. Did you agree with him? If not, why? How would you have handled it differently?

6. Who was your favorite character and why?

7. Allison is a presence throughout the book. How did you feel about her perspective?

8. Was there anything that surprised you about this story?

9. Everly found a group of people who accepted her as she was. What did her character add to the story?

10. Finally, would you live at Sunny Pines? And if so, would you ride on the van? ☺

About the Author

© 2024 Andrea Flanagan Photography

Melissa Payne is the bestselling author of six novels, including *The Wild Road Home*, *A Light in the Forest*, and *The Night of Many Endings*. After an early career raising money for nonprofit organizations, Melissa began dreaming about becoming a published author and wrote her first novel. Her stories feature small mountain towns with characters searching for redemption, love, and second chances. They have been three-time Colorado Book Award finalists and Colorado Authors League 2020 and 2023 winners for mainstream fiction. Melissa lives in the foothills of the Rocky Mountains with her husband and three children, a friendly mutt, a very loud cat, and the occasional bear. For more information, visit www.melissapayneauthor.com.